CANDLELIGHT
Supreme

"I'M NOT WORTH CRYING OVER," HE SAID SOFTLY.

"There'll be other men, Carrie. Men who want what you want—marriage, a family, a home . . ."

"I expect so," she whispered, tears filling her eyes.

"I want you to know that if I ever settled down, I'd want to live my life with you. I've never felt that about any other woman before. And I've never said 'I love you' to anyone else, Carrie. And in my own way, I mean it."

"I love you, too, Asa," Carrie whispered helplessly.

"Don't! Don't love me, Carrie. Forget me. Tuck me away somewhere deep in your mind and live your life without thinking about what might have been."

"Is that what you're going to do?" she asked searchingly.

Asa could hardly bear to look at her. "That's all there is to do, Carrie."

CANDLELIGHT SUPREMES

DARK PARADISE

Jackie Black

A CANDLELIGHT SUPREME

Published by
Dell Publishing Co., Inc.
1 Dag Hammarskjold Plaza
New York, New York 10017

*To Charles and Kim and Karen, thanks for the
memories.*

Dell ® TM 681510, Dell Publishing Co., Inc.

Candlelight Supreme is a trademark
of Dell Publishing Co., Inc.

Candlelight Ecstasy Romance®, 1,203,540, is a registered
trademark of Dell Publishing Co., Inc., New York, New York.

ISBN: 0-440-11744-5

Printed in the United States of America

February 1987

10 9 8 7 6 5 4 3 2 1

WFH

To Our Readers:

We are pleased and excited by your overwhelmingly positive response to our Candlelight Supremes. Unlike all the other series, the Supremes are filled with more passion, adventure, and intrigue, and are obviously the stories you like best.

In months to come we will continue to publish books by many of your favorite authors as well as the very finest work from new authors of romantic fiction. As always, we are striving to present unique, absorbing love stories —the very best love has to offer.

Breathtaking and unforgettable, Supremes follow in the great romantic tradition you've come to expect only from Candlelight Romances.

Your suggestions and comments are always welcome. Please let us hear from you.

Sincerely,

The Editors
Candlelight Romances
1 Dag Hammarskjold Plaza
New York, New York 10017

Author's Note

Public television held me spellbound recently with their excellent series on China titled "Heart of the Dragon." I used some of the information I learned from that series in this book, but nothing short of experiencing the reality of China in person could compare with the visual and audio opportunity to visit that country from one's own living room that this fantastic program offered the viewer night after night.

I also wish to thank James P. Sterba, the *Wall Street Journal* staff reporter, for his hilarious article on sea slugs, a so-called treat for the palate I doubt very seriously will ever achieve the popularity in the Western world that it obviously enjoys in China.

Though I lived in Hawaii for two and a half years once and have since returned there for a short vacation, I never learned on either of my visits to that luscious state some of the things I learned about it from Fodor's 1986 Travel Guide. I appreciate the excellent help I received from that knowledgeable source.

CHAPTER ONE

"Carrie, you won't just sit around and brood now that you won't have me to look after any longer, will you?"

At hearing her younger sister, Julie, address her as Carrie, it suddenly occurred to Carolyn Winters that she wouldn't be hearing her nickname pronounced a hundred times a day in Julie's bright, cheerful voice anymore. The pain of the realization made Carolyn tighten her grip on the half-full cup of coffee she was clutching and force back the tears waiting to engulf her once Julie was safely aboard her plane to England.

"I mean," Julie continued, her usual expression of joyous preoccupation with herself and her life temporarily missing from her gamine face, "I know you're going to college at last to get your degree, but I'm hoping you'll do something about your social life now, too, since you won't have your responsibility to me as an excuse to avoid getting serious about a man. You ought to meet some good prospects at the university."

Carolyn had acted as Julie's parent for the past fourteen years, and the beginnings of the empty-nest syndrome were affecting her as violently as though she were Julie's mother rather than her sister. Nevertheless, she tried, for Julie's sake, not to sound as depressed as she felt when she answered.

"I think most of my fellow students will be a little young for me, don't you?"

Julie's small, pretty face tightened with annoyance. "There you go again," she said impatiently. "For years, you used me as an excuse for not dating anyone seriously. Now you're going to pretend the men you meet will be too young for you." Shaking her head with disgust, she asked, "Don't you ever look in a mirror, Carrie? You're beautiful. And when I went with you to

9

enroll at the university, I saw more than one of those young men ogling you as though you were a banana split and they were ice cream addicts. I was downright jealous!"

Carolyn lifted one finely arched eyebrow in an expression of patent skepticism. "Don't exaggerate, Julie," she said in the same automatic parental tone she'd used on her sister from Julie's infancy.

Julie cast her eyes at the ceiling and let out an exaggerated sigh of exasperation. Then she lowered her eyes, which displayed her impatience with Carolyn quite clearly, and said, with a firm lack of apology, "All right, so I wasn't jealous. But I *did* see the looks you were getting, and they weren't the sort guys give to doddering grandmothers, which is what you sounded like a minute ago. For heaven's sake, Carrie, you're only thirty-two years old. And now that you won't have me hanging around your neck anymore, I suggest you start living your life for a change. You've put it off long enough!"

Carolyn concealed her thought, which was that Julie's suggestion had such a facile ring to it, as though all one had to do was snap one's fingers and *voilà!*—a complete change of life was possible. *It's a shame it isn't that easy,* Carolyn thought, her panicky depression abruptly escalating as she heard the announcement that Julie's plane was now boarding.

When a look of excited anticipation sprang up in Julie's expressive green eyes, Carolyn tried to stifle her resentment that her sister was so obviously anxious to leave her.

I'm just being selfish, she excused Julie's attitude. *I should be glad Julie is independent enough to want to go to school in England in order to be completely on her own for a change. She can find out who she is without me hovering over her telling her who she's supposed to be . . . which is funny,* she added wryly as she picked up her purse and got to her feet to follow Julie . . . *since I'm not even sure who I am now that the whole basis of my identity is about to fly out of my life.*

Julie's pace was brisk and eager, as was her conversation. She chattered every step of the way, assuring Carolyn that she would write regularly, and that she would be careful with her allowance. Carolyn feared the last was a useless promise, since Julie had always been an enthusiastic and careless spender.

She'd had cause to be grateful too many times that though their parents hadn't been around to raise them, they had left a great deal of money to support their daughters financially at least.

Maybe I'm wrong, Carolyn thought abstractedly as she relinquished her purse to the X-ray machine and followed Julie through the metal detector. *Maybe being on her own will help her grow up in all sorts of ways.*

But Carolyn's efforts to look on the bright side of Julie's decision to go across the Atlantic to finish her education were only desperate attempts to fight off the panic that was hovering at the edges of her mind. In reality, she wanted to order Julie to stay home and go to the local university where she herself was enrolled. She knew she could back up the order, since she controlled the family purse strings and would until Julie was twenty-one. But she also knew that Julie was just stubborn enough to head for England without money, and passionate enough to loathe her sister for forcing her to do so.

"Julie . . ." Carolyn said, and at hearing the pleading note in her own voice, she fell silent, afraid if she continued to speak she would start to beg her sister not to go.

Julie faced her, the expression in her eyes suddenly half-guilty, half-wary, as though she understood what Carolyn was feeling, yet was determined not to let her sister interfere with her plans.

"This is best for both of us," Julie said quickly, a strained plea for support in her voice and expression. "If I stayed here, you'd go on mothering me forever, never letting me grow up and never making a life of your own. You'd go on living through me instead of for yourself."

Carolyn could feel her face whiten at the implied accusation. "Have I really been that possessive?" she asked faintly.

Julie took a step as the boarding line moved forward, her expression a mixture of guilt and loving determination.

"No, you haven't been possessive," she admitted softly, and again there was that plea for understanding in her voice and eyes that wrung Carolyn's heart. "Just the opposite, in fact. You've been too giving. You're the best friend, the best substitute parent, the best sister anyone ever had. But I've known for a long time that you were too caught up in sacrificing yourself

11

for me to take care of your own needs, and I can't live with that anymore. It makes me feel like a creep."

Startled, Carolyn instinctively protested. "Oh, Julie, no!" she exclaimed softly, conscious of the other people within listening range. "I've never felt I was making a sacrifice. I love you. I've loved taking care of you. You give meaning and purpose to my life."

Julie looked sadly impatient. "But don't you see that that's not right?" she asked with gentle firmness. "You deserve a life of your own—a career, a husband, children—everything you hope I'll have someday!" she said urgently as she glanced up and saw that she was almost at the boarding tunnel. "I don't want you making any more sacrifices for me," she added with a tinge of desperation in her voice. "I want you to think of nothing and no one but yourself for a while."

Carolyn swallowed down the rising sob in her throat, wondering how she could make Julie understand that it wasn't that easy. How could she function thinking only of herself?

"I'm not going to worry about you," Julie then said with deliberate brutality, a brutality Carolyn knew was foreign to her sister's basic nature. "I'm going to have a ball. I'm going to live my life to the fullest. I'm going to have it all!"

Unthinkingly, Carolyn nodded, her eyes brimming with tears that wouldn't be held back any longer. "Yes, Julie," she said, meaning it. "You do that. I want you to."

"Oh, *God!*" Julie groaned with frustration. "See what I mean? I'm tearing you apart by leaving, but all you can think of is my happiness! Why can't you concentrate on your own?!"

Carolyn blinked fast, trying to keep her tears under control. "I am," she said, referring to her selfishness in wanting to keep Julie with her rather than letting her go.

"Sure," Julie mocked frustratedly, then grimaced as she saw that it was her turn to have her boarding pass checked and go through the tunnel to the plane. "Carrie, I have to go," she said, her tone mournful. "Kiss me good-bye and then forget about me for a while. Please?"

The tears were streaming down Carolyn's face now, but she was unconscious of them. "Don't be stupid," she choked out as she reached for Julie and pulled her into her arms to hug her tightly, just as she'd hugged her for eighteen years. "How can I forget my baby?"

Julie hugged her back briefly, then straightened, and though there were tears brimming in her eyes, the look on her face was firm and unyielding. "I'm not your baby, Carolyn," she reminded her sister gently. "I'm your sister. But I'd like nothing more than to be an aunt to the babies I hope you will have someday . . . someday soon," she added on a pleading note.

Carolyn lifted a hand to swipe at her eyes. "Okay," she said in a quavering, tear-laden voice. "I'll go out and get myself pregnant as quickly as possible."

Her joke fell flat. Julie didn't laugh. She merely said, with a seriousness beyond her years, "I wish you would, with or without marriage, though I think for the baby's sake, a husband would be nice. I've missed our Dad all my life, though I never knew him."

And then Julie leaned forward and kissed Carolyn quickly on the cheek, before stepping away to show her ticket and boarding pass to the impatiently waiting airline employee.

Julie, don't go! Carolyn screamed silently, the agony of parting rising up inside her with devastating force. *Don't leave me alone! I don't know how to live without you to look after!*

Julie looked back at the entrance to the tunnel, her small face so woebegone it reminded Carolyn of the time she thought she'd lost her kitten, Calico, before they discovered it huddling in the fork of an old oak tree in the backyard, unable to get down without help.

" 'Bye, Carrie." She mouthed the words without sound and lifted a hand in a farewell wave.

And Carolyn stood stunned as the child she had helped raise from infancy disappeared down the tunnel. Now Carolyn would be alone, forced to try to find some new meaning in life . . . some way to fill the interminable hours she had been accustomed to lavishing on Julie.

I'm a caretaker, Carolyn thought with numb realization. *That's who I am . . . that's all I know . . . that's all I've ever wanted to know. But who do I care for now?*

There was no answer, and slowly, Carolyn walked over to the

13

windows to watch with dull, streaming eyes as the plane that would carry Julie out of her life headed for the runway.

Carolyn felt ill. She felt achingly alone. She could hardly stand the idea that she might feel this way for the rest of her life. She had not the slightest desire to go home to the house she and Julie had shared for the last eighteen years. It was empty now, empty of everything but memories. And she had two long weeks to get through in that empty house before classes started at the university.

I don't even want to go to school, she acknowledged with dull resignation. *It will just be learning for the sake of learning. I've never wanted any career other than being a homemaker, but there's not much use of hoping for the husband and children Julie thinks are so easy to find. They might be at her age, but not at mine.*

She found a tissue in her purse and wiped her eyes and blew her nose, then finally headed for the exit, walking slowly, her eyes down, gazing sightlessly at the shining wooden surface of the floor. She raised her head only when she began to wonder if she had walked too far past the doors leading out to the parking area, and then found herself staring at a huge travel poster advertising vacations in Hawaii.

Carolyn stood still, her eyes fixed intently on the poster as vague memories filled her mind. Her parents had taken her to Hawaii once before Julie was born. And though Carolyn had been very young and didn't remember many details of the vacation other than how much fun it had been to swim in the ocean, she did recall that it had been an extremely happy time for her.

I could stand a vacation right now, she thought wryly, *as well as some happiness.*

But Carolyn was so unaccustomed to thinking in terms of her own pleasure that she didn't take her thoughts seriously, and with a shrug of her shoulders, she automatically rejected what she regarded as a momentary, and foolish, attempt to run away from her circumstances. Turning her back on the poster, she left the terminal, walked to the parking lot, and climbed in the red Mercedes sports coupe that had been Julie's eighteenth-birthday present, purchased before Carolyn had been informed that Julie wouldn't be around to drive it.

So what are you going to do with yourself for the next two weeks, Carrie? The question revolved in her head as she drove away from the airport, followed relentlessly by another one. How in the world had she ever let herself believe that things would go on as they had been indefinitely?

Nothing stays the same forever, she thought with angry self-disgust at her own shortsightedness. *And no one but me seems to want to live in a time bubble, safe from change. But I guess it's time to get with life now,* she thought with irritable self-mockery. *Time to make something of myself besides a housewife without a husband. And maybe one day I'll forget that today, all I want to be is an old-fashioned caretaker, happy to nurture someone else without stint . . . subject to all the disappointment that placing my happiness in another's hands can bring.*

Despite Carolyn's attempts to deal with reality, her mood didn't lighten, and the closer she got to home, the worse she felt. Finally, upon pulling into the driveway of the comfortable, attractive home that had sheltered her and her sister for so many years, her eyes began to fill with tears again.

Carolyn blinked them away and activated the garage door opener, pulled into the garage, killed the motor, and forced herself to get out and face the task of entering the house that no longer seemed so welcoming.

It took exactly five minutes of wandering around the silent, deserted rooms to push Carolyn to the brink of desperation. At the end of that time, she realized she had made a decision only when she started fumbling for the telephone book to look up the number of a travel agency. Two hours later, feeling somewhat dazed by the uncharacteristic speed and boldness of her own actions, she handed two suitcases to a limousine driver and climbed into the vehicle to be carried right back to the airport where she had said good-bye to Julie such a short while earlier.

Well, Carrie, she thought, clenching her hands together in her lap and trying to control her agitated breathing, *maybe there's hope that you'll do all right on your own yet.*

But it was easier to say the words than to adjust to the unfamiliar sensation of doing something so spontaneously self-centered. Indeed, Carolyn remained vaguely astonished at what she was doing until she finally fell asleep somewhere far out over the Pacific Ocean, soothed by the drone of the plane's jet engines into a dream of blue skies, warm sands, and pounding surf . . .

CHAPTER TWO

Asa Bradley came completely awake all at once, as he had trained himself to do over the years, with his mind clear and his senses braced to test the atmosphere around him for danger. It took only a second for him to realize that, as had been the case for the last two months, there was nothing more dangerous to face in this small, efficient apartment the Company was providing him in which to recuperate than the prospect of having to drink his own rotten coffee for breakfast.

Though there was no danger for Asa to face, there was pain . . . enough pain to make him aware every morning upon first opening his eyes of what he had lost at the hands of a scared double agent who, upon being caught red-handed, had chosen to shoot his way to safety rather than be sent to prison for the rest of his life. In a situation where Asa had come out with very little to be happy about, he had at least the minor satisfaction of knowing that the double agent who had cost him his career as an active field agent had been caught anyway. But he had also learned that revenge was not nearly so sweet as having two good legs to get about on.

Grimacing, Asa slowly and carefully straightened out his bad left leg, wishing to hell as he did so that he'd quit curling up into a fetal position in his sleep. He knew what the position disclosed about his state of mind, but he preferred not to think consciously about his emotional condition. The dreams that haunted his sleep were bad enough, and he couldn't do anything about them. But he could control his thoughts while awake and he wasn't about to indulge the self-pity that had swamped him when he'd first learned his wound wasn't ever going to heal enough to get him out into the field again.

Gritting his teeth to keep from groaning out loud, Asa maneuvered himself up in the bed, swung his right leg over the side of it, then grasped his bad left leg with his hands and lifted it to join the other one. With his right hand, he took hold of the bedpost and used it to steady himself as he stood up on his right foot while he held his left leg straight. Then, putting as little weight as possible on his left leg, he hobbled to the kitchen to put on a pot of his abominable coffee.

While the coffee was brewing, he did a series of exercises with the help of a machine which was designed to strengthen his already formidable arm and shoulder muscles and his one good leg. He kept his eyes off the scarred appendage that had taken the bullet which had ended his career as a field agent.

As he exercised, Asa thought about the visit he'd had from the local representative of the Company the night before, and his hard mouth curved into a humorless smile. He couldn't help wondering if the assignment he'd been given was legitimate or if his superior, Don Hubbard, had thought it up as a form of mental therapy to prepare the "patient" for the sort of tame life he would be forced to lead from now on. But upon further reflection, Asa decided Don Hubbard's character wouldn't permit him to waste Company time or money on anything that wouldn't eventually pay off. There wasn't an altruistic bone in Hubbard's body.

Finished with his exercising, Asa turned the bathtub taps on, and while waiting for the tub to fill, he forced down a cup of the brew he couldn't seem to get right no matter how many times he varied the amount of coffee granules and water.

As he drank, he continued to think with a certain distaste about the assignment he'd been given to ease him back into the fold.

It wasn't that he was unqualified to lecture at the University of Hawaii about modern China. He knew as much as any Westerner *could* know about the place and its people. Hadn't he been running agents in and out of there for the past ten years? But he had no desire to switch the danger of fieldwork for the serenity of the academic world, even if the lectures were only a coverup to find and cultivate Li Chang's grandson in order to get to Li Chang.

Asa doubted if finding Li Chang would do the Company any good anyway. If the old man had intended to talk to the American authorities, he wouldn't have slipped into Hawaii illegally and hidden himself away among the Chinese community here. Finding him and threatening him with deportation wouldn't scare a veteran of the Long March. The old man had no doubt come to Hawaii to die among his relatives and Asa was inclined to grant him the anonymity he craved. But he wasn't being paid to form policy, Asa acknowledged wryly, and never had been. His job was to follow orders, and he knew he would keep on following them. It was either that or find some kind of job that was even more boring and stifling than the sort of assignment he would be condemned to from now on with the Company.

After bathing in water so hot as to be almost unbearable, but which eased the ache in his knee considerably, Asa awkwardly climbed out of the tub and prepared to shave. Because he wore a full beard, he didn't have to shave anything other than his neck, which was a blessing because standing in one position too long hurt.

As he shaved, he absently noted that his dark hair was about two weeks past due for a cut. He realized he was getting careless about such things, which was another indication that his emotional condition was bad. Maybe he needed this assignment more than he wanted to admit.

Asa avoided looking at his eyes in the mirror above the sink. The bleak, hostile expression in the dark brown depths was too vivid a reminder of his state of mind. One of his many attributes as an agent had been the ability to project a warm friendliness which put people off guard. Seldom had anyone in the past ever suspected that a man who appeared to be so charming and lighthearted could be a trained spy, and if necessary, a trained killer.

Back in the bedroom, Asa put on his current working costume—a pair of jeans faded to light blue, a short-sleeved red aloha shirt decorated with wild Hawaiian designs, and instead of the thong sandals he would normally have worn, a pair of casual lace-up shoes which were more practical for a man unsteady on his feet.

In the kitchen, he sat at a small butcher block table, drank another cup of coffee, ate a couple of cold leftover Chinese eggrolls, and scanned a local newspaper printed in Mandarin with a speed that would have astonished a casual observer. When he'd finished devouring the newspaper, he heaved himself to his feet and went to gather up the materials he would use in a series of lectures on modern China to be held in a couple of weeks when the fall semester at the University of Hawaii began. He might not need the materials today. But if the professor at the university whom the Company had pressured into setting up the lectures wanted to see the material, it would help to establish Asa's credentials as a competent teacher.

Finally, a briefcase in one hand, the strong cane he despised but couldn't do without in the other, he let himself out of the apartment and started the three-block walk to the University of Hawaii. The Agency had given him a car, but he disdained its use for such a short walk, telling himself he wanted to enjoy the beautiful Hawaiian landscape and weather and to exercise his bad leg. With bitter self-mockery, he wondered now if the real explanation might be that he simply wanted to prove to himself he could still accomplish something so trivial as walking a mere three blocks without giving in to the pain that was his constant companion.

As he walked to the university, he eyed with unconscious envy the fresh eager faces and healthy bodies of the young men and women of various racial backgrounds who politely stepped out of his way at spotting his limp and cane. Their effortless mobility embittered him. Their innocence made him feel jaded and old.

As Asa entered the Administration Building for his interview with the professor forced by the Agency to hire him, he was under no illusions that Dr. Wu would be feeling amiable about the situation. The good doctor, whose family had emigrated to the United States after Mao's overthrow of Chiang's government, was more touchy about civil rights under the U.S. Constitution than many native-born Americans were, and he hadn't liked having to agree to something without being told the underlying reasons for the request.

Still, Asa knew that Wu was considered a devout American patriot, and that it was his patriotism which had won the day for the Company. Asa only hoped he wasn't going to have to use a lot of time and energy saving face for Dr. Wu, because despite his understanding of and respect for the Chinese psyche, he had about used up his store of patience getting over the first trauma of the loss his wound had caused him. In fact, he was finally admitting to himself that the Agency doctors had known what they were doing bringing him from Hong Kong to Hawaii for a long recuperation.

Asa's thoughts shifted abruptly as he entered a small conference room, where he found Dr. Wu standing with his back to the door, gazing out the window. Asa took the opportunity to study the man before the doctor became aware of his presence.

Small-framed and tidily dressed in a white shirt and neat, lightweight gray suit, Dr. Wu gave the impression of being a scholar even from the back. Amused by the impression, Asa thought it must be the way the small man had his hands clasped behind him, the way a college lecturer might do as he paced before a class. He thought probably Dr. Wu would be fussy and pedantic, a conclusion he amended immediately when, apparently sensing Asa behind him, Wu turned quickly and fastened his intelligent, piercing black eyes upon his visitor.

For a long moment, neither of them said anything. They merely stood sizing one another up, and Asa's respect for Wu rose when the man showed no sign of agitation or nervous energy. His dignity, Asa saw, was innate and not likely to be ruffled by a visit from a man he must know was an agent for the CIA.

"Dr. Wu?" Asa inquired, projecting a quiet and respectful confidence into his voice he knew instinctively would provoke a favorable response, no matter how reluctant Dr. Wu might be to feel favorable toward his visitor.

Dr. Wu nodded his head, and now there was a slight tinge of wry amusement in his dark eyes. Instead of answering in English, he rattled off a greeting in Mandarin.

Asa knew the doctor was testing him, hoping to put him off balance, yet he was careful to keep any answering amusement out of his expression and tone as he responded just as rapidly in flawless Mandarin. He had initially learned the language from the adopted daughter of his missionary aunt and uncle, who had

21

brought the girl back from China with them when they'd had to flee the mainland after Mao's successful revolt. Later, at the behest of the Company, he had polished his knowledge of the language through formal study.

Asa couldn't tell whether he'd managed to surprise Dr. Wu or not. The man's calm seemed undisturbed as he again nodded his head and gestured with one hand to a nearby table where there were chairs upon which they could sit.

Asa hobbled to one of the chairs, conscious of Dr. Wu's eyes on him all the while, and stood waiting for the other man to seat himself first, a gesture of respect. Now Asa was certain the doctor was secretly, perhaps ironically, amused by Asa's display of manners. But he became aware of a sense of gratitude toward Dr. Wu when the man ignored Asa's handicap. Instead of insisting that Asa sit down and rest his leg, he merely stepped to the table and sat, whereupon Asa gratefully followed suit.

"I sense that you are not unqualified to give this series of lectures I have been . . . ah, shall we say, *strongly invited* to sponsor," Dr. Wu commented in an accent almost as American as apple pie. But there was still a touch of China in his voice, as well as a definite flavor of pique in his tone indicating that the man was not happy about the situation he had been forced to accept.

"I am not unqualified," Asa agreed simply, keeping his gaze level as he stared into Dr. Wu's piercing eyes.

"That is a relief," Dr. Wu responded with a wry twisting of his lips. "I was not looking forward to being blamed for sponsoring a complete ignoramus who represented himself to be an expert on China."

Asa sensed a question behind the statement and knew that Dr. Wu was obliquely inviting him to explain how he had become an expert. Since he had no intention of making such an explanation, he merely smiled, and said, "I will not embarrass you, doctor. You can be sure of that."

If Dr. Wu was disappointed by Asa's reply, he didn't show it. Instead, he continued to study Asa for another long moment before he shrugged his slight shoulders and pulled a folded paper from his pocket.

"Here is the schedule of your lectures, Dr. Bradley," he said, addressing Asa by his title for the first time, and making Asa feel uncomfortable when he did so. For while it was true that the title was perfectly legitimate—Asa had indeed obtained his Ph.D. in Asian Studies with the backing of the Agency years before—and often provided him cover for assignments, the nature of his work in the past was so far removed from the academic world that Asa always felt like a fraud when he had to hide behind his scholarly credentials.

"Thank you," he responded levelly, concealing his thoughts with hard-earned skill as he reached to take the paper Dr. Wu was offering.

"You will notice, of course," Dr. Wu drawled with that wry twisting of his lips again, "that there is no specific topic listed under each lecture period other than the overall subject of Modern China. That was impossible in such a short time, especially when no one offered me the information."

Dr. Wu's drawl deteriorated into downright irony as he spoke the last phrase, and Asa hid a smile.

"That fact may possibly reduce the number of students you attract," the doctor concluded, with what Asa thought was a bit of unworthy satisfaction.

"I expect I'll attract enough," he responded with bland calmness. He would, of course, not explain that there was only one particular young male student he was interested in attracting and that he was certain the young man would be at his lectures. His interest in all things Chinese had been noted by the Agency for some time.

Asa made it obvious that as far as he was concerned, the interview was over, but his sensitivity to Chinese manners prevented him from standing up until the older man rose first. When Wu ignored Asa's signal, Asa told himself that he should have known he wouldn't get away from his host so easily.

Wu leaned forward and placed his small hands palm down on the flat surface of the table.

"I have asked myself," he said with calm irony, "why your superiors have gone to so much trouble to set these lectures up." He nodded his head, holding Asa's eyes with his own implacable stare. "And I have concluded," he went on, "that there can be only one reason."

Asa stared at Dr. Wu in a calm fashion, keeping his expression absolutely neutral. He said nothing, and after a moment, Dr. Wu continued.

"I think there must be someone at this university whose attention you wish to attract." He spoke musingly, never taking his eyes from Asa's. "And since I must, as your sponsor, attend these lectures myself," Dr. Wu allowed a slightly malicious amusement to glint from his black eyes for an instant, "I shall be most interested to see who interests you so much."

Inwardly, Asa permitted himself a weary sigh. Why was it, he wondered, that practically every one of the few people outside the Agency who had suspected who he was and what he did for a living, had reacted with a desire to pit their wits against his. Was it the same sort of thing that happened when a certain type of man met a movie actor whose screen reputation was that of a tough guy? That type couldn't wait to test themselves against the image, and usually tried to provoke a fight.

Whatever the reason for Dr. Wu's curiosity, it was simply an added complication Asa could have done without. Now he would have to waste time cultivating several students in order to hide his real objective.

"You will be most welcome at my lectures," Asa said politely, though he smiled only with his lips while extending the invitation.

Looking challenged rather than disappointed by Asa's manner, Wu smiled back.

"I'll look forward to it," he said with equal politeness, and then at last got to his feet. When Asa had struggled to his own and stood leaning on his cane, the doctor extended a hand.

Somewhat surprised by the gesture, Asa nevertheless kept his expression bland and took the extended hand to shake it.

With a polite nod, Dr. Wu then left the room, and Asa followed more slowly. He had nothing to do except kill time. He wasn't hungry, so that cancelled out finding a restaurant, and he knew his leg wasn't up to a long walk, so with a fatalistic shrug, he headed back to his apartment, thinking he would pass the time sitting out on his minuscule balcony. Maybe the hot Hawaiian sun would bake some more of the ache out of his knee.

And maybe, Asa thought with self-mocking humor a short while later as he sat in his brief swimming trunks with his bad leg propped on the railing of his balcony, sipping a beer and idly inspecting the few passersby who ambled beneath his second-floor perch, fate would be kind enough to send him a mature woman with whom to dally away a few lonely hours that evening.

By mature, Asa meant a woman who could look at his bad leg without oohing and aahing her sympathy and ending up falling madly in love with him. Women now seemed to consider him some sort of a wounded knight who needed tender loving care, and they all, sooner or later, wanted to dispense such care in a manner that made him feel smothered. He was thoroughly sick of that particular reaction from the women he'd met so far in the friendly atmosphere of Hawaii.

He also included, in the description of maturity he favored, a woman who wanted nothing more from him other than a few hours of casual fun, followed by a mutually satisfying physical encounter, followed by a set of mutually enthusiastic good-byes. If Asa had ever entertained the idea of marriage and family, it had been so long ago he'd forgotten when or why, and even the change in the risks of his career from prevalent to almost non-existent hadn't penetrated his habitual perception of himself as a loner. It had been years since he had needed anybody in an emotional sense, and he certainly didn't want to be in a position where some woman thought she needed him. He abhorred the clinging vine types and steered clear of any female he thought might be afflicted with that particular disease, no matter how attractive she was. Women's liberation was the greatest thing to come along since the wheel as far as he was concerned, and he had no intention of ever changing that opinion.

A short while later, as though fate were on the alert to fulfill his wishes, Asa was presented with an opportunity to make the acquaintance of a very attractive woman. But as Asa well knew, fate often carried a sting in her tail, and what at first looked like an answer to his wishes soon became an irritant that made him wish fate had, on this particular occasion, minded her own business and left him in peace on his isolated balcony.

When Carolyn had called the travel agency, she had been informed at first, somewhat indignantly, that reservations for a prime vacation area like Hawaii should be made at least three months in advance. But as luck would have it, one group going out that day had had a cancellation and the agent agreed to put Carolyn with them. The agent had neglected to say that the tour was made up of elderly retirees, and Carolyn had known upon joining the group at the airport that she wasn't going to fit in.

Upon arriving in Hawaii, however, she was grateful to be part of any group, for she felt groggy from sleeping sitting up, and thoroughly disoriented at finding herself alone and so far from home. She was therefore grateful to be guided by the local tour director, along with the rest of her fellow travelers, to a bus and driven to a hotel.

The hotel didn't seem to be very prepossessing and when Carolyn reached her room and closed the door to it behind her, she was instantly seized with a severe case of claustrophobia. The room couldn't have been over ten by ten, and since the bed was a double and there was also a dresser, there was barely room for Carolyn to squeeze between the two pieces of furniture to get to the sliding glass door leading onto a tiny balcony where, if she took only one step past the doors, her toes poked through the protective railing. But at least she could breathe out there, even if the view did consist of the back of another hotel rather than the beach and ocean.

Obviously, Carolyn thought with half-hysterical humor, *one should plan a trip to Hawaii more carefully rather than taking the first (and only) tour available on two hours' notice. Next time, I'll pay more attention when the travel agent describes a tour as their "rock-bottom bargain."*

Admitting her mistake was one thing. Living with it was quite another proposition, however, and Carolyn braced herself to step back inside the tiny cubicle the hotel had the nerve to call a "deluxe" room and remedy her mistake.

She was somehow not all that surprised to find that the room didn't come equipped with a telephone, and with a sigh, she slipped her handbag over her shoulder and rode the rickety elevator down to the lobby, where the reception desk was manned by a truly gargantuan Hawaiian swathed in a wildly patterned aloha shirt who produced a wide, white smile as she approached him.

"Aloha!" he pronounced in a booming voice, but his smile quickly disappeared when Carolyn stated her request for a larger room.

"Ain't no more rooms, lady," he declared in an accent Carolyn was shortly to learn was peculiar to native-born Hawaiians. "We been booked up long time."

As he spoke, the man's brown eyes were studying Carolyn's attire with a hint of incredulity, which only served to inflame her already short temper. She would have been aware that a black linen Evan Picone suit was not the preferred attire of choice on a tropical island from the fact that she was fairly smothering in it, even if she hadn't belatedly remembered that Hawaii is noted for its informal dress. But she didn't need to be looked at as though she were a specimen in some exotic museum by a man who had just denied her what she considered a necessity—a room large enough to permit her the small comfort of being able to breathe.

Carolyn's chin came up in a gesture intended to convey firmness, and her blue eyes glinted sparks of fire as she responded, "Not only is my room too small, it's too hot."

The man shrugged his massive shoulders. "We havin' a hot spell," he informed her, though his expression plainly indicated that she would find her room less uncomfortable if she would change clothes. "Don't need no air-conditionin' here normal time."

Carolyn sighed as she realized she wasn't going to get anywhere with the man. "Then please tell me the name of some other hotel where I might be able to get a suitable room." She stressed the word *suitable*, but the Hawaiian merely stared at her in a bland fashion as though her plight impressed him not at all.

"Ain't no rooms noplace else neither, lady," he informed her with another shrug of his mountainous shoulders. "Big tours all over de place dis time of year. You lucky you got room here. Better keep it."

Carolyn had no intention of "counting her blessings," as the desk clerk seemed to be trying to convince her she'd better.

"Where is a telephone?" she asked coolly.

The man shook his head. "Ain't got no pay phone here," he informed her, and when Carolyn looked pointedly at the office telephone behind him, he again shook his large head. "That for business," he said somewhat piously. "Management don't let customers use it."

Carolyn inhaled a deep breath to keep from saying something she would later regret, spun on the heel of one mid-sized black pump, and left the hotel, intending to find a pay phone nearby and check every hotel on the island of Oahu if necessary in order to find herself other accommodations.

An hour later she hung up the phone after spending her last coin in a vain attempt to find what she sought and leaned against the cubicle in an attitude of defeated, overheated exhaustion, thinking she might just as well call one of the airlines and book a seat home rather than go back to the hole she was expected to call her home-away-from-home on this so-called island of paradise. But the telephone had just swallowed her last coin and she couldn't call an airline without obtaining more change, and so she dredged up the strength to leave the telephone booth.

As she did so, she looked up and saw an inviting vista that swept away some of the gloom that had descended upon her so recently. A mere few yards away was a lovely beach being swept by curling blue waves that looked so cool, Carolyn immediately felt a longing to plunge into them. But a black linen Evan Picone suit was no more suitable for swimming than it was for anything else here, and so she merely stared longingly at the water, debating whether she couldn't, after all, stand that crummy little hotel room at least for a couple of nights in order to enjoy what she'd come here for—sand, surf, and sun.

While she stood trying to make up her mind, a severely dented automobile pulled up directly in front of her, and a grinning young man with dark olive skin and a cap of black hair rolled down his window and stuck his head out of it.

"Want a tour, lady?" he called cheerfully. "I take you everywhere cheap."

Carolyn blinked at the young man and then at the dented, rusted car. "Is this a taxi?" she inquired on a note of incredulity.

The young man hesitated for a breath before his grin widened and he nodded enthusiastically. "Yah, lady," he agreed. "Best taxi on the island."

Carolyn was tempted. It would be nice to get off her feet if nothing else . . . and perhaps this young man might know of a better hotel?

"Is your . . . ah . . . taxi air-conditioned?" she asked hopefully.

"You bet!" he nodded, his white grin splitting his face. "It's cool in here, mama . . . I mean, lady." He corrected himself when Carolyn gave him a sharp look.

"And you know Oahu well?" Carolyn probed further. "Including all the hotels?"

"Nobody know this place better'n me," the young man boasted as he thrust his door open and hopped out of his car. He was dressed in cut-off jeans, a dirty T-shirt with a palm tree in the middle of it, and ancient thongs which looked as though they were going to fall apart at any moment.

"Well . . ." Carolyn wavered. "How much do you charge for this tour?"

The young man held out his hands in a gesture denoting innocent hurt and asked, "What you think? I'm a crook? I charge reasonable, lady. Real-reasonable."

At that moment, a dribble of perspiration trickled down Carolyn's right side beneath the clinging silk blouse she wore, and all she could think of was getting somewhere—anywhere—that was cool.

"All right!" She made up her mind and dove for the door handle on the rear door of the car. "Just hurry, will you? I'm so hot I'm about to faint."

With her back turned, Carolyn missed the slightly feral gleam that appeared briefly in the young man's black eyes before he hopped into the driver's seat, rolled up his window, and took off with a roar that threw Carolyn backward against the rear seat.

Alarmed, she glanced at the back of the young man's head, then raised her eyes to the mirror. He was looking into the mirror as well and met her glance with a cheerful grin which made Carolyn relax.

It was blessedly cool in the car, and for a few moments Carolyn was occupied taking off her jacket and placing it neatly on the seat beside her, then pulling the material of her blouse away from her perspiration-slick skin. When she finally looked up, expecting to see exotic scenery out the car window, she was puzzled to see that they were traveling down what seemed to be a perfectly ordinary street if one didn't take into account the distinctly Hawaiian flora, such as numerous hibiscus flowers in vibrant colors that abounded everywhere.

"Where are we going?" she inquired of her cheerful driver.

"I show you our university," he responded in a bland tone. "I'm a business major there."

While Carolyn thought it admirable of the young man to be proud of his ambitions, she had no desire to see a university on her vacation when she would be seeing all too much of one when she got back home.

"Ah . . . well." Carolyn started to tell her driver of her thoughts, when he suddenly whipped the car down an alley and came to a screeching halt in the back of a dilapidated four-story apartment building that looked as though it were one step from being a candidate for demolition.

"What in the world?" Carolyn spoke in a tone of astonishment, unable to fathom what her crazy young driver was doing now.

The young man turned around to grin at her again, only this time there was a look in his eyes Carolyn instinctively shied away from.

"Gotta go to my apartment for a minute and get somethin'," he said with casual blandness. "You come in with me. It's not safe to sit out here. Got some bad people in this neighborhood."

"Are you kidding?!" Carolyn responded indignantly, beginning to suspect that her young taxi driver might be one of the "bad people" he'd mentioned. "I'm not going anywhere with you. In fact, I want you to take me back to my hotel right this minute!"

At that, her driver's expression lost its friendly cheeriness

30

with an abruptness that strengthened Carolyn's already heightening suspicions.

"What—" the young man sneered, "you too big a snob to visit a place like mine? You mainland haole women are all snobs anyway, right?"

Carolyn was angry, but she was also becoming frightened. She had read stories in the newspapers about tourists to Hawaii being robbed by young, angry native-born Hawaiians . . . robbed or worse.

"I'm not a snob," she said with a careful lack of expression while she gathered her jacket and purse in one hand, trying to do it in such a manner as not to raise her driver's suspicions about what she intended to do. "But I'm hot and tired, and I'd like to go back to my hotel . . . please."

The grin came back then, but the expression in the dark eyes stayed hostile.

"Sure," he said. "You come in with me for a minute, then I take you back. Okay?"

No way, Carolyn rejected the idea mentally while she managed to paste a thin smile on her lips. Then, before the young man could react, she had seized the door handle and thrown herself out of the car, stumbling a little as her high heels came in contact with the rough dirt of the alley. Recovering her balance, clutching her purse and jacket to her middle, she was off and running as fast as her shoes and the rutted surface of the alley would allow.

She heard the young driver's door open and then he was yelling at her and she hurriedly glanced back, grateful to see that the alley was so narrow there was no chance he could turn his car and come after her. A second later, she realized he was more resourceful than that. He simply climbed back into his car, started the motor, put it in reverse, and started backing after her!

Oh, God! Carolyn prayed as she ran for dear life, stumbling and lurching over the red dirt ruts. *Please don't let him catch me!*

She felt slightly safer as she came out of the alley and turned left, back the way they'd come. It was easier to run on the sidewalk that edged the street, and Carolyn frantically kept running, all the while searching the surrounding area with her eyes, looking for someone—anyone—who might help her. She knew her pursuer wasn't far behind, and she thought he might just be daring enough to kidnap her on a city street in broad daylight if there was no one around to observe him.

Just as she was giving up on spotting anyone, she saw a man sitting in a chair on a small second-floor balcony of another apartment house which seemed much newer and more respectable than the one the young driver had claimed as his own. With a leap of gratitude in her pounding heart, Carolyn yelled at the man with all her might and was rewarded for her efforts when she saw him turn to look at her in a startled manner.

At the same moment, Carolyn heard the roar of an engine coming up behind her with a speed that turned her bones to water, and she looked over her shoulder. Her pursuer was right on her heels!

Carolyn turned back around and put on a burst of speed, grateful beyond reason when she saw the man on the balcony stand up and lean his hands on the railing as he watched the scene below him.

"Help!" Carolyn yelled at the top of her lungs, then promptly stumbled and almost fell down. As she was recovering her balance, she heard the car behind her come to a screeching halt and then the sound of a car door opening.

"Hey, lady!" the young driver barked at her in an angry tone, causing Carolyn to turn to face him again. Her face was white with fear, and her breath was sobbing in her throat as she began backing up while the young man strode toward her with an ugly look on his face. "What you gonna do, huh?" he sneered angrily. "You gonna tell the police I tried to rape you or some-thin'?"

Getting away was Carolyn's first priority. She hadn't had time to think about what she would do afterward, but now that he mentioned it, contacting the police seemed like a pretty good idea.

She was about to say so, hoping to scare the young man off, when the man on the balcony spoke first.

"Leave her alone, son!" Asa Bradley said in a tone that

wasn't a yell, but nevertheless carried clearly to Carolyn's pursuer.

The young man stopped short and looked up at the balcony where Asa stood watching him, and now the look on his face was even uglier. But after studying Asa for a long moment, he glanced back at Carolyn, who had used the opportunity to keep backing closer to Asa's balcony, and with a sneering smile on his face, he shrugged.

"You lucked out," he told her as he started walking backward to his car. "Next time, maybe you won't."

And after expressing that chilling thought for Carolyn's benefit, he climbed into his car and rapidly backed the vehicle away so that neither Carolyn nor Asa could read his license tag until he was far enough away to turn a corner and drive out of sight.

Carolyn stood still now, shakily regaining her breath and forgetting about her rescuer for the time being. She was hot, exhausted, and furiously disgusted with herself for being so foolish as to get in the car with the young hoodlum in the first place. Now she was lost, stranded and vulnerable to someone just like him.

Then she remembered her rescuer and turned to gaze up at him, only to realize with absolute incredulity that the man was naked! Was everybody on Oahu crazy, she wondered hysterically.

Unaware that the woman below him considered him nude because the railing hid his brief swimsuit, Asa watched her with amused contempt. While he found her blond hair, wide blue eyes, and perfect skin attractive, he knew at once that she wasn't his type. She resembled a refugee from the nearest Junior League meeting cast out into the sordid world to fend for herself, and Asa hadn't the slightest inclination to get further involved with her troubles. Judging by the look of shock on her face, he decided she wouldn't welcome his further involvement anyway. But some chivalrous instinct he would have sworn he didn't have came to the forefront, and he found himself leaning further over the railing to yell down at her.

"Are you all right now? Do you need some help?"

The nude man's attractive voice startled Carolyn. He

sounded too cultured to be dangerous. But then the young driver had appeared to be nice at first, too, hadn't he?

"I beg your pardon?" she responded, pretending she hadn't heard him clearly while she tried to decide whether to trust him to call her a taxi . . . a *real* taxi . . . or not.

"I said," Asa repeated, his impatience rising, "do you need some help?"

Carolyn hesitated until she saw that her indecision had worn the man's patience thin, and that his face displayed absolutely none of the lust she had glimpsed in the eyes of the young man who had picked her up earlier. In fact, she could see that this man was about to wash his hands of her entirely. Relief brought a stunning smile to her mouth, and she yelled up to stop Asa, who was in the process of turning away.

"I could use a taxi," she called to him. "Could you call me one?"

Asa was caught off guard by the charm of Carolyn's smile and the warmth in her voice. She looked the type to drip ice when she spoke, but she wasn't displaying the cool, condescending attitude he expected from a Junior League type.

Maybe the kind of scare she's just had knocked some humanity into her, he thought with sarcastic amusement. An instant later, he was telling himself, *Oh, hell, get it over with, Sir Galahad. She'll be running true to form once she's had time to recover, and when she does, you don't want to be around her.*

"I'll call one for you," he agreed, his tone short and unpleasant. "Wait there. It'll be around to pick you up soon."

Before Carolyn could thank him, Asa had disappeared inside his apartment, and feeling much relieved, but still stickily hot, tired to the bone, and thoroughly put off by her reintroduction to Hawaii, which she had assumed would offer her the same sort of freedom from care she remembered from her childhood trip here, Carolyn hobbled to a tree fronting the street and leaned against it.

With her eyes closed as she rested, Carolyn heard a car pull up in front of her, and thinking, *My, that was quick*, she opened her eyes, expecting to see a legitimate taxi at the curb. Her breath literally stopped in her throat when she found herself staring at the same young man who had deceived her earlier.

She straightened upright with a jerk as he started getting out of his car.

"I'm warning you," he sneered unpleasantly at her over the hood of his vehicle. "Don't tell the police about what you *think* I had in mind. I didn't do nothin' to you, and you don't know that I was goin' to, so just button up. Otherwise . . ."

He left the word hanging in order to inflame Carolyn's imagination as to what he might do to her, then started to move.

Carolyn didn't wait to see whether he was going to climb back into his car or come after her again. In a flash, she had spun around and was running for the door of her rescuer's apartment building. He hadn't invited her in to wait for her taxi, but as far as Carolyn was concerned, nudist or not, he was a far better risk than the young man behind her, and she had had as much risk in one day as she cared to encounter!

CHAPTER THREE

As Carolyn pounded on an apartment door she fervently hoped belonged to the man on the balcony, she was aware her knees were shaking like jelly from a combination of fear and climbing a set of stairs so fast that her feet had hardly touched the concrete. On another level she was also aware that she seemed to have lost control of her thought processes. Her mind was darting from worry to worry so fast, everything was a blur.

She wondered if she was experiencing a form of hysteria. She wondered what she would do if she'd misjudged the location and this wasn't her rescuer's door at all. She wondered what she'd do if it *was* her rescuer's door, and when he opened it, he was still naked. And finally, she wondered why it was taking her rescuer so *long* to open his damned door!

Asa hadn't opened the door because after calling for a taxi, he had started to draw a tub of hot water in which to soak his knee and he was naked now where he hadn't been before. When the knocking on his door began, he waited a couple of minutes, hoping whoever was there would go away again. But when the knocking became more of a pounding than a knock, he had an idea who it might be, and he wasn't pleased. Obviously, the woman on the street had disintegrated into hysteria for some reason, and he was in no mood to deal with her.

When it became obvious that the woman wasn't going to leave him in peace, Asa turned off the taps, donned a terry-cloth robe with impatient movements and hobbled slowly to his front door. There was a distinct scowl on his rugged features when he flung the door open, which disappeared quickly in favor of a grimace when Carolyn threw herself across the portal into his arms, dropping her purse and jacket at his feet and almost knocking him off balance in the process.

"Thank God!" she babbled as she clung to the solid wall of terry-cloth-covered body she recognized as security at last. "He came back! He was coming after me! Oh, my God, I'm so glad you're here!"

Asa would have preferred to be just about anyplace else than standing on the polished wooden floor of his apartment supporting 120 pounds of perspiring, hysterical woman with his body, but he was nothing if not a realist, and from the strength of the woman's grip, he was aware he wasn't going to regain his privacy again until he calmed her down.

"Okay, Okay," he snapped, aware that his rough tone probably didn't sound very reassuring, but unable to help it just yet. "You're all right now. Calm down and hush up, for Pete's sake!"

A tremendous quaking went through Carolyn's body in reaction to gaining safety, and strangely enough, her rescuer's gruff, unsympathetic tone was more reassuring than if he'd acted concerned. Since he didn't, it was as though there wasn't anything to be concerned about, and Carolyn was able to lighten her grip on him and look up at his face, though she didn't let go of him entirely.

Asa was no stranger to fear, though he'd long since learned to control his own, and the trembling of Carolyn's body got through to him as nothing she could have said would have. He felt a reluctant sympathy for her, which he demonstrated by awkwardly patting her back.

"Everything's all right now," he said, looking behind her through the open door at the hallway outside. "There's no one here except me. Whoever your young friend was, he's gone now."

"Friend?!" Carolyn drew back slightly and sputtered the word through her clattering teeth. "He's no friend of mine!"

Asa glanced at her face and smiled slightly at the wide-eyed look of indignation on her pretty face.

"Just a form of expression," he apologized, and seized the opportunity to step out of Carolyn's grip and move to look up and down the hallway. As he had expected, there was no one there.

Carolyn was reluctant to let him go, but she made herself clench her hands together rather than grab him again and watched fearfully as he made his inspection of the hallway. Her shoulders sagged with relief when he stepped back inside shaking his head.

"Nobody there," he said lightly.

A thought made Carolyn tense up again. "Maybe he's still outside though," she suggested, her tone anxious. "Will you look?"

Asa stifled a sigh of impatience and turned to do as his unwelcome visitor requested, figuring that was the fastest way to reassure her. He forgot about his limp as he hobbled across the room to go out on the small balcony where he could see the street and sidewalk below clearly. When he had ascertained that the young man had disappeared, Asa came back inside the apartment and limped toward Carolyn, saying, "He's gone. You don't have to worry about him anymore."

Carolyn barely heard him. She was staring at Asa's bare, scarred knee and feeling consumed with pity at seeing such a strong, fine-looking man having to hobble so awkwardly when she could picture quite clearly how he must have walked before his injury.

When she lifted her eyes, the expression in them absolutely clear to Asa's discerning gaze, she saw that he was scowling at her in such a ferocious manner, she should have been frightened to death of him. But she wasn't. She was merely ashamed of herself for letting him see how she pitied him.

"Thank you," she said quickly in order to keep him from saying something about her rudeness. "I can't tell you how grateful I am that you were around to scare him off."

Asa's scowl didn't lighten appreciably and he merely grunted a response as he came to a stop directly in front of Carolyn where she still stood at the door. He was feeling even less friendly toward her than he had before, and he didn't take the trouble to keep his feelings out of his expression.

Carolyn looked up into his dark brown eyes and saw his hostility, but she saw something else as well—pain and frustration and a deep disappointment that wrung her heart.

"Does it hurt much?" she asked gently, surprising herself with the question. She hadn't known she was going to risk his anger by asking it.

Thoroughly angry now, Asa reacted in a manner he would later admit was inexcusable.

"Yeah, it's agonizing," he said in a gratingly brutal tone. "I can't get any sleep because of it. I have to use up a platoon of women every single night to get my mind off my poor little wound. Wanta volunteer? I think I have an opening between midnight and 1:00 A.M. if you're interested."

Carolyn instinctively drew herself up in an attitude of affronted dignity before something in Asa's face dispelled that reaction. And suddenly, though the situation was one in which bantering seemed inappropriate, she smiled and quipped in a nonchalant fashion, "Sorry. I enjoyed running for my life so much, I plan to stake myself out and give it another try tonight." She shrugged her shoulders. "What's a vacation for, anyway, if not to get out of the old rut and find some excitement in life?"

Reluctantly, Asa reacted to her manner and smiled back at her. He hadn't meant to, but he couldn't help it.

"Then do me a favor," he retorted without thinking, "and choose another location for your fun, all right? I'm not very well equipped to play the knight in shining armor these days."

"You couldn't prove it by me," Carolyn responded, only half-teasing, and quickly added, hardly knowing why, "How'd you do in the old days?"

Asa frowned. "What do you mean?" he demanded out of the paranoia that went with his profession.

Carolyn's eyes widened at his manner. "You said you weren't equipped to play a knight *these* days," she explained. "I was merely wondering how you did when you had . . ."

Appalled at what she'd been about to say, Carolyn abruptly shut her mouth and stared at Asa in consternation.

"When I had two good legs?" Asa supplied the rest of what Carolyn had been about to say. "I did just fine," he drawled in a dry manner. "Averaged two or three rescues a day at least."

Before Carolyn could decide whether to apologize or let it go, Asa took her arm and turned her toward the door.

"But since this particular rescue seems to be finished, I suggest you go downstairs to wait for your taxi and let me get back to my bath," he said with a firmness that annoyed Carolyn. He was making her feel very unwelcome, which was out of character for a knight in shining armor. Still, he *had* rescued her, and she owed him her gratitude.

"Thank you again," she said soberly when Asa paused at the open door and stood waiting, obviously impatiently, for her to leave. "Is there anything I can do to show my gratitude?"

She had said the words with complete innocence. It was not in her makeup to drop double entendres, nor was she in the habit of flirting. But the expression that came into Asa's eyes brought a flush of embarrassment to Carolyn's cheeks when she realized he had misinterpreted her offer.

"What'd you have in mind?" Asa inquired dryly, slanting his mouth into a mocking smile. He was acting out of sheer perverseness. The blush had told him she hadn't meant what another sort of woman would have.

"Dinner or a gift!" Carolyn snapped indignantly.

Asa shrugged, regretting for a moment that his visitor, however attractive, wasn't the "mature" type he favored.

"Don't worry about it," he said in a dismissing tone. "I have everything I need."

Even as he said the words, he realized they were a lie, and he was annoyed with himself suddenly. Then he became annoyed with Carolyn when he saw she was as aware as he was that he quite obviously didn't have everything he needed and wouldn't unless some miracle occurred to give him back the full use of his left leg.

"I'm sorry, but I'm in a hurry," he said stiffly, "and if you don't get downstairs, you may miss your taxi. I'm glad to have been of help."

Carolyn knew she should have been as anxious to leave as this man was obviously anxious to get rid of her, but she felt an extreme reluctance to see the last of him for some strange reason. She hesitated, staring up into his dark eyes, wanting something from him without knowing what it was, and absolutely positive he wouldn't give it if she should discover what she wanted.

Asa impatiently shifted from one foot to another and immediately experienced a stab of pain as a result of his careless movement. Before he could control it, he felt his eyes close and his lips move into a grimace of reaction.

Carolyn sucked in her breath and instinctively took a step toward him, lifting a hand to place it on his robed arm.

Asa's eyes came open immediately at her touch, and he stepped back out of reach, his expression becoming hostile again when he saw the look of sympathy in her large blue eyes.

Carolyn let her hand drop and swallowed down what she wanted to say. Instead, she substituted, in a gravely sincere tone, "Thank you. I'm sorry. I'll be going now."

Asa didn't respond as Carolyn picked up her purse and jacket, turned away from him and stepped across the threshold. As she walked away, he was surprised that he didn't slam the door behind her, but instead stood where he was watching her until she disappeared down the stairwell. He was even more surprised when, after closing the apartment door, he moved to the double windows leading out to the balcony and stood just inside until she came into sight out on the sidewalk below.

Who in their right mind comes to Hawaii dressed like that, he thought angrily, then became aware that the anger was directed more at himself than at his maiden in distress. *And who but a complete idiot gets into a car with a stranger,* he added for good measure, aware now that he was also, for some reason, trying to denigrate the woman who had erupted into his life so unexpectedly and unwelcomely.

But when a taxi drew up at the curb a moment later, and Asa watched the woman he'd rescued climb into the back of it and be driven away, he was really astonished at himself when he realized he was wishing he'd at least gotten her name.

Don't be a sap, he told himself as he returned to the bathroom and his now lukewarm bath water. *She's an ooher and an aaher if I ever saw one, and that's the last type of woman you want to get to know, Bradley. Once they get their hooks in a man, they cling like glue, and if there's anything you don't need in your life*

41

right now, it's 120 pounds of glue . . . no matter how attractively packaged it is.

Despite his satisfaction with his conclusion that the woman who had landed unexpectedly on his doorstep was unsuitable to pursue, her image continued to distract him, even when he tried to blank his mind of all thought and meditate while he waited for the ache in his knee to ease.

He wasn't really surprised though uneasily wary when he finally began wondering if there would be any real harm in trying to find her again. Looking for a reason to justify such foolish behavior, he told himself that there was little likelihood that a woman on vacation, clinging vine or not, would be able to sink her hooks deeply enough into any man in only a few short days to do him any lasting harm.

On the drive back to her hotel, Carolyn was disturbed at the nature of her thoughts and feelings. The incident with the young hoodlum should have been at the forefront of her mind, but his part in the episode she'd just experienced seemed somehow to have slipped into insignificance, while the contact with the man who had rescued her was somehow vividly important.

Why didn't I ask him his name? she wondered disconsolately. *Or give him mine,* she added, trying to forget that he had seemed very anxious to get rid of her. But as much as she would have preferred to think differently, she knew that if he had reacted to her as strongly as she had reacted to him, he would have asked her who she was and where she was staying, and the fact that he hadn't was proof that he wasn't interested.

What do you care? Carolyn asked herself, growing cross with her own preoccupation with a man she would never see again and who, though he'd rescued her, hadn't treated her in a very gentlemanly-like manner afterward.

Despite her attempt to turn her thoughts elsewhere, however, she immediately began wondering how he'd hurt his leg. Thinking about his injury made her feel such intense sympathy for him and such indignation that a man as magnificently male as he was had to suffer the injustice of undeserved pain and disfigurement that she was genuinely upset by the time her taxi deposited her at her hotel.

After she'd paid the driver, she stood on the sidewalk staring at the place she had hated earlier.

It doesn't make sense to come all this way only to turn around and leave again without seeing anything of Hawaii at all—except a back alley and a stranger's apartment. And are you so spoiled and petty that you can't put up with a little discomfort for a few days?

Oh, damn! she at last gave up lying to herself and admitted the truth. *I want to see that man again. I know where he lives, after all, and I could go back there in a day or two on some pretense or other and hope he won't humiliate me by throwing me out.*

Her decision made, Carolyn strode into the hotel, glared at the desk clerk who had been of such little help to her earlier, and entered the creaking, rattling elevator to go up to her room.

As she shut her door behind her and faced the tiny, hot cubicle where she would live for the next few days, she told herself she'd gone completely around the bend to endure such discomfort just on the hope that she could see again a man she'd barely met and who didn't seem even to like her very much.

Well, if you have gone round the bend, Carrie, you might as well enjoy it instead of heading back home to an empty house and an empty life! she told herself with grim amusement, and began ripping off her sodden clothes in order to take a shower.

Much to her surprise and relief, the one thing that was any good about her room was the shower. After luxuriating in the cool streams of water for a solid fifteen minutes, Carolyn collapsed on the lumpy mattress of her bed and let herself sink into a healing, restoring nap. When she woke several hours later, however, she was absolutely astonished at the nature of the dreams she had had while wrapped in the so-called safety of her unconscious.

Sitting up straight in the middle of the bed, Carolyn blinked at her dim image reflected in the mirror across the room.

"My God, Carrie!" she whispered in a tone of awe. "What's happened to you? One meeting with a rude, unpleasant knight in shining armor, and you throw off your inhibitions like they

43

were an old, worn-out dress. I think you'd better be careful, don't you?"

And feeling more than a little shaken by what was happening to her as a result of acting completely on impulse for the first time in her life, Carolyn rose from her bed to take another shower and get ready for dinner.

While she was bathing, however, a slight, mischievous smile began curving her sleep-softened lips, as she realized that while she had had to face a certain amount of danger as a result of acting out of character, she had at least felt glad to be alive for a while that afternoon.

The grim reality of going home to nothing would have to be faced soon enough. Meanwhile, freedom from her mundane life beckoned, and Carolyn decided to ignore the staid little voice in the back of her mind which always preached caution, and see what happened.

CHAPTER FOUR

When Carolyn gave herself a last look in the mirror that evening before leaving for dinner, she was pleased. In her pale blue cotton sundress, and with her shoulder-length champagne-colored hair tied at the nape of her neck with a wide clasp, she looked like someone on a vacation. The black suit was tucked away at the back of the room's minuscule closet, and she had no intention of remembering it was there until it was time to pack up and go home.

Grabbing up a straw purse, along with a white cardigan in case the constant trade winds grew chilly after dark, Carolyn left her room and ventured down the hall to the elevator. A few moments later, she was a little taken aback when the elevator doors swung open to disclose a lobby thronged with the elderly members of her tour group.

With a mental shrug, she began making her way through them when she felt a hand on the bare skin of her shoulder and she jumped a little before swinging around to find out who had touched her. Her nerves settled down when she realized the hand belonged to a comfortably plump woman who was perhaps in her early sixties and who had a warm smile on her lips and a twinkle in her intelligent blue eyes.

"Sorry to startle you," the woman said in a pleasant voice and now she was patting Carolyn's arm, "but I noticed you on the bus that brought us here from the airport. You do sort of stand out in this group," she said in a lightly teasing way as she indicated the elderly population in the lobby with her eyes.

Carolyn smiled at the woman, liking her immediately. She seemed that rare type of woman whose personality was ageless, even if her body showed the effects of time.

"Forgive me for being a busybody," the woman continued simply, "but are you traveling alone?"

Carolyn's smile turned into a slight grimace. "I'm afraid so," she admitted just as simply as the woman had asked.

A look of kindly curiosity came into the older woman's eyes, but she didn't inquire as to why someone so lovely and, relatively speaking, so young, should be vacationing alone in the first place, much less why she had joined a tour of senior citizens. Instead, she issued an invitation.

"Well, don't think you'll hurt my feelings if you'd rather be on your own, because you won't. But if you'd like some company for dinner, you're welcome to join Celie and me." Here, she indicated with her hand another elderly woman who was standing off to one side looking somewhat bewildered and helpless. "We're heading for the International Market Place first and then we're going to find a good Chinese restaurant. I'm dying for some chicken and snow peas. By the way," she added cheerfully, "I'm Martha Goggins."

As Carolyn took the hand Martha offered and shook it, murmuring "Carolyn Winters" in turn, she was trying to decide whether to accept the invitation or not. Had Martha proposed that just the two of them go, she wouldn't have hesitated. But Celie looked an entirely different sort of person than Martha. Clad in a rather faded print housedress, and wearing sensible black lace-up shoes, she looked not only elderly, but old-fashioned. However, despite her misgivings about Celie, and despite Martha's assurance that her feelings wouldn't be hurt if Carolyn refused the invitation, Carolyn was too polite to do so.

"Thank you," she said lightly. "I'd be very pleased to have dinner with you, Martha."

The twinkle in Martha's eyes sparkled brighter and she nodded and said, "Good. Then let's collect Celie and find a taxi."

The mention of a taxi brought to Carolyn's mind the man who had called one for her that afternoon, but she determinedly pushed the thought aside, knowing she did not yet have the courage to look him up again. Besides, she admitted to herself wryly, though she had no idea how he would go about it should he decide *he* wanted to look her up, it would certainly be preferable if he made the first move.

As Carolyn had feared, Celie was a fretter. After being introduced to Carolyn, Celie immediately commenced to fret about whether the sweater she'd brought along was going to be warm enough, then she fretted about how much the taxi ride was going to cost, and once they were in the taxi, she fretted about whether her digestion was going to stand up to Chinese food.

"Are you sure you don't want to eat something more normal?" she inquired of Martha, who smiled and shook her head.

"Chinese food *is* normal." She cheerfully dismissed Celie's worries. "The Chinese have been eating it for centuries. Besides, dear," she added in a comforting way as Celie continued to look fretful, "some of it is very bland and easily digestible. I'll show you what to choose on the menu, and I know you're going to love it once you've given it a chance."

Carolyn had to smile when Martha turned her head slightly toward her and gave her a wink, but she still wished she and Martha could have dined together without the dampening presence of Celie White.

At the International Market Place, the three of them wandered around looking at the variety of shops and the international wares they offered, but Martha was the only one who bought anything: a dragon kite for her grandson and a wildly patterned scarlet muumuu for herself.

Typically, Celie disapproved. "You'll never get that kite in your luggage," she predicted sourly, "and where in the world can you wear that awful dress except here in Hawaii?"

Cheerfully undaunted, Martha responded, "If I have to, I'll carry the kite instead of packing it, and the dress is so comfortable and versatile, I can use it as a robe, and just wear it around the house."

"And it will look lovely on you," Carolyn put in, annoyed by Celie's rudeness. "The color suits your complexion."

Martha flashed Carolyn a look of amused comprehension and gratitude, then both Martha and Carolyn were distracted as Celie gave a small, audible gasp. Fortunately, before either of them could ask what was wrong, they followed the direction of Celie's outraged gaze and discerned what was bothering her. A handsome young man of obvious Asian ancestry and a pretty young Caucasian girl with long blond hair were strolling past with their arms around one another.

The couple was dressed in an extremely casual manner, both wearing thongs and shorts and matching short-sleeved cotton Hawaiian shirts, but Carolyn knew instinctively that it wasn't their attire that bothered Celie so much as their mixed backgrounds.

"Well, I never . . . !" she exclaimed, making no effort to lower her voice, and lifted her nose in the air while her faded blue eyes flashed her disgust.

Embarrassed, Carolyn was grateful when the couple didn't look their way. She was even more grateful when Martha voiced a dryly impatient rebuke to Celie.

"Well, if you haven't, I'm surprised," she drawled. "How have you lived over sixty years without realizing that love has a way of striking blows against prejudice?"

Celie looked even more outraged, but Martha took her arm firmly and started pulling her in the opposite direction from the one the couple had taken. "I'm starved," she said, ignoring Celie's sputterings. "Let's find a restaurant."

Carolyn reluctantly followed the two women, wondering how Martha had gotten stuck with Celie and why she put up with her. But since she herself was stuck for the time being, she said nothing, though she made up her mind to refuse any further invitations if Celie was to be included in them.

Possibly out of respect for Celie's worries about money, Martha chose a Chinese restaurant that looked clean and yet inexpensive, and when the three of them were settled in a booth, Carolyn concentrated on her menu while Martha helped Celie with hers, but without a great deal of success.

"I don't like the sound of that," Celie kept repeating, until with a sigh, Martha shrugged.

"Well, there are some American dishes listed at the bottom of the menu, Celie," she said, pointing at them. "I give up. Choose something familiar, then."

Celie ended up ordering a hamburger and black coffee, Martha chose the chicken and snow peas she favored, and Carolyn selected Almond Chicken, though as she did so, she felt a

48

pang of loneliness, since that was Julie's favorite Chinese dish as well.

After their Chinese waiter had taken their orders and hurried away, Carolyn noticed with surprise that Celie was staring with moistened eyes at a young couple in a nearby booth who had a baby perhaps six months old in a highchair at the end of the table.

At noticing Carolyn's gaze on her, Celie quickly brushed at her eyes. "That child is about the age of my granddaughter," she said stiffly, "but of course I've never seen her."

"Why not?" Carolyn asked, surprised by the emotion Celie was displaying.

"Because my youngest daughter married a sailor," Celie replied bitterly, "and they're living in Guam. He wouldn't even let her come home to have the baby! I suppose he was afraid she wouldn't want to come back to him, and if I had my way, she wouldn't!"

Carolyn wished she hadn't asked, especially since Martha was giving her a warning look as though trying to tell her to drop the subject. But apparently, it was too late. Celie was off on a long discourse which lasted throughout the delicious dinner, complaining unceasingly about the ingratitude of children these days who went off and left elderly parents to fend for themselves.

Carolyn's eyes were glazed and she wished she could turn off her ears by the time they were served their fortune cookies. Fortunately, Celie's kidneys were unreliable, and Carolyn and Martha received a break when Celie started scooting out of the booth.

"I suppose the restroom will be filthy," she said grimly as she got to her feet, "but I can't wait. I'll be back in a few minutes."

When Celie was out of earshot, Carolyn looked at Martha and grimaced. "I'm sorry," she apologized, "but I had no idea—"

"I know," Martha said on a sigh as she patted Carolyn's hand. "Celie married late, you see, and her husband died early, which made Celie cling to her children even more than she might have normally. Her youngest got married and left home a couple of years ago very much against Celie's wishes. I suppose

49

she wanted her daughter to stay with her forever. I thought she would have gotten over the empty-nest syndrome by now, but it seems she prefers to nurse her misery rather than make the best of things. I thought this trip might shake her out of it, but it doesn't seem to be."

Carolyn felt a pang of recognition at hearing Martha's explanation of Celie's behavior, and she felt guilty at realizing that if she could have, she would probably have kept Julie at home with her for the rest of their lives, just as Celie had wanted to hang on to her own daughter.

"Have you and Celie been friends a long time?" she asked Martha, trying to distract herself from her unpleasant thoughts.

The twinkle in Martha's eyes appeared again, and Carolyn thought how attractive the older woman seemed when her eyes smiled that way.

"Actually, we're cousins," Martha explained, "and I sort of got stuck with Celie over the years because no one else could put up with her for long."

Carolyn softened further toward Martha. "And how do you manage to put up with her?" she asked bluntly, then felt a little chagrined by her lack of tact.

Martha merely chuckled, however. "Well, it's never been easy," she confessed, "but I've sort of made Celie into a project of mine."

"A project?" Carolyn was both amused and puzzled.

Martha nodded. "I've promised myself I'll teach Celie to enjoy life if it takes the rest of our lives," she said with a mischievous grin. "And it may just take that long."

Carolyn couldn't help laughing. "Good luck," she said with amused skepticism.

"I need it sometimes," Martha responded in a dry tone. "You wouldn't believe how hard it was to persuade Celie to come on this trip. And it isn't as though she had anything better to do at home. She spends most of her time moping around her apartment feeling sorry for herself because she's all alone." Martha shrugged and shook her head in disgust.

Again, Carolyn felt a twinge of recognition, which she determinedly pushed out of her mind.

"And what about you, Martha?" she asked. "Do you have much family?"

Carolyn was surprised when Martha's expression changed, displaying a sadness that didn't fit her cheerful personality.

"I did," Martha said quietly. "My husband and son were drowned ten years ago. They were fishing in a boat together and a storm came up. Now, I just have my daughter-in-law and a grandson."

Carolyn was appalled at having reminded Martha of such a tragedy, but then her curiosity began to rise as she watched Martha fight her sadness and conquer it.

"I'm sorry," she said softly.

Martha gave her a warm smile and patted her hand again. "Thank you, dear. I am, too," she said simply. "But since I can't change things, I make the best of them."

Carolyn blinked at Martha, marveling at her calm acceptance of such a tragic loss and feeling ashamed of her own self-pity over losing Julie when her sister, unlike Martha's loved ones, would eventually come back.

"Now it's my turn," Martha said lightly, the twinkle back. "I'm dying to know how such a pretty young woman ended up in a group of senior citizens. Why aren't you vacationing with a handsome husband and a brood of rowdy children instead of hanging out with the likes of Celie and me?"

Carolyn smiled ruefully, thinking that in some ways, she had more in common with Celie than she cared to admit.

"I guess I'm suffering from the empty-nest syndrome, too," she admitted reluctantly, ". . . like Celie."

"Nobody's like Celie," Martha snorted, but there was a puzzled look in her eyes. "But you're much too young to have grown children," she added, her curiosity evident in her tone.

"That's true." Carolyn shrugged. "And I've never even been married."

Now Martha's attractively shaped eyebrows rose, and Carolyn laughed.

"I raised my sister," she quickly explained, aware that Martha was probably wondering if she'd been an unwed mother. "Our parents were killed when Julie was a baby and I

51

was fourteen. An aunt looked after Julie until I graduated from high school and then I took over."

Carolyn frowned then as she felt the pang of separation anew. "Julie just left to go to college in England," she added sadly.

Now Carolyn saw a look of comprehension come into Martha's wise eyes.

"And you couldn't face the empty house, so you ran away to Hawaii?" she asked gently. When Carolyn nodded, Martha again speculated. "I have the feeling you took raising your sister a little too seriously."

Carolyn looked at Martha in surprise. "How can you take such a responsibility too seriously?" she asked. "And besides," she added, frowning with sadness again, "I loved taking care of Julie. It wasn't as though raising her was a burden. I'd do it all again willingly."

Martha nodded, her warm gaze perceptive. "But Julie's gone to find her own life now." She stated the obvious. "Don't you think it's time to concentrate on yourself for a change?"

Carolyn unconsciously scowled, failing to wonder how Martha knew so much after such a brief acquaintance. "That's what Julie said," she answered somewhat indignantly, "but it's not that easy."

"Not if you've never done it," Martha murmured, drawing Carolyn's attention, "but it's not impossible."

"I'm not so sure," Carolyn sighed. "I don't have any idea how to start."

Martha smiled broadly. "Well, coming on this trip is a start," she teased, "though if I'd been advising you, I wouldn't have recommended this particular tour group . . . not unless you have a peculiar fancy for much older men, that is."

Carolyn grimaced. "I made up my mind rather quickly, and this was all that was available on such short notice," she confessed.

Martha laughed. "That makes me feel better," she chuckled. "I was afraid you did like the grandfatherly type."

Carolyn had to laugh, too, before she realized Martha was implying that a man could solve all her troubles, which Carolyn wasn't at all sure was the case. She did want a family, though. It was just that it had been so long since she'd dated anyone seriously, it felt awkward now thinking about getting involved with a man. Of course, there was that inexplicable attraction she'd felt toward her rescuer, but nothing would probably ever come of it. Even if she did get up the nerve to contact him again, his manner hadn't been encouraging. Still . . .

Celie arrived back at the table just then, interrupting Carolyn's thoughts, and as the other two women started to fish in their purses for money to pay for their food, Carolyn quickly offered to treat them.

Martha started to protest strongly, but Celie's protestations were decidedly unconvincing. Carolyn gave Martha a private look, which made her protestations die away, though she was obviously disgusted with Celie's willingness to have Carolyn pay for the meal.

As they came out of the restaurant, Carolyn was thinking it was far too early to go back to the hotel, but predictably, that was Celie's intention.

"We're supposed to go to that Polynesian Village tomorrow," she said, sounding as though she regarded the prospective trip as a chore rather than something to look forward to, "and I know it's going to wear me out. I want to try to get a good night's sleep, though I never sleep well in a strange place."

To Carolyn's disappointment, Martha agreed.

"Yes, I think an early night is in order," she said, sounding tired as she began to look up and down the street for a taxi.

Carolyn said nothing, though she had hoped that she and Martha could leave Celie at the hotel and then do some exploring together.

After arriving back at the hotel, Carolyn couldn't face staying in her room on such a lovely evening, so after Martha and Celie had gone up to their rooms, she stepped outside again and headed for the beach.

The crowds of people on the sidewalks made Carolyn feel secure about walking alone, and in a very few minutes, she was on Waikiki Beach with her sandals in her hand as she walked along the shoreline and delighted in the feel of the wet sand squishing under her toes and the warm ocean waves surging over her bare feet. It recalled to her mind her earlier visit here with her parents, and then she wished that she had thought to bring Julie here for a vacation.

Maybe next summer, she thought wistfully, and then wondered if Julie would even come home the next summer. Perhaps she would want to explore other places in Europe with the English friends she would make at college.

Carolyn grimaced as she realized her thoughts were about to plunge her into another bout of depression, and she determinedly turned away from her contemplation of the lonely ocean spreading in front of her to look at the people who were enjoying their walk on the beach as she had been.

Many of the people around her were couples, however—perhaps honeymooners—and Carolyn's depression escalated instead of abating as she found herself wishing she had someone to hold her hand and gaze at her as though she were the only other person in the world.

This is exactly how Celie would feel, she thought dryly, trying to shake herself out of her mood by comparing herself to a woman she so far hadn't found the least bit attractive as a fellow human being. *So cut it out, Carrie,* she instructed herself impatiently. *If you want to emulate someone, take Martha as an example. She wouldn't mope around feeling sorry for herself when there's all this beauty to enjoy.*

Determinedly, Carolyn continued walking and concentrated on the tactile pleasure of the sand, the waves, and the gentle caress of the wind against her skin. She was thinking how nice it would be to go swimming the next day when she spotted an ice cream vendor on the sidewalk nearby and smiled with anticipation. She'd had no dessert after her Chinese dinner and an ice cream sounded wonderful.

At the edge of the sidewalk, Carolyn brushed the sand from her feet and donned her sandals before approaching the ice cream stand. And a few minutes later, as she stood licking the edges of an ice cream sandwich, she was unaware that she was being watched by a man with a cynically amused expression in his deep brown eyes.

Asa Bradley sat on a low stone wall nearby congratulating himself on the correctness of his deduction that he would find a woman as obviously inexperienced as the one he'd rescued earlier that day in the vicinity of the best-known tourist attraction Hawaii offered: Waikiki Beach.

She looks about 13, Asa thought as he watched Carolyn enjoying her ice cream treat with the simple pleasure of a child. But then his gaze scanned the outline of her body under the blue sundress and the long length of her attractively shaped legs and he revised his estimate upward. *Thirteen going on thirty*, he decided, and abandoned the idea of disappearing before she discovered him, which was just as well, since it was at that moment that Carolyn turned to retrace her steps to her hotel and started toward him.

Asa sat on the stone wall, his bad leg stretched in front of him, his folded hands on top of the cane he held in front of him, and waited to see if his damsel in distress would look his way or pass by without noticing him. He was uncertain which he wanted her to do, and he decided to let fate determine whether they would become acquainted for the short time his little tourist would be in Hawaii. Asa wasn't sure what had drawn him to look for her, but he meant for any relationship they might develop to be a brief one, naturally.

Carolyn glanced in his direction, looked away, and then quickly turned her head toward him again, peering at him in the uncertain light as though she weren't sure he was who she thought he was.

Well, here we go, Asa thought with wry humor as the fate he had trusted decreed Carolyn would come toward him rather than pass him by. *I just hope she's reasonably mature. I'm not in the mood to waste my time with a naïve innocent.*

"Hello?" Carolyn said hesitantly as her excitement grew when she became positive the man sitting on the wall staring at her was the same one who had rescued her earlier that day. "Haven't we met?"

Asa almost laughed out loud. In anyone else, her words would have been a not-very-original line, designed to promote a pickup. But Asa knew better than to believe that this particular female was practiced at picking up men.

"I believe we have," he drawled, letting his inner amusement come through in his tone. "Is this where you decided to stake yourself out?"

Carolyn was blank for a moment until she remembered her flippant remark earlier that day and smiled, feeling more and more lighthearted at finding again the man who had made such an impression on her.

"No, there are too many people around," she said lightly. "No self-respecting abductor would choose such a place for a kidnapping, would he?"

"Don't be so sure." Asa shrugged, remembering some cases where there had actually been such bold kidnappings. "Good kidnappers can usually overcome any obstacles in their paths."

Carolyn's smile broadened. She didn't dream he was speaking from experience.

"Well, but you're here now, aren't you?" she teased. "And I believe you said you used to average one or two rescues a day?"

"When I was younger . . . and more fit," Asa replied, daring her with a look to show pity for his injury.

Carolyn carefully schooled her expression so that she wouldn't show the pity she knew he would hate, and was surprised when she realized she wasn't actually feeling pity now, merely outrage that such a man should have to endure a handicap.

For a long moment, Carolyn stared at Asa, noting the intelligence and cynicism in his dark eyes, the strong planes of his very masculine face, the thick, gray-flecked beard which needed a trim, and the dark abundance of his hair, which curled slightly at the nape of his neck, indicating he also needed a haircut. Despite his casual attire and his obvious lack of concern with timely grooming, he exuded an aura of subdued power, which Carolyn realized was probably what had discouraged her pursuer that day; that and the large, powerfully muscled frame of a man who kept himself physically fit. The young taxi driver would not have known the man who had told him to leave her alone was handicapped.

"I'm Carolyn Winters," she found herself saying in an effort to prolong this unexpected encounter.

Asa hesitated, thinking that his options for abandoning this foolish pursuit of a woman who wasn't his type were narrowing with every moment he spent in her company.

"Asa Bradley." He nevertheless introduced himself and held out a hand.

Now Carolyn hesitated without being certain why, before she took Asa's hand and shook it. His skin was disturbingly warm, his palm firm, almost rough, but she was somehow convinced he didn't work with his hands.

"Have you had dinner?" Asa asked, half hoping she had, or if she hadn't, that she would refuse the invitation implicit in his question for the very good reason that he was a stranger, which would let him off the uncomfortable hook she'd somehow sunk into him. He hadn't liked the small jolt of electric sensation he'd felt when she had taken his hand. That hadn't happened to him since he was a teenager, at the mercy of hormones that he had long since learned to control.

Carolyn was amazed at herself when she opened her mouth and told an out-and-out lie.

"No, I haven't," she said simply. "Have you?"

"No," Asa answered somewhat grimly, and carefully got to his feet with as little awkwardness as possible. "Do you like Chinese food?"

Carolyn managed to keep a straight face. "Very much," she answered, hoping he wasn't going to take her to the same Chinese restaurant where she'd eaten earlier with Martha and Celie and where the waiter might recognize her and comment upon her return visit. It was awkward enough to be accepting a dinner invitation from a man she'd barely met, if Asa's words could be construed as an invitation, much less have him find out just how much she wanted to be with him.

"My car's parked on the next street over," Asa said, resigned now that for whatever reason, fate was determined that the two of them would spend some time together. "Do you want to walk to it with me or stay here and let me pick you up?"

His reference to picking her up made Carolyn flush with embarrassment. She'd never been picked up by a man before in her life, but wasn't that exactly what was happening?

"I'll walk with you," she said quietly, aware that she was afraid to let Asa Bradley out of her sight. He might not come back.

As she matched her steps to Asa's slow pace, Carolyn felt as though she'd somehow stepped into a twilight zone. No one who knew her, least of all herself, would have believed even twenty-four hours before now that she would be behaving so totally out of character. For all she knew of Asa Bradley, he could be a more formidable opportunist than the young man who had scared her so badly that afternoon. But she didn't sense any menace from him. Indeed, if anything, she sensed a certain reluctance in him that piqued her ego. But if he wasn't attracted to her, why ask her to dinner?

"When did you get here?" Asa asked, certain that she was a fairly new arrival in Hawaii. Otherwise, why wear the garb he had seen her in that afternoon?

"Today," Carolyn answered absently. "And I was about to turn around and go straight back home until—"

Abruptly, she caught herself up, appalled that she had been about to blurt out that *he* was the reason she'd decided to stay.

"Until what?" Asa prodded warily as he automatically took her arm to escort her across the busy street.

Carolyn felt his touch send shafts of warm pleasure through her body, but she also heard the note in his voice that told her he wouldn't like hearing the truth.

"Until I realized it was silly to spend money on airfare to come all this way and then leave without having my vacation," she answered lightly and felt Asa's fingers on her bare arm relax a little. She wasn't sure whether she should be angry at what that told her. All she was sure of was that she wanted to be with Asa for a while longer.

"Yes, I guess that's true," Asa said, unconsciously sounding as relieved as he felt.

Carolyn tightened her lips and remained silent as they finished crossing the street and stepped up on the curb. When Asa led her down a dark side street, she didn't hesitate.

Am I going crazy? she wondered somewhat irritably. *Here I am accompanying a total stranger down a dark street and dying to get wherever he's leading me. Maybe if he acted a little more as if he were accompanying an attractive woman instead of accepting a burden with reluctant dread, I'd behave more sensibly. But if this is some tactic of his, it's working. He's fooling me into believing he's not interested in me as a woman.*

The car Asa led her to, though fairly new, was a nondescript color and make, and Carolyn reflected that it suited his present manner. A sports car would have worried her . . . or encouraged her. She wasn't certain which at this point.

She watched out of the corner of her eye as Asa started the engine, then relaxed when she realized the car had an automatic shift and he wouldn't have to use his injured left leg to drive.

"The restaurant I have in mind is not close," Asa said, glancing at her as he stopped at a stop light.

"Does it have good food?" Carolyn replied, sensing that he was again giving her the option of backing out, which irritated her unreasonably.

"It has excellent food," Asa answered gloomily, aware that she wasn't going to back out when he'd been wishing she would.

"Then it doesn't matter how far it is," Carolyn said in a firm voice and turned away to look out the window, trying to understand why a man would invite her to dinner, then act as though he wished she had refused his invitation. Asa's behavior was beyond her capability to interpret. But though her pride was dragging in the dust by now, she was adamant that she wasn't going to allow her reluctant suitor to disappear into the night as he apparently wanted to do . . . at least not until she found out what was going on inside him.

And Asa, who didn't need to look at Carolyn to hold her lovely image in his mind, was convinced he would spend this evening growing more and more attracted to her, only to end it frustrated by her refusal to go to bed with him. And he was not about to make any promises to end the frustration he sensed was in store for him. No sir, he decided grimly. He would ride out this situation he'd gotten himself into as though it were any other dangerous assignment. Then he'd say good night to the lovely lady, forget he'd ever met her in the first place, and thank his lucky stars that she was as naïve as the thirteen-year-old he²d compared her to earlier. Better that than to be in her arms and find they were a beautiful, silken trap he couldn't escape.

CHAPTER FIVE

As Asa neared Hotel Street, he wondered whether he should have avoided this rough part of town considering Carolyn's frightening experience that morning. Then he dismissed the thought. She was in no danger, and, though he knew she'd been teasing, she had said she'd wanted to get out of her normal rut while on vacation, hadn't she? He was willing to bet Hotel Street was about as far from her "normal rut" as it was possible to get.

He watched out of the corner of his eye and was amused to see that she didn't seem frightened. She was gazing fascinatedly at the tattoo and massage parlors, the rowdy sailors on liberty from Pearl Harbor looking for excitement, and the other assorted (and sordid) business establishments. Then he headed for a quieter area of Chinatown where there were more respectable shops and restaurants.

Normally, Carolyn would have been extremely uneasy finding herself in such an environment. But in Asa's company, she felt safe enough to indulge her curiosity and stare to her heart's content at a way of life that was completely foreign to her usual staid, suburban life-style. In fact, she was almost disappointed when he drove into a quieter area and parked, but she said nothing and, in consideration for Asa's leg, let herself out of the car rather than wait for him to come around, meeting him at the curb in front of the vehicle.

Asa noted her gesture and was both amused and slightly irritated by it. He also noted the way she was inspecting the surrounding area and wondered if, despite her obvious interest, she was also uneasy.

"There's nothing to be afraid of here," he said, wanting to

60

reassure her that she was safe. "At least, not when you're with me," he added, suddenly alarmed that she might take him too much at his word and come down here alone sometime.

"I know," Carolyn replied, looking at him with such simple trust that Asa felt uncomfortable. He suspected she could begin to depend on him all too easily, and what was worse, judging from the fact that her trust pleased him more than he wanted to admit, he might begin to like having her depend on him. That was a trap he didn't want to fall into.

At that moment, a small gust of wind tugged a strand of Carolyn's champagne-blond hair out of the clasp at the nape of her neck and as she lifted a slender hand to push it back behind her ear, she smiled at Asa in an unselfconscious way he found charming. He discovered himself really liking her for the first time since they'd met, and he smiled back at her more naturally than he'd managed to smile for quite some time.

"Come on," he said lightly, sliding his fingers around her bare upper arm and wishing an instant later that he'd had more sense than to touch her. Her skin was warm and smooth and too seductive to the touch to risk prolonged contact. He made himself let go of her, and was immediately irritated by the situation he'd gotten himself into. Had he been with a woman more his type, he wouldn't have to be careful about such things.

Carolyn was disappointed when he let go of her. His warm, strong clasp had made her feel protected, as well as provoking a little thrill of excitement down her spine she found extremely pleasant.

"They have both Mandarin and Szechuan cooking here," Asa said as he paused outside a small restaurant that looked much more intriguingly authentic than the Americanized Chinese restaurant Carolyn had eaten at with Martha and Celie. "Some of it is hot and spicy. Can you handle it?"

Carolyn looked into Asa's dark eyes and sensed another question in them about what *else* she could handle that was hot and spicy. She felt a dart of excited fear, quickly suppressed it, and answered both the silent and the verbal questions as calmly as she could manage, surprising herself as much as Asa in the process.

"I can handle it, Asa," she said simply, deliberately using his

61

name for the first time and pronouncing it familiarly, as though they'd known one another—perhaps intimately?—for a long time.

Asa immediately felt a rush of sensual pleasure and he went quite still, not trusting his ears for a moment. But the expression in Carolyn's eyes before she looked away told him he'd heard right and taken her meaning correctly. He wished he knew whether to be pleased or alarmed.

Carolyn, disturbed now by her uncharacteristic boldness, made somewhat breathless by the immediate glow of male sexuality she'd seen in the depths of Asa's dark eyes, was grateful when, after a slight pause, he ushered her into the small restaurant without further comment.

As they walked inside, a tiny, bent Chinese gentleman looked up, said something in Chinese to the Asian couple he'd been visiting at their table, then hurried forward with a beaming smile, chattering in Chinese to Asa as he approached.

Carolyn couldn't believe her ears when she heard Asa's deep voice replying in the same language. Startled, she tilted her head over her shoulder to look up at him, staring in fascination at his mouth as the foreign, staccato sounds continued to issue from it.

Asa paused and glanced down at her, a faint smile appearing on his lips as he noted her surprise. But now the elderly Chinese gentleman was gesturing at them to accompany him to a table, again chattering in his native language as he pulled out a chair at a plain wooden table for Carolyn.

She seated herself, her eyes never leaving Asa's face as he and the proprietor conducted a conversation while Asa seated himself across from her. Then Asa, glancing at Carolyn, switched to English and said, "The lady doesn't speak Chinese, Lei. Can you tell her in English what you recommend to eat this evening?"

The little man bowed, and in a strong accent suggested shark fin soup to begin with.

Carolyn swallowed, hoping she had misunderstood him, which wouldn't have been hard considering his garbled English pronunciation, but at catching a look in Asa's eyes that was somewhat mocking, she strengthened her backbone, or rather

her stomach, and nodded with a pleasant smile at the elderly man, who looked delighted that she had taken his suggestion.

"I'll have the same, Lei," Asa nodded as well, and when Lei had hurried away, Asa returned his attention to Carolyn.

Carolyn decided time was too short to be coy about asking what she wanted to know, and said, "Where did you learn to speak Chinese?" in a blunt fashion that made Asa's pupils widen at first. Then a somewhat vague look came into his eyes that made Carolyn feel uneasy. She had the strangest feeling, which she immediately tried to dismiss, that he was searching for a lie to tell her!

"My aunt and uncle were missionaries in China before the Communists took over," he said in an offhand manner. "When they had to leave China, they brought a young Chinese girl with them who'd been abandoned at the Mission and whom they adopted. She taught me the language."

To Carolyn's relief, Asa's explanation sounded truthful, and she relaxed. "Can you read and write it as well?" she asked.

Asa nodded, but he shifted his eyes away at the same time in a manner that again made Carolyn feel uneasy. The gesture didn't fit him. And if Carolyn had only known it, Asa was cursing himself for his uncharacteristic behavior. Had he been on a job, he would never have shown in any such manner that he was uncomfortable, even had he been telling out-and-out lies, which was not exactly the case now. He simply wasn't explaining that the Company had paid for him to learn to read and write Chinese.

"What do you do, Asa?" Carolyn again elected to be blunt. And when Asa hesitated for an instant, she added, "Do you use your knowledge of Chinese in your work?"

Asa couldn't understand why he was suddenly finding it difficult to play the game that had been a part of his life for over ten years. All he had to do was use part of the truth and toss it off glibly as though it were all of it. Annoyed, he gave his answer in a manner that was sharp and discouraging, which could have been a sure tipoff to Carolyn that he was trying to conceal something.

"Yes, I use Chinese in my work," he answered, unaware that he was looking at her in an almost hostile way. "I have a doctorate in Asian Studies, and I'll be lecturing at the University of Hawaii this fall about modern China."

Carolyn was taken aback by Asa's hostile attitude, and while ordinarily she would have been delighted to learn his profession and would have wanted to ask him questions about China, now she felt discouraged from asking him anything further at all.

Fortunately, Lei arrived with their soup at that moment, and Carolyn abstractedly noted it looked perfectly ordinary, which was a relief. She had half expected to be faced with a bowl of miniature sharks swimming around in a mock sea.

Asa and Lei were again speaking in Chinese while Carolyn wondered how she was going to force down another dinner on top of the one she doubted she'd digested as yet. Even if she hadn't already eaten once this evening, the change in Asa's attitude would have robbed her of her appetite anyway, so why should she have to feel uncomfortable about simply admitting that she wasn't hungry? It was absurd to let Asa's mockery provoke her into doing anything she didn't want to do.

"We're talking about the main course," Asa remarked to her during a pause in the conversation with Lei.

"I'm not very hungry," Carolyn answered, staring straight at Asa in a calm fashion, almost daring him to mock her for being, as she suspected he thought she was, too finicky and unadventurous about strange food to risk Lei's offerings. "And I'm not feeling in the mood for anything hot and spicy anymore," she added, her gaze never wavering as she delivered her double message to Asa, not caring whether he would take it as an excuse to become even more abrupt with her. As far as she knew, she hadn't given him an excuse to be abrupt with her in the first place.

Asa kept his expression blank, though he felt annoyed with himself for letting his uncharacteristic behavior spoil what had looked like a promising evening.

"Then I suggest a serving of gau chee min after you've finished your soup," he said without showing his annoyance. When Carolyn looked blank, he added, "They're soft dumplings stuffed with meat. I'll eat what you leave."

Carolyn shrugged and nodded, Asa indulged in another spout

of Chinese conversation with Lei, and then the elderly proprietor left them to go back to the kitchen.

Carolyn picked up her spoon and gingerly tasted the shark fin soup. It wasn't bad, and she glanced up at Asa, who was smiling at the cautious way she'd tested the soup.

His smile seemed natural and Carolyn felt the tension inside her easing, though she was reluctant to trust his mood just yet. For someone who seemed so masculinely assured, she was finding him remarkably temperamental.

"Do you come here often?" she inquired politely, behaving more as though they were the strangers they actually were than she had since she'd met him.

Asa regretted that his manner had precipitated this distantly polite attitude in Carolyn. He had liked her earlier spontaneity even if it had caused him some uneasy moments.

"Here and other places," he said quietly. "There's a large population of other Asians besides Chinese in Hawaii, and I enjoy variety."

Carolyn's dark lashes swept up in a smooth motion that fascinated Asa as she gave him a cool look that said she suspected he liked variety in women as well as food.

Asa kept his expression blank and unrevealing but he was thinking that he *didn't* like variety in women . . . at least he hadn't until meeting her. Before she had sprung into his life in such a tumultuous way that morning, he had stuck with the sort of "mature" woman it was safe for a man in his profession to love and leave. And since he had been in the Orient for most of the last ten years, he had found his relaxation mostly among Oriental women who had dark hair and eyes and were generally delicately petite.

As Asa studied Carolyn's smooth peaches-and-cream complexion, the lovely blond shade of her hair, the wide blue eyes that contained an innocent expression which shouldn't have been there at her age, and the tall, slender, perfectly synchronized perfection of her body, he mentally shook his head at his own foolishness in becoming attracted to her. Was it just because she was so very different from the women he was used to? But there had been a blonde or two since he'd arrived in Hawaii and gotten back on his feet. They just hadn't been Carolyn's sort of blonde. He'd had more sense than that until she'd exploded into his life uninvited.

Carolyn was aware that Asa was staring at her, and that his stare was both malely appreciative and yet distancing. Feeling slightly fed up with his ambivalence, she caught his gaze and asked, bluntly again, "Why did you ask me to dinner, Asa?"

Asa smiled, but he wouldn't be hurried by her bluntness. He took his time, continuing to study her as he decided whether to be honest with her or not. Finally, he shrugged. "I'll be damned if I know," he said softly, unaware that his answer humiliated Carolyn past endurance until he saw her face whiten and her body stiffen.

Suspecting that her next reaction would be to get up from the table and leave him, Asa quickly leaned forward and caught her clenched left hand in his fingers, tightening his grip when Carolyn instinctively tried to pull away.

"Maybe I like to live dangerously," he said, keeping his tone soft as he stared into Carolyn's eyes with an intensity that distracted her from the blow to her pride he'd just delivered.

"Dangerously?" Carolyn sounded as incredulous as she felt, but she kept her tone as low as his. "You consider me dangerous?"

"More than you know." Asa smiled faintly, and now he relaxed his grip on her hand slightly without entirely letting her go and absently began to stroke his fingers over her soft skin.

His touch disturbed Carolyn, producing that breathless feeling inside she'd had when he'd taken her arm out on the street.

"In what way?" she asked absently, her attention diverted to their hands. Asa was rubbing his thumb lightly across her palm now and as her eyes remained caught in his dark gaze, she felt the tingle of his light touch running all the way up her arm to her breasts, where it seemed to lodge and create even more havoc with her breathing.

"We aren't suited, you know," Asa murmured, caught himself in the sudden intense intimacy they were sharing to the point where he forgot caution for perhaps the first time in his entire adult life. "It isn't wise for either of us to pretend we are."

His words puzzled Carolyn, bringing her slightly out of her

preoccupation with the senses Asa was stroking with his hand, his eyes, and his enveloping voice.

"We don't know one another," she replied, her tone faint. "How can we tell if we're suited yet?"

"I don't have to know you well to realize the type of woman you are," Asa said quietly, and to Carolyn's ears, he sounded regretful.

"And what type is that?" she asked, frowning slightly at hearing that tone of regret in his voice.

Asa's lips twisted in a slight grimace. "The type who wants marriage, home, and children," he shrugged, and dropping Carolyn's hand, he leaned back in his chair, putting a physical distance between them that Carolyn realized was also his way of putting some emotional distance between them.

She tilted her head, studying him as intently as he had studied her earlier. "Is there something wrong with being that type of woman?" she inquired softly, her puzzlement and disappointment clear in her tone.

"Not for some other man," Asa said, sounding firm as he attempted to strengthen his resolution that after this dinner, he would take Carolyn Winters directly to her hotel and forget about the fantasies of making love to her that kept springing up in his head every time he touched her.

Carolyn felt a heavy sensation in her chest. "Are you already married, Asa?" she asked soberly.

Startled by the question, Asa said, "No!" before he realized it might have been wiser to pretend he was, since he was certain that would put a stop to any fantasies Carolyn might have been spinning about him.

Carolyn felt relieved, and she couldn't keep her relief out of her expression, nor could she keep from saying, "I'm glad," with simple honesty.

Asa felt annoyed with himself again. Where the hell was his ability to think on his feet that had kept him alive and his cover intact for the last ten years?

Lei returned to the table and looked disappointed when he saw that neither Asa nor Carolyn had eaten their soup. He said something in Chinese to Asa, and Carolyn assumed he was asking if there was something wrong with the soup.

Asa shook his head and with a smile for Lei, picked up his spoon while he said something to the elderly man that sounded reassuring.

At viewing Asa's kindness toward Lei, Carolyn felt a spurt of warmth for him flood through her. She wished that he would display some of that kindness toward her. Then she ducked her head and began to eat her soup so that he wouldn't see how disappointed she was that he obviously had no intention of pursuing a relationship with her.

He's obviously changed his mind about having even a vacation romance with me. And then, remembering how ambivalent he had been all evening, she added, *That is, if he had romance in mind at all where I'm concerned. I must have been projecting what I wanted onto him. Maybe he just wanted company for dinner and nothing else, and the ambivalence came in when he saw that I wanted more than that.*

Chagrined by her thoughts, Carolyn decided it was time she picked her pride up from the dust where she had let it drop and followed Asa's lead in letting this episode between them flow on harmlessly until it was time to let it end for good.

Raising her head, she said in a politely casual manner, "Have you ever been to England, Asa?"

Asa had his blank expression on again, and he shook his head.

"My sister's there now, preparing to attend college," Carolyn said, and in a polite, casual way, proceeded to chat about Julie for a few moments before going on to other safe topics, as though nothing had happened between Asa and herself to change their status from that of polite strangers to two people who had skirted, for an all too brief few moments, an intimate awareness of one another that could lead to something more involving than a casual dinner.

They finished their meal in that fashion, but all the while Asa was telling himself he should be grateful for Carolyn's efforts to act obligingly upon the message he had given her that this was what he wanted, he was instead becoming more and more irritated by the distance that her polite conversation was creating between them.

Hell, man, you can't have it both ways! he told himself disgustedly as he put money on the table for the meal, stood up, and came to draw Carolyn's chair back for her. But when she got to her feet, he deliberately didn't move away, so that she ended by standing quite close to him, and the clean scent of her body tinted with the seductive wrap of her perfume enveloped him, while the momentarily unguarded look in her eyes was an invitation every male instinct he owned wanted to accept.

Lei broke the spell by hurrying over to speak in Chinese to Asa. While he answered, somewhat absently, Carolyn moved to stand a few feet away, carefully concentrating on Lei rather than looking at him. He suspected she was determined not to fall again into the trap of thinking of him as other than a passing acquaintance and he couldn't blame her, considering the conflicting signals he had been giving her all night.

Let it go, he told himself grimly as he voiced a few polite phrases to Lei. *Get her back to her hotel and let it go!*

When they were finally in the car driving in the direction of Waikiki, Asa was grateful that Carolyn remained quiet. He couldn't have taken much more of her polite conversation when he wanted to hear her say his name in that soft voice she had used during the intimate episode they'd experienced briefly at the table.

Hell, he wanted a lot more than to hear her say his name, he admitted bleakly as he tried to concentrate on his driving. He wanted to take her in his arms, feel that delectable body of hers against his, and crush that perfect mouth of hers beneath his own until she kissed him back as passionately as he suspected she could.

She had let her reserve slip away for a few moments there, he realized, and he had forced her to take it up again, fool that he was. But he would have been an even bigger fool to start something between them there was no way to finish. Right?

He didn't feel right, however. Not when the silence between them stretched all the way back to Waikiki until he'd parked the car. Not when she turned to him with that polite, remote look on her face, not when she started to mouth all the correct, polite phrases that would thank him for dinner and a pleasant evening.

"Carolyn, for God's sake, cut it out!" he interrupted before she could break his patience altogether, and then he ran a hand through his hair in an irritable manner and looked away.

Carolyn hesitated, sensing something of what was going on inside him and uncertain how to respond. "My nickname is Carrie," she finally said, wondering where the words came from. What difference would it make to him what her nickname was? she wondered bleakly. What was it he wanted from her, anyway? She had given him what she thought he wanted and now it seemed she'd been wrong . . . again!

Asa looked at her, his expression taut, before he relaxed slightly, a faint smile coming to his lips.

"Carrie . . ." he repeated her nickname softly, liking it, thinking it softened her Junior League image in a very attractive way.

Carolyn stared at his face in the shadows, feeling enormously frustrated. She wanted to ask him so many things: how he'd injured his leg, why he seemed to reach out for her one moment and push her away the next, whether their meeting that evening had been completely accidental or whether he'd made it happen. She somehow knew he was the sort of man who could make that sort of thing happen where other men couldn't.

But he had set enough barriers between them that she couldn't ask him anything at all . . . couldn't feel comfortable and safe with him the way she had at the beginning of the evening, couldn't anticipate the kiss she had been longing to have from him every time she'd looked at his firm mouth and wondered if it could soften against hers.

"I . . . it's getting late." She forced the words out and reached for the door handle on the car. "I believe my tour is going to the Polynesian Village tomorrow, so I should get some sleep."

She wondered at her ability to voice such a lie so convincingly. She wouldn't sleep that night. Furthermore, she doubted she would accompany the tour to the Polynesian Village either. Maybe if she simply lay on the beach, the sun would bake the wild longings Asa Bradley had woken in her away and they would disappear forever.

"Good-bye. Asa," She unconsciously voiced a farewell she

considered valid rather than saying "Good night," which she would have said had circumstances allowed it.

Asa didn't answer, and Carolyn barely noticed that he didn't. She got out of the car, shut the door, and walked away, refusing to look back. When she reached her hotel, she stared at it, unable to contemplate entering that small room which would simply enclose her tightly in the vise of empty disappointment she felt.

Turning sharply, she headed for the beach instead. The crowds of people had thinned out, but there were still a few couples around, whom Carolyn ignored. Slipping out of her sandals, she crossed the sand to the water's edge and stood with the waves breaking over her feet and ankles as she stared out at the moonlit Pacific, willing the peaceful scene to enter her heart and erase the emptiness there.

A few moments later, she heard at the very edge of her consciousness the sound of shifting sand as someone came up behind her, and she felt a wild fury engulf her at the idea that she might be going to have to endure the sort of advances she was positive her young taxi driver of the morning had had in mind.

Stiffening, she whipped around, then went still as she came face to face with Asa Bradley. He stood there, leaning on his cane, staring at her with a sort of grimly amused resignation on his rugged face, before he said, very softly, "I wanted to kiss you good night. You didn't wait. Have I walked all this way for nothing?"

Slowly, the sound of the waves became audible to Carolyn again, she felt the smooth sand under her feet again, she felt the blood moving under her skin again.

"I wouldn't dream of putting a man with an injured leg to the trouble of walking here for nothing," she said with quiet solemnity, then waited, without daring to breathe, to see if he was going to accept her insistence on this sort of honesty between them.

Asa understood. She didn't want to play the sort of avoidance game he had insisted on earlier, then come to realize he didn't want any more than she did.

He let the cane fall to the sand and stood braced on his good right leg, waiting.

Carolyn let out her breath, stepped forward, and placed her hands lightly on his shoulders, her eyes on his.

"I'm not sure if I remember how to go about this," she whispered. "It's been a long time since I kissed a man."

Asa's hands came up to her waist and he drew her to his body. "You'll remember," he answered, his voice low and husky with desire. "It only takes the right man to bring it all back."

As he lowered his head, and then his mouth closed over hers, Carolyn felt a distinct jolt, as though her whole body had experienced a pleasurable shock. And she knew Asa was wrong. She wasn't remembering anything. She was experiencing for the very first time what it felt like when the right man kissed her.

Her hands slipped over Asa's shoulders to cup the back of his head, and she let his mouth lead hers in a duet filled with pleasurable sensations. Then she felt another jolt when his arms tightened around her and he melded her body against his own in a way that was possessive and familiar, as though he were certain she would welcome such familiarity.

This time he wasn't wrong. Carolyn was sensually enchanted by Asa's confidence. She relaxed against him, assenting to his handling of her body with no thought of protest, feeling a net of trust and safety undergird the excitement beginning to flow through her veins.

For his part, Asa was aware of a sort of grim warning in his brain telling him that beneath the tremendous physical pleasure he was experiencing was something more. Feeling. Carolyn was dangerous to his whole life. He knew he had been right to fear having her in his arms, and he cursed his weakness in following her to the beach. But the warning wasn't sufficient to make him stop kissing Carolyn until a burst of laughter came from behind the two of them and he reacted with instincts honed by years of anticipating a greater sort of danger than the woman in his arms represented.

Carolyn was stunned when Asa broke the kiss and spun around in an extremely fast motion, throwing her off balance for an instant. Then she was horrified when he gave a groan of agony and collapsed onto the sand, clutching his bad knee.

"Asa!" She said his name in a choked voice, then was on her

knees beside him, placing her hands over his as though her touch might ease his pain somehow.

Asa gritted his teeth, aware now that his instincts had played him false. The noise that had spun him around and resulted in the fiery agony he was experiencing had been nothing more than the lighthearted laughter of a couple passing behind him and Carolyn on the sand. But more important, the incident had demonstrated clearly to him how poorly equipped he would be to handle the sort of emergency he might have to someday if he was ever allowed to return to the field, a possibility he had been unconsciously clinging to without acknowledging even to himself what he was doing.

"Stop it!" he bit out as he roughly brushed Carolyn's hands away from his. "I'm all right!"

Clearly, he was not all right. His face was still drawn into a grimace of excruciating pain. But Carolyn was too shocked by his tone and the almost brutal way he had brushed her hands aside to protest his statement. She sat back on her heels, watching with anxious empathy as Asa fought to get control of himself.

Finally, the shafts of liquid fire darting through his knee dissipated enough that Asa felt he could stand up without being pitched onto the sand again. He was bitterly aware as he struggled to his feet that Carolyn was holding her hands out to him, as though to catch him if he fell. Far from appreciating her desire to help, however, her awareness of his helplessness filled him with fury.

When they were on their feet, Asa looked around for his cane, and at seeing it some distance away, his pride received a further blow when he realized he was going to have to ask Carolyn to get it for him.

He should have felt grateful when she realized without his having to say the words what he wanted and crossed the sand to pick up the cane, then brought it back to him, holding it out silently, her eyes displaying all the sympathy Asa could least tolerate just then.

"Can you get back to your hotel alone all right?" he grated as he took the cane and leaned heavily on its support, looking through her rather than at her.

"Yes," Carolyn answered in a shaken tone, "but don't you want me to . . ."

"I don't want anything from you!" Asa bit out harshly. "I don't *need* anything from you or anybody else . . . understand?"

Feeling as though her heart were breaking, Carolyn gripped her hands together to still their shaking and nodded. She could empathize with what Asa must be feeling, but she hated the helplessness his pride forced on her. She had never wanted to help anyone in her life the way she wanted to help Asa Bradley at this moment.

When Asa started to turn away, his slow, careful movements tore at Carolyn, making her reckless.

"Couldn't I just walk with you back to your car?" she asked, trying her best to keep emotion out of her voice and sound calm when she felt anything but calm and unmoved.

Asa paused, and since Carolyn couldn't see his face, she didn't know it bore an expression of bitter self-contempt. Forgotten completely was his former appreciation of women's liberation. In this situation, all he could think of was that it was his place to offer Carolyn protection and escort her back to her hotel, not hers to take care of him. But he knew he would barely make the distance to his car, and it was out of the question to try to behave like the man he used to be and provide a lady the escort she deserved.

"I—don't—need—you," he spaced the words deliberately and imparted a harshness to his tone he hoped would make Carolyn Winters forget about pitying him and be glad to see the back of him instead.

Without turning to see how she had taken his words, he started walking again, clenching his jaw as each step shot bolts of pain through his leg.

Asa was concentrating so hard on staying upright and mobile long enough to get to his car that he was oblivious to everything else around him. And when he at last reached the vehicle, he had to lean against the driver's door for a moment to rest before he attempted to climb inside.

When he raised his head, he experienced a jolting shock at seeing Carolyn standing a few paces away, her face white, her

74

body rigid, as though following him had cost her every bit as much physical pain as it had cost him to walk the short distance to his car.

Asa suddenly felt ashamed of the way he'd spoken to Carolyn on the beach. He also felt unexpectedly moved by the concern she'd shown for him by risking his anger and following him to make sure he reached safety. But before he could find the words to apologize, Carolyn spoke first.

"You were right," she said with a quiet simplicity that was tinged with sadness. "You didn't need me."

An instant later she was gone, leaving Asa staring at the empty sidewalk where she'd stood, feeling torn. Should he go after her in the car or end things between them on a discordant note that might be easier in the long run than parting with a kiss?

Unable to decide one way or another for the moment, he shook his head and opted to postpone the decision. He would have his hands full that night trying to get his knee into a condition where he could sleep, much less use his energy stewing about hurting a woman's feelings . . . especially when she was the type of woman who could cause him as much emotional pain as his knee caused him physical pain . . . if he let her.

CHAPTER SIX

Carolyn lay curled on her lumpy bed fighting tears as she tried to sort out the confusion reigning in her mind.

I lost Julie yesterday, she thought, *and it hurt. It's natural that it should hurt, isn't it?*

Having decided that yes, it was perfectly natural to hurt over losing Julie, especially when it was evident that things could never be the same as they had been even when Julie came home for visits, Carolyn turned her mind to wondering how natural it was to hurt as badly as she did over what had happened with Asa.

I barely know him, so why is he able to cut me to the heart this way? Why should I care that he doesn't need me?

Turning onto her back, Carolyn stared up at the dark ceiling searching for the sense of it all. Had she presumed that Asa's injury made him so vulnerable that he needed someone? Had her own desperate need to have someone to take care of in place of Julie made her assume she could substitute Asa into the emptiness Julie had left behind her? Was that what was going on?

Carolyn closed her eyes in self-disgust and shook her head. Even if they had known one another for longer than a day, it would have been presumptuous to think a man like Asa Bradley would tolerate such an expectation from a woman. He had made it brutally clear that, injured or not, he wasn't looking for that sort of relationship with anyone. She had hurt his pride. She had left herself open to hurt. And all because she couldn't stop behaving like a damned caretaker!

She stewed over that for a few minutes as though she had reached the only conclusion to explain why she felt so depressed, but after a while, another possibility occurred to her, though it didn't make as much sense as the first one, considering the brief acquaintance she and Asa shared.

I don't believe in love at first sight! she scoffed and would have abandoned this train of thought entirely if she hadn't remembered how she had felt when Asa touched her . . . especially when he'd kissed her.

But I suppose there's such a thing as infatuation at first sight, she admitted thoughtfully, remembering how she hadn't wanted to leave Asa that morning after he'd rescued her, how she'd been thinking of some way to get in touch with him again, how delighted she'd been to find him on the beach that evening.

Would I have been so drawn to him if he'd had two good legs? she speculated. *Or am I so much the mother hen looking for a chick that his injury counted for more than his other attractions?*

Deliberately, Carolyn relived in her mind the kiss on the beach. She couldn't remember worrying about his injured leg then! And he certainly hadn't seemed handicapped in any way when it came to making love.

She felt her skin flush with heat as she remembered the power in his arms as he'd molded her against him, the solid wall of his chest against her breasts, the dominance of his mouth on hers.

No, Asa wasn't a helpless cripple needing a nurse or a mother. He was definitely a man who'd had, at the time he'd kissed her anyway, other needs—very adult, very male, needs.

And I wasn't thinking about mothering him then, either, Carolyn admitted with wry honesty. *I wanted him as much as he wanted me . . . or more. And I suspect that's why I'm really hurt and depressed: because Asa Bradley won't be kissing me, and wanting me, again like that.*

The truth left a dull ache inside her chest, and Carolyn turned on her side, wishing she could go to sleep and wake up in the morning feeling all right again. Asa Bradley had made her forget for a while how much she missed Julie. But then he'd gone away and left her doubly lonely, and that just wasn't fair!

She fell asleep at last, only to dream of what had been on her conscious mind, so that when she woke in the morning, she felt resentful at not having gained a respite.

A knock on her door startled her out of her groggy morning thoughts, and she was quickly on her feet.

"Who is it?" she called through the door.

"It's Martha Goggins, honey," a familiar voice replied. "If I woke you up, I apologize, but the bus is picking us up in thirty minutes. Did you plan to go to the Polynesian Village with us?"

Carolyn unlocked the door and pulled it open, hiding behind it in case there was anyone else in the hall, since she was still in her nightgown.

"Come in, Martha," she invited, managing a smile.

Martha's smile was as warm as Carolyn remembered it as the older woman came into the room, and for just a moment, Carolyn was plunged back into her teenage years after she'd lost her parents. There had been so many times back then when she'd longed to have her Mom and Dad to talk to. Her elderly Aunt Helen had done her duty by her young nieces, especially the infant, Julie. But she hadn't been the sort who could offer advice about boys or any other problems a teenage girl had, and Carolyn had had only her girlfriends to confide in, which hadn't always been satisfactory.

"You didn't get much sleep, did you?" Martha asked as she inspected Carolyn with a maternal eye. Before Carolyn could say anything, she added, "My room's right next door. I had slept for a while, then woke up and was reading my Bible when I heard you come in."

Carolyn shrugged. "It's always hard to rest in a strange bed the first night away from home."

She winced inwardly at telling Martha a little white lie, and then again as she realized she had sounded like Celie. But Martha merely nodded her agreement.

"If you're coming with us, you'd better hurry," she then reminded Carolyn. "I'm afraid you won't have time to eat breakfast before we leave, but I expect there'll be something to eat where we're going."

Carolyn hesitated. She didn't feel like being rushed, and she certainly didn't feel like enduring Celie's company that morning.

Martha's eyes twinkled at her. "Celie won't be coming with us," she said, straight-faced. "Says her arthritis is bothering her too much to walk around all day. She's going to go sit on the sand and let the sun bake her aches and pains, though I'm not sure how the sun's going to get through all the clothes she's wearing. It would be too much to expect her to put on a bathing suit, though. She thinks the styles have been indecent for the last fifty years."

When Carolyn found herself joining in the grin Martha gave at the end of her explanation, she suddenly realized it would be far better for her peace of mind to spend the day with someone as able to take her out of herself as Martha than to sit around moping over a man who'd made it clear he wasn't interested in her.

"It won't take me a minute to get ready," she assured Martha, and then they both burst out laughing at the alacrity with which she'd made up her mind when she'd learned that Celie wasn't coming.

Martha made herself comfortable on the side of the bed and read through a brochure on the Polynesian Village they were to visit while Carolyn rushed through a quick shower and dressed in a pair of white shorts and matching tank top. Then she pulled back her hair from her face and fastened part of it in a ponytail at the back of her head while leaving the rest of it on her neck to shade it from the sun.

"Better put on some sun cream if you have it," Martha said mildly. "You're fair, and they tell me this Hawaiian sun is powerful."

"I have a hat," Carolyn said, dragging a visored white tennis hat from the drawer where she'd put her things, "and I've played tennis all summer. I don't think I'll burn."

She tossed the hat on the dresser, then applied foundation to her skin, and a light layer of blue eyeshadow to her lids, patting it all with a dusting of powder before smearing on a colorless lip coating.

"I'm ready," she informed Martha as she clapped the hat on her head, slipped her feet into a pair of comfortable thong sandals, and grabbed up her straw purse.

Martha, who was clad in a sensible dress and comfortable tennis shoes, stood up and shook her head with admiration as she gave Carolyn a once-over. "You look like a model for one of those high-fashion magazines my daughter-in-law is always buying," she declared. "I don't know how you've managed to stay single so long. The men in Kansas City must be crazy."

Carolyn laughed, appreciating Martha's compliment because she had a good idea that Martha didn't give insincere ones.

"You'd be surprised how fast the ardor died when they learned I came with a ready-made family," she teased, though she wasn't telling the absolute truth. Though it had been true that one or two of the men she'd dated casually over the years hadn't been willing to take Julie on along with Carolyn, there had been a few who would have gotten serious if Carolyn had allowed it. But one of the reasons she had never allowed that to happen was that she knew she couldn't stand some outsider disciplining Julie. And besides, she admitted to herself as she and Martha left the hotel room and Carolyn closed the door behind her, there hadn't been one man in all those years who had made her feel like Asa had when he'd kissed her last night.

Don't think about him, she instructed herself somewhat grimly as she followed Martha to the elevator. *No doubt it's the romantic atmosphere here and being on vacation that made you react to him so strongly, and even if it wasn't, "you're not suited," as Asa put it, so that's the end of that.*

In the lobby, where the rest of the tour group was milling around waiting for the bus, Carolyn was surprised when the huge Hawaiian clerk brought her a Styrofoam cup of coffee.

"Thank you," she said, wondering if he was trying to make up for being so unhelpful the day before.

"In Hawaii, we say *mahalo.*" He flashed his white grin at her, while his large dark eyes inspected her from head to toe, seemingly with pleasure.

"Mahalo," Carolyn echoed agreeably, wondering if he liked what he was seeing from a strictly male viewpoint or if he was merely approving her change of clothing to something more sensible for Hawaii's climate.

"You're welcome," he beamed. "You goin' to Polynesian Cultural Center today?"

Carolyn noted the odd emphasis of syllables he used as she nodded. It sounded very different from mainland speech, more colorful.

"You betta put on sun lotion then," he advised, inspecting

80

her fair skin in a doubtful manner. "Haole wahines burn here sometime."

Carolyn merely smiled and said *"mahalo"* again without explaining that her skin was more immune to the sun than it looked.

The clerk went back to his duties behind the desk and the bus arrived just as Carolyn was finishing her cup of coffee. Martha came back from inspecting a rack of postcards and joined Carolyn, and together they boarded the bus.

As they got started, the tour director explained that they would take in the Nuuanu Pali and a few other sights on their way to the Polynesian Cultural Center, and within a short time, Carolyn was climbing off the bus with the rest of the party, hanging on to her hat to keep the violent winds from snatching it away, and viewing a scene she didn't think she would ever forget.

The lookout point was carved from the wall of a cliff in the Koolau Mountains and as Carolyn gazed out over a panorama of razor-edged mountains, several shades of red earth, and fields of an incredible green to the distant ocean where it met the sky in a joining of blue upon blue, she forgot everything other than the awed appreciation she felt for nature at its most vibrant.

The tour director spoiled things for her somewhat by explaining that the Pass was the setting for a battle between Kamehameha the Great and the defenders of Oahu, and that many of the resisting warriors had been forced over the precipice to fall to their deaths on the jagged rocks 1,000 feet below.

Grimacing at the description, Carolyn wondered if there was anything beautiful in the world that hadn't been soiled at some time or another by the violent emotions of man.

Then they were back on the bus, and were shortly passing through a tunnel to get to the windward side of Oahu. After a while, they were on a road that skirted the ocean and Carolyn and Martha marveled that the views could be so stunning. They agreed that reality outdid the pictures they'd both seen which had looked too perfect to be real.

As they neared the Cultural Center, the guide explained that it was a living museum consisting of authentic native structures and inhabitants, featuring the arts, crafts, skills, sports, and customs of six Polynesian groups: Hawaiian, Tahitian, Samoan, Fijian, Tongan, and Maori.

When they learned that it covered forty acres, Martha gave a dramatic sigh and looked down at her shoes. "Thank goodness Celie didn't come," she whispered to Carolyn, who broke up laughing, then held up one of her own feet.

"I've got room to swell and nothing to blister," she said to Martha, feigning smugness.

"Famous last words," Martha retorted, looking at Carolyn's bare arms and legs and shaking her head.

After lunching at the Gateway Restaurant, Carolyn put on her hat again, Martha clapped the large straw one she'd brought along on her head, and the two of them started off together at a smart pace, disdaining the trams and the canoes some of the other members of the tour were taking.

By the time a couple of hours had passed, however, they were grateful to pause at every attraction and when they saw a large young Samoan split a coconut on a stake fixed in the ground, they agreed it was time for something to drink.

As they sipped the colas they'd bought, Martha looked at Carolyn with a grin. "How come you look as tired as I do?" she teased. "You're young!"

"Ha!" Carolyn groaned as she sat back on a bench and stuck out her feet, which were not only swelling, but had a pink cast over the top of them which told her her skin wasn't as immune to the Hawaiian sun as she'd thought it was. "I don't feel very young right now."

"You ready to take a canoe?" Martha inquired blandly.

"Am I ever!" Carolyn agreed, but by the end of the tour, she still felt as though she'd been dragged around forty acres in the wake of a hot steamroller which periodically backed over her just to remind her who was boss, and she didn't in the least care that the group wasn't staying for dinner and a show being held that evening.

Carolyn and Martha were definitely dragging their feet by the time they arrived back at the hotel, and it didn't help that they found Celie waiting for them in the lobby, looking triumphantly cool and rested.

"Did you have a nice time?" Celie inquired with sweet malice.

"Couldn't have been better," Martha said serenely. "You really missed something, Celie, but I'll show you my snapshots when I get them developed."

Carolyn could hardly keep a straight face, but the urge to laugh departed immediately at Celie's next words.

"Well, hurry up and get dressed for dinner," she said, back to her usual sourness. "I'm hungry. And I don't want any of that Chinese garbage tonight either, Martha."

"I don't either." Martha didn't lose a beat as she headed for the elevator. "I was thinking of trying Japanese food tonight. I've heard their sushi is marvelous."

"I want *American* food, Martha," Celie insisted, trailing after her. "What's sushi, anyway?"

"Raw fish," Martha said with succinct satisfaction as the elevator doors closed on her and Celie.

Carolyn had paused at the desk when the Hawaiian clerk had gestured at her. She couldn't imagine what he wanted and was wondering irritably if he merely wanted to flirt when he held up a pink telephone message sheet, and her heart jerked painfully in her breast. All she could think of was that something might be wrong with Julie, forgetting for the moment that Julie didn't even know where she was.

As she looked at the message, her heart gave another jerk, less painful than the first one, but no less surprising. The message was from Asa and merely said "Call me," followed by a telephone number.

Carolyn glanced up, her expression vague, as she wondered whether she would be wise to call Asa. She had barely thought of him today. Well, she admitted sheepishly an instant later, at least she hadn't thought of him as often as she might have if Martha hadn't been around to distract her. But there was no use even thinking about ignoring his message, she realized with a resigned sigh as she turned to head outside to find the pay phone she had used the day before. She didn't have the willpower.

Asa sat on his balcony with his leg propped up, scowling at nothing as he told himself he hoped Carolyn . . . Carrie—he amended his thoughts, preferring the nickname to the formal one—ignored his message and didn't return his call. He didn't know why he felt it necessary to apologize to her anyway. In a week or so, she would depart for the mainland, he would get on with his life, and soon he would find it difficult to recall her name at all . . . or her face . . . or the way she kissed.

Grimacing with impatience at remembering the pleasure of kissing Carrie, he brought his leg down, got up, and hobbled into the kitchen for a cool beer. As he stood in the kitchen taking a long draft, he found himself gazing at the clock over the refrigerator, figuring how soon Carrie might get back from the Cultural Center the hotel clerk had informed him was on the tour's agenda for the day, before he stopped himself and uttered an audible curse.

You're bored, man, he told himself irritably. *That's all it is. You're well enough to feel like doing something active, but you can't because of the leg, so you're looking for something to distract you. Better look in another direction, Bradley,* he thought with grim irony. *Carrie Winters is a sight too dangerous to play with, even for a big, brave CIA man.*

Since his leg, and his mind if he wanted to be honest about it, hadn't allowed him much sleep the night before, Asa decided to take a nap. What else did a crippled ex–field man do when he was bored out of his skull, he asked himself dryly as he flopped on the bed. If he was lucky, maybe he'd have an erotic dream about Carrie Winters and get her out of his system that way.

The ringing telephone brought him out of just such a dream a couple of hours later, and Asa resented the intrusion. His voice expressed his resentment when he had fumbled the receiver off the hook and answered the call.

"Hello!" he snarled, forgetting in his irritation at losing his dream of Carrie, that his caller might be Carrie in the flesh.

"Asa?" Carolyn was alarmed by his tone, thinking he might still be having a lot of pain with his leg. "Are you all right?" she inquired in an anxious way that showed her concern.

The sound of Carrie's voice blended with Asa's dream, and

though he was fully awake, he hesitated about answering until he had subdued the pleasure that had shot through him at being in contact with her again.

"Yeah," he finally said, just when Carolyn was beginning to get really worried. "I'm fine. How are you?"

Carolyn actually held the phone away from her ear and looked at it in puzzled astonishment. What did he mean, how was she? How was she supposed to be when he'd practically torn her head off the previous evening just for trying to help him! Now that he sounded all right, her relief allowed her anger to surface.

"I'm fine," she said coldly. "And you? How's your leg?"

"Better," Asa answered, suddenly amused by Carolyn's quick change of attitude. He supposed it was like a mother whose child had been lost and then recovered. While worried, she was frantic. When the worry was over, she wanted to kill the little bastard. Asa thought it might be wise to refrain from mentioning that his leg was as recovered as it was ever likely to get.

"Just better?" Carolyn was back to being worried.

"Hey . . . I'm all right," Asa said softly, a reluctant smile curving his lips as he became aware that having someone care about him felt good. He was torn between enjoying the real pleasure Carrie's concern gave him, apologizing for his behavior the previous evening, and getting off the phone—permanently.

"You're sure?" Carolyn persisted, then realizing that she might be playing the motherly role she seemed addicted to, she quickly added, "Well, of course you are. You wouldn't say so if you weren't, right? So . . . why did you call, Asa?"

Asa hesitated. Carrie's bluntness took him by surprise at times, and he reacted by refusing to give in to what he considered pressure.

Carolyn forced herself to remain quiet, though she was beginning to want to scream at Asa. Why did he have to be so damned difficult?

"I wanted to apologize for last night." Asa finally got to the point. "I'm sorry I behaved badly to you."

Now it was Carolyn's turn to hesitate. Asa's apology disarmed her, and she began to melt toward him. But she was reminding herself that she shouldn't trust Asa when he was being disarming. It never lasted.

"Carrie?" Asa sat up on the bed, forgetting for a moment that he should want her to stay angry with him, that he shouldn't have called her to apologize in the first place. And especially that he shouldn't be wanting to see her again.

"It-it's all right, Asa," Carolyn opted for grudging graciousness. "The circumstances were . . . well, I might have yelled at you if I'd been hurting the way you were."

"I doubt it," he drawled, unable to picture her losing her temper, no matter what the provocation.

"Why should you doubt it?" Carolyn demanded, about to prove Asa wrong as her temper rose. "Asa, you're the most frustrating man I've ever met! Are you under the impression I don't have feelings like everyone else? If you are, why bother to apologize to me?" she interjected quickly before he could break in. "Why assume there's a need to?" *And why bother to kiss me?* she added silently, her temper rising another notch.

"Hey . . . hey . . ." Asa, somewhat astonished by her outburst, automatically tried to soothe her.

"Don't 'hey' me!" Carolyn snapped. "You're like a yo-yo, Asa Bradley! You make me feel totally off balance!"

Silently, Asa admitted there was truth in her assertion, and that she had good reason to be confused about him. He was confused himself, for God's sake! Aloud, he continued to try to soothe her.

"I'm sorry," he said quietly. "I'm going through a bad time right now, Carrie."

Asa didn't consider he'd given her a valid excuse for his behavior, but Carolyn immediately quietened.

"I'm sure you are," she said soberly. "And I accept your apology, Asa." She paused, and then couldn't help herself. "Asa, is your leg really better?"

"Yes," he assured her, smiling again at her concern. "Did you have a good time today at the Cultural Center?" he said to get off the subject of his leg.

"Yes, but it was tiring," Carolyn answered. Then, frowning, "How did you know where I was?"

"The desk clerk."

"Oh . . . yes, I see. Have you ever been there?"

"No." Asa was amused by the question. He hadn't had much time in his adult life for such amusements, even if he were the type to be inclined toward them.

Carolyn started to say that he should go, then bit her tongue just in time. A forty-acre stroll was not the sort of venture you recommended to a man with an injured leg.

A silence between them developed as Carolyn fought her inclination to ask Asa questions she knew he wouldn't appreciate, though she had no idea why he resented such questions, and Asa fought his inclination to invite Carolyn to dinner again.

"Ah . . . I, uh, should probably get back to the hotel and shower." Carolyn finally couldn't stand the silence any longer. "I haven't had dinner."

Immediately, Carolyn regretted bringing up dinner. It sounded too much as if she were trying to get him to ask her out again. In truth, she would have loved to have dinner with him. There was no use in pretending differently, despite the fact that she found Asa a very difficult man to deal with. But she wished it didn't sound as if she wanted an invitation from him.

"What do you mean, get back to the hotel?" Asa asked in order to keep himself from extending the invitation that was on the tip of his tongue. "Aren't you in your room?"

Carolyn sighed. "My room doesn't have a phone," she explained. "And there isn't one in the lobby either. I'm outside on the street using a pay phone."

"I'm sorry to have put you to the trouble," Asa said, and indeed he was sorry. So sorry that he began to think he should make things up to her for that inconvenience, as well as the way he'd behaved the night before, by going ahead and asking her out.

God, aren't you clever, Bradley? he addressed himself with ironic self-disgust. *Why not just admit that you want to be with the woman?*

"It's all right, Asa," Carolyn sighed, beginning to think that if there were a possibility of the two of them having a relationship, it might always be like this—Asa apologizing while she accepted his apologies. Perhaps it was just as well if they didn't see one another . . .

"Carrie, have dinner with me," Asa said, abruptly making up his mind. He'd be damned if he'd sit in this depressing apartment all evening wishing he'd done what he just had. She'd be leaving in a few days. He could sit in his depressing apartment then!

Carolyn started to ask, "Are you sure—" but she quickly decided against it. He might say he wasn't sure at all.

"Fine, Asa," she said, taking care to sound coolly casual. "Can you give me an hour or so to get ready?"

"Sure," Asa said in a brusque way he regretted immediately. Why was it, he wondered grimly, that if he was going to behave like a fool, he couldn't do it gracefully, instead of performing like the yo-yo Carrie had described? He made up his mind to change his ways, starting immediately.

"I'll pick you up about eight," he said, softening his tone. "And I'll try not to do anything I have to apologize for tonight," he added with dry purposefulness.

I'd rather you did, Carolyn sighed silently, thinking he might be referring to making love to her. If he should, that was one apology she wouldn't accept!

"See you soon, then." She elected to ignore his last comment. "Oh . . . ," she added quickly. "Is there any particular way I should dress?"

"Something like what you had on last night will be fine," Asa drawled, thinking, *more than fine—beautiful.*

When Carolyn had hung up, Asa sat on the side of his bed, his expression intent as he sorted out where he was going with this. He'd never faced this sort of situation before. He'd been too smart. Now, it seemed as though fate, by throwing Carrie Winters into his lap at a time when everything else in his life was going wrong, was conspiring to get him in over his head.

Asa didn't like the feeling of losing control of his own destiny the injury to his leg had produced. And he didn't like the feeling of losing control of his willpower that Carrie produced in him. But, he admitted grudgingly, he liked even less the thought of letting her slip away out of his life without experiencing what he suspected would be a very special encounter.

Would it be special enough for her though? he wondered.

Special enough for her to take it for what it was without getting hurt when she couldn't have more?

Don't be so egotistical, he told himself irritably. *What makes you think she'll want more than a short affair? She may be the marrying kind, but you may not be the one she wants to marry . . . not if she has any sense.*

It didn't occur to Asa that his worries on Carolyn's behalf could be applied to himself. Oh, he was fairly sure he wouldn't get out of this one with as few regrets as he always had before. But that he might ever want marriage was out of the question. After all, there was always the chance that someday, something could be done about his leg that would allow him to get back in the field. New medical miracles occurred every day. And a field man had no business with a wife.

Take what's offered, Bradley, and let Carrie make her own decisions, he told himself as he got to his feet and hobbled toward the shower. *As the old Spanish proverb says, "Take what you want . . . and pay for it if you have to." That holds true for women nowadays as well as men. And I doubt the price will be more than either of us can afford.*

The question settled in his mind, Asa whistled cheerfully as he showered, refusing to consciously acknowledge how his mood had changed now that he had given himself permission to take what he wanted, nor how much more he was looking forward to the dinner date than he had looked forward to anything since a bullet had ripped into his knee two months ago and ended everything he considered made life worthwhile.

CHAPTER SEVEN

Her eagerness to be with Asa again was evidenced by the fact that Carolyn was dressed, made up, and standing in front of her dresser mirror inspecting herself half an hour before he was due to pick her up.

Tonight she wore a white sundress, and the sun she'd gotten that day imparted a glow to her skin the color of the dress emphasized. She'd used a curling iron on her hair, so that it looked slightly windblown instead of smooth and sleek the way she normally wore it, and she'd applied her makeup with a skillful hand so that her smooth, regular features and large eyes were dramatically emphasized.

As she sprayed herself lightly with an expensive perfume, Carolyn supposed her appearance was as good as it was going to get and there was no point staying in her room to fidget.

Also, Asa's telephone message had made her feel slightly guilty about being out of pocket in case Julie should need her. She'd left word with one of Julie's friends where she was, but her little sister wouldn't know that Carolyn was on vacation in Hawaii unless she called Kansas City. Yet Carolyn was reluctant to call Julie and speak directly to her over the phone. Hearing her little sister's voice might plunge her into a state of depression again, which would negate the purpose of the vacation. So she decided instead to go down to the lobby, buy a postcard, and send it to Julie. The vacation would be all but over before the card arrived in England, but writing and sending it would make Carolyn feel less guilty about dropping out of sight.

She'll probably think I've gone completely around the bend, Carolyn shrugged, not certain that Julie would be too far off the mark. Since making her decision to take this trip in such an off-the-wall fashion, then meeting Asa after she'd gotten here, Carolyn had the feeling at times that she had somehow stepped completely out of the real world and was temporarily living a dream.

If I am, I'd just as soon not wake up for a while. She smiled at herself in the mirror, then pivoted, grabbed a sweater and her purse, and left her room feeling more optimistic than she had in ages.

The Hawaiian clerk had been replaced by a delicately pretty young Oriental woman, and after exchanging smiles, Carolyn thumbed through the rack of postcards and finally chose one picturing Waikiki Beach. Seating herself in one of the rattan lobby chairs and thinking for a few moments, she finally penned:

> Missed you and came here to distract myself. It's lovely. Will be here two weeks. We'll come here together sometime. Hope all is well with you.
>
> > Love you,
> > Carrie

Satisfied, Carolyn got up and went to the desk for a stamp.

When the clerk had sold her one, Carolyn stamped the postcard, handed it to the clerk, then went back to her chair to await Asa.

From Carolyn's point of view, Asa's arrival was badly timed. He came through the hotel door just as Martha and Celie stepped out of the elevator, and Carolyn realized the two women might be expecting her to dine with them. She wouldn't have cared if it had just been Martha, but she had an idea Celie's evil little mind would begin hatching all sorts of questions about how Carolyn had met Asa.

She was on her feet when both Asa and the two women descended upon her at the same moment.

"Hello, Asa," she greeted him first with a friendly smile, but before he could respond, she then turned to Martha, who was looking Asa over with what Carolyn thought was surprised approval. She ignored Celie for the moment, which turned out to be a mistake, because Celie spoke before Carolyn could, eyeing Asa with definite *disapproval* as she did so.

"Are you ready to go to dinner with us, Carrie?" she inquired, and Carolyn thought she sounded belligerent.

"Actually, no." Carolyn kept her irritation out of her voice and spoke with calm dignity. "I'm dining with Asa Bradley tonight. Asa"—she turned to him and winced inwardly when she saw an expression of amused mockery in his dark eyes—"this is Martha Goggins and Celie White. Martha . . . Celie . . . Asa Bradley, a friend of mine."

Carolyn could have killed Celie when she saw the woman give Asa an up-and-down look filled with disdainful suspicion. Perhaps it was his beard she didn't like, or perhaps Celie was just a man hater, but whatever the reason, Carolyn was exceedingly grateful to Martha when she held out her hand to Asa, gave him a warm smile, and said, "It's nice to meet you, Mr. Bradley. Doesn't our Carolyn look lovely tonight?"

"Indeed she does," Asa responded politely in his attractive voice as he flashed Carolyn an encompassing look of approval.

Carolyn didn't know if he was being sincere or merely polite, but she was pleased to see him shake hands with Martha. She was also amused when neither he nor Celie offered their hands to each other and, as though by mutual consent, each ignored the other's presence altogether.

"Well, we'd better get on our way, Celie." Martha took charge of ending the episode by taking Celie's arm as though to pull her away by force if necessary. "I hope the two of you have a pleasant evening." She nodded to Asa, gave Carolyn a sincere smile and a twinkling look filled with mischievous encouragement, then dragged the scowling Celie away with her out the hotel door.

Carolyn faced Asa and was immediately aware that he was amused by, and curious about, her relationship with Martha and Celie.

She lifted her shoulders in a shrug. "I decided on the spur of the moment to come here," she explained, "and the only thing available was a cancellation on a tour of retirees. Martha took me under her wing. She's a darling, don't you think?"

"She seemed very nice, yes," Asa said gravely, though his

eyes were shining with laughter. "But the other one seemed to have doubts about me."

Carolyn grimaced. "Celie's a sourpuss, and I'm not sure she likes men, period."

"Good," Asa responded, his eyes fairly dancing with laughter now. "I was afraid there was something about me that didn't seem respectable . . . my beard perhaps?"

Carolyn inspected him in a wry manner. "Well, as far as that goes, I don't know you well enough myself to vouch for your respectability," she drawled. "All I really know about you is that you rescue maidens in distress, you speak Chinese with a great deal of assurance, and you're as temperamental a man as I've ever met. Does that about sum it up?"

Asa raised an eyebrow, and the wicked glow in his eyes reminded her of something else she knew about him.

Carolyn flushed a little as she took his meaning. "Oh, yes," she added faintly. "And you kiss strange women on the beach."

"*Strange* women?" Asa teased in a low, suggestive voice. "Are you strange, Carrie? Should I look for a reference concerning *your* respectability?"

Carolyn scowled at him. "Let's go to dinner," she suggested, ignoring his question. "I'm starved."

A grin tugged at Asa's mouth. "But you haven't told me how I rate at kissing strange women on the beach," he said as he took her hand, and started toward the exit. "It seems to me . . ."

"It seems to *me*—" Carolyn interrupted firmly, ". . . that it would be wise to drop the subject for now."

"Does that mean we can talk about it again later?" Asa quickly riposted, his smile wicked.

Carolyn sighed, aware from the tingle in the hand that Asa held that she would be disappointed if they didn't get back to the subject of kisses later in the evening.

"Only if I get a rating, too," she murmured, casting a teasing glance upward at Asa's smiling face.

As he dropped her hand to push the door of the hotel open for her, the expression in Asa's eyes made Carolyn's pulse escalate.

"I can give you that right now," he murmured back, his voice seductively caressing. "Shall I?"

Carolyn, aware that her whole body felt flushed and tingling now, shook her head and looked away as she stepped through the door into the soft Hawaiian night. She was grateful for the breeze which cooled her skin as Asa followed her out, again took her hand, and guided her toward his car.

To distract herself from his touch, Carolyn glanced at his leg, relieved to see that Asa wasn't walking any differently than he had before he'd hurt himself the night before.

Asa caught her at it. "I'm fine," he assured her quietly.

Carolyn looked up at his face, and at failing to see any expression of pain there, she felt herself relax.

"I'm glad," she said simply, and was rewarded with another charming smile from Asa.

As they walked, Asa reflected that he seemed to be doing a lot of smiling since he'd met Carrie. It felt good to be able to smile again. He wondered, however, if he would continue to feel like smiling when she left to go back to the mainland. Then he shrugged the thought away and concentrated on the pleasure of having her company now. He was used to taking his pleasure in concentrated doses, and relinquishing it easily when it was over. He didn't think things would be any different where Carrie was concerned.

In the car, before he turned on the ignition, he sat back and gave Carolyn a long look that brought the tingle back to her skin.

"Martha was right," he finally said in a soft drawl. "You do look lovely tonight."

Carolyn had to swallow before she could say anything at all. "Thank you," she finally replied faintly, bringing another smile to Asa's lips as he detected the disturbance inside her—a disturbance that pleased him, since it was an indication that she was very aware of him as a man.

He gave her a few moments to recover as he started the car and pulled out into traffic. Then he startled her again.

"How do you like my beard?" he asked in a thoughtful way.

Surprised by the question, Carolyn inspected his face, her eyes wide and curious. "I like it," she shrugged, "but then I don't have anything to compare it to since I've never seen you without it." She hesitated, then asked, "Do *you* like it?"

Asa shrugged. "It just seemed easier for a while," he said, the vagueness of his reply puzzling Carolyn.

"You mean while you were recuperating from your injury?" she inquired, and was immediately aware of a certain tension in Asa that told she had once again asked something he didn't want to answer. She felt extremely frustrated by his reaction. Why didn't he want to tell her how he'd hurt his leg? And why didn't she have the courage to ask him straight out?

"Yes," Asa nodded, his tone distant. "It was hard to stand up long enough to shave at first." Then he quickly changed the subject. "I thought we'd have steak tonight. Is that all right with you?"

Inwardly, Carolyn sighed at this indication that Asa's behavior tonight was apparently going to be as puzzling as it had been the previous night. Aloud, she merely said, "Yes. Steak sounds wonderful."

"Good." Asa glanced at her with a smile, then started asking her about her day.

Carolyn didn't believe Asa really cared about how she'd spent her day, but she obligingly offered up a few tidbits about what she and Martha had seen at the Cultural Center. Then she remembered the Pali and asked Asa if he'd ever seen it.

He nodded. "Yes, it's impressive."

"And absolutely beautiful," Carolyn agreed. "But I liked it better before the guide told us about the Hawaiian warriors being thrown off it."

Asa glanced at her, his gaze thoughtful. "You don't like violence," he said in a casual way, not as though he were asking a question but had reached a conclusion.

Carolyn shook her head and shuddered. "I hate it," she said soberly. "I've never understood why wars were necessary, why people have to hate one another."

Asa's smile was cynical. "Wishing it weren't so doesn't change anything," he commented dryly.

"I suppose not," Carolyn agreed, her tone wistful. "But it still doesn't make it any easier for me to understand how one human being can kill another, or rob them or . . ."

She paused, thinking about her encounter with the young man the previous morning, wondering if she should have contacted the authorities about him. Might he hurt someone else because she hadn't?

But Asa was speaking again, distracting her.

"Maybe it's because you've never wanted for anything in your life," he said, giving her a look that Carolyn found disturbing. It was as though he found her thinking incredibly naïve. "If your family were starving or freezing, wouldn't you be tempted to fight to feed and clothe them?" he asked, but without waiting for an answer, he continued, "And then there are the fanatics—the ones who think they've found *the* answer to the world's problems and want to force that answer onto everyone else. Would you suggest people like us just sit back and let them dictate our lives for us?"

Carolyn was a little astonished by how seriously Asa spoke, and she felt uncomfortable because she sensed he was feeling impatient with her. Admittedly, she had led a sheltered, comfortable life and aside from donations to charities, she'd never given much thought to the material needs of other people, nor had she bothered much about world politics. She had concentrated almost totally on her responsibility to Julie and her love for her. But was that a crime? She had the uneasy feeling that Asa thought so.

In fact, Asa *was* feeling impatient with Carolyn. He considered her wrapped up in her own safe, comfortable life with no true conception of the total world picture.

"Asa?" Carolyn drew his attention, and when he looked at her, frowning with his thoughts, he realized how uncomfortable he was making her. He didn't feel particularly repentant about it, however. Maybe it was time someone made her uncomfortable, he thought irritably.

Nevertheless, he gave her a perfunctory apology. "Sorry," he shrugged, and Carolyn knew he wasn't sorry, not really.

"No, you aren't," she said in a quiet way that made him jerk his head around to gaze at her. "There's no need to apologize to me without meaning it, Asa," she added, her gaze troubled. "I suppose I understand your impatience with me. I admit I don't pay much attention to world affairs and that I'm fortunate and

never had to worry about where the next meal was coming from
—" She lifted her shoulders in a shrug then. "—or even how I
would pay for my next new dress."

Asa was torn between admiring her quiet admission and his
impatience with the complacency she was admitting to. He supposed she was no different from thousands of other Americans,
though, too many of them in Asa's opinion. She was the one he
was attracted to at the moment, however, and he would have
preferred her to be more politically aware. He wondered cynically how she would take knowing just how politically aware he
was. Would she cringe away from him in horror because he'd
been trained to combat the violence she hated with a violence
of his own?

Carolyn was staring at his hard expression with dismayed
confusion, aware that this discussion had somehow derailed the
pleasant beginning of their evening. She didn't know how to get
things back on track, and in any case, Asa was now pulling into
the parking lot of a restaurant so there was no chance to say
anything further for the time being.

When he'd parked the car, Asa looked over at Carolyn, and
at seeing the subdued bewilderment in her eyes, he felt a little
ashamed of himself, as though he'd been browbeating an innocent child who couldn't be expected to behave like an adult.
But damn it, she wasn't a child and it wasn't a child he wanted
in his bed that night! She was a woman, and he wanted her to
think like one.

"Asa, please . . ." Carolyn was frowning at him in consternation, and Asa realized he'd been scowling at her. "What's the
matter with you? Why are you so angry?"

Asa took a deep breath and forced himself to relax, thinking
that even if his injury hadn't taken him out of the field, maybe
he'd been due for a respite anyway. The constant danger of
living on the edge had a way of making agents forget that it was
people like Carolyn they were trying to protect—people who
had a right to a certain amount of innocence. He'd made a
bargain when he'd joined the Company that he'd exchange his
innocence to protect theirs, and it was time he remembered that
bargain.

"I guess I didn't get through the evening without doing something I have to apologize for, did I?" he asked.

Carolyn shook her head. "Asa, I don't like feeling that I'm the sort of person who is always due apologies," she said soberly. "It makes me feel—" She hesitated, then remembered Julie's expression about how she'd been feeling. "—like a creep," she finished in a wryly thoughtful manner.

That brought a smile to Asa's lips, and he leaned forward, sliding his hand under her hair to rest it on the nape of her neck, a gesture which immediately turned his thoughts, as well as Carolyn's, away from everything but their physical attraction for one another.

The smile disappeared as Asa held Carolyn's gaze and slowly pulled her toward him while he leaned further forward. When he was a breath away from her mouth, he scanned her face with his eyes. The slumberous sensuality in their dark depths produced a languorous feeling of expectancy in Carolyn, and her lips parted slightly to receive his kiss.

"Forgive me," he whispered, and received his answer when Carolyn closed the distance between them and placed her mouth lightly against his.

Asa quickly deepened the kiss, and the sensations he produced in Carolyn with his lips and the gentle probing of his tongue, as well as the light stroking of his fingers against the nape of her neck, brought a shuddering submission from her.

She raised a hand up to his neck. He was wearing a white open-necked shirt and she slid her fingers inside the opening to touch the slope of his neck as it joined his shoulder.

Her tentative exploration brought a surge of arousal into Asa's loins, and he drew back slightly to stare into her eyes, the lambent glow deep in the depths of his own alerting Carolyn that she was playing with fire. She supposed she should feel cautious about that, but it was beyond her to feel anything but a deeply feminine pleasure at his response to her.

Without saying anything, Asa slowly released her, but Carolyn couldn't feel disappointed when she interpreted his gaze to mean that he was only forcing a temporary intermission upon himself and her, and she was silent as he got out of the car and limped around to open her door.

When she stood beside him, she felt almost overwhelmed by the variety of emotions he caused in her. She had never felt her own femininity so strongly until she was forced to contrast it against Asa's masculinity. It was a good contrast, she decided as he took her arm to lead her to the restaurant. She appreciated the male power in him.

But there was more to her feelings than a basic awareness of him as a man, she realized. She felt a tenderness toward him as well. Indeed, she felt so many things about Asa Bradley, and there was such depth to those feelings, that she was suddenly frightened as she became aware that he wasn't the type of man she could forget easily when her stay in Hawaii was over. Because he wasn't going to ask her to stay when her vacation was over. She was abruptly, devastatingly sure of that.

Carolyn was wrapped in her own thoughts as they entered the pleasantly decorated restaurant and were seated at a table beside a glass window looking out on a wildly beautiful garden. She was trying with a sort of desperate urgency to decide whether to play it safe with Asa while there was still time, or risk her fragile emotional well-being by plunging into an all-out experience with him she suspected wouldn't leave her unscarred.

"Shall I order for you?" Asa asked quietly, sensing Carolyn's mood and empathizing with it to a certain degree. The kiss they'd exchanged in the car had shaken him more than he cared to admit.

"Please." Carolyn nodded, her gaze abstracted as she fought to turn off her mind against her feeling that it was desperately important to decide something before dinner was over. Surely she was exaggerating the situation, she thought in a haze of bewildered confusion. Surely Asa couldn't have gained such power over her in the brief time they'd known one another.

But as she looked across the table into his eyes, she knew he had. And she knew as well that there was absolutely nothing she could do about it now. She had somehow crossed over that imaginary line that separated control of her own fate and safety, into a wild country—wilder than the beautiful junglelike growth outside the window—where only emotion reigned and where Asa pulled the strings.

A waiter appeared and Asa ordered steak dinners. When they were alone again, Asa looked across at Carolyn, and as though sensing her emotional disturbance, reached his hand across the table with the palm up.

Carolyn stared at his hand a moment, then slowly placed her palm against his, closing her eyes briefly when she felt her fear drain away as though Asa were pulling it out of her.

When she opened her eyes, his were smiling at her.

"All right?" he murmured, and Carolyn nodded, letting out the breath she had been holding without realizing it.

"Yes," she said, feeling tension draining out of her body as her fear had drained a moment earlier. "I suppose I am."

"Good," he said quietly, and squeezed her hand lightly before letting her go.

Later, for the life of her, Carolyn could never remember what they talked about as they dined in a leisurely fashion on fresh pineapple in a marshmallow sauce, followed by steak, baked potato, crusty bread, and fresh coconut pie.

She ate well. She could remember that. And she could remember that the sound of Asa's quiet voice had wrapped her in a protective haze of serenity and that she had presumably answered him appropriately from time to time. But the words were missing.

Asa wouldn't have been surprised had he known that Carolyn wasn't really taking in his small talk. He couldn't remember later what he'd found to say for the hour and a half they'd sat dining together. He was focused on the future—the immediate one which would occur after dinner—when he was going to make love to Carrie and reality would take on meaning again. Meanwhile, he was content to sit in his haze of expectation and eat the dinner that seemed to have no texture and mouth words that seemed to have no meaning at all.

At last, the bill for the meal was in front of him, and he paid it, and then he stood up, barely feeling the ache in his leg that had developed from sitting in one position too long, grasped his cane, and escorted Carrie out to the car.

"We'll go to my apartment," he said with simple directness as he started the engine, glancing at Carrie as though for confirmation, though he knew it wasn't necessary.

"Yes." Carolyn, still wrapped in a hazy world where reality was on the other side of an impenetrable glass, gave her assent as simply as Asa had asked for it.

They didn't bother to talk until the door of Asa's apartment closed behind them. Then, as he leaned back against it and pulled Carolyn into his arms and she met his kiss as naturally and hungrily as he gave it, reality exploded inside both of them with stunning force.

Asa found himself wanting to do something foolishly dramatic, such as he had previously thought happened only in novels and movies. He wanted to pick Carolyn up in his arms and carry her to his bedroom like the proverbial conquering male. He noted his unreasonable disappointment that his leg prevented carrying out the ridiculous gesture, and was amused, thinking he must be in deeper than he'd thought to even entertain the notion at all. It had never been his style.

But then Carolyn nestled her head in the curve between his neck and shoulder, and her warm lips touched his skin, and Asa ceased worrying about what was ridiculous and what wasn't.

"Come to bed, Carrie," he whispered huskily, holding her tighter for a moment before he straightened and pulled her resisting arms from around his waist so that they could walk to his bedroom.

She hugged his arm against her as they moved to the bedroom, walking with her eyes half-closed until Asa shut the door behind him. Then she opened them wide in the room lit softly by a streetlight outside, in order to see Asa and the bed where he would make her his own.

Her eyes adjusted as he drew her to the bed, and she saw his expression plainly as, after unzipping her sundress and letting it slip down her body, and discovering she wore no bra, his eyes took on that same exciting sensuality she had seen in them in the car earlier.

He lifted his hands to touch her, and Carolyn thought she might faint as his warm palms cupped her breasts and his thumbs traced an erotic pattern lightly across the tips of them.

"You're beautiful, Carrie," he murmured, his soft, seductive tones weaving a spell in her head as effective as the one his hands were weaving on her body.

Then his mouth was on hers and he was following her down onto the bed where he continued to kiss her and stroke her with hands she thought must be magical to elicit the delicious sensations they brought to life inside her. She wondered if her touch affected him that way, and was deeply pleased when, after unbuttoning his shirt, she heard him groan and felt him shudder as she drew her fingers lightly over his shoulders and chest.

"Carrie, wait . . ." For the first time in his life, Asa was uncertain about maintaining control over his body, and he wanted so intensely to keep control and bring pleasure to Carrie.

He drew her hands away from him, pleased when she was plainly disappointed at the loss of contact, and got up to shrug out of his clothes. Nude, he bent to slide the delicate lace panties she wore over her hips and tossed them aside, then rejoined her on the bed, his sexual excitement pounding in his head and in his loins.

Carrie arched up to meet him and caught her breath when she felt the warmth and strength of his body against hers, then gasped as she felt his full weight on her, pressing her back on the bed.

She felt the escalation in his need and gloried in the difference of his approach as his caresses dominated her body and demanded her response. Her own need had risen to meet his, and she encouraged the scope of his kisses and the urgency of his hands on her with a response calculated to drive him further.

"Carrie . . ." The roughness of desire in his voice wasn't echoed in the gentleness of his hand as he parted her thighs and slid searching fingers into her.

Carolyn gasped and arched, then clasped his wrist with her fingers to make him stop.

"You don't like that?" he murmured, tender, sensual amusement underlying his deep tones.

"Asa . . . please . . ." she panted, digging the fingers of her free hand into his shoulder and loosening her clasp on his wrist as she lifted her mouth to his and accepted the thrust of his tongue with a total submission that pushed Asa to the brink of release.

He moved the hand she was now holding in a light grip and, linking his fingers with hers, pushed her arm to the side, pressing it to the mattress as he quickly shifted his body and nestled between her thighs. Carrie instinctively raised her hips and accepted the thrust he made in one smooth motion, inhaling sharply as she felt him enter her.

"Oh, Carrie . . ." Asa whispered against her lips. "Carrie . . . Carrie . . ."

And then there were no more words as he brought her, with sure swiftness, the satisfaction she craved, delaying his own until she triggered his release by shuddering in his arms in a surrender that was as devastating to his emotions as to his body.

It was a long time afterward that Asa at last began to believe what his uncharacteristic reactions to Carolyn Winters had been trying to tell him all along. He wasn't going to get out of this relationship as easily as he always had managed with women before . . . if he managed to get out of it at all.

CHAPTER EIGHT

Asa lay on his back dozing when Carrie made a slight movement in her sleep and brought him wide awake, his muscles tensed for action. It had been a long time since he'd woken in a bed with someone beside him.

He relaxed as he realized it was Carrie who had moved, and turned his head to glance at her and see if she was awake. She wasn't, and as he stared at her slightly parted lips and the way she was curled up like a child, he felt an uncharacteristic tender, protective feeling come into his heart that he enjoyed for a moment before the implications of that feeling brought a frown to his lips.

Quietly, he slipped from under the sheet and got to his feet, realizing as he did so that his knee wasn't aching as badly as it normally did when he first woke. He smiled with somewhat grim amusement, wondering if he should tell his doctors to start recommending sleeping with a beautiful woman as an effective pain reliever for male patients with his problem.

In the bathroom, Asa gazed thoughtfully at his reflection in the mirror over the sink, thinking he looked decidedly scruffy. No wonder the old biddy—what was her name? Celie something, wasn't it?—had eyed him as though he were a rapist on the prowl earlier that evening. His hair was way past due for a cut, and his beard definitely needed a trim. But at least his eyes had lost some of the hostility he'd avoided looking at for the past two months.

Somewhat absently, Asa searched in the vanity drawer for a small pair of scissors that were part of a manicure set he seldom used and when he had them, he started trying to trim his beard, making a botch of it because he'd never worn a beard before, and therefore had had no experience at trimming one. He'd planned to have a barber do it when he'd gotten around to going to one.

Finally, he looked at the mess he'd made, grinned, shrugged, and got out his razor to shave the whole thing off. When he was done, he was surprised to realize that looking at his clean-shaven face made him feel more like his old self.

He began to wonder if his improved mental outlook was a natural result of time passing and being well enough to be given a new assignment, or if Carrie Winters had something to do with the change.

He mouthed a silent curse as he realized he needed to do some more thinking about Carrie. He'd thought he had the matter settled in his own mind, but making love to her had scrambled everything up. He hadn't expected the damned earth to move! But it did. So much for simple sexual encounters. And on top of that was this new protective feeling he had toward her, which made him more than a little uneasy and demanded that he look at things from her point of view again.

But wasn't this the age of women's liberation? He didn't have to be responsible for her feelings, he thought irritably.

Damn it, he'd had enough responsibilities connected with his work. Running a network was something like playing father to a whole group of people, only worse, because the situation they were all in was a life and death one. It was a series of relationships built on trust and respect, and every time he'd sent one of his people on a mission, he'd had to sweat it out until they were back safe. And he'd felt guilty as hell getting shot up and having to leave them to someone else . . . someone who might not care as much or know the ropes the way he did . . . someone new for his people to get used to, which might unsettle them and play on their nerves, perhaps causing a disastrous mistake.

Asa leaned on the sink with his head down, eyes closed, teeth clenched, as he dredged up all the things that had made his life a living nightmare for two months, thinking he sure as hell didn't want to have to worry about a spoiled little socialite getting her feelings hurt when there were people he'd left behind him whose lives were at stake!

Asa lifted his head and shifted his body with unwise impatience and got a stab of pain in his knee as a reward. He grimaced, then caught sight of his face in the mirror and went still as the knowledge of his impotence to do anything about those people he'd left behind crashed in on him again.

What was the good of taking out on Carrie his fury at what fate had dealt him? he wondered bleakly. It wasn't her fault. If it was anybody's, it was his own for not recognizing in time that he was nurturing a traitor in his network—a traitor who, for all Asa knew, might already have blown that network he was so concerned about before he'd gotten caught.

Asa sighed and straightened, suddenly longing to forget everything again for a while, the way he had at times since Carrie had come into his life. Especially the way he had when he'd made love to her. Didn't he deserve a little forgetfulness? Hadn't he put his life on the line for his country, for people just like Carrie? Didn't she owe him something, even if it cost her a little emotional pain?

Asa shook his head, knowing his thinking was off-center. The truth was that neither Carrie Winters, nor anyone else, owed him a thing. He'd made his own decision about how to live his life, and despite the danger and the hardship he'd had to endure at times, he would go right back to it if the Company would let him, because it was the life he wanted.

It was also the life he couldn't have anymore.

On that bleak thought, Asa moved, turning off the bathroom light, letting himself quietly back into the bedroom, seeking the comfort and forgetfulness Carrie could give him. He would worry about her later. Right now, he needed her.

After slipping into bed, Asa scooted over under the sheet. Carrie had her back to him, and he slid his arms around her, gathering her up close to his body, curving his legs into the curve of hers spoon-fashion, uncaring that the position made his knee ache.

Carolyn stirred and came groggily awake. She was disoriented for a moment, then smiled with sleepy contentment as she recognized that it was Asa's arms and body that sheltered her. She turned her head and as he lifted his to look at her, she kissed his cheek, then shifted around to face him.

106

Smiling, Asa raised up on his elbow and rested his head on his hand, content for the moment just to look at her.

"I fell asleep," she murmured, smiling sleepily back at him.

"So did I," he answered softly. "For a while."

Carolyn frowned then, blinking up at him. There was something different about his face, but for a moment she didn't realize what it was. Then she caught the scent of his aftershave and her eyes opened wider.

"Asa, you shaved off your beard," she said with quiet amazement. "Why?"

"Don't you like it?" He managed to sound offended, but he couldn't contain his smile at the look of surprise on her face.

"I don't know yet," she said simply, reaching a hand up to stroke his smooth cheek. "It feels sort of strange to fall asleep with a bearded man and wake up with someone else."

Asa's smile broadened momentarily and then he took her hand in his, turned it over and kissed the palm. "I'm still the same man," he whispered huskily. "Want me to show you?"

"Maybe you'd better," Carolyn agreed, a sweetly complacent smile tilting her mouth.

Asa leaned down and kissed away the complacency, moving his body to half cover hers as he did so. When he let her breathe again, her smile was gone, but her eyes were slumberously welcoming.

"Feel familiar?" he murmured, kissing each corner of her mouth.

"Not quite as tingly," Carolyn demurred in a teasing whisper.

"Oh, is it tingles you want?"

Carolyn started to nod, but Asa caught her mouth in a kiss that definitely produced tingles. She arched in a delicious stretch, which brought the length of her close against the warmth and strength of Asa's body, ending the stretch by turning on her back and bringing her arms around his shoulders to pull him over her.

"I think I detect tingles," Asa teased with soft humor as he propped his weight on his elbows and looked down at Carolyn's smiling face.

She nodded and wriggled a little, seeking a more comfortable position beneath him, and immediately felt his response to her movement. Looking into his face, she saw the rugged lines of it tautening with sexual arousal, and she went still, eyes wide with fascination at what she was seeing and feeling happening as a result of a simple movement of hers.

"Why the surprise?" Asa muttered, his voice thickening. "I would have sworn you knew what happens to men when they want you."

Carolyn frowned a little. "I'm not all that experienced, Asa," she said with soft hesitancy, as if uncertain he would believe her.

"You weren't a virgin," he pointed out, hurting her a little.

Emotionally, she withdrew a little from him, and Asa sensed it and frowned.

"Hey." He spoke more softly now. "What does it matter? Neither was I . . . and I try not to be too much of a male chauvinist when I can help it."

His attempt to smooth things over didn't help. Carolyn wasn't particularly pleased to be reminded that there'd been other women for Asa, nor was she in particular agreement with his subtle endorsement of sexual freedom, despite the fact that she was in Asa's bed after knowing him for two short days. She hadn't as yet had time to sort out rationally why she had allowed that to happen so spontaneously.

But she had once felt the way he apparently did, though she'd never been promiscuous by any stretch of the imagination. Her views had changed when Julie had become a teenager, and Carolyn had had to start worrying about things like teenage pregnancy. She had had to decide then what sort of an example she was going to be for her young sister, and it hadn't taken much effort to decide for celibacy, especially when the men she'd dated had been types she hadn't found it difficult to refuse.

Carolyn became aware that Asa was frowning at her, and that his arousal was diminishing, and she stirred uncomfortably.

"What is it?" he asked, a slight impatience in his voice, which came from the fact that her behavior was a subtle, and unwelcome, reminder that she wasn't the "mature" type of woman he normally favored. He preferred not to think about that. "Why the second thoughts?"

Carolyn could understand his impatience with her, considering his viewpoint concerning casual sex, but his attitude didn't help reduce her discomfort.

She doubted an explanation would make much of an impression on him, which dampened her own ardor considerably, but she decided to give him one anyway.

"Asa, I haven't been with a man in over six years," she said soberly.

"Why not?"

As she had half expected, he sounded more disapproving than curious. Carolyn sighed and continued her explanation, however useless she felt it would probably be.

"Because I was raising my young sister—Julie, the one I told you was going to school in England," she reminded him, "and I had to provide an example for her. I didn't want her thinking it was all right to be too casual about such things. She was so young, and I knew what it was like to have a child to raise when you were barely out of childhood yourself."

Asa stared at her with a curious frown on his face, and Carolyn spoke hastily, fearing she'd given him the impression she'd made a tremendous sacrifice in raising Julie. Somehow, it was important to be honest with Asa. She would worry later about why it was so important.

"Not that I minded raising Julie," she insisted. "I didn't. I enjoyed being a substitute mother to her . . . very much. In fact, I'd be glad to do it all again," she added somewhat wistfully. Then she shook her head a little and continued. "It's just that it meant giving up some things, and I didn't want her to have to do that. She's not as . . . as maternal, I guess you could call it, as I am."

The more Carolyn spelled out the type of woman she was, the more Asa's ardor cooled. He felt almost guilty at having made love to her earlier. Despite the fact that he'd known since first laying eyes on her that she wasn't the sort he should get involved with, he'd managed to forget it while gripped in his need for her. And part of him couldn't regret what had happened even now. But part of him did, and Carolyn was both dismayed and resentful at sensing his mood.

Before she could say anything more, however, Asa had a thought that brought him bolt upright in the bed.

"Good God, Carrie!" he rasped harshly. "If you haven't been with a man in that long . . . Don't tell me you're unprotected!"

Carolyn bit her lip, her expression filled with uncertainty, and looked away, and Asa raked a hand through his hair in an exasperated fashion.

"Hell, it never occurred to me . . . !" he said. "Well, damn it, if it had, *I'd* have done something . . ." *Or stayed right the hell away from you!* he added mentally, filled with a sort of righteous fury he couldn't comprehend.

Carolyn scooted over and drew the sheet up over her breasts, feeling momentarily miserably embarrassed by her own carelessness until she realized she wouldn't have been so careless if she had really minded the idea of becoming pregnant. That realization hit her hard, and she stared at Asa with an incredulity that matched his own while she wondered if her subconscious desires could really control her conscious actions in such a serious matter.

Asa misunderstood her expression and immediately felt defensive.

"Well, damn it, you could have told me!" he bit out. "I admit I've gotten out of the habit of taking precautions of my own with the way things are these days, but I would have if you'd just had the decency to tell me!"

Asa's accusation made Carolyn go cold with shock, but the coldness was quickly followed by a hot fury that consumed her. She sat up with a jerk, clutching her sheet protectively, glaring at him as though she hated him, which at the moment, she almost did.

"Don't you worry about a thing, Mr. Asa Bradley!" she practically snarled at him. "I haven't forgotten that you consider us *unsuited!*" She spoke the word with contempt. "Just remember that 'the way things are these days,' " she mocked his words, again with contempt, "if there are any consequences to take care of, I can handle them! I've already raised one child, and she turned out beautifully, a result that I had quite a lot to do with, if I do say so myself! I can do it again!"

Asa's eyes narrowed and he clenched his jaw. "Maybe that's what you had in mind all along," he spoke with dangerous coldness. "Maybe my only purpose was to provide you with a replacement for that little sister of yours!"

Carolyn drew back as if he'd struck her. His accusation was, for all she knew, too close to the truth to be tolerated!

"I wouldn't . . . !" she started to say, then choked on the words. Had she? she wondered with a sort of guilty horror.

Giving Asa a stricken look, she threw back the sheet and bounded out of bed, intent only upon getting away from him. She had to think. And without Asa Bradley around to confuse her.

Her clothes were on Asa's side of the bed, however, and as she came around to snatch them up, he reached out and caught her arm. She gasped as he dragged her back on the bed with him and pinned her down beneath him.

"Let me go!" she gritted, struggling to loosen his hold. But the muscles Asa had honed to a fine pitch, and which Carolyn had admired a short while earlier, were more than adequate to defeat her pitiful attempt to get away from him.

"Not so fast!" he said hostilely. "Let's get something straight before we part company, Miss Spoiled Brat!"

Carolyn subsided, staring up at Asa with incredulity again. She might be a lot of things, she thought with amazed grimness, but a spoiled brat was definitely not one of them! At least not in the sense that he obviously meant.

"If I wanted children," Asa grated, his hard eyes boring into Carolyn's hostile gaze, "I would get married and have them and raise them myself. But I don't happen to want children," he continued more quietly but no less grimly, "nor do I appreciate having someone else take the decision out of my hands. Any child you might have conceived tonight would be half mine, and whether I like it or not, if there is a child, I'm going to have to worry about him or her for the rest of my life. I would have liked to have been consulted about a little matter like that!"

Carolyn blinked, swallowed, and finally accepted the crushing accusation as just. Miserable now, she closed her eyes in shame, unable to look into Asa's accusing eyes any longer.

Asa hesitated, another thought occurring to him which in-

111

creased the self-disgust he was already feeling at having treated Carolyn to what he could only describe to himself as caveman tactics. He was still angry at her, but he tried to keep his anger out of his voice as he dealt with the possibility that had just occurred to him.

"I wouldn't like to think of you getting an abortion though," he said levelly. "I realize it's your body and your decision. But it's still my child, and I wouldn't want it disposed of as if . . ."

Carolyn's eyes had flown open and she gaped at him in horror, causing Asa to hesitate.

"I wouldn't do that!" she stated with absolute conviction.

Asa continued to hesitate for a moment, then he loosened his grip on her slightly and shrugged, not knowing what else to say.

Somewhere in this upsetting confrontation, Carolyn had done a little mental arithmetic, and now she frowned at Asa and said, much more quietly, out of respect for his justified concern, "Asa, I doubt there's anything to worry about. I don't think it's the right time of the month."

He shrugged again, his face blank. "But you're not sure." He stated the obvious.

Carolyn closed her eyes and shook her head. "No, I can't be positive," she admitted with soft regret, knowing now that whether her subconscious had been dictating her actions or not, and no matter how much she would like to have a child of her own, she didn't want one this way. Not when the child's father would resent her so much.

Asa stared down at Carolyn's sad face, and a totally unexpected regret for all the normal things of life he had chosen to miss out on when he'd chosen his career filled him. Had he been a normal man with a normal job, he would have wanted someone like Carolyn as his wife and he would have wanted children with her.

You could have them now, the thought lodged in his mind, tempting him somewhat, yet confusing him as well because the idea was so new to him. *But if you did, you could never go back to the field.*

Despite all the indications that he would never go back to the field anyway, Asa wasn't ready to give up the possibility yet.

But he suddenly despised himself for browbeating Carolyn simply for being a normal person with normal wants and wishes.

"Carrie . . ."

Carolyn's eyes came open, her expression puzzled at the soft way Asa had said her name.

"I'm sorry . . . again. . . ." Asa apologized, his frown self-directed now.

Carolyn relaxed a little, but she shook her head.

"No," she said with quiet firmness. "I was wrong, Asa. I can't explain it." She shook her head again, closing her eyes in sad bewilderment. "Maybe you're right . . . maybe I ignored caution because subconsciously I wanted a child. I don't know," she said simply. Then, opening her eyes to study his face, she added, "But I do know one thing."

"What?" Asa's question was posed absently. He was once again admiring Carrie's ability to admit when she was wrong with such simple dignity.

"I wanted *you*, Asa," Carolyn said softly. "And not just as a . . . a stud, as you called it. I wanted you because you're the man you are . . . because I'm attracted to you. I couldn't have—" She paused and swallowed, then made herself finish. "I couldn't have made love with you simply to get pregnant. I just couldn't have."

Asa studied her open, honest gaze and finally smiled faintly. "No, I don't believe you could have," he said in a low, husky voice. He was stunned an instant later to realize he was becoming aroused again.

Carolyn felt it, too, and inadvertently sucked in her breath.

Asa made a wry movement with his lips. "I guess the attraction's still there," he said.

"But . . ." Carolyn started to stammer.

"I know . . . I know," Asa grimaced. "I'm not going to do anything about it . . ."

He hesitated, staring at her, wanting her, realizing he was going to keep on wanting her until it was physically impossible to have her because she wasn't on this confounded romantic island any longer.

"Carrie . . . I know I've been an ass, but . . ."

Carolyn started smiling, then a little burst of laughter burst out. "Oh, God, Asa, I still want you, too," she choked out, suddenly on the verge of tears.

Asa saw the glitter of moisture in her eyes and, without thinking, bent down to kiss the tears away, ending at her mouth, where he hesitated, then gently brushed his lips against hers.

Carolyn couldn't help her response, nor the fact that she curled her arm around his neck and pressed against him.

"I'd better take you back to your hotel now," he muttered, part of him pleased at seeing the disappointment come into Carolyn's eyes, part of him mentally shaking his head at how foolishly she made him behave. He demonstrated that foolishness an instant later by saying, "Tomorrow, Carrie, I'll take care of the precautions."

His reward was the absolutely stunning smile Carolyn gave him, telling him without words that she was as foolish as he.

CHAPTER NINE

Asa parked near Carolyn's hotel, shut off the engine, then turned to look at her. She was gazing at him in that trusting, accepting way that made him feel uneasy, and though he was wishing his conscience would shut up and leave him alone, it wouldn't, so he decided he had to voice the warning he thought was only fair to give her. Maybe telling her straight—as straight as he could afford to be, anyway—about how it was with him, would chase away an attack of the guilts if she started taking things too seriously.

"Carrie . . ." he started out slowly, leaning back in his corner of the car as he looked at her in a troubled way that captured Carolyn's attention. "Remember how I said that we weren't suited—"

He paused as he saw Carolyn stiffen, clasp her hands together tightly, and turn her head away to look out the window.

"I remember," she replied in a voice that sounded muffled to Asa's ears.

"Carrie, look at me," he said softly, wanting to see if she was upset.

Carolyn reluctantly faced Asa again, struggling to keep her expression blank. She didn't want to let him know how badly she'd taken his reminder that he didn't intend for things to get serious between them.

Men don't take a little bedroom fun and games as seriously as most women do, she reminded herself unhappily, and then suddenly remembered that before she had decided to practice celibacy for Julie's sake, there had been a couple of men who could have made that same observation about her. She knew for sure that one of them had been on the verge of proposing when she'd

115

broken off their relationship and that he had suffered for a while over losing her. So what right did she have to feel resentful toward Asa because he didn't want to get serious? she wondered bleakly.

"Carrie, it doesn't have anything to do with you," Asa said truthfully. "You're a beautiful woman, and I suspect you'll make some man a fantastic wife one day."

Carolyn managed to keep an ironic expression from flittering over her face. This was exactly the sort of spiel she had given a man or two in the past. In the lexicon of romantic relationships, it was called "letting someone down gently."

"But there are reasons why I can't be that man," Asa went on in a soft, gentle voice that made Carolyn feel wistfully drawn to him. "All I can offer you is my company for however long you're here in Hawaii on vacation."

Asa paused, wondering if he was being presumptuous in warning Carrie off this way. Maybe all she wanted was his company for a brief time—a holiday romance to add a zing to her vacation. The thought made him feel irritable for some reason.

"It's all right, Asa." Carolyn forced her voice to conceal the disappointment raging through her. She was overwhelmingly curious as well concerning Asa's reasons for remaining unmarried. His air of mystery was frustrating for her, but she thought it would do little good to question him. She'd already had several tastes of his attitude when she got too curious.

Asa studied her, trying to discern if she really was accepting his warning in the spirit she appeared to be. Her face looked calm and composed, but she was twisting her hands in her lap in a way that made him frown.

"Do you want to see me again . . . on those terms?" he asked thoughtfully, dragging his eyes away from her hands to focus on her face. He didn't want to receive the message those hands were trying to give him.

Carolyn hesitated, then shrugged. What was the use of debating the question? Of course she wanted to see him again, despite the heartache she sensed was looming ahead for her when it came time to say good-bye.

"Yes, Asa," she said quietly, her gaze steady as she looked into his eyes. "I want to see you again."

A feeling of intense relief surged through Asa, alerting him to the fact that he'd been dreading hearing her say "no" more than he'd realized.

"Good," he said softly, his eyes caressing Carolyn in a way that made her pulse speed up. "Then I'll pick you up tomorrow morning, say around eight o'clock. We'll have breakfast together, then do a little sightseeing if that's what you want."

"I'd like to go swimming," Carolyn said, ". . . and perhaps have a picnic? Would that be possible?"

Asa grinned. "If you want to take a chance on what I can manage to throw together from the scant supplies in my kitchen," he teased.

Carolyn forced herself to smile back at him. "I'll chance it," she said with mock dread, "though the way this vacation started out, I wouldn't be surprised if you gave me food poisoning."

"Brave woman," Asa said soberly before smiling again. "But don't worry. I'll try to keep you healthy. I wouldn't want to spoil your vacation."

You already have, Carolyn thought instantly before mentally chastising herself for the observation. After all, even if her vacation ended with her being miserable because Asa was willing to let her go, the time they would spend together in the meantime might be worth the price.

"Good," she said aloud in a lightly teasing way as she reached for the door handle. "Then I'd better get some sleep so I'll be rested for tomorrow."

Asa leaned forward, placing his fingers lightly on her shoulder. The touch on her bare skin brought a sinking feeling of physical arousal into Carolyn's stomach.

"Don't I get a good-night kiss?" Asa murmured in a low voice that heightened the sexual tension Carolyn was experiencing.

"Of course," she whispered, leaning toward him as though pulled by an irresistible force.

Asa's mouth on hers was as warmly exciting as she'd feared it would be, making her long to be back in his bed so that they could make love again. She had to force herself to draw back and fumble the car door open before she begged him to take her back home with him.

"Good night, Carrie," Asa said reluctantly. He didn't want to let her go.

"Good night, Asa," Carolyn murmured over her shoulder before she climbed out of the car, shut the door, and gave him a little wave of her hand before turning to walk away toward the entrance of her hotel.

Asa watched her, admiring her slender body and graceful walk. When she'd disappeared inside her hotel, he started the car, heading for a drugstore he knew would be open.

He felt a little foolish making his purchase. It had been a long time—all the way back to his teenage years—since there'd been a need to buy the sort of protection he carried back to the car with him, and in a way, he resented the artificial barrier between him and Carrie his purchases would present. But it was better than the alternative: being forced to give up making love to her for fear that lovemaking would result in a child he was in no position to love and raise the way it deserved.

Just hope it isn't too late, he thought, feeling uneasy when he realized the thought of Carrie having a child of his wasn't arousing the bitter feelings of outraged self-righteousness he had experienced earlier. *For your own peace of mind,* he acknowledged what was happening to him somewhat grimly, *cut out the sentimental claptrap. You wouldn't be feeling any of this if you still had going back in the field to look forward to, and who's to say that won't eventually be possible? So take the week or two of pleasure for what it's worth and then don't look back. You won't be doing Carrie Winters any favors by playing with the idea of turning into a model husband and father. That just isn't in the cards.*

Carolyn let herself into her hotel room as quietly as possible in case Martha was up next door reading. After shutting the door behind her, however, she realized she was wishing she had someone to talk to about the dilemma she faced, and Martha, if she wasn't shocked to the core, would no doubt be an excellent source of wise advice.

Grimacing, Carolyn rejected the idea and began to take off her clothes. While it might be nice to have a friend to advise her, it was probably too much to expect that a woman of Martha's age would be sympathetic toward Carolyn's intention to have a short-term affair with a man she barely knew.

When she had on her nightgown, Carolyn climbed into bed, but she didn't feel sleepy. She wished Asa were beside her in the bed right then preparing to make love to her again.

You apparently stayed celibate too long. She tried to explain away the longing for Asa that consumed her. *Or maybe it's just a case of wanting what you can't have. If Asa were available as a potential husband, would you continue to want him this badly?*

She felt disquieted when the answer that came into her mind was a resounding "Yes!" Then she frowned, wondering why Asa *wasn't* available as a potential husband. What were those reasons he'd said put him off limits for that sort of relationship?

She doubted she'd ever know, and the conclusion brought a scowl to her lips. Why did he have to be so damned mysterious? Was he a crook on the run?

Carolyn immediately shook her head, positive that Asa Bradley wasn't the criminal type. But maybe he was the type who liked to seem mysterious so that he could have what he wanted from women without losing his freedom? That seemed more likely.

A light tap on her door made Carolyn jump.

"Who is it?" She composed herself and called softly without unlatching the door.

"It's Martha," came the answer, voiced as softly as Carolyn had spoken. "May I talk to you for a minute?"

Carolyn hesitated, then shrugged and let Martha come in. The older woman was dressed in a pink chenille robe. Her gray hair was slightly mussed, as though she'd been sleeping, but her blue eyes displayed an expression of alert interest that didn't seem sleepy at all.

"I heard you come in," she said softly, as though to keep from disturbing the rest of the occupants of the hotel. "Did you have a good time with your Mr. Bradley?"

Carolyn sighed as she led the way to her bed. There were no chairs in the room, so she and Martha would have to sit on the bed to talk.

"Yes and no," she said, a touch of forlorn indecision in her voice.

119

Martha settled herself at the foot of the bed, her warm, intelligent blue eyes fixed on Carolyn's face. "Well, that's an interesting answer," she said with mild humor. "Do you want to talk about it, or would you prefer I mind my own business and get myself back to my room where I belong?"

Carolyn smiled faintly, debating about how much to tell Martha. She decided simply to ask her new friend, in a roundabout way, how much she wanted to hear.

"Martha, how shockproof are you?" she asked, studying Martha's kind face for a reaction.

Martha tilted her head, looked thoughtful for a moment as she returned Carolyn's gaze, then shrugged her well-padded shoulders.

"I've lived a long time," she finally said in a simple fashion, "and I've seen a lot of facets of human nature in my life. And though I have my own standards of behavior that I try to keep, I try not to judge anyone who may have different standards too harshly."

Inwardly Carolyn winced, certain now that Martha would consider what had happened between her and Asa that night as outside acceptable standards. But then, Martha reached across the bed and patted her knee, and when Carolyn looked at her, unaware that her expression was slightly woebegone, Martha smiled kindly at her.

"In your case, honey," she said with firm conviction, "I'm satisfied you're as decent as they come. If you've done something you're reluctant to tell me about, don't be so hard on yourself. I was young once . . . and I must say, that Asa Bradley you went off with tonight has a look about him that made even my old heart speed up a little. I wonder if he has a father running around on the loose somewhere?" she teased.

Carolyn couldn't help laughing, but though she felt considerably more relaxed about having Martha know what she'd done than she had a moment earlier, she was still a little leery about spelling things out.

"You've got something on your mind and no one to talk to about it, haven't you?" Martha said kindly, her face creasing into a warm smile. And as Carolyn looked at her with both reluctance and hope in her eyes, Martha's gaze became a little sad. "I'd be willing to bet you haven't had anyone to talk to in a long while," she added soberly. "Not since you lost your parents?"

Carolyn nodded in a glum fashion, feeling just a little sorry for herself. Martha's sympathy made it easy to feel that way.

"Well, honey," Martha said with level firmness, "I may not be a qualified psychiatrist or psychologist, but I'm a darned good listener, and if you want to get something off your chest, you don't have to worry that I'll disapprove of you. Oh, I'm not saying I might not disapprove of something you've done," she added with a smile to soften her words, "but I won't disapprove of *you* . . . understand?"

Carolyn smiled gratefully. "I understand," she said quietly. "And thank you, Martha. It's just that I'm not certain what good talking about my problem will do. I've already decided to . . ." Carolyn paused, dropped her eyes, and hugged her knees to her chest while she searched for a way to put her decision which wouldn't sound crude.

"You've decided to make hay while the sun shines, so to speak," Martha said dryly, "and worry about the consequences later."

Carolyn looked up quickly, startled by Martha's perceptiveness.

Martha shrugged. "I told you I was young once," she said lightly, and then she gave Carolyn a thoughtful look that made Carolyn slightly uncomfortable. "I suppose Mr. Bradley isn't available for a long-term commitment?" she asked with muted curiosity.

"How did you know?" Carolyn responded, puzzled and alarmed at how quickly Martha was getting to the point of things.

"Because if he were, you wouldn't have a problem," Martha said in a simple way that made Carolyn relax.

She sighed, then shrugged. "No," she admitted. "Asa isn't available for a long-term commitment. He's already told me that."

"Did he say why?" Martha asked, frowning a little.

Carolyn shook her head. "He just said there were reasons,

121

and asked me if I was willing to spend my vacation with him on that basis or if I'd prefer not to see him again."

"Do you think he's already married?" Martha asked, sounding concerned.

"No." Carolyn frowned again. "But, of course, I can't be certain. However," she added, brightening a little, "he appears to be living alone. I didn't see any signs of a woman's touch in his apartment."

Carolyn became aware that Martha was looking at her in that perceptive way she had again and flushed a little. Now Martha would have to be exceedingly dense not to figure out what had happened while Carolyn was in Asa's apartment.

"Well, I doubt if he'd have taken you there if he was married," Martha said practically. "So I don't think we have to worry about that. But if he's already told you he can't get serious about you, I suppose your problem is whether to continue to see him and take the chance that you might end up very serious about him."

Carolyn nodded, her expression glum. "That's about it," she admitted reluctantly.

"And you've decided to keep seeing him," Martha gently prompted.

Carolyn sighed. "That's about it," she repeated.

Martha stayed silent for a long moment, merely studying the troubled look in Carolyn's large eyes.

"Carolyn," she then said with soft sympathy in her voice, "have you ever heard that old Spanish saying about taking what you want and then being willing to pay for it if you have to?"

Carolyn nodded, a far-off expression coming into her eyes as she thought about the possibility that she might already be pregnant, while the father of her child wanted no part of her or the baby on a permanent basis.

"Are you willing to pay what you might have to if you continue to see this man and end up falling in love with him?" Martha inquired gently.

Carolyn didn't answer right away. She was thinking of the pain she might have to face—the pain of loss. And at remembering how it had felt to lose Julie, she wasn't certain if she

122

could take a double dose of that sort of pain. But then, realizing she could no more refuse to see Asa again than she could refuse to see Julie, she had to face the fact that she must already be more than a little in love with him, and that loving someone didn't mean you could throw a chain about them and tie them to your side.

"I guess I don't have any choice but to pay," she admitted softly, "since I can't imagine not seeing Asa while I'm here, and he doesn't seem the type of man who would change his mind about a thing like marriage."

Martha remained silent for a second, then, giving a big sigh, she stood up and came around the bed to take Carolyn in her arms and give her a comforting hug.

"I wish I could tell you you're right to take such a chance," she said softly, "but I'm not sure you are. On the other hand, at my age, it's easy to forget how impossible it can be at times to refuse to seize the moment when you're young and in love. So what it boils down to, honey, is that it's your decision, just as it will be you who'll have to live with that decision. And while I don't like to think of you hurting, I wouldn't dream of telling you to stay safely away from what life has to offer."

"Thank you, Martha," Carolyn murmured, feeling comforted somehow, though nothing Martha had said should have comforted her. She supposed it was just that she was grateful for Martha's concern, and it felt very peaceful to be held and hugged and made to feel as though Martha cared and wasn't going to be judgmental.

Martha straightened and patted Carolyn's shoulder. "I guess it's time I went back to my own bed and let you get some sleep," she said.

Carolyn watched as Martha moved toward the door, fidgeting with the belt of her tatty old robe as she walked. At the door, she paused for a moment looking thoughtful. Then she shook her head and when she looked at Carolyn, there was nothing in her eyes other than a warm smile.

"Good night, honey," she said. "I guess you won't be coming with us to Pearl Harbor tomorrow to see the Arizona Memorial?"

"No," Carolyn admitted. "Asa and I are going to have a picnic and go swimming."

Martha then got a faraway look in her eyes, as though she was thinking of past picnics of her own. Her smile was dreamy and soft and a little sad.

"Good night, Martha," Carolyn said, wishing her friend hadn't lost her family the way she had. It hurt to think of the pain she must have suffered, in spite of the fact that she seemed determined to live her life to the fullest anyway.

"Good night, dear," Martha said absently, and let herself out, closing the door quietly behind her.

Carolyn turned off the bedside lamp and settled into bed, feeling wistful. If there were any justice in life, she thought sadly, Martha would still have her beloved family about her, and Asa Bradley would be a marrying kind of man, ready to fill Julie's place in her life with love and children and a happy future to look forward to. But it seemed that there was no justice in life—not for her, not for Martha—and possibly not for Asa Bradley, whom fate had already deprived of physical independence, and who was himself voluntarily shutting the door on the sort of emotional commitment that seemed as natural as breathing to Carolyn, and that might have made up to Asa for the injury to his leg.

You can't dictate his life for him, she thought groggily as sleep began to cloud her mind. *But, oh, don't you wish you could? Wouldn't it be lovely to say to Asa Bradley, "You will love Carolyn Winters, marry her, have children with her, and live happily ever after with her" and have it work out just like that?*

Yes, lovely, she thought on the last breath of consciousness. Lovely, but totally, irrevocably unrealistic. Asa Bradley was a man who would live on his own terms, and it was just too bad that his terms were a world away from her own.

CHAPTER TEN

As Carolyn stood at a railing looking down at Hanauma Bay while Asa got the picnic basket out of the car, she realized she was falling in love with Hawaii. Aside from the fact that she would have to contend with a midwestern winter back in the States, the natural beauty to be found in Hawaii called to something in her soul.

Stretched out below, the transparent turquoise water of Hanauma Bay, which had formed in a volcanic crater located at the base of Koko Head, was fronted by white sand and palm trees—truly a tropical paradise—and Carolyn could hardly wait to sample what awaited her there.

"Ready?"

Carolyn came out of her absorption with the view and glanced at Asa, who was standing beside her looking fantastically virile in his shorts and aloha shirt, the picnic basket he'd scavenged his kitchen to fill in one strong hand.

"I'm ready," she agreed with wholehearted enthusiasm, giving him a brilliant smile that made Asa catch his breath.

Indeed, Carolyn was ready. She had woken that morning determined to live for the moment. She would enjoy life to the fullest for these brief two weeks while she had Hawaii and Asa and she wouldn't spoil any of it by thinking about the future. The future would come in its own time and she would deal with it when she had to. Meanwhile, it couldn't be allowed to interfere with the present.

Asa had caught her mood immediately after picking her up, and recognizing a philosophy that had been his own for almost all of his adult life, he had felt a sense of relief and anticipation. Maybe Carrie Winters was more his normal type of woman than had been apparent at first. If so, it would make things a hell of a lot easier and give him a brief interval of enjoyable forgetfulness before he had to get back to work.

"Come on, then." He grinned at her and with the picnic basket in one hand and his cane in the other, led the way toward the paved path leading down to the beach.

The path was steep, and Carolyn glanced at Asa doubtfully because of his leg.

"We'll take it slow going down." He shrugged in an easy manner, not taking offense over her concern, "and I think there's a shuttle we can take back to the top when we're ready to leave."

Carolyn hoped so. As she unobtrusively watched Asa slowly maneuver his way downward, and felt the strain in her own calves the slope caused, she couldn't help feeling concerned for him. She would have liked to offer to carry the picnic basket, but she was afraid to offend his male pride.

By the time they reached the beach, Carolyn had to pretend she didn't see the beads of perspiration on Asa's tanned forehead and the strain in his face.

"This looks like a good place," she suggested, pleased when she managed a calm, unconcerned tone. She had chosen a spot quite near the path so that Asa wouldn't have to carry the picnic basket any farther.

"But that one looks better," he replied, pointing farther on where there was a palm tree they could sit under.

"Oh, yes," Carolyn said brightly, ignoring the indication that Asa was aware of what she'd been trying to do. "We'll get the shade."

When he had set the basket down under the palm tree, Asa shrugged out of his shirt, tossed it aside, and sat down and leaned back on his elbows to rest.

Carolyn stared at the smoothly bulging muscles of his tanned shoulders and torso, then her eyes moved to his legs. The right one was as tanned and muscled as the rest of his body, but the tan of the left one disappeared around his knee where there was a mass of scar tissue, and the muscles were less pronounced in that leg.

The sight of the damage marring what was otherwise one of the most magnificent physiques she'd ever seen made Carolyn want to cry. Her throat closed, blocking off a rising sob, and she quickly pivoted as though to admire the view while she struggled to get her emotions under control.

Behind her, unaware of her feelings, Asa sat up. His knee was beginning to recover from the long climb, and as he absently massaged it, his eyes swept Carolyn's back in an appreciative survey.

She had her hair in a ponytail to anchor it against the wind, her posture was straight, her derriere enticing, her long tanned legs elegant. Asa thought she had the look of a thoroughbred, which while nice to admire from a distance, was slightly offputting as a lover. But then he remembered how uninhibited her lovemaking had been the night before, and a slow smile curved his lips while his body involuntarily tautened in anticipation of making love to her again.

Carolyn began to pull her Navy blue T-shirt over her head. She tossed it aside, then unzipped her white shorts and stepped out of them, unaware that Asa was watching her disrobe with a deepening gleam of arousal in the depths of his eyes. Under her clothes, she had on a two-piece turquoise bathing suit that stopped just short of being an all-out bikini, and Asa smiled at this indication of her modesty while he reminded himself that in bed the modesty conveniently disappeared.

"I'm going in for a quick dip," Carolyn tossed over her shoulder as she started toward the water. She daren't look at Asa directly yet. There were tears in her eyes. She intended to blame any redness that remained after her swim on the salt water, and she hoped the physical activity of swimming would chase away her sudden plunge into emotionalism and leave her free to enjoy the rest of the day.

"I'll join you in a minute," Asa called after her, his eyes sweeping her figure with a lazy, encompassing possessiveness he didn't identify as the sort a man who regards a woman as his own might display.

As Carolyn had hoped, the swim helped her get back in control, and when Asa joined her a few moments later, she was again as lighthearted and cheerful as she'd been when he'd picked her up that morning.

Asa's knee didn't bother him in the water. In fact, the constant ache of it lessened into a dull, remote pain he found it easy to ignore as he swam. Soon, he was splashing Carolyn in a playful way and they both began to laugh and splash and dunk one another.

Finally, Asa caught Carolyn around the waist and as she struggled laughingly to get away, he growled, "A kiss or another dunking! What's it going to be, lady?"

"Ha! I don't trust you!" Carolyn sputtered. "You'd probably take the kiss and dunk me anyway."

Asa gave her a benign smile that was tinged with evil intent.

"See what I mean?" Carolyn pointed a dripping finger at his face. "Anyone who can smile like that has to have a sneaky personality! I'll bet you're really a spy in disguise instead of an innocent college lecturer the way you pretend to be!"

The change her words wrought in Asa's face for an instant astonished Carolyn. But before she could even be certain she'd seen what she thought she had, Asa's hand was on the top of her head and he had dunked her so quickly, her open mouth filled with water and she began to choke.

Flailing with her arms and legs, Carolyn finally succeeded in bobbing to the surface, no thanks to Asa, who, not realizing she was choking, had tried to keep her submerged.

Coughing and choking, struggling for breath, her eyes wide and frightened, Carolyn was backpedaling in an attempt to get away from Asa before he drowned her completely.

Asa was in water he could stand in, and at seeing the state Carolyn was in, he quickly grabbed her and bent her over one arm while he pounded her back with his free hand. Now, Carolyn thought he was going to beat her to death and she commenced to struggle against his hold again.

Frowning his concern, Asa began to head for shore, dragging Carolyn with him. Carolyn continued to struggle until she realized where he was heading and then she relaxed in his grip and went into another coughing fit that lasted until Asa hauled her onto the white sand of the beach.

"Hey . . . hey . . ." He soothed her and patted her back as she bent over at the waist with her eyes closed and her hands on her knees, waiting to see if she was done coughing. "You're all right now, Carrie," he said, sounding shaken to Carolyn's water-logged ears. "I'm sorry. I didn't mean to half drown you."

Didn't you? Carolyn found herself thinking and then was appalled by the thought. Where had it come from? Hadn't she imagined the unnaturally still, dangerously tense expression on his face when she'd accused him of being sneaky? Or had she?

Asa interrupted her thoughts as he gently placed his hands on her shoulders and pulled her upright so that he could look into her face.

"All right now?" he asked, and there was such a wealth of tender concern in his deep voice and in his expressive dark eyes that Carolyn's hysterical imaginings went right out of her head.

"Yes," she replied shakily. "I think so." And Asa pulled her into his arms, letting her rest against his broad chest while he rubbed her back in such a soothingly protective way that she began to feel completely safe again.

Reluctantly, out of concern for his leg rather than because she really wanted to leave the safe haven of his arms, Carolyn straightened and leaned back in his embrace.

"I could use something to drink," she said. "There's still a tickle in my throat."

Asa nodded. "I'll bet there is." And he turned, slipping his arm around her waist to lead her to where they'd left the picnic basket.

Fetching a Thermos bottle from the basket, Asa unscrewed the top and poured a small amount of cold lemonade into the matching cup. Carolyn took it from him and sipped gratefully.

"Better?" Asa asked when she'd lowered the cup, which was now empty.

With a smile on her lips, Carolyn nodded. "Sorry to be such a baby." She shrugged.

Asa shook his head, his expression grave for a moment. He was feeling guilty about the action he'd taken to hide his reaction at hearing Carolyn playfully, innocently, hit upon the truth concerning him. He certainly hadn't meant to hurt her though.

"It was my fault," he said truthfully. "I wouldn't have hurt you for the world, Carrie," he said, meaning it, and because he did mean it, he sounded utterly convincing to Carolyn.

"I know," she said softly, smiling up into his eyes. "Let's forget it and eat. That swim gave me an appetite."

Returning her smile and feeling relieved, Asa helped her sit down, then settled beside her.

"What have you got?" Carolyn said mischievously, pointing at the basket.

"Nothing that any chef worth his salt is going to steal for his repertoire," Asa grimaced. "Some cheese, crackers, fruit, a couple of peanut butter sandwiches and the rest of the lemonade."

"Sounds delicious." Carolyn eagerly came up on her knees and started rummaging in the basket.

Asa looked at her skeptically, but when he saw she wasn't pretending—that she really was looking forward to the meager repast he'd provided, he had to grin, surprised again by the difference in her appearance and her character. She looked like the caviar, champagne, and strawberries type, but she was already munching on a piece of cheese like a starved little mouse.

"Hey! Do I get any?" he teased with mock resentment.

Carolyn shifted her eyes at him slyly and shook her head as she bent to wrap her arms around the basket, pretending she was going to keep it all for herself.

Asa raised an eyebrow and made a movement as though he were going to force her to give up the basket, and Carolyn sat back on her heels and held up a hand in surrender, her blue eyes sparkling with laughter. She swallowed the bite of cheese at last and said, "Help yourself, mighty hunter. This mastodon you killed and brought back to the cave is so yummy, I couldn't resist. But now I give place to the warrior."

Again, her words seemed to skirt the truth of Asa's life and though he kept a bland expression on his face and nodded in a superior way, inside he was amazed. Did she sense something about him that gave rise to her teasing remarks? Or . . .

For just an instant, the paranoia that went with Asa's profession made him wonder if she was more than she seemed. Then he dismissed the idea, feeling like a fool for letting his imagination run away with him. If Carolyn Winters was an enemy agent, he thought dryly, or even a friendly one sent to keep an eye on him, he'd eat the palm tree he was leaning against and then turn in his credentials for good, certain he'd lost any attributes he'd ever had as an intelligence agent.

"Well?" Carolyn asked impatiently. She was on her knees with her hands on her hips, waiting for him to share the food.

"Woman getting uppity?" he growled in a threatening caveman voice.

"You betcha!" Carolyn nodded, unintimidated. "Get with it, Og, or I'll start hunting the food myself and let you sit around starving until I'm ready to share."

Asa glowered at her, but he hauled the picnic basket between his legs and rummaged in it for one of the peanut butter sandwiches, which he held up while he searched with his other hand for a banana to go with it.

Carolyn snatched the sandwich from him, unwrapped it, and took a big bite, closing her eyes in ecstasy over the taste.

Asa shook his head in mock amazement. "I never thought a mastodon sandwich was all that great," he grumbled.

"It must be that special sauce you concoct out of berries and honey," Carolyn suggested after swallowing the bite.

"Uh-huh," Asa drawled as he unwrapped a sandwich for himself. "That's my talent, all right. I'm known in every cave of the clan, far and wide, for my cooking."

Carolyn shrugged. "Don't knock your talents," she said gravely, "or God may take them away from you. How would you like to eat a mastodon sandwich *without* your special sauce?"

Asa glanced at Carolyn thoughtfully, resigned now to her offhand way of phrasing things so that they hit uncomfortably close to the core of truth. To his knowledge, of course, he hadn't done anything to deserve having his talents taken away from him, if you wanted to describe a solid, dependable leg as a talent, and he didn't connect God with the injury that had robbed him of the sauce of his life, but the bare bones of her statement were accurate: he was reduced to the sort of mundane life he could barely tolerate.

Asa had to admit, though, that in Carolyn's company, his tolerance level was a good deal higher than had been the case before she appeared on the scene, and with a mental shrug, he ate his sandwich, determined once again to take the forgetfulness she offered with both hands while it was available.

As they were eating, other people began drifting onto the beach, and Carolyn viewed their appearance with disfavor. When it had just been the two of them, Asa and herself, she'd been able to imagine they were in a Garden of Eden with no one else in the world to disturb their paradise.

Julie would be a little upset with me about that, she thought humorously as she popped the last bite of a banana into her mouth and lay back on the sand to stare up through the fringes of palm leaf at the fluffy white cloud formations and the unbelievable blue of the sky.

"Sleepy?" Asa asked with quiet companionableness.

"A little," Carolyn answered dreamily. "But I hate to waste my time oblivious to all this beauty. I wonder if the people who live here full-time appreciate it the way visitors do, or if they take it for granted?"

Asa stared out over the turquoise water, his eyes narrowed against the sun. "How do you think you'd feel if you lived here full-time?" he asked in an idle fashion.

Carolyn blinked up at the sky, the question taking her by surprise because the idea had never occurred to her. She knew Asa wasn't suggesting that she move to Hawaii . . . she could tell by his tone. But, Carolyn realized with a sense of astonished pleasure, if she wanted to move here, what was to stop her?

"I think I'd continue to appreciate it," she replied absently, her thoughts dwelling on the fantasy of living in paradise forever. It shouldn't be too difficult to sell the house, she mused, or if Julie didn't like the idea of that, it could be rented. And since Julie was gone, there was no one she would regret leaving all that much. The few close friends she had would love the idea of visiting her here anyway.

She could even go to college here, she realized as she sat up and propped her chin on her knees, her eyes blankly staring out over the bay.

"What are you thinking about?" Asa asked, his eyes searching her expression. "You look a million miles away."

Carolyn blinked and came back to the present. Then she

smiled. "Not that far," she said lightly. "I was right here as a matter of fact."

Asa shrugged, then glanced at the beach and grimaced when he saw how the place was filling up with people.

"Eden is becoming populated," he announced, startling Carolyn by referring to this place the way she'd thought of it. He sat forward and turned his head toward her again. "Would you prefer to stay here with the crowd or go for a drive?" he asked.

The way he phrased the question told Carolyn what he wanted, and she smiled inwardly as she agreed to the drive. "I'm eager to see everything," she nodded as she began clearing up the debris of their lunch.

They took the shuttle back to the parking lot, and Carolyn was grateful for the fact that Asa was willing to ride instead of insisting on walking.

When they were back in the car, still in their bathing suits, he said, "We'll just go as far as the Blow Hole, then start back to the apartment to shower and change. I'll take you to Pearl Harbor this afternoon, and we can have dinner at the Pearl City Tavern. It's a good place to eat."

Carolyn shrugged agreeably. She had brought along a relatively wrinkle-free sundress in her tote bag, so they wouldn't have to go back to her hotel, and she was in a mood to just sit back and enjoy, letting Asa make the decisions. Just being with him amid all the beauty Hawaii had to offer was enough to make her heart sing with contented satisfaction.

The Blow Hole was just a hole in the rugged lava coastline where the action of the waves forced the water up through a lava tube, and Carolyn watched it interestedly for a few minutes until she sensed Asa was ready to go.

"It reminds me of a mini–Old Faithful," she said as they walked back to the car hand in hand.

"Hmmm, I suppose so," Asa answered absently. He was beginning to anticipate getting back to his apartment, where he intended to make love to Carrie. He didn't understand why he was feeling like a kid caught in the throes of youthful lust. He could barely even remember his teenage years, they were so buried beneath layer after layer of harrowing adult experiences, and he wondered at his own comparison. Had he ever been a

133

carefree, foolish young man with nothing more important on his mind than how far his present inamorata would allow him to go in the backseat of his secondhand Ford?

"What are you thinking, Asa?" Carolyn asked, smiling at him as they paused beside the car. "Now *you* looked as though you were a million miles away."

Asa gave her a lazy grin. "I was," he admitted simply, without going into a detailed explanation of what he'd been thinking. "A million miles and a million years away."

He opened the door for her and Carolyn got into the car, accepting that Asa wasn't going to explain his cryptic answer any more than she had been willing to explain her thoughts about moving to Hawaii earlier. If she had, he would have thought she was doing it because of him, she realized with a wistful inner sigh. And maybe that was it. Maybe she was fooling herself that it was only the beauty and the pleasant climate that had brought the idea into her head. Would it all be so lovely without Asa as part of the scene?

Yes, Carolyn realized thoughtfully. The beauty would remain without Asa. It was just that his presence completed her enjoyment of what there was to be appreciated on its own merits.

They fell into a companionable silence on the way back, both anticipating the privacy which would allow them to hold one another again.

When the apartment door had closed behind them, and Asa had set the picnic basket on the small butcher block table, he turned to Carolyn, his eyes taking on the warm sensuality that inevitably triggered her senses into full-blown life.

"Will you shower with me?" he asked huskily.

Carolyn nodded, her eyes softening as Asa came to take her hand and lead her into his bedroom with its adjoining bathroom.

Unselfconsciously, Carolyn stood with passive acceptance as Asa stripped away the bathing suit she wore, then stepped out of his own. His eyes never ceased their encompassing, possessive sweep of her body, and Carolyn's skin began to glow with warmth wherever his gaze touched her, while, in her turn, she gazed with helpless fascination at the masculine beauty of Asa's body.

"Come on," he murmured, his voice thickening with passion as he took her hand and led her into the bathroom.

While he adjusted the water to the correct temperature, Carolyn raised her hands to the back of her head to pull out the elastic band holding her ponytail so that she could shampoo her hair in the shower.

Asa straightened and went still, held by her beauty, until she dropped the elastic band and circled his neck with her arms, stepping close to his body. The contact set fire to his senses.

"Carrie . . ." He said her name, his voice thick, and then his mouth found hers and he was molding her against him in a way that made Carolyn feel as though her skin were melding with his, forming a delicious unity.

Asa raised his head, and the heat of his sexual arousal was in his dark gaze as he searched Carolyn's eyes and found the echo of his need there.

"Let's get the shower over with," he said, his voice low and ragged.

Feeling languorously contented, Carolyn nodded, and stepped into the tub with Asa right behind her.

Asa wanted to bathe Carolyn himself, but he didn't trust what would happen if he touched her. Nor did he dare allow her to soap him as she started to do.

Her understanding in her drugged, smiling eyes, Carolyn bathed, her eyes never shifting from Asa's eyes and body as he quickly soaped himself. When she was done with her body, she reached for a bottle of shampoo Asa had left on the side of the tub and regretted having to close her eyes as she worked up the suds in her hair.

To her surprise, she felt Asa's hands on her, turning her, and when she had her back to him, he gently pushed her hands away and rubbed the suds into her scalp himself.

Carolyn was completely bemused. No one other than a hairdresser had ever shampooed her hair for her, and Asa's touch was light and deftly thorough, sending her into a dreaming haze of absorption in her senses.

Then he was rinsing the suds away, and Carolyn came out of her haze as the water cascaded over her head, making her squinch her eyes and mouth shut to keep the soap out.

"That's got it," he said softly as he bent to turn off the taps.

As he dried her, Carolyn went rocketing back into a heady state of arousal she saw, with a glorious fascination at the sight, that Asa was experiencing as well.

She stood, her legs apart for balance, her arms held laxly at her sides, and watched with total concentration as Asa dried himself.

When he'd tossed the towel away, he caught her hand, holding her gaze as he led her back into the bedroom. He kissed her, then gently pushed her down onto the bed. But instead of following her down, he straightened, opened the bedside table, and quickly donned the protection he'd bought the night before.

Carolyn watched, feeling both a little awed by the power of Asa's masculinity, and a little sad that the precaution he was taking was necessary. How lovely it would be, she thought abstractedly, if there was no need to prevent the conception of a child. How she would love to be gloriously pregnant with Asa's son or daughter, filled with the anticipation of bringing a new life into the world.

Then Asa was on the bed beside her, and she lost track of such thoughts as she became absorbed in the intense pleasure of touching him as freely and possessively as she wished, while he brought her with slow sureness up the path of mounting ecstasy with his searching hands and wandering mouth, and his erotically whispered praise for her beauty and her impassioned responses to him. She felt the subdued strength in his body and exulted in her power over his masculinity. His responses to her kisses and her glancing touches made her feel like a goddess, while her own reactions to his caresses made her feel like a humble slave, subject to a powerful king whose wishes were her command.

Asa was completely lost in the lovemaking, in a way he never remembered experiencing before. Always in the past, while he allowed his body the pleasure it craved, there had been a part of him that remained detached and alert.

He would tell himself later that it was natural he had let go so completely with Carrie. He wasn't on the line, as he had been in the field in Hong Kong. He was safe in Hawaii, there was no danger to guard against, and he could relax completely for the first time in years. He would tell himself that and try to believe it. But while he was making love to Carrie, there was no room for self-deception.

"I love you," he whispered as he moved over her. "I love you," he said again as he slipped into the luscious welcoming haven of her body, and he heard his voice in his mind repeating that low litany to the rhythm of their lovemaking until the words were torn audibly from his throat at the moment of completion. They reverberated in the otherwise silent room, and the remembrance of how they'd sounded would come back to haunt him when he would later try to explain away what he'd felt.

Just now, however, as he lay sprawled with Carolyn beneath him, his breath rasping from his exertions, all that mattered was the fact that he heard an answer to his declaration.

"I love you, Asa," Carolyn murmured shakily, and then pressed her lips to his cheek while she held him safe from reality in arms as smooth and warm as life itself, as binding as the deceptive strength of silk.

CHAPTER ELEVEN

Carolyn studied Asa's somewhat grim expression as he stared at the memorial of the sunken battleship Arizona, and wondered at it. Thinking of the 1,177 sailors entombed there was enough to make anyone feel solemn, even sad enough to cry perhaps, but there was something different about Asa's reaction that worried her. But then, she realized on a wave of sad frustration, Asa's mood had been distant ever since he'd made love to her earlier at his apartment. The burst of optimistic joy that had filled her then, when he'd said he loved her, was fading rapidly as a result of his behavior since he'd risen from the bed.

Asa's thoughts were far from Carolyn as he stared at the monument to what he considered fellow travelers. The sailors trapped in their watery grave might have died before he'd been born, and their mission, unlike his, which had always been shrouded in secrecy, might have been open for everyone to know about, but he felt a kinship toward them just the same. They'd laid their lives on the line for their country, just as he had, and the fact that they'd had to pay the price without even a chance to fight back, filled him with shame concerning his self-pity over his injury.

Carolyn slid her hand in his, bringing Asa out of his thoughts, but the glance he gave her was so remote that she felt a chill settle in her heart. She quickly dropped his hand and turned away so that he wouldn't see the hurt in her eyes, and the chill deepened when he didn't say anything or move toward her.

Carolyn stood silently, seeing nothing, and thought about Asa's complex personality and the strain it had put on their relationship almost from the first moment they'd met. She couldn't begin to come up with an explanation for his swift mood changes . . . the way he pulled her toward him one moment and pushed her away the next. She had thought that would end when she'd agreed not to expect anything of him after her vacation was over.

Though Carolyn thought the emotional adjustment Asa must be having to make because of the injury to his leg might have something to do with his paradoxical behavior, she somehow didn't think that was all there was to it. But what else could there be? It felt decidedly odd to have shared the ultimate physical intimacy with a man—to be more than half in love with him—when she knew almost nothing about him other than that he spoke Chinese like a native and was going to lecture about China at the University of Hawaii.

"The boat's ready to leave. Are you ready to go?"

Carolyn bristled at the lack of emotion in Asa's voice when he spoke to her, but she said nothing, merely nodded and allowed him to help her into the shuttle boat that would take them back to the Pearl Harbor Naval Base. One glance at his face as they settled into the boat told her he wasn't in a mood for conversation, so she stayed silent until they were back in his car.

"Where are we going now?" she asked quietly after he'd started the engine.

"Pearl City," Asa answered absently. He was still in the reflective mood he'd been in at the memorial.

They'd driven a few miles before Asa realized Carolyn was unusually silent, and when he glanced at her, he saw that she was wearing an unhappy expression. He started to ask what was wrong, then realized he didn't have to ask. He'd been behaving badly to her again, as though her feelings weren't important enough to be considered.

With an inward sigh of self-disgust, Asa debated about giving her another in what looked like a long string of apologies stretched over the short length of their time together. Then he rejected the idea, deciding instead to make up to her for his boorishness.

"Do you like monkeys?" he asked in a teasing way, reaching over to take her hand and squeeze it as he gave her a warm

139

look. He pretended he hadn't seen the look of astonished star-tlement she'd given him as he turned back to watch the road.

"Why, yes. I guess so," she said slowly. "Why?"

"Wait and see," he said in an exaggeratedly mysterious way. Switching subjects, he added, "People don't add much to the scenery around here, do they?"

He was referring to the stretch of rather tawdry shops and housing they were passing by on their way to Pearl City.

"No." Carolyn shook her head, her thoughts still centered on Asa's most recent change of mood. He was like a chameleon, she thought with a good deal of exasperation. Still, when he was in his present mood, she couldn't think of anyone she'd rather be with . . . not even Julie, which was downright amazing when she considered she'd only known Asa a couple of days and a good portion of their time together he'd acted like a boor. It was even more amazing when she realized she wanted to be with him even when he was being rude and inconsiderate!

"It would have been great to see all this when it was virgin territory," he was going on. "Or even when it was only popu-lated by the native Hawaiians, although from what I've heard and read, there were some drawbacks to their culture."

"Drawbacks?" Carolyn was listening with only half an ear.

Asa shrugged. "Bloody battles—a lot of taboos where the punishment was death." He smiled slightly and gave her a sly glance. "I believe they considered women allied with the nega-tive principle of darkness and restricted them quite a bit."

That got Carolyn's attention, and giving him a cool glance, she said dryly, "The similarities among cultures separated by thousands of miles which never came in contact with another is amazing, isn't it?"

Asa adopted an innocent look. "In what way?"

"You know very well what way," Carolyn retorted. "The sup-pression of women seems to have been almost universal. It's still in favor over most of the world, even in the twentieth century as a matter of fact, even in the United States."

"Oh, so you're a women's libber?" Asa teased, not at all put off by the idea.

Carolyn frowned, searching for a clarification of her views in

140

her mind. She'd never thought that much about it before, despite her remarks to Asa.

"Not the way some people think of it," she said thoughtfully. "I mean, I've never wanted a career for myself. I'm happiest as a homemaker."

Asa immediately frowned, but Carolyn wasn't looking in his direction.

"But if I did want a career," she went on more surely, "I certainly wouldn't want anyone telling me I couldn't have one simply because I'm a woman. Julie—my younger sister is studying for a degree in economics, of all things." Carolyn shook her head. Julie's choice of study still amazed her, especially considering her carelessness with money. "And I would be furious if she were denied employment because of her sex."

"So you want the opportunities open for other women," Asa commented. It made him uncomfortable when Carolyn brought up her penchant for homemaking and taking care of children. He supposed it made him feel as though he were wasting her time by being with her, even if only for a short period, when she could be looking for the husband who thought as she did and would be thrilled to find a woman who wanted to stay home and cook and clean and make babies.

Carolyn shrugged and nodded. "I suppose so," she agreed. "I feel a little guilty about going to college this fall when I don't even know what I want to study."

"You haven't been to college?" Asa asked, sounding a little astounded.

"That was one of the things I gave up to raise my sister," Carolyn said, her tone slightly curt because of Asa's reaction. "One of the things I didn't mind giving up," she added truthfully.

Asa shrugged, wanting to get off this subject somehow, though his next remarks weren't the sort to end the conversation.

"I would think your choice of study would be obvious," he said a little impatiently.

Carolyn bristled, but held on to her temper. "Such as?" she replied in a cool tone.

"Home economics, child psychology, sociology . . . there's

a whole list of subjects for someone interested in taking care of people." Asa softened his tone, thinking he deserved that note of coolness in Carrie's.

Carolyn relaxed and frowned thoughtfully. "When I was a child, I used to want to be a doctor like my father," she said, a tinge of sadness entering her voice as she added, "but after my mom and dad were killed and I had Julie to look after, I forgot about it."

Asa felt himself softening toward her again. His little Junior League refugee hadn't had it all as soft as he'd thought she had.

"It's not too late," he ventured.

Carolyn shook her head, but she didn't reply out loud. She was thinking, *I don't have the motivation and dedication it would take, especially if Julie's wish for me should come true and I eventually do find someone to marry. When—if—that happens, I want to start a family right away. And if I do have children, I want to have the time to enjoy them—watch them grow—be there for them when they're sick or—well, just be there for them—the way I was for Julie.*

But what if her dream wasn't going to come true? she wondered bleakly. She glanced at Asa and was filled with sadness because he was uninterested in helping her fulfill her dream. He would have been perfect, but . . .

"What about being a social worker, then?" Asa continued to pursue the subject, though he couldn't have said why. "There are people all over who need someone to care. You can't pick up a paper nowadays without reading about them. If you need to be needed, the field's wide open."

Carolyn went still inside, focusing on Asa's perhaps unconscious revelation that he had somehow zeroed in on the central core of her character.

"Why do you think I need to be needed?" she asked quietly, wondering how Asa could have come to know that about her in such a short time.

He gave her a surprised look. He'd been trained to pick people apart and search out their hidden motivations, he wanted to say. But he couldn't, of course.

"Ah, you just seem the type," he answered somewhat lamely.

"Am I wrong?" he then asked. He supposed he wanted confirmation that he'd picked her apart correctly.

Carolyn hesitated, looking away to stare out the car window. "No," she finally answered quietly. "No, I guess you aren't wrong, Asa."

Though he was pleased to have been right on one level, on another, Asa wished he'd been wrong. He was beginning actually to hate the guilt Carrie stirred in him. He had enough guilt to last him a lifetime, he thought bitterly. There might be people who'd depended on him lying dead in their graves right now because he'd let them down.

"Then you ought to give some consideration to my suggestion," he said almost curtly. "You'd be perfect as a social worker."

Carolyn winced at his tone, and once again, felt helplessly bewildered by his attitude. He sometimes behaved as though he didn't even like her, much less love her, the way he'd said he did when he'd made love to her. But maybe Asa Bradley was simply the type of man who tossed words like "love" around in bed with no true conception of the emotion he labeled so carelessly.

The thought was bitterly sobering and Carolyn stared at him with the objective scrutiny she might have given a complete stranger.

"How do you feel about needing someone . . . or having them need you?" she asked in a flat, level tone. "I'd like to know." But *like* didn't describe what she wanted, she realized an instant after she had spoken. She *needed* to know what Asa Bradley was really like.

Asa clenched his jaw, torn two ways about giving Carrie a straight answer. If he told her the truth, he suspected some of the magic they created together would dissipate. But if he didn't tell her the truth, he would feel like a hypocrite.

"I haven't needed anyone, at least on a personal, emotional level," Asa finally said in a flat voice, "since I was a kid. And I haven't wanted anyone to need me," he added, feeling somewhat brutal as he did so, "since I got to be an adult. I don't expect that to change." He paused, unable to look at Carolyn, before he added with soft finality, "Does that answer your question?"

Carolyn felt slightly sick . . . certainly empty. "Yes, Asa," she answered in a faint voice after a moment. "That answers my question."

The rest of the drive to the Pearl City Tavern, where they would dine, was accomplished in complete silence.

"Can they breathe in there?" Carolyn asked in amazement as she stared at several monkeys swinging on branches behind a glass wall behind the bar at the Pearl City Tavern.

"Obviously," Asa said, his voice tinged with humor. "They look healthy to me. Don't they to you?"

"I guess," Carolyn said absently, unable to get over seeing monkeys in such an unusual setting. She wasn't sure she approved. But then she'd never felt quite comfortable at zoos either, always feeling slightly sorry for the caged animals.

"Come on." Asa took her arm. "Let's sit down."

They dined on Maine lobster, which struck Carolyn as funny when they were on an island in the middle of the Pacific. She thought the price of their meal was an indication of how far their poor dinner had had to travel before landing on the plate in front of her.

"Aren't you hungry?" Asa asked. He'd been starved and hadn't noticed for a while that Carolyn wasn't eating with a great deal of enthusiasm.

"Not really," she admitted. "I'm only eating because these cost so much and it would be a shame to waste them."

Asa laughed. "Spoken like a true housewife," he teased.

Carolyn wasn't amused by the joke. "One needs a husband to be a housewife," she said coolly. "I've been a homemaker, not a housewife."

Annoyed by her reaction, Asa merely shrugged and concentrated on his lobster. Annoyed by *his* reaction, Carolyn gave up eating entirely.

On the long drive back to his apartment, Carolyn debated about asking him to take her straight to her hotel. She wasn't in the mood to make love right now. She doubted if Asa was. But she had left her bathing suit and clothes at his apartment, so she stayed silent until they arrived there.

"After I've collected my things," she said as they climbed the

144

stairs, "perhaps I should go back to my hotel. The poor tour director must have been beside himself when he counted heads this morning. I'm sure he'd appreciate my checking in with him."

"That friend of yours—Martha, wasn't it?" Asa replied as he inserted his key in the lock of his apartment door. "She would have explained things, wouldn't she?"

Carolyn hesitated, annoyed at being caught in a white lie. Actually, she had asked Martha to reassure the tour director.

While she was trying to think of something to say, Asa got the door open and ushered her inside. When she started to walk away from him, however, he held on to her hand as he shut the door behind him.

Her eyes were wide and wary as she turned and looked into his and discovered the lambent glow in their dark depths that meant he wanted her.

"I don't want you to go," he said softly, and his simple directness sparked a dart of warm response inside Carolyn she wanted to reject.

"Why?" she asked, her tone as soft as his, her gaze steady. "You haven't acted as though you enjoyed my company very much this evening."

After a slight hesitation, Asa answered. "I can't deny that I'm not always easy to be around," he said quietly. "But there are other times . . . like now . . ." He stopped, his gaze finishing the explanation for him as he gently pulled her into his arms.

His kiss undermined Carolyn's desire to assert herself, to show him that she wasn't going to be a punching bag for his verbal assaults or his silences one moment and a willing body to share his bed the next. Besides, she thought a little wildly as Asa's hands and mouth stirred her senses into life, what's the point of this relationship? Casual sex? That isn't good enough . . .

But under the direction of Asa's skilled onslaught, her body disagreed, and soon Carolyn found herself in Asa's bed again, completely caught up in the illusion he could create that what they shared together was anything but casual.

Again, his voice whispered, "I love you, Carrie." And again, she believed him . . . because she wanted to. Because he sounded so convincing, she was helpless to remember that his actions and his words after the lovemaking was over always made what he was saying now seem like lies.

It made no difference. In Asa's arms, the illusion was complete. The joy was whole. The completion was devastatingly real. He was hers as much as she was his in that darkened bedroom, and Carolyn knew the truth of that without question. It was enough . . . for a while.

They collected the rest of her clothes the next morning and checked her out of the hotel. The tour was leaving for Maui shortly, and Carolyn had only a few moments alone with Martha to make her explanations and say her good-byes.

"I don't want to lose track of you, Martha," she said a little forlornly as she and Martha exchanged addresses.

"You won't," the older woman said simply. "We're not that far apart, as you can see. And I'll be disappointed if you don't call me when you get back to Kansas City."

"I will." Carolyn nodded firmly.

"If you don't," Martha said, the twinkle sparkling in her eyes, "I'll call you and give you a real dressing down. Then, I'll have you over and give you dinner and we can have a long talk."

"I'll look forward to it." Carolyn smiled, thinking she was going to need a special friend when she got back to Kansas City —someone who didn't need a lot of explanations and who would understand if Carolyn was experiencing the letdown she was positive she would when her affair with Asa was over.

"Be careful, dear," Martha said quietly, glancing at Asa where he stood near the door staring outside. "He seems a decent man, but he's a heartbreaker as well, I think."

Carolyn nodded, her expression sober. "Yes, Martha. I've already accepted that about him."

Martha opened her mouth to say something else, then closed it, shaking her head as she gave a big sigh. Carolyn was certain her friend wanted to give her some motherly advice but had wisely decided otherwise in view of the fact that Carolyn's mind was made up.

"Martha, this is *my* time," Carolyn attempted to explain in an awkward manner. "My time to be foolish—to do something I want that's completely irresponsible, I suppose. Something that I'll no doubt have to pay for ten times over when it's done and I have to go back to being sensible." She shook her head, the expression in her eyes troubled. "I can't really explain, but I need these two weeks, don't you see? It's the first time in years I've had only myself to think about . . ."

"I know," Martha said soothingly. "I know, honey. You deserve your time. Take it without thinking you owe a foolish old woman any explanations. You don't even owe that little sister you raised an explanation, you know. You have your own life to live now. It really is *your* turn to make a life for yourself."

But not with Asa, Carolyn immediately thought, and then was impatient with the sadness the thought brought with it. *But it doesn't matter,* she assured herself with firm conviction. *This is my time out of time. Just a brief episode to bridge the gap between the old life and my new one.*

"Good-bye, dear," Martha said and leaned forward to kiss Carolyn's cheek. "I'm so glad to have met you."

Carolyn hugged Martha back and echoed the sentiment. "I'll see you again soon," she promised.

She felt a little bereft as she watched Martha walk away and rejoin Celie despite that assurance, however. But then Asa was looking at her, waiting for her to come to him, and she joined him, determinedly putting thoughts of Martha aside.

"Your bags are in the car," he said quietly, his eyes scanning her face. "Unless you've changed your mind?"

Carolyn shook her head. "No, Asa. I haven't changed my mind."

"Good," he said, hoping she would never discover that he had amazed himself by asking her to stay with him for the remainder of her vacation. It certainly hadn't been his plan to go that far. But now that it was done, he couldn't be sorry. He felt a lot of things, some of them on the negative side, but regret that Carolyn had taken him up on his offer wasn't one of them.

When they were in the car, heading toward his apartment, Carolyn made a request she couldn't explain even to herself.

"Asa, could we drive by the university?" she asked abstractedly, and was relieved when he didn't ask her why. She wouldn't have known what to say.

"Sure." He shrugged, though he was frowning at being reminded that in less than two weeks he would be lecturing there, attempting to establish contact with a young man who he hoped would lead him to another one: an old man who had once been part of the inner circle surrounding Mao, and whom the U.S. government wanted to question about why he had left his position of power.

As he drove, an airplane zoomed overhead, making Asa feel restless. The feeling departed as an idea came to him and which he immediately broached with Carolyn.

"That tour of yours," he said questioningly. "They're going on to Maui today, right?"

She nodded, glancing at him curiously.

"Would you like to see something of the other islands with me?" he then suggested, and grinned when Carolyn's face lit up with enthusiasm.

"I'd love it!" she exclaimed, then looked at him curiously again. "Are you going just for me, Asa, or haven't you seen any of the other islands yourself before now?"

"No, I've never been anywhere other than Oahu," he said with a smile, glancing at her. "But even if I had, from what I've heard, it wouldn't be any strain to see them again."

Carolyn smiled happily. "No, I suspect it wouldn't be," she agreed. And as they later drove around the University of Hawaii before going to the apartment to pack Asa a bag and make reservations to fly to the Big Island of Hawaii first, she wondered with puzzled disinterest why she had asked Asa to show her the university. It hadn't much to offer when she was about to see the rest of what the wonderful island chain of Hawaii was like.

CHAPTER TWELVE

For the first time since their exploration of the other islands in the Hawaiian chain had begun over a week ago, Carolyn rose before Asa, in fact before the dawn. But then, she hadn't slept much anyway for thinking about how soon her idyllic vacation was going to end.

After donning a light robe, she let herself out onto the patio adjoining their room and sat in a lounge chair, staring at the white tops of the ocean waves cascading onto the shore nearby, listening to their muted thunder, trying to fight the depression that rose inside her whenever she thought about leaving all this . . . and Asa.

Three more days, she thought soberly. *Only three more days.*

Until now, she had been able to keep the bargain she'd made with herself to live only for the moment. In fact, it had been ridiculously easy to pretend that she and Asa, like so many other couples they'd seen, were on their honeymoon. The days had been filled with adventure as they viewed the still active volcanoes on the Big Island of Hawaii and the moonlike lava fields and black beaches those volcanoes had created. There were orchids there, too—22,000 varieties of them, many of which they'd seen.

On Maui, they'd explored the old whaling town of Lahaina, seen the acres of sugarcane that seemed to go on forever, and Carolyn had been awed by the beauty of Iao Valley Park and the Iao Needle, though once again, her enjoyment had been dampened at learning that at one time in Hawaii's tumultuous past, the Iao Stream had been dammed with human bodies and the water reddened with the blood of Maui warriors who'd died in battle. She'd been careful not to mention her reaction to Asa, however. They were getting along much too well to take the chance that he would react as he had when she'd talked about the Pali to him, which might have spoiled the beautiful nights they were sharing.

As Carolyn leaned her head back and closed her eyes, letting the sound of the ocean, the delicious scents of Kauai and the tropical breeze soothe her into a more peaceful frame of mind, she realized it was the Hawaiian nights she'd shared with Asa she would remember most of all when this trip was over.

Oh, there had been beauty to spare during the days. Carolyn couldn't deny that. But the nights . . . the nights were an enchanted idyll that she thought must come only once in a lifetime to those who were lucky enough to have it at all, and she didn't expect, if she ever did marry, to have a honeymoon to compare with the mock one she and Asa had been having. The only way it could have been better was if they really had been married, with a future together to look forward to.

Instead, the ending of everything was coming soon, and Carolyn wasn't certain how she was going to be able to bear it. How did one say good-bye to a person who had become lover, friend, confidant . . . the husband of her heart, in everything but name?

A tear slid down her cheek, catching her by surprise. Impatiently, she brushed it away, but another followed—and another—until there were too many tears to fight and she gave up trying, concentrating instead on keeping her lapse a silent one so as not to wake Asa.

Asa came awake slowly, and when he was fully alert, he frowned at realizing his old habit of waking instantly had been slipping steadily away since the first night he'd spent with Carolyn on the Big Island.

It'll come back, he told himself uneasily and turned to seek comfort from Carolyn, a new habit he was developing in the mornings to replace the old one of searching for danger upon first waking.

She wasn't there.

Asa sat bolt upright, panic swimming at the edges of his mind until he subdued it. There was nothing here to fear, he reminded himself. She had probably woken early and gone for a walk or . . .

He heard a faint sound coming from the direction of the patio and in an instant he was out of bed and pacing silently to the double doors leading outside.

Asa relaxed at spotting Carolyn's robed figure huddled on the lounge chair. He couldn't see her face, but he didn't need to. She was all right and that was all that mattered.

Although the sky was just lightening and there wasn't likely to be anyone around to see him, since he was nude, he didn't step outside to join Carolyn. Instead, he headed for the bathroom to run a tub of hot water. His leg was aching, and though he would have preferred to start this morning the same way he'd started each one for over a week—making love to Carolyn—he was willing to let the ritual of the hot bath supersede the new one of making love for a change.

As he relaxed in the tub of hot water, Asa let his mind wander, thinking back with pleasure over the past week. Normally, he wasn't the type to behave like a tourist, but with Carolyn for company, he had actually enjoyed seeing the sights that thousands of other people came to the islands to see—especially when the days always ended with such romantic evenings and nights.

He had been aware from time to time that strangers viewed him and Carolyn as honeymooners, and he had suspected once or twice that Carolyn was indulging such a fantasy in her own mind. Since fantasy was not his style, the illusions she weaved both amused and troubled him. He hoped she was going to be able to face reality when the time came.

At that thought, and one that followed it, Asa opened his eyes and stared unseeingly at the tiled wall at the end of the tub. It wasn't going to be easy for him to go back to the old life once Carolyn was gone either. Unlike previous women he'd known, she'd somehow managed to breach a few of his defenses . . . some fairly important ones, in fact, such as his habitual view of himself as strictly a loner.

As a loner, he hadn't appreciated waking up with someone else in his bed. But since he'd been with Carolyn, he'd enjoyed waking up next to her warmth and this morning, when she hadn't been there, besides being worried, he'd felt . . . bereft?

Asa frowned, disliking the word that had occurred to him. Maybe he'd been a little lonely, but bereft? That word smacked too much of experiencing a definite loss—a loss of something that had become too important to him. It was the way he'd felt when he'd learned his leg wasn't going to heal completely and be as strong as ever.

You'll miss her for a while, sure, he told himself somewhat grimly. *But you'll get over it, especially when you get back to work.*

He turned to wondering what had woken Carrie so early, but when an explanation occurred to him, he avoided acknowledging it. He didn't want to spend their last three days together worrying about how she was going to be when their time together was over.

She'll get over it, too, he told himself. *She'll have to, since she won't have any other choice. It's not as though you've given her any reason to hope there's a chance for anything permanent to develop between us. There isn't, and she knows it.*

His attempt to soothe his conscience was only partially successful, but Asa turned his mind away toward what they would do today. Living for the moment was the whole secret of making the most of his infrequent opportunities to relax from the responsibilities he normally carried, and Asa had learned the art well.

Carolyn heard the water running in the bathroom and knew Asa was up. Hurriedly, she brushed the tears from her cheeks and searched in her robe pocket for a tissue to blow her nose.

When she thought she had eliminated the signs of her crying session to the best of her ability, she slipped back into the room and stood wavering uncertainly for a moment. It felt strange not to have awakened in Asa's strong arms with the warmth of his body against her back and his soft whispers of love in her ears.

Briefly, she wondered if he'd missed their early-morning lovemaking as much as she was missing it now, but if he had, wouldn't he have come out on the patio to get her? Unless he'd seen her crying and didn't want to deal with her tears.

That cold thought held her frozen for a moment before she relaxed and shrugged. He slept in the nude, and probably just hadn't wanted to put something on to come outside. Besides, his leg always ached in the mornings, and he always took a hot bath to ease it.

A mischievous thought seized her then, bringing a smile to her lips. It was still early, and they weren't on any hard and fast schedule anyway. She could join Asa in the tub and they could add a little variety to their lovemaking.

Carolyn entered the bathroom quietly, and at seeing that Asa had his eyes closed and his head tipped back at the end of the tub, her smile broadened. He was a perfect target. Slipping out of her robe, she tiptoed to the side of the tub and was leaning down to scoop some water in her hand, intending to sprinkle it on his face, when he moved with the speed of lightning and grabbed her wrist.

She gasped, nearly fell overboard, and looked up to glare at him. He had one eye open and a sly smile on his lips.

"Good morning, Carrie," he said innocently. "Did you need the tub?"

"I was going to *join* you in the tub, actually," she said irritably, "but you . . ."

"Now, why do I get the impression you're not telling me the strict truth," Asa interrupted in a musing tone. "If I were a detective, and someone had snuck up on tiptoe to the side of a tub I was in and dipped her dainty little hand in the water, I would have said she had something unworthy in mind . . . such as splashing water in my face?"

"I wasn't going to splash," Carolyn responded virtuously. "I was going to sprinkle."

"Oh, I see," Asa said solemnly. "There's a difference."

"A *big* difference." Carolyn nodded.

"Well, why don't you come on in here and we'll discuss it," Asa suggested. "You look uncomfortable all hunched over the tub like that."

"I wouldn't be hunching over if you'd let go of my arm," Carolyn responded dryly.

Asa immediately let his fingers spring open, lifted his hand, turned the palm in and out as though to show it was empty, and smiled like an innocent cherub.

Carolyn ostentatiously rubbed her wrist for a moment before stepping into the tub in a prim, dainty fashion. When she was settled between Asa's legs facing him, she had to smile.

"It's a little cramped in here, isn't it?" she said lightly, revising her plan for them to make love. There just wasn't room.

Asa was staring at her face, wondering why her lashes were damp and the normal clear white of her eyes was reddened. But if she'd been crying, he didn't want to start the tears again by saying anything, so he merely smiled evilly.

"A little cramped for what?" he asked, wiggling his eyebrows in a parody of a leer.

Carolyn looked down her nose at him. "Never you mind," she said dismissively. "It wasn't a good idea anyway."

"What wasn't a good idea?" he demanded, quickly sitting upright.

Carolyn eyed him askance. "Washing my back?"

"Oh, is that what you had in mind?" he said in a brisk fashion as he grabbed the cake of soap. "Why, honey child, that's no problem at all."

Asa's method of washing Carolyn's back turned out to be interesting. He seemed to have a great deal of trouble locating and reaching the target, so that it was Carolyn's front that got most of the rubbing.

At last, she was gigglingly aroused and decided it was time to fight back.

"My turn," she demanded, and grabbed the soap out of his hand.

Asa stretched his head up and thrust out his chest. "Easy on the right shoulder," he warned with pomposity. "I strained it once."

Since that part of his anatomy wasn't on her plan of attack, Carolyn assented agreeably and dived for his waist instead.

Fifteen minutes later, there was a great deal of soapy water on the floor of the bathroom and Carolyn had discovered that, with a little bit of ingenuity and quite a bit of agility, amazing things could be accomplished in tight spaces.

"I hope you're satisfied," Asa panted in an exaggeratedly gloomy fashion as he lay back in the tub feigning exhaustion. "I got in this tub to relax and soak out my aches and pains."

"How *is* that knee of yours?" Carolyn murmured dreamily against his chest.

"What knee?" Asa grinned, then broke out into a chuckle as he hugged her close.

For the rest of the day, as they explored the garden island of Kauai, Carolyn was able to keep the low spirits she'd woken with at bay, and Asa made a special effort to keep things light and cheerful.

At dinner that night, however, when they sat on a lovely terrace and drank wine and gazed at the ocean, Carolyn's mood quieted steadily until Asa, looking across the table at her pensive expression, knew what was on her mind and that it would do no good to try to joke the inevitable away. He didn't feel in a jovial mood himself anymore anyway.

"It's been something, hasn't it," he said quietly, his dark eyes somberly warm as he gazed at Carolyn, storing away memories of how she looked this night in the red and white figure-hugging muumuu he'd bought her and with a red hibiscus in her soft hair.

She understood what he was saying, and her gaze was open and vulnerable as she stared back at him.

"It's been wonderful, Asa," she said with quiet sincerity. "The most wonderful days of my life."

He frowned slightly then, wondering if she meant her words. Then he wondered if he could say the same. The answer, when it finally came, was disturbing, for he discovered he felt the same. But, of course, nothing like this could last, he reminded himself. One couldn't live on moonlit nights of love forever. The nature of the world wouldn't allow it.

"I'll miss you when you're gone," he said, meaning it, unaware that his words drove a nail through Carolyn's heart.

She hadn't really expected anything else, at least consciously. But hearing the finality in Asa's voice was still heartbreaking.

"I'll miss you, too, Asa," she answered in a voice husky with tears, and quickly looked away to try to get herself under control.

Her tears made Asa feel helpless and a bit angry. Damn it, he thought, I spelled it out for her . . . and for myself, he added grimly.

"Are you finished eating?" he asked a moment later in an awkward manner.

That awkwardness made Carolyn feel almost sorry for him. He was so uncomfortable with emotion, she thought sadly, and wondered what sort of family he'd grown up in. One where all the members were supposed to be strong and immune to ordinary human weaknesses, no doubt. One where independence was encouraged and dependence on anyone or anything was frowned upon. He'd said he hadn't needed anyone since childhood and didn't want anyone needing him. Carolyn thought that was a sterile, empty way to live, but perhaps it was safer than her own way where she loved too deeply and left herself much too vulnerable.

"Yes, I'm finished," she answered at last, thinking the words might be appropriate in more ways than one. She was having a great deal of trouble finding a point to her life at that moment.

"Then let's go to our room," Asa said, feeling relieved. In the room, they could make love and when they made love, they forgot everything else. Carolyn wouldn't cry, and he wouldn't have to feel like a damned heel.

As it turned out, Asa was wrong. The lovemaking was as tender and exciting as it had ever been, but afterward, Carolyn's tears soaked his shoulder, and he not only felt like a heel, he felt that damnable sense of bereavement he'd woken with that morning and which he cursed steadily in his mind as being weak and unrealistic and a waste of time.

Neither of them got much sleep that night.

CHAPTER THIRTEEN

Two nights later, Asa lay propped on the bed in his apartment watching, almost against his will, as Carolyn neatly and methodically folded each piece of her clothing and tucked it away in her suitcase. He'd come to know her well in the time they'd been together, and he was aware that the blankly controlled expression on her face concealed a wealth of emotion. For while she might be able to control her face, she couldn't do the same with her hands, and Asa could see how they trembled.

"I'm not worth getting upset about, you know," he said abruptly, precipitating the very discussion he'd intended to avoid.

Carolyn paused for a second, then put the shorts she'd folded into her bag and straightened to look at Asa, keeping her expression blank. She felt slightly numb, but an emotional maelstrom trembled at the brink of her control, waiting to engulf her if she let it.

"If you weren't worth getting upset about, Asa," she said in a quiet monotone, "I would never have gotten close enough to you to risk becoming upset."

Asa became aware that he was clenching his jaw and he made himself relax as he realized he was fighting a battle for control of his own. *And what can you say to that, Mr. Intelligence Agent,* he thought with a trace of self-mockery, *since the same holds true for her. If she wasn't special enough to make you risk getting involved with her against your better judgment, this parting would be as easy as the dozens like it you've gone through in the past.*

Only it was a mistake to classify any of the previous partings he'd experienced in the same category as this one, Asa knew.

Because Carrie Winters wasn't like any woman he'd ever known.

"There'll be other men . . ." he said, his normal awkwardness at discussing emotional matters coming through in his voice. "Men who are more suitable for the type of woman you are."

Carolyn felt her mouth curve into a smile filled with irony. "I expect so," she answered as matter-of-factly as she could manage, thinking silently, *and of course, there will be other women for you Asa . . . women more suited to the type of man you are—footloose and fancy free.*

Asa hadn't expected her to agree with him quite so matter-of-factly when she was obviously torn up over their parting, and he had to wrestle with an illogical surge of jealousy as he stared at her, so femininely lovely in her lacy nightgown, and pictured another man seeing her like this.

"Well, that's done," Carolyn said with an attempt at lightness that failed as she looked around and discovered everything was packed except the gown she wore now and the slacks, summer sweater, and shoes she'd left out to wear on the plane the next morning.

"Good," Asa said softly as he sat up and held out his hand. "Then, come here."

Carolyn slowly turned in his direction, feeling a curious reluctance to join him in bed, perhaps because this would be their last time together.

But she could no more resist his outstretched hand and the look of warm beckoning in his dark eyes than she could have stood fast against one of the tsunamis that sometimes swept the shores of Hawaii as a result of an earthquake somewhere on the ocean floor.

When she had reached the side of the bed and placed her hand in Asa's, he drew her down to sit beside him and for a long moment, he simply inspected the lovely classic planes of her face, the tousled champagne-colored hair, the solemn expression in her wide blue eyes, and the slim, graceful lines of her body outlined under the pale pink gown.

"Let me love you through the night, Carrie," he said with an uncustomary note of emotion in his deep, quiet voice that caught at Carolyn's heart and brought the tears she'd been fighting to her eyes.

"Don't cry," he whispered, gently drawing her down to lie beside him and bending to kiss her eyelids with his lips. "I want to remember you smiling. You have the most beautiful smile I've ever seen."

As he drew back slightly, Carolyn blinked her eyes rapidly, fiercely willing the tears away. At last, she was able to bring forth a wavering smile that was a parody of the ones Asa had been receiving all week, and which he knew he would never be able to forget.

Tenderly, he brushed his mouth against hers until instead of smiling she was returning his kiss, her lips as temptingly soft and delectable as Asa could wish for. He deepened the kiss, feeling his loins tightening with the special desire Carolyn always brought forth in him. She tasted like sunshine and exotic flowers and romance lost, and he unconsciously held her tighter, attempting to dispel the almost panicky feeling he had that she was already slipping away from him before it was time.

"Hold me, Carrie," he grated roughly against her petal-soft ear. "Hold me tight!"

Carolyn clung to him, not only because he'd demanded it, but because she was also gripped by a feeling of premature loss. She became aware that she was taking a sort of despairing inventory with her hands of his hard body, his beloved rugged face, the thick hair that grew long on his neck.

But it wasn't enough to touch him with her hands. Soon, she was kissing him everywhere, her mouth feverishly urgent as she committed the taste of him to memory.

"God, Carrie . . . don't . . . ." Asa protested, his desire trying to surge past his control as a result of Carolyn's impassioned lovemaking.

But Carolyn wouldn't be stopped, and Asa, recognizing the reason for her actions, forced himself to relax and permit her to have her way. His time to do the same to her would come before the night was over. Of that, he had no doubt.

At last, she was on her knees beside him, as she drew the nightgown up and over her head while Asa watched, his eyes glazed with desire and reverence for her beauty. The gown was tossed aside, and Carolyn lithely straddled him.

He gazed up into her flushed face, into the drugged expression of her wide-open eyes, and then he groaned and shut his eyes as she took him inside her.

"Carrie . . ." He whispered her name as his eyes opened to a narrow slit and his hands came up to her hips, aiding her in the smooth, gliding motions of her rhythm. "Carrie—my beautiful Carrie—" He repeated a litany of praise that died on a rasping intake of breath when she began to rock in her release of passion. Then he was joining her, forgetting everything, and simply feeling with every inch of him as the glory of union burst upon him.

Afterward, he cuddled her trembling body against his chest, feeling a tender protectiveness that shook him. He couldn't avoid the realization of how far along he'd come in this relationship that was about to end.

He didn't want to think about it ending—not now—not while they still had this last long night together. He could return to reality in the morning—but not now . . . not now . . .

And so, when the trembling in Carolyn's body ceased, he began to stroke it into passionate life again, as he did throughout this last night together, until the morning came, finding them exhausted and dully numbed against the parting that would come at the airport soon.

"Are you sure you have everything?" Asa asked quietly as Carolyn closed the last suitcase and wearily straightened.

"I seem to." She shrugged, wondering if Asa wanted to be certain she didn't leave any reminders around his apartment. She had an idea he wanted to forget her just as totally as he had immersed himself in being with her throughout the night that had just passed.

"Then let's go have some breakfast before we have to get you to the airport," he said, moving to pick up her bags and carry them into the front room.

Carolyn followed him, pausing as he set the bags down by the front door. She remembered how he had looked when he'd opened that door to her the day they'd met—so irritable and scowling. Would it have been better or worse, she wondered, if that had been both the beginning and the end of their acquaintance? Certainly, if she'd never seen him again after that day, she wouldn't be feeling this sense of helpless despair.

Asa stepped close and took her shoulders in his hands, staring down into her eyes with a look she dared not classify as the sort of love she felt for him.

"I want you to know," he said with soft firmness, "that if it were possible for me to live . . ." He hesitated, afraid he was about to say too much, then gave a mental shrug and finished anyway. "If I could live like a normal man," he said gently, "I'd want to live my life with you. I've never felt that about any woman before . . . never said that to anyone else. Nor have I said 'I love you' to another woman, Carrie. And in my own way, I mean it."

Carolyn stared up at him, loving him to the depths of her soul, yet wanting to scream at him and demand an explanation of why he couldn't live a normal life and keep her with him. Her bewildered turmoil showed in her eyes and Asa sighed and shook his head.

"I can't explain," he said gently, but with such firmness that Carolyn knew he wouldn't be dissuaded from keeping his secrets. "Just remember that I've shared more of myself with you than I have with anyone in my entire adult life . . . though instead of remembering anything about me, it would be better if you forgot me entirely."

"I can't," Carolyn whispered helplessly, her eyes moistening with tears, though she was trying hard to hold them back.

Asa's gaze probed hers, and finally he nodded. "No, I won't be able to forget you either," he admitted with a small, humorless smile.

And then he drew her into his arms and held her for a few long moments. Carolyn held him just as tightly, her face in the crook of his neck, her eyes closed, as she let her senses register the feel of him, the scent of his aftershave, the smoothly rough texture of his skin.

He held her away from him at last, reluctantly. "Let's get it done," he said in a tone rimmed with grim inevitability, and he

161

turned, opened the door, picked up her bags and stepped outside.

Carolyn hesitated a moment, turning to look at the apartment where she'd learned the depth of her womanhood, then silently stepped across the threshold and closed the door behind her. She followed Asa downstairs, out to his car, and waited while he stowed her bags in the trunk.

In the car, she sat turned toward him, her gaze never still as she looked at his face, his strong hands on the wheel, the casual male grace of his body while he drove them to a small restaurant where they would eat breakfast.

They talked very little while they waited for their food to arrive, and when it did, Carolyn felt her stomach turn over with nausea.

"I can't eat," she said, shuddering as she looked at the eggs on her plate. "I'd be sick if I did."

She didn't realize how Asa had taken her words until she looked at his face and saw a wary question in his eyes that made her both sad and angry. She shook her head. "I'm not pregnant, Asa," she assured him dryly, without explaining that upon waking that morning there had been familiar signs that she was about to start her period.

"Just drink your juice and your coffee, then," Asa gently suggested, feeling ashamed of having shown her how worried he had been for a moment there. But his worry had been as much for her as for himself, he admitted as he pushed his own eggs aside and finished his coffee.

He paid the bill and then they were back in the car heading for Honolulu Airport, and this time Carolyn stared out the window, afraid to look at Asa for fear she would burst into tears.

Carolyn felt each moment that ticked inexorably by as though her life were draining away like the sands of an hourglass trickling downward. She was aware of almost nothing other than Asa as he checked her bags, obtained her boarding pass, and escorted her to the departure gate.

Finally, it came time to walk down the tunnel to the plane that would take her away from paradise and deposit her back into mundane, lonely reality.

"I love you, Asa," she whispered with simple honesty as she

stared up into the taut planes of his face for the last time. "I love you desperately."

A spasm of something she couldn't identify passed over his face, and then his eyes were boring into hers as he said with rough intensity, "Don't! Don't love me, Carrie. Forget me. Tuck me away somewhere deep in your mind where I can't get out and live your life without thinking about what could have been."

"Is that what you're going to do?" she asked quietly, searching his eyes for an answer.

Asa could hardly bear the look in her eyes, but he forced himself to hold her gaze as he nodded. "That's all there is to do, Carrie," he said with quiet finality.

A last call for Carrie's flight boomed out, and Asa used its cover to pull Carolyn into his arms for a last kiss. He couldn't keep from showing the desperate hunger he felt for her in that kiss, and it was the hardest thing he'd ever had to do when he broke it, stared into her eyes one last time, then turned her toward the boarding tunnel.

Carolyn walked slowly, turning her head to look at him again and again until she reached the plane and was hurried inside and pointed toward her seat by the stewardess.

Asa stood where he was long after Carolyn had disappeared, and when he did move, it was toward the window where he could watch her plane taxi away.

He stood straight, but the expression in his eyes was bleak as he said a silent good-bye to his Carrie, the woman he should have resisted but couldn't. He'd taken what he wanted, and now it was time to pay, and he acknowledged the justice of the bargain. Hadn't he gotten by for years without having to pay for his pleasure with the sort of emotional bondage Carrie was leaving him as a legacy? Yes, and it was past time for the account to come due, he acknowledged with stoic realism.

Inside the plane, Carolyn sat staring out the window through a film of tears, wondering if Asa would wait until she was gone, or if he'd already left to go back to his apartment. She wouldn't have been surprised by either behavior from him. He was not a man one could slip neatly into a hard and fast category . . . nor was he a man she could forget, as he'd tried to tell her to do.

She stared out the window until the plane was roaring down the runway and then she closed her eyes and endured the muted terror of takeoff. When the plane was in the air, however, she was back at the window, scanning the tropical paradise below her with sad regret. She felt as though she were leaving a large part of herself on that island floating in the deep blue Pacific. She had adopted Hawaii as her own for a brief two weeks—she had found someone to love there—she could have stayed forever if . . .

If, she thought with bleak bitterness. One of the biggest words in the English language. Too big to defeat easily, too small to base any hope on. "If" was a word she would learn to despise over the next few weeks while she wrestled with a deep-seated depression that would finally drive her to seek a cure for the legacy of despair Asa Bradley had given her as a going-away gift and which she couldn't get rid of no matter how hard she tried.

CHAPTER FOURTEEN

"Yes, married couples experience domestic turmoil in China."
Asa answered the question of a young Eurasian girl who'd been
using her large dark eyes to flirt with him throughout his lecture
and who had been the first to hold up her hand when he got to
the question and answer period. "There's even divorce, though
it's handled differently there."

Asa stood with relaxed confidence at the podium, and sensing
the interest of his audience in the topic the flirtatious coed had
brought up, he mentally shrugged and gave the people what
they wanted. He had nothing better to do, after all. The young
man who interested him hadn't shown up for this first lecture,
much to Asa's disappointment.

"For instance," he went on, "it's the policy of the Chinese
government these days to restrict families to one child. That
policy is unpopular enough as it is, but should that one child
turn out to be a girl, the disappointment is often bitter."

A wave of indignation went through the female members of
the audience, and Asa smiled and shrugged.

"I know," he said matter-of-factly, "it's hard for Americans
to sympathize very much with such an attitude. But in China,
female children have never been appreciated the way male children are. In fact, in the past, little girls were often sold to
anyone willing to buy them, or even left to die."

Now the indignation in the audience was palpable.

"You have to understand," Asa said firmly, "that boys represented security to parents. They could work when they got old
enough and help put food on the table. Girls simply ate and
created a burden on the already strained resources of the family

165

unless they were fortunate enough to marry well and bring good fortune to the parents that way."

The young woman who'd been flirting with him was pouting now, in a provocative way that amused Asa without creating any real interest on his part. He suspected he wouldn't be ready for the sort of fun and games his admirer most likely had in mind for some time. Carolyn had cured him of the desire for brief casual encounters for the time being.

"Now, suppose a Chinese couple has their one child and it turns out to be a girl," Asa continued. "And suppose the father considers it his wife's fault that the child is a girl."

A few protests rose from the audience and Asa held up his hand for quiet.

"Of course, we know that it's the male who determines the sex of a child," he said amiably, "but not every culture is aware of it, or if they are, are willing to accept that premise as true." He shrugged. "I've heard of one case where the father was so disappointed, he could barely be civil to his wife, or to his mother-in-law, which is truly disgraceful behavior in China. Eventually, his wife tired of his behavior and wanted a divorce, which, in China, like almost everything else, is handled by a committee."

Asa grinned as some in the audience looked puzzled.

"Think of it as group therapy," he said in a joking manner. "Several people on a committee appointed to handle such matters listen to the wife's side of the argument, then to the husband's side. Then the head of the committee tries to bring about a reconciliation. If it works, everyone is pleased, since divorce is frowned upon in China. If it doesn't work, and the spouse who wants the divorce has a good enough case, the divorce is reluctantly granted."

Asa raised a finger to point at a young Caucasian man in the audience who had his hand up.

"What about the Cultural Revolution?" the young man inquired. "What was it like and how are things different now?"

Asa took a deep breath. "That's a large subject to be handled in a few sentences," he said ruefully, provoking a slight wave of laughter from the unexpectedly large group who had come to hear him lecture.

"I'll handle the Cultural Revolution more extensively in another lecture," Asa promised. "For the time being, let me just say that it was a social experiment that got out of hand and created years of chaos from which China is now trying to recover. Some of the young people who missed out on a decent education during that period may never recover, however, which is a shame."

He was starting to raise his hand to acknowledge another questioner when out of the corner of his eye he noted a latecomer heading toward one of the few empty seats in the back of the lecture hall. Asa felt an inner tension rising inside him as he recognized the young man he was here to find, but he was careful not to show that tension in his manner as he pointed at a young Filipino woman who had a question.

"What do the Chinese think of Mao now?" she asked. "Is he still their hero?"

"Oh, yes." Asa nodded. "Mao managed to give the impression he stood apart from the so-called Gang of Four, which included his wife, and their instigation of the Cultural Revolution. In my opinion, the average Chinese man and woman needs Mao to look up to. After all, if he has feet of clay, who can they trust? He's the Revolution personified."

Though Asa would have preferred to go on, simply because the young man he sought was now in attendance at the lecture, a glance at his watch showed him he was already ten minutes over his allotted time, and a glance at Dr. Wu, who stood against one wall looking impatient, told him the good doctor would end the discussion for him if he didn't wind things up.

"I'd like to go on, but we're running late," he said to the audience, giving them a pleasant smile. "My next lecture is on Wednesday at three o'clock. I hope to see you all again then."

A burst of applause greeted his dismissal, and it seemed sincere, so Asa was pleased with his performance so far. He only wished his young man hadn't missed the best part of his performance.

As he gathered his notes together, he was not surprised to see that the young woman who'd been flirting with him was coming toward the podium, no doubt prepared to pretend her interest in his knowledge of China was all that was on her mind. Asa sighed inwardly, dreading the little scene he would have to play to discourage the young woman from suggesting a cozy chat over coffee. Then he forgot the young woman when he saw the young latecomer he was here to stalk threading his way through the seats of the auditorium toward the podium.

"Mr. Bradley!" the young woman was calling to him, giving him her best smile. "Oh, Mr. Bradley! Can I talk to you for a moment?"

"Certainly," Asa said with absent politeness, while inwardly he was cursing his bad luck in having sparked her libido.

As the young woman came to stand far too close to him and gazed earnestly up at his face, Asa listened to her with half an ear and kept up with the young man's progress out of the corner of his eye.

"I need to do a paper on China for one of my classes," the young woman explained predictably. "And you're so wonderfully knowledgeable about the country and its culture, I was wondering if . . ."

"Cut it out, Leilani," the young man, who was now standing quite near, interrupted, giving the young woman a look of disgust. "It isn't China that interests you, and you know it."

The young woman Li Chang's grandson had addressed as Leilani swung toward him with a fiercely hostile look on her pretty young face.

"What do you know about what interests me, Jimmy Li?" she demanded.

"I've known you since grade school, remember?" Jimmy Li answered with a snort of disgust, "and the only time you've ever taken an interest in your studies was when the instructor happened to be male, reasonably presentable, and young enough to flirt with."

Asa, suspecting that young Jimmy Li was quite correct about Leilani, hid a smile as he studied his target in a way that wasn't humorous at all.

Jimmy, like many young male Chinese, was of average height but slightly built. And unlike the majority of his classmates, who dressed in a casual Hawaiian fashion, Jimmy was dressed in dark trousers and a white shirt, indicating that he was more serious and traditional than his peers, which was in accordance with the briefing Asa had received on him.

As Leilani engaged in an arguing match with Jimmy, Asa noted the intelligence in the young man's dark eyes, the neat haircut, and the somewhat sulky curve of his lips. And Asa noted something else about young Jimmy Li that made him hide another smile. While he castigated Leilani for being a flirt and a bubblehead, he was by no means disinterested in her as a female. Asa wondered if he'd been the attraction that had brought Jimmy to the podium after all. It was possible the young would-be swain had merely been jealous of Leilani's attempt to make a conquest other than himself.

"Ah, excuse me," Asa broke into the heated argument, using a mild tone that got their attention. "How would the two of you like to continue your argument over a cup of coffee or a Coke? I'm buying."

Jimmy Li immediately curled his lip. "I have to be in class," he said with a great deal of haughty dignity, "but I'll bet Leilani will be *glad* to take you up on your offer."

Inwardly, Asa sighed. His ruse had backfired on him. He had only included Leilani in the invitation to entice Jimmy to accept. Instead, Jimmy, after giving Leilani a look of fiery indignation, spun on his heel and walked away, leaving Asa stuck with Leilani, who was glaring at Jimmy's retreating back.

Asa was hoping Leilani would refuse his invitation, but she suddenly seemed to remember him, and turning back, she gave him a brilliant smile, though he thought he detected a hint of bruised pride—as well as something more sincere—in her large dark eyes.

"I'd love to have coffee with you, Mr. Bradley," she said sweetly. "Shall we go?"

As they walked to a nearby cafeteria, Asa let Leilani's chatter wash over him without replying other than giving an acknowledging grunt from time to time. He was thinking that all was not lost if he could get her to talk to him about Jimmy. Since they'd known one another for a long time, she might be able to give him a clue as to what would be the best way to approach his young target.

When they were settled at a table, Asa with a cup of coffee,

Leilani with a cup of pineapple juice, Asa set himself to the task of charming her to a point where she would trust him.

"Who was your friend back there?" he asked mildly.

Leilani immediately began to pout, which Asa thought absently was probably just one of many weapons she carried in her arsenal of female lures. Her lips were full and sensuous anyway and pouting only made them more so, which Asa figured Leilani was very well aware of.

"Oh, that's just Jimmy Li," she said with disgusted dismissal. "He's a real brain and a real jerk. He can't understand anybody wanting to have a good time now and then. All he cares about is his studies."

Asa decided to flatter her with the truth. "Oh, I wouldn't say that," he disagreed mildly, giving Leilani an admiring smile.

She preened a little as a result of his smile, but there was a puzzled look in her eyes as well.

"What do you mean?" she asked, gazing at him soulfully.

Asa shrugged. "Well, I got the impression that Jimmy . . . Li, is it?" And when Leilani nodded, her curiosity evident in her eyes, Asa said innocently, "I got the impression he liked you—maybe that he was a little jealous even."

Leilani flushed and for the first time, her expression became natural instead of put on to seduce Asa with her charms.

"Ha!" she said spontaneously. "Jimmy Li doesn't like anybody, much less me, and he's certainly not jealous!"

Asa raised a skeptical eyebrow and shook his head. "I admit that on the surface, he seemed hostile," he agreed lightly. "But I'm a man myself, Leilani . . . may I call you Leilani?" he interrupted himself to ask, again smiling at the young woman with as much charm as he dared to use.

"Of course." She perked up immediately, but before she could start to flirt again, Asa went on.

"Well, as a man, Leilani, I saw something in Jimmy's attitude that certainly resembled jealousy to me."

Leilani frowned now, and Asa saw the sudden ray of hope in her eyes quickly fade to disappointment.

"You must be wrong," she said quietly, and Asa found himself liking her all at once.

"Why must I be wrong?" he asked in a gentle way.

Leilani shrugged, an unhappy expression in her eyes now. "Well, I admit that Jimmy and I dated for a while our senior year of high school," she said reluctantly, "but he kept trying to change me into somebody I'm not, and we finally broke up."

Asa nodded understandingly. "Yes," he said quietly, "it's hard when someone doesn't seem to like you for yourself. What did he want to change about you?" he then asked, though he was sure he knew the answer to his question already, and Leilani's betraying blush made him even surer.

"He said I was a flirt," she admitted, looking over Asa's shoulder rather than at his face. She shrugged. "And he'd get angry with me because I'd want to go to a movie or a dance instead of studying for a test we had coming up—stuff like that," she added, sounding somewhat miserable to Asa's ears. "We fought about the same things we fought about today."

Asa nodded, his gaze thoughtful. "In other words, he takes life too seriously," he suggested with quiet sympathy. But when Leilani nodded vigorously, obviously delighted to find a sympathizer, he added, "And you don't take it seriously enough."

Leilani stopped nodding abruptly, and now the pout was back.

Asa ignored the pout. "It seems to me if he could lighten up a little, and you could be a little more serious, then you two would have something going for you."

Leilani scowled. "He's not likely to lighten up," she predicted, but Asa noted that she didn't protest that they wouldn't have anything going for them, which convinced him Leilani still cared for Jimmy.

"He might," he said with lazy disinterest.

"How?" Leilani immediately pounced on Asa's words, which made him want to laugh. Of course, he didn't.

"In a case like this," Asa said musingly, "someone has to make the first move." He could see that Leilani resented the idea of having to make the first move, but he continued. "I have an idea that if you were to act a little more serious, Jimmy would respond by acting a little more like the young man he is rather than the aged scholar he seems to want to be."

Leilani giggled at that, and Asa smiled back at her. Then the giggles died away, and she looked annoyed.

"I don't see why I should have to make the first move, as you call it," she said resentfully.

Asa shrugged. "It's just the way men are," he said, as though it were a fact that couldn't be disputed. "They're not as sweet and generous and forgiving as women," he added somewhat gravely, inwardly wincing at laying things on a little thick.

Leilani preened again, obviously enjoying the idea that she was sweet and generous and forgiving.

"Well," she said with a certain virtuousness that amused Asa enormously, "I suppose I could give it a try . . . if I decide I want to get Jimmy back, that is, which I'm not at all sure that I do."

Uh-huh, Asa answered with silent skepticism, while he merely smiled encouragingly at Leilani.

She suddenly got a look of dismay on her face, which grew as she brought her wrist up to inspect the face of her watch.

"Oh, no!" she exclaimed as she started gathering her books up in her arms. "I'm late for my accounting class, and that old witch would just love to flunk me if she gets the chance!"

As she got to her feet, her books twisted every which way in her arms, she barely paused to deliver a farewell to Asa.

"Thanks, Mr. Bradley," she said hurriedly as she started backing away from the table. "I'll be at your lecture on Wednesday, okay?"

"Great," he said amiably, giving her another smile. "And it would be even better if you brought Jimmy with you."

Leilani smiled a little uncertainly, wiggled her fingers at him, then took off in a graceful run toward the business section of the university.

Asa sat on, finishing his coffee while he hoped that Leilani would be his ticket to getting close to Jimmy Li . . . if she didn't make him so jealous he refused the bait.

Later, walking back to his apartment, Asa's thoughts veered from Leilani and Jimmy to Carrie Winters. He was feeling the dread that came upon him every time he returned to his empty-feeling temporary home now and realized Carrie wasn't there to welcome him.

This too shall pass, he reminded himself. But all the same, he stayed in his apartment only long enough to take a shower and

172

change clothes before he left it again and drove to Chinatown to dine at one of the Chinese restaurants he favored and exchange a little harmless gossip with the proprietor who was delighted by the novelty of finding a haole who spoke flawless Chinese.

"Honey, you barely touched your roast beef," Martha Goggins said gently to Carolyn, who immediately got a guilty look in her large blue eyes that made Martha ache for her young friend.

Carolyn and Martha had gotten together several times since Carolyn's return to Kansas City, and Martha, who had thought it natural that Carolyn should seem so depressed at first over losing her nice Asa Bradley, was growing increasingly alarmed now that she thought enough time had passed for Carolyn to be getting over her unhappy love affair.

"Carrie," she said gently, "let's leave these dishes, take our coffee, and go into the living room. I think it's time we had a heart-to-heart talk."

Carolyn looked dully at her friend before agreeing. Part of her wanted to confide in Martha, but another part of her kept thinking, "What's the use?"

At last, however, she nodded and got to her feet, bringing the cup of coffee she didn't want with her. When they were settled on Martha's comfortable sofa, Martha looked gravely at Carolyn.

"How's college going?" she asked, having decided to approach Carolyn's real problem in an oblique manner.

Carolyn sighed and lifted her shoulders in a fatalistic shrug. "It's okay, I guess," she answered. "I just can't seem to get very interested in composing sterile little essays for my English class, or cutting up harmless little frogs in Biology, or . . . Well, you get the picture," she finished in a lifeless voice that made Martha want to shake her.

"I certainly do," Martha responded dryly. "And I suppose your social life still consists of playing tennis with one of your married girlfriends or going to a movie with one of your divorced ones?"

Carolyn frowned at Martha, disliking the faint hint of accusation she thought she heard in her friend's voice.

"I haven't met any men I care to date if that's what you mean," she said, sounding a little defensive even to her own ears.

"Of course you haven't," Martha responded in a light way that didn't ease Carolyn's suspicion that she was about to receive a lecture. "I suspect that Robert Redford couldn't drag you out of your self-pity long enough to make an impression," she added, confirming Carolyn's suspicion.

"That's an exaggeration," she bristled, more out of a natural desire to defend herself than because Martha was wrong.

"Is it?" Martha said, again in that dry way that made Carolyn feel guilty.

"Martha, please—" She started to demand they drop the subject, but Martha wasn't in a tactful mood for the present.

"No," Martha shook her head as she leaned forward and put her empty cup on the coffee table. "I've sat and watched you droop around, and I've kept my mouth shut because I knew you wanted me to, but it's about time I stopped helping you stay mired in your swamp of depression."

Carolyn scowled at Martha, who ignored her displeasure and simply studied her for a long moment, during which Carolyn became increasingly uncomfortable.

"Carrie, if you could have anything you wanted besides Asa Bradley, what would it be?" Martha asked at last, her tone thoughtful.

The question stumped Carolyn for a while. Then she shrugged. "Having Julie home again, I guess," she said dispiritedly.

"Besides that, too," Martha responded, making no secret of how impatient she was growing with Carolyn.

Carolyn sighed and thought again. "I guess . . ." she finally said in a slow, thoughtful way, "I would like to have a husband and children and a home . . . in Hawaii." She said the last two words with the surprise she was feeling. They had just slipped out without her knowing they were going to.

Martha brightened a little. "So you were really taken with Hawaii?" she asked, ignoring the reference to the husband and children, since she considered Carolyn wasn't likely to find the right man until she'd gotten over Asa Bradley.

"Yes, but that's impossible, of course," Carolyn said, again sounding depressed in a way that made Martha want to scream.

She didn't. She merely said, "And why is it impossible, may I ask?" in a rather tart manner that surprised Carolyn.

"Well, because . . . because Kansas City is my home . . . and Julie's," she added more firmly, aware that her first argument didn't carry much weight with Martha judging by the impatient look on her matronly face.

"Julie's in England," Martha pointed out crisply, "and she'll be there for another few years."

"Well, then," Carolyn spoke up, almost glaring at Martha, "I couldn't possibly move to Hawaii while Asa's there!"

"Why not?" Martha said, her very tone making it clear she found Carolyn's arguments specious.

"He'd think I came back to try to . . . well, to try to . . ."

"Catch him?" Martha interjected.

Carolyn didn't answer, but her silence spoke for itself.

Martha shook her head and sighed. Then she held up her fingers and began to enumerate the reasons why Carolyn's thinking was off base.

"Number one," she said with exaggerated patience, "Asa Bradley doesn't even have to know you're there."

"He'd know," Carolyn broke in, the look in her eyes coming close to breaking Martha's soft heart. "He lectures at the university there, and if I did move to Hawaii, I'd go to college there because I promised Julie I'd get my degree . . . and because I wouldn't have anything better to do," she finished rather lamely.

Martha glanced at the ceiling as though gathering strength. "And if he does know?" she asked in an exasperated fashion. "So what? He doesn't own the place, does he? And he can think what he likes as long as you don't make it obvious that's what you're doing there."

Carolyn looked at Martha, a frown in her eyes.

"The trick to the whole thing," Martha went on, "is not to go there with the idea of starting up with him again. If you do that, you're digging your own grave. The man has made it clear he doesn't want to marry you," she said with deliberate cruelty, though her nerve almost faltered when a stricken look came into Carolyn's eyes.

"Well, hasn't he?" Martha demanded, feeling like a monster when the stricken look began to dissolve into tears.

"Ye-ye-yes." Carolyn gulped over the sob rising in her throat.

"Honey, don't cry just yet," Martha said with firm gentleness it cost her a lot to call up. "You can cry later after we've finished talking."

Carolyn looked at Martha in astonishment, her mouth open, her eyes brimming with tears. Then, instead of continuing to cry, she began to chuckle. Martha smiled back at her, and finally the two of them were laughing until the tears Carolyn wiped from her eyes were of mirth, not unhappiness.

"Oh, Martha," Carolyn choked out over her chuckles. "That's the first time I've laughed in a month. It feels marvelous."

"Of course it does," Martha said with mock sternness. "Now let's get back to deciding how we can keep you laughing. You don't want to be like Celie, do you?" she added, adopting a little crafty psychology.

Martha was rewarded when Carolyn's expression became horrified.

"I didn't think so"—Martha nodded firmly—"and I hate to say it to anyone, much less someone I like as much as I do you, Carrie, but you've been skirting the edges of Celiedom lately, and it's time you stopped."

"God, yes!" Carolyn agreed with a shudder. "How is Celie, anyway?" she asked, her expression showing the distaste she felt for Martha's cousin.

"As self-involved, self-pitying, and hard to take as ever," Martha said promptly, eager to use this new lever she'd found to get Carolyn out of her depression.

"Like me," Carolyn said grimly, accepting the comparison without liking it one little bit.

"Well . . ." Martha hesitated, but she saw she didn't have to rub it in anymore. Carolyn already looked at least fifty percent better than she had when she'd arrived for dinner that evening.

"All right, Martha," Carolyn said quietly. "I get your point.

176

But I'm not sure moving to Hawaii would do any good other than rub salt in my wounds."

"Salt is a good healer," Martha said, more gently this time.

Carolyn smiled faintly, wishing she could be as brave and resourceful at overcoming life's disappointments as Martha was.

"There's Julie to think about." Her thoughts shifted direction. "Our house is half hers, and she's entitled to a say in what I do with it."

"You don't have to sell it," Martha shrugged, then frowned, "that is, unless you can't afford not to?"

Carolyn shook her head. "I have enough money to live where I like, and I suppose instead of selling my house here, which might not be wise anyway should I find Hawaii less appealing than it seems and want to come back, I could rent it out. That way, it would always be here for Julie, too, should she want to settle in Kansas City when she finishes school."

Martha was delighted that Carolyn had reached the point of mulling over details instead of refusing to consider a change at all.

"Wonderful!" she exclaimed heartily. "That sounds like the sensible thing to do. Leave your options open, so to speak."

Carolyn eyed Martha with growing suspicion. "If I were inclined to be paranoid," she said with mock belligerence, "I would suspect that you've been staying up nights trying to think of some way to get me thinking about all this."

Martha adopted a look of affronted innocence. "Who, me?" she huffed. "Why, I sleep like a baby. Besides," she added with feigned virtuousness, "what would be so wrong about trying to think of some way to erase that pitiful look you wear pasted on your face these days? It would be an act of public service to—"

"All right, all right!" Carolyn laughed, feeling chagrined at learning how Martha had perceived her since her return from Hawaii. "So I've been a pain in the—"

"Heart!" Martha quickly intervened with a smile. "I've hated seeing you suffer, honey. I really have. Especially when there's no need for it if you can just look at things the right way."

"The right way?" Carolyn grimaced.

Martha nodded. "If you could be objective," she said quite

seriously, "you'd realize that, as much love as you feel for Asa Bradley, it doesn't mean the world has come to an end because you can't have him. Pity him if you must for what he's missing, but don't pine for him. There are too few days in our lives to waste them wanting things we can't have."

Carolyn glanced sharply at Martha as she heard the slightly wistful note that came into her friend's voice during the last sentence she spoke.

"You're right, Martha," she said soberly, thinking that if anyone had cause to pine for things she couldn't have, it would be her wonderful friend. And there was no one else who could provide a better example of how not to waste the days than this lovely woman.

"Martha, I'll try," she added, her expression distant as she began to focus on the future for the first time since saying goodbye to Asa with some hope instead of dread and depression. "I really will try," she added quietly, almost to herself.

"I know you will, Carrie," Martha said, her gaze proud and warmly accepting. "You just needed some time to grieve. But the grieving has to end sometime. Life is supposed to be lived. You're too young and beautiful and vital, with too much to give, to spend your time vegetating. Don't you agree?"

Carolyn suddenly grinned. "If I did, I'd be immodest, wouldn't I?"

"Nonsense!" Martha objected stoutly. "You look in the mirror every day, don't you? Why indulge in false modesty? You *are* beautiful, you *are* vital, and you're going to make some man a wonderful wife and some children a perfect mother one of these days. Now don't argue with me!" She held up a hand when Carolyn opened her mouth to say something.

"I wasn't going to argue with you," Carolyn said with exaggerated meekness. "I was merely going to point out that if I *don't* make some man a wonderful wife and some children a perfect mother, I can always take the advice of a certain elusive fellow who's already escaped my clutches and make a fantastic social worker."

Martha grinned and soon the two of them were giggling like two schoolgirls.

They discussed the idea of Carolyn's moving to Hawaii for a

little longer, and then, as Carolyn was about to leave, she couldn't resist putting her arms around Martha for a fervent hug.

"You're the best substitute mother I ever had," she told Martha in a solemn voice, but with a twinkle of loving humor in her eyes.

"It seems to me I'm the *only* substitute mother you ever had," Martha responded with cheerful tartness, but there was a pleased look in her faded blue eyes that made Carolyn glad she'd been able to give such a compliment with complete sincerity.

"Let me know what you decide," Martha said as Carolyn donned her light jacket and stepped outside into the mild chill of the September night.

"I will." Carolyn smiled. "After all, if I take your advice I'm going to have to give you *some* reason for refusing any future dinner invitations you care to extend."

Martha sobered a little at that before she began to smile again. "Well, I can't deny I'll miss you," she said with simple directness. "But if you get settled over there in paradise, maybe I'll save up my pennies and pay Hawaii another visit one of these days."

"I wish you would." Carolyn nodded, meaning it. "You'll always be welcome wherever I am, Martha, and that's a fact."

"Bless you, honey, I know it is," Martha said, her voice a little wavery with emotion now as she leaned forward to give Carolyn still another hug. "Now get yourself home safely and finish up your homework. If I'm going to have a substitute daughter, I guess I'm entitled to do a little scolding now and then, aren't I?"

Carolyn laughed and nodded, and with a little wave of her hand, she walked away to find her car and go home to the homework Martha had reminded her was waiting.

Later that night, as she lay in her bed and thought things over, however, she realized with a little pang of anxiety that her mind was more than halfway made up to make some drastic changes in her life. She would think things over carefully, of course, before making a final decision, and she would have to talk it over with Julie, but Carolyn was well aware that in her mind she was already on her way to Hawaii and a new life. All that really remained to be settled was the little matter of the part Asa Bradley would play in that new life. She couldn't afford to resettle herself hoping to resume a relationship with a man who'd made it clear he wasn't available. And she couldn't wallow any longer in the hopeless inertia she'd been experiencing since saying good-bye to Asa. As Martha had pointed out, that was no way to live a life.

CHAPTER FIFTEEN

"Got any progress to report?"

Asa and the man the Company had assigned as his contact strolled along a deserted beach in the early hours of a Monday morning, looking out to sea at the pinkening horizon.

They had chosen this hour and this particular beach as a meeting place because it was usually empty.

"Not so far." Asa answered the question his companion had posed. "He didn't show up until the end of my first lecture, and though he came to the podium afterward, I think it was because a girl he used to date was making a play for me, rather than because he wanted to talk to me about anything."

As his companion gave him an inquiring look, Asa understood what was on his mind and nodded.

"Yes, I'm keeping in contact with the girl, encouraging her to get back together with young Li in the hope that she'll bring him to me. But so far he isn't biting."

"Has he been to any more of your lectures?"

"He's been coming"—Asa shrugged—"but he sits in the back and disappears as soon as they're over. That doesn't give me a chance to get to him afterward because there are always a few students who want to talk to me about China after the lecture and I have to stay in character."

"So you think your best bet is still the girl?"

"It looks like it," Asa said, sounding weary even to his own ears. He was tired of the assignment that was keeping him in Hawaii, especially since he didn't seem to be making any progress. He wanted to get away from this place that reminded him of Carrie at every turn and get to Langley, where he would eventually be assigned. He didn't expect to be overjoyed by the type of work he would be doing at Headquarters either, but it was past time for him to get started on making the adjustment from field man to desk jockey.

He became aware that his companion was looking at him in a sharp manner and he wasn't surprised by the next question.

"How's the leg? I notice you've still got a hell of a limp. Is it giving you a lot of pain?"

Asa clenched his jaw in frustration. He'd been doing his best to walk as normally as possible, but the leg was still giving him trouble, and obviously it showed. And what the hell was he trying to hide it for anyway? he thought bitterly. The doctors would always have the final say-so about his fitness to return to his field position, and he couldn't fool them.

"Yeah," he admitted grimly. "It still hurts."

His companion shrugged. "Tough luck," he said in a somewhat awkward manner, but Asa understood that the man really did sympathize, and probably was damned grateful at the same time that it hadn't happened to him.

Then it was back to business.

"How many more lectures have you got to go?"

"Only two," Asa answered. "And that's stretching it. I'm already repeating myself once in a while, so there's no question of trying to drag things along for another lecture or two. If Jimmy doesn't bite by the time I'm done, I can't see any choice other than to make a direct approach to him."

"If it comes to that, we'll let the FBI do it," the contact grunted. "We'll let them think we just got onto it ourselves and are turning it over to them just like the book says we're supposed to. That way, they'll have to return the courtesy and keep us advised of any progress they make instead of holding everything close to the vest like they normally do."

"Like *they* normally do?" Asa mocked in a dry manner.

For answer, his contact merely shrugged. "I doubt if they'll get anything from the kid anyway," he went on. "Family loyalty comes first with those people. So we'll keep our eyes open around Chinatown the way we've been doing, not that we're likely to find an old fox like Li Chang that way, either."

"And if we do find him, he's not likely to tell us anything of value anyway," Asa pointed out. "If he'd intended to talk to us, he would have gotten in touch with us already."

"Maybe he just needs some incentive," the contact said, his voice hard.

"You mean deportation?" Asa shook his head. "That won't scare him."

"No, but maybe a threat to his family's welfare will."

Asa took a deep breath, then turned a harsh gaze on his companion. "They're citizens," he said in a dangerously quiet voice.

The contact held up his hand, a grimace on his face. "I know, I know," he said with a shrug. "I'm not saying we'd actually do anything to his family. But the old man won't know that, will he?"

The idea still left a bad taste in Asa's mouth. Coming from the sort of environment Li Chang had, Asa didn't doubt that that sort of threat would be effective. The old man would probably find it a natural way to behave. But it might alienate Jimmy Li and the rest of the family, and Asa had an idea Jimmy might be a good recruit for the Agency. He didn't intend to propose such an idea, however, until he got to know Jimmy better . . . if he ever did.

"Well, keep trying," the contact said, pausing as they came to the path leading up to where they'd parked. "It will be a real feather in your cap if you can find that old man and get him to talk, you know."

Asa wasn't much interested in collecting feathers for his cap and never had been. Agency politics left him cold. All he'd ever wanted, and all he still wanted, was to do as good a job as he could of protecting his country by gaining information the U.S. needed to have.

The contact seemed to realize such tactics weren't effective with Asa, and he shrugged. "Let me know immediately if anything happens," he said briskly without offering to shake hands. And he strode off up the path toward his car.

Asa lingered for a while, pacing to the shoreline to watch the sun pop up over the horizon. The colors were spectacular and he found himself thinking about bringing Carrie here sometime to share the view with him. Then he realized what he was doing and his mouth twisted into a self-mocking grimace.

Suddenly, loneliness overwhelmed him, astonishing him in the process.

You should never have gotten involved with her, he castigated himself. *Look what it's doing to you. Why the hell couldn't you have left her alone!*

But there was no satisfying answer to that question and Asa's enjoyment in the morning was gone, so he slowly made his way back to his car, trying to concentrate on the notes he needed to make for his next lecture.

As he drove back to his apartment, he silently, in a grimly impatient way, addressed the young man he was stalking.

Jimmy, get off your high horse and come talk to me. You know damned well you want to, and I'm a hell of a lot easier to talk to than the FBI, if only because I speak your language and understand your culture.

Carolyn listened to the phone ringing across the Atlantic and tried to relax. Surely Julie would be pleased for her, she thought nervously, so why the anxiety? Before she could think more about why she was reluctant to tell Julie about her plans, however, the receiver was being lifted on the other end and a youthful female British voice was saying, "Hello?"

"I'd like to speak to Julie Winters, please," Carolyn answered. "I'm calling from the United States. Is she in?"

"Just a sec," the young woman on the other end of the line responded cheerfully, and within a few minutes, Julie was on.

"Hello? Carolyn?" she said, sounding anxious.

"Yes, darling, it's me," Carolyn said in a light, affectionate tone. "How are you?"

"I'm fine!" Julie said with a touch of exasperation. "How are you? Why are you calling? Is anything wrong?"

Carolyn made a face at the phone good-naturedly. "No, nothing's wrong, honey," she said soothingly. "I just wanted to talk to you about something."

"Oh," Julie relaxed. "That's good. Say, listen, Carrie, I'm sorry about not writing more, but you wouldn't believe how busy I've been. The courses here are really tough, and I spend a lot of hours studying, and when I do have a little time off, there's so much to see—"

"Julie," Carolyn interrupted humorously, "I didn't call to bawl you out for not writing." Indeed, Carolyn had resigned herself to the fact that Julie wasn't much of a correspondent before she'd ever left home.

"Oh . . . okay . . . that's great," Julie said, but she still sounded wary. "Did you call about my allowance, then?" she asked, and without giving Carolyn a chance to respond, she quickly began one of the rapidly paced explanations Carolyn had gotten used to over the years.

"See, I had to buy a good raincoat and a decent umbrella because it rains a lot here, and then there were some expenses I didn't count on furnishing the flat—"

"The flat?" Carolyn interrupted. "What flat?"

"Oh, I guess I didn't tell you about that yet," Julie said innocently. "You just wouldn't believe how dreary this dormitory is, Carrie, and if you could see it, I know you would hate the thought of me having to stay here, so a couple of friends and I are going in together to rent a place of our own. It's the cutest place you ever saw, and we've about got it furnished. We'll be moving in over the weekend as a matter of fact, and I'm glad you called because I haven't had a chance to write you about it yet, so you wouldn't have found me here if you'd called next week instead of now and—"

"Julie . . . Julie . . . *Julie!*" Carolyn rushed to stem the flow of words. "Who are these friends you're moving in with and where is this flat?"

"Oh, you'd love Sally and Helen, Carrie," Julie said blythely, "and the flat is in a sort of rundown neighborhood because we couldn't afford anything in a nice one, but it's a *decent* neighborhood even if it is a little rundown, Carrie, and you'd love the place if you could see it."

I doubt it, Carolyn thought dryly, while aloud she merely said, "You *will* be careful, won't you, Julie? You know how I worry."

"Oh, sure," Julie responded with easy assurance. "You know me."

That's why I'm worried, Carolyn thought exasperatedly, but she managed somehow to keep from loading Julie down with her worries and a lot of advice her young sister probably wouldn't take anyway.

"So you didn't call because I'm overdrawn on my allowance?" Julie now asked, her tone curious.

"No," Carolyn sighed. "I didn't know you were overdrawn. The bank statement hasn't come yet."

"Oh," Julie said, and Carolyn knew she was feeling disgruntled because she'd made an unnecessary confession. Julie's philosophy encompassed putting off telling bad news until you couldn't get out of it.

"Actually, Julie," Carolyn said, trying to sound nonchalant, "I called because I have some news about a move of my own."

"A move?" Julie said, obviously not comprehending at first. Then she fairly exploded over the phone. "What?" she demanded. *"What* move?"

"That's what I'm trying to tell you, honey," Carolyn said gently. "Remember the postcard I sent you from Hawaii?"

"Remember it?" Julie said somewhat indignantly. "I couldn't believe it. You've never gone off like that in your life, Carrie. I was astonished!"

"Well," Carolyn explained, "the house was so lonely without you, I just decided to get away for a while. After all, there wasn't anything to keep me here. The fall semester didn't start for a couple of weeks . . ."

The silence on the other end of the line told Carolyn that Julie was feeling guilty and resenting it, and Carolyn quickly hurried on to dispel any ideas Julie might be getting that she was being emotionally blackmailed.

"Anyway, Julie, I loved it in Hawaii," she went on, hoping she didn't sound as wistful as she felt about just how much she had loved it and why, "and I've about decided I'd like to live there."

"Live there?" Julie responded blankly. "In Hawaii?"

"Yes, honey," Carolyn said brightly. "Wouldn't you love coming home for vacation to a beautiful tropical island instead of Kansas City?"

"You must be kidding," Julie responded, sounding shaken.

"No . . ." Carolyn said calmly, "I'm not kidding, Julie. I'm perfectly serious."

"But—but—Kansas City is *home*," Julie said, sounding as though she were extremely puzzled that Carolyn didn't know that.

"Well, yes, it has been home, Julie," Carolyn responded, her heart beginning to sink a little at Julie's attitude. "And I don't intend to sell the house, since it's half yours and you might want to live in it someday. I'm just going to rent it out."

"Rent it out?" Julie exclaimed. "To *strangers?*"

Carolyn raised her eyes to the ceiling, feeling a little helpless at the way this conversation was going. "Yes, I imagine it will be to strangers, Julie," she said, holding on to her patience. "After all, we don't know anyone personally who would want to rent it. Our friends all own their own houses."

"Of course they do!" Julie responded, her voice wobbling a little now, demonstrating to Carolyn how upset she really was. Carolyn just didn't know why her little sister was reacting so negatively to her plan.

"Julie, listen," Carolyn said soothingly, "I need a change in my life right now. You can understand that, can't you?"

"But you're going to college!" Julie said, as though that were enough of a change for anybody.

Carolyn sighed. "Yes," she agreed, "I'm going to college. But they have a university in Hawaii, too, Julie, and I plan to enroll in it. And this may only be a temporary move, Julie," she added, hoping that would ease whatever insecurities Julie might be feeling about the situation. "If, after a while, I want to move back to Kansas City, there's no reason why I can't. This is just an . . . well, an experiment, sort of. It may work out and it may not. I'll just have to see."

"And meanwhile," Julie said somewhat bitterly, "I won't have a home!"

Carolyn blinked, finally understanding why Julie was so upset.

"You can't just pick up and leave like that, Carrie," Julie said tearfully. "I count on you being there. I'd feel like an *orphan* if you weren't where you're supposed to be!"

Carolyn felt a surge of conflicting emotions. She had always been there for Julie, and she could understand that Julie might be feeling abandoned without the security of having Carolyn waiting where she'd always been—a haven to come home to. But for the first time in all the years she'd taken care of Julie, Carolyn also felt a tiny prickling of resentment that her sister, who had done what she wanted to in going off to England without displaying a qualm about her decision, apparently expected Carolyn to order her own life around what Julie wanted as well.

"Carrie, you've always been there for me," Julie now said in a pitiful tone that Carolyn viewed with a certain amount of suspicion. Julie was not above using any means available to manipulate events to her own satisfaction. "How can you think of just going off like this and leaving me to fend for myself?"

"Julie, you won't be fending for yourself any more than you're doing right now in England," Carolyn pointed out reasonably. "I'm not planning to disappear off the face of the earth, after all. Hawaii is a state, for heaven's sake, and I'll make a home for us there that you can come to."

"It won't be the same," Julie responded sulkily. "I won't know anybody there except you."

"Did you know anyone in England when you arrived?" Carolyn asked, her patience beginning to wear thin.

"It's not the same," Julie said, a stubborn note in her voice that Carolyn recognized with a somewhat despairing sense of déjà vu. Julie could be like an immovable rock when she was in this mood. "I didn't expect to know anybody here," Julie continued, "but home is different. Home is . . . well, just *home* . . . where I know people and where things are and can look forward to being where I belong again."

With one part of her mind, Carolyn sympathized with Julie. But with another part, she felt an unaccustomed stubbornness of her own beginning to assert itself.

"Well, if I'm still in Hawaii next summer, I don't see why you can't come back here and stay with one of your friends if you'd rather do that than come to Hawaii," she said quietly.

There was a short silence on the other end of the line before Julie admitted, grudgingly, "Well, actually, some of my friends here want me to go on a tour of Europe with them for part of the summer."

Carolyn had suspected that might be the case, and her impatience with Julie rose another notch.

"How much of the summer did you plan to spend in Kansas City?" she asked dryly.

Again there was a short silence on the other end of the line. "What does it matter?" Julie then burst out defensively. "That isn't the point. The point is, I count on you being where you're supposed to be!"

"For how long, Julie?" Carolyn said, a tinge of indignation leaking into her voice. "What if I get a proposal someday, and the man lives somewhere other than Kansas City? Am I supposed to turn him down because my little sister expects me to stay where I *belong?*"

"That's not fair," Julie said, sounding tearful again.

"Not fair to whom, Julie?" Carolyn asked, forcing herself to keep her voice quietly reasonable. "Oh, honey," she then sighed as her shoulders slumped, "I know how you feel. We all want a secure nest somewhere we can come back to if we need to. But I can be your security in Hawaii as well as in Kansas City, Julie. I realize it will take some adjustment for both of us, and I may end up back here eventually anyway. But don't you think I deserve at least a chance to spread my wings a little, honey? I've never . . ."

But there Carolyn stopped, afraid she would make Julie feel guilty about the years Carolyn had put her first.

"Did you meet someone in Hawaii, Carrie?" Julie asked, her tone almost accusing. "Is that what this is all about?"

Carolyn hesitated. Julie's words had sent a sharp pang of loss through her . . . too sharp to make the prospect of arguing about Asa with Julie acceptable for the time being.

"If I had, would that be a crime, Julie?" she answered indirectly. "You sound as if you think it would be, which is hard for me to understand when you said you wanted me to find someone."

Julie was silent, and Carolyn smiled a humorless little smile. Julie wasn't used to being put in a bind like that, she knew.

"This just isn't like you at all, Carrie," Julie said sadly. "You only do things for other people, not for yourself. That's why I thought a man might be involved. I've always thought that if

189

you ever did fall in love, you'd sacrifice yourself for your husband just the way you did for me. People get used to taking what's offered, Carrie," she said dully, "and though it may not be fair, it's hard to keep from resenting someone like you who suddenly does an about-face and starts thinking of themselves for a change."

Carolyn went very still, disliking the picture of herself Julie had just drawn for her.

"You mean," she said slowly, "when a doormat stands up and refuses to be walked on anymore, the people who've been accustomed to using it resent the loss, even though they might not have respected the doormat in the first place?"

"Oh, Carrie!" Julie exclaimed, and Carolyn could hear both guilt and reproach in her voice. "It isn't that I didn't respect you. I did—and I do! It's just that I got used to you being one way, and it's hard for me to relate to the way you're acting now."

"I see," Carolyn said, her voice quiet and abstracted.

"Carrie, I didn't mean to hurt your feelings," Julie said anxiously.

"No, I'm sure you didn't," Carolyn agreed, sounding remote even to her own ears. She wanted to come out of the introspective mood Julie had precipitated, but she couldn't seem to for the present.

"Carrie, you can see what I mean, can't you?" Julie pleaded. "The way I'm feeling is natural, isn't it?"

"I suppose it is," Carolyn responded, a note of surprise in her voice. "I guess you're simply behaving the way I brought you up: expecting me to put you first the way I always have."

Carolyn could almost feel Julie wincing on the other end of the line.

"I'm not trying to make you feel guilty, Julie," she said calmly. "I'm trying to understand what's happening here. And when I do, I'll make my final decision about moving to Hawaii."

"You mean you haven't decided for sure?" Julie asked, a small note of hope in her voice she couldn't hide.

"Not for sure." Carolyn nodded, though Julie couldn't see her. "But, Julie . . ." she said very quietly.

"Yes?" Julie sounded subdued.

"If I do decide to move to Hawaii, I don't want to be accused of selfishness, do you understand? Even if you think I am being selfish, I'd like you to give me the right to be that way this once."

There was a small silence, then Julie responded as quietly as Carolyn had spoken. "I'll try, Carrie. I'll really try."

Carolyn smiled faintly. "I guess that's as much as I can ask considering I'm responsible for your upbringing," she said, a shrug in her voice. "Now, Julie, I'd better hang up, or I'll soon be going over *my* allowance. What kind of an example would that be for you, right?"

Julie gave a rather feeble chuckle.

"Take care of yourself, honey," Carolyn said, putting her normal warm affection into her voice for Julie's sake. "And write when you can."

"Yeah . . . sure . . . I'll do that," Julie answered, sounding forlorn to Carolyn's discerning ear.

For a moment, that forlorn note in Julie's voice triggered instincts in Carolyn that had been fostered over years of playing the role of Julie's parent. She wanted to keep any disappointments, any hurts, away from her baby sister by giving in to whatever would make Julie happy.

The moment passed when the thought occurred to Carolyn that there wasn't any way on earth to give anyone, no matter how dearly loved, everything they wanted in life, while the constant habit of sacrifice was not necessarily the best way to love. As Julie had explained, the recipient got in the habit of taking, and sometimes, as was happening to Carolyn now, the giver began to experience a certain resentment over not getting anything back—not even a modicum of understanding.

"Good-bye, honey," Carolyn said softly.

" 'Bye, Carrie," Julie said with unaccustomed soberness, and the connection was broken when she hung up the phone.

Carolyn sat where she was for a long time, thinking over the conversation she'd had with Julie, and the discoveries she'd made about herself as a result of it. It wasn't the first time the shortcomings in her own character had been pointed out to her. The elderly aunt who had taken care of Julie when Carolyn had still been at school had accused her more than once of spoiling Julie.

"You'll live to regret it," she'd predicted in that tart voice that had always grated on Carolyn. "Spare the rod and spoil the child is the way of it, Carrie Winters, and you'll find that out one of these days."

Since Carolyn had always felt a need to make up to Julie for the lack of parents, she had ignored her aunt's advice. And Julie had the sort of innate, sunny, charming nature that made it easy for her to get what she wanted without having to stage stormy rebellions.

Yes, Carolyn admitted to herself, Julie was somewhat spoiled. But she was also basically a decent, admirable human being who didn't have the sort of character problems some young people did. Sparing the rod might have encouraged a certain amount of her cheerful self-centeredness, but Carolyn didn't think she would have gotten a result she could be as proud of had she taken her aunt's advice.

She smiled at the thought of how indignant Julie would have been at receiving a spanking. Her pride would have demanded she be twice as bad the next time if she was going to have to pay for her behavior in such an undignified manner anyway.

The smile faded as Carolyn acknowledged that another sort of child might be different. She didn't know. She had only Julie to go by. And since she wasn't likely to have a child of her own the way things were going, she might never know. The real problem to be considered at the moment was not whether she had made mistakes in raising Julie, but whether she was going to compound those mistakes by giving in to Julie's unfair demand that Carolyn continue the behavior Julie had gotten used to.

"I understand how she feels," Carolyn whispered, looking at the room around her that was as familiar to her as her own face or Julie's. "It took a long time for me to stop resenting Mom and Dad for leaving Julie and me alone like that, even though I knew rationally that they couldn't help it. They didn't commit suicide, after all. They were killed in an accident. But if I move to Hawaii, it won't be by accident, and Julie will feel justified in resenting me for taking away her home."

192

Carolyn closed her eyes and leaned her head back on the sofa, trying to sort out the pros and cons of what she wanted to do, the rights and the wrongs of it.

Finally, her eyes flew open and there was a light of determination in them.

"I'm sorry, Julie," she whispered to the empty room around her. "But it's time I stopped living my life for someone else. Not you—not even Asa Bradley—have the right to determine what I do and what I don't do, where I live or don't, how I feel or don't feel. I'm way past due to grow up and assert my independence. It's my time now, and I'm going to grab it with both hands."

Her decision made, Carolyn reached for the phone to call a realtor friend she knew she could trust to find decent renters for the house. When that call was over, she realized she couldn't bear the thought of continuing at the local university until the semester was over. She would lose this semester's credits, of course, and she wouldn't get a refund, but she didn't care. She'd waited fourteen years to go to college anyway, and another few months were nothing to worry about. Besides, it would take her that much time probably to find a place to live in Hawaii, get settled and get the paperwork taken care of to enable her to attend the University of Hawaii during the spring semester.

Her next call was to Martha. When her friend answered, Carolyn's message was very simple.

"Martha," she said, a certain relish for the future in her voice, "I think I'm over my depression."

"You certainly sound like it," Martha responded cheerfully. "Made your decision, have you?"

"I certainly have." Carolyn chuckled. "Start saving your pennies so you can come visit me in Hawaii, Martha."

"Good for you!" Martha said. "But you aren't going to count on anything happening with Asa again, are you, Carrie? I wouldn't like to see you get in the state you were in when you came home last time."

"No, Martha," Carolyn said calmly. "I'm not going to count on a thing from Asa Bradley, but I don't intend to hide from him either."

"But do you think you can resist temptation if he wants to

. . . well . . ." Martha hesitated, but Carolyn understood her meaning.

"I'm not sure," she said aloud, and silently added, *but I at least know better now than to face his sort of seductive skills unprepared, and if he decides to use them on me again, neither of us will have to worry about my getting pregnant this time.*

"Well, I wish you luck," Martha responded, but there was a certain tinge of worry in her voice that made Carolyn smile a wry acknowledgment.

"Ah . . . now luck is something I can use," she teased lightly, "and if there's any justice at all in life, that's exactly what I'll get."

CHAPTER SIXTEEN

Carolyn was a little amazed at herself the way she took charge and got everything arranged so that she could leave.

The realtor saw no reason why Carolyn had to stick around waiting for a potential renter to show up. Since Carolyn was willing to settle for a six-month rather than a year's lease and was willing to rent the house furnished rather than go to the expense of having things shipped to Hawaii, the realtor was confident she would find someone suitable quickly. Carolyn didn't explain that she was willing to make such concessions as a form of insurance. If the allure of paradise waned fairly quickly, it would make it just that much easier to return to Kansas City.

The realtor also contacted another realtor in Hawaii for her, and when Carolyn found out how much it would cost to rent the small beach house she'd envisioned in her mind, she quickly settled for a decent furnished apartment near the university instead.

A letter came from Julie a few days after their telephone conversation, and Carolyn was amused when she discovered it read something like a subtle bribe that her little sister would be more thoughtful in the future if only Carolyn would stay put instead of traipsing off to Hawaii.

She wrote back immediately, explaining as gently as possible that she wasn't going to be dissuaded from trying life in Hawaii, but that the move was an experiment, not a hard-and-fast commitment. She doubted Julie was in a mood to appreciate the difference, but she resolutely put her sister's objections out of her mind as she continued making arrangements to leave.

Dropping out of the university was no problem. In fact, Carolyn was amused to detect a certain amount of envy on the part of her instructors and those fellow students who came to know about her move, perhaps because winter was coming on earlier than usual in Kansas City.

At last the day before her departure arrived and everything was in order. Julie's car (Carolyn had sold her own), a few pieces of furniture, and some family mementoes that Carolyn didn't want to trust to renters were in storage, along with her winter clothing. She had boxed up and shipped to Hawaii some things she wanted to have with her there, and her bags were packed. There was nothing left to do except kill time.

In the end, she called Martha, who was more than happy to take her on a pilgrimage to say good-bye to some of her favorite places in Kansas City. When Carolyn found herself becoming a little homesick in advance, Martha bolstered her courage.

"It's only an experiment, remember," she reminded Carolyn with firm cheerfulness. "If you don't like it, you can come home anytime you want. A lot of people would envy you that freedom, Carrie. There aren't too many of us who can pick up and move wherever we like without having to consider employment and finances, you know."

Carolyn nodded, suddenly feeling a little guilty at remembering the talk she had had with Asa about her advantages and how she took them for granted. Martha wasn't trying to make her feel guilty, she knew, but the implication was the same. What sense did it make to cry over what she was leaving when she hadn't been happy here lately and had the freedom to come back to it whenever she wished?

"It's nice that you'll have time to get settled before you start school." Martha continued accentuating the positive.

"Yes." Carolyn had to smile. "I have a lot to be grateful for, Martha, and I'm going to try using you as an example and count my blessings instead of behaving like your opposite, Celie."

Martha grinned. "Oh, even Celie has her uses," she said smugly.

"Such as?" Carolyn's tone contained the skepticism she felt.

"Such as providing a negative role model to hold over your head and make you shape up, of course," Martha answered.

Carolyn laughed, and her mood was light for the rest of the evening, only deteriorating when it came time to say good-bye to Martha.

"I'll miss you," she said, swallowing her tears.

"And I'll miss you," Martha nodded, tearing up herself. "But we'll write, and one of these days, I'll be coming to see you . . . that is, if you don't decide to come back before I get enough pennies saved for the trip."

Carolyn wanted to offer to pay for Martha to come see her, but she knew Martha wouldn't stand for it, so she merely hugged her friend, kissed her cheek, then let the tears come without hindrance as she watched her drive away.

Carolyn slept very little that night. Her mind was in turmoil as she pondered the wisdom of what she was doing. Only the realization that she didn't have to live with the decision forever if she didn't want to kept her from jumping up and canceling everything she'd set in motion.

The next morning, as she shut the door of the home that had sheltered her for more than eighteen years and locked it behind her, her face was pale and set, but she didn't falter.

I can come back, she kept telling herself periodically until she was in a plane over the Pacific Ocean. Then it seemed appropriate to let her small talisman against her fear of the unknown go, and start concentrating with some degree of optimism on what the future held for her.

At the end of his next-to-last lecture, Asa looked out over the crowd of students to where Jimmy Li and Leilani sat and was determined to make some progress with the young man today. Time was running out.

He went through the question-and-answer period somewhat mechanically, and was relieved when it was over. He hoped there wouldn't be anyone who wanted to talk to him when the session broke up this time, because he didn't want Jimmy and Leilani to get away before he could invite them to go for coffee with him.

His hopes weren't realized. A number of students came forward to talk to him after his lecture, and by the time he had forced himself to display a patience he didn't feel for half an hour before they began to thin out, his mood was foul. But his spirits lifted when he heard Leilani's feminine voice coming from behind him.

"Come on, Jimmy. It looks like he's about done."

He finished with the last student, then turned around with a smile. "Leilani." He greeted her pleasantly, and nodded at Jimmy. "I'm glad to see you two. How about getting something to drink with me?"

Leilani returned his smile. "We'd love to . . . wouldn't we, Jimmy?"

Jimmy Li nodded, but though his gaze was somewhat admiring as he stared at Asa, Asa suspected it would take a while to win the young man's confidence.

"Did you enjoy the lecture?" he inquired amiably of the two of them as he tucked his notes in his briefcase.

"Jimmy hung on every word," Leilani spoke up before Jimmy could answer. "Especially when you talked about the Cultural Revolution. He likes all that political stuff."

Jimmy gave Leilani an annoyed look, and Asa was amused to see that she quickly fell silent and lowered her gaze in a demurely feminine way that didn't fool Asa in the least, though he suspected it did Jimmy.

Jimmy cleared his throat, and sounding a little formal, he said, "I found your lecture very interesting."

Asa smiled casually. "Thank you, Jimmy," he said as he closed and picked up his briefcase and the three of them started walking toward the cafeteria. "You're of Chinese ancestry, aren't you, Jimmy?"

Jimmy nodded, his dark eyes taking on a wary expression.

"I thought so," Asa smiled in a friendly manner and let it rest for a moment.

As they walked, Asa noticed that Jimmy was intrigued by the cane and the way Asa limped, but he didn't volunteer any information about how he'd gotten his injury. He'd already had to lie to Leilani and say he'd been hurt in an automobile accident, and if Jimmy was curious, he could ask her what had happened.

At the cafeteria, Asa noted that Jimmy displayed a courtesy toward him that was typical of the way Chinese young people treated their elders. He offered to get the drinks and seemed relieved when Asa didn't try to give him money to pay for them.

When they were at last settled at the table, Asa with coffee, and the two young people with fruit juice, Jimmy eagerly leaned forward, an expression in his eyes that Asa recognized as that of an intense student.

"Have you been to mainland China?" Jimmy asked.

With prey as sharp as Jimmy, Asa had always found that it was better to stick as close as possible to the truth.

"I've been to Hong Kong and Taiwan," he answered quietly, which was the truth, but not all of it. Asa's ventures into mainland China had been very brief and covert and Asa had no intention of telling Jimmy about them.

Jimmy grimaced. "Taiwan," he said dismissively. "That's not China. It's just an attempt by Chiang Kai-shek to recreate the China he lost."

Asa shrugged. "Technically, you're right," he agreed.

Asa was pleased by Jimmy's eagerness to talk about China and he let the conversation go on for some time, skillfully turning it in the direction he wanted it to go, which was toward the part Jimmy's grandfather had played in the government of China.

Leilani sat silently between them, and Asa was aware that the young woman was bored out of her mind, but he was also aware that she was careful to conceal her boredom from Jimmy. Apparently, she had taken the advice Asa had given her and was making the first move toward reconciliation, but Asa had an idea her pose wouldn't last unless Jimmy met her halfway soon.

When the time was right, Asa made his move.

"There was one member of the Chinese government I've always admired," he said amiably, and noted the gleam of wary interest that appeared in Jimmy's black eyes. "I don't know if you've heard of him," Asa went on, "though he has the same name as yours. Li Chang?"

"What about him?" Jimmy responded without acknowledging that he had or had not heard of his own grandfather. His face was an inscrutable blank now, giving nothing away.

"Only that it takes an exceptional amount of political skill to survive the successive purges that periodically sweep through the Communist hierarchy." Asa shrugged. "From what I know of Li Chang, he seems to have been a pragmatist rather than a real fanatic, though he was adept at giving the impression he was as dedicated as anyone."

"Perhaps he was simply dedicated to the best interests of China," Jimmy responded levelly, but Asa's sharp eyes noted a certain amount of pride in Jimmy's seemingly blank gaze.

"Perhaps he was," Asa agreed amiably. "I'd love the chance to ask him, but he seems to have disappeared from the scene, and I've been wondering if his political skill finally failed him. He may be inhabiting a Party prison somewhere these days, being reeducated, as I believe the Party puts it, or perhaps they've put him to work on a communal farm somewhere, though he's getting up in years now, and I can't imagine that he could handle much hard physical labor."

Now, Asa saw a definite flash of annoyance in Jimmy's eyes, but it was quickly gone . . . so quickly that Asa had to admire the young man's ability to hide his thoughts.

"What would you talk to him about if you could see him?" Jimmy asked, as though he were merely idly curious.

Asa smiled and shrugged. "A hundred things," he said simply. "There are a lot of gaps in my knowledge of China he could fill in, and I'm always looking for new information."

"Why?" Jimmy quickly inquired, sounding almost suspicious.

"China is my specialty, Jimmy," Asa answered quietly. "I've always been fascinated by the Sleeping Giant. Someday I may write a book about it. Isn't it natural that I want to gather information wherever I can?"

Now Jimmy was frowning at him thoughtfully. "What do you do when you aren't lecturing at universities?" he suddenly inquired.

Asa smiled. "I'm a fortunate man, Jimmy," he said lightly. "I have a private income that enables me to spend my life studying China without worrying too much about expenses. From time to time, I share what I've learned with institutions like the University of Hawaii. But mostly, I'm too busy learning to do anything else."

And that was about as neatly obscure a way of defining his profession as Asa could come up with.

Jimmy relaxed visibly, and after that, as the conversation wound down, Asa had the feeling Jimmy was watching him closely, perhaps evaluating the risk of introducing Asa to his grandfather? Asa fervently hoped so. But he knew it would take time. First, Jimmy would have to talk it over with Li Chang and obtain permission to divulge his whereabouts.

Leilani was obviously relieved when it was time to go. Since Asa appreciated her part in getting him and Jimmy together, and even for her silence during the talk they'd had, he gave her a warm smile as they said good-bye, then wished he hadn't when Jimmy's eyes showed jealousy.

Later, after Jimmy and Leilani had gone and Asa was walking home, he decided that the young couple really weren't suited to one another, and he almost regretted his part in getting them back together. Then he mentally shook his head, wondering what the hell right he had to make such a judgment. He was an expert on loving and leaving women, but that was all. When it came to forging a permanent relationship, he was totally inexperienced.

Carolyn stood in the middle of the living room of her new apartment admiring the decor. There was a shining hardwood floor under her feet, the furnishings were a good quality white wicker with the cushions covered in a colorful fabric, and there were carved wooden effigies of Hawaiian gods hanging on the walls.

She stepped to the double glass doors and peeked out onto a balcony which was festooned with various plants and contained a small table and a couple of chairs. Immediately, she imagined dining there in the evenings with the cool trade winds providing atmosphere, and as she turned to glance at the realtor who'd met her at the airport and driven her here, there was a delighted smile on her lips.

"You like it," the plump, dusky-skinned Hawaiian woman said with satisfaction.

"So far, it's marvelous," Carolyn agreed as she headed for the kitchen, which was compact, but had everything she'd need. The two bedrooms were nothing out of the ordinary, but considering the charm of the rest of the place, Carolyn didn't care.

Fifteen minutes later, she was signing a six-month lease and accepting the keys from the realtor.

"Do you know a reputable car dealer?" Carolyn inquired as she escorted the woman to the front door. "I'm going to need transportation."

"You want big American or small foreign?" the woman asked.

"How about small American," Carolyn grinned, "preferably one I can lease for a while until I make up my mind whether I want to buy it."

"I find out for you." The realtor nodded, and when she was gone, Carolyn began to put her things away.

She was pleased that the apartment was near enough to the university so that she could walk to classes if she didn't want to drive and worry about parking. Of course, it was also quite near Asa's apartment, but Carolyn refused to think about that for the present.

By the time she had unpacked, bought enough food to fix herself a light supper, eaten, and then showered, she was exhausted and was in bed and asleep by 9:30.

The next morning, she woke feeling rested and optimistic, and she thoroughly enjoyed eating her toast and coffee on the small balcony. She was on the second floor, and though she was too far from the shore to see the ocean, there were flowers and trees in abundance to gaze upon, as well as the most amazing variety of people to be found anywhere in the world . . . at least it seemed so to Carolyn. She looked forward to meeting some of those people with a great deal of enthusiasm.

Within four days, Carolyn was completely settled in. She had a Hawaiian driver's license, a small compact car to drive, her boxes had arrived and been unpacked, the refrigerator and cupboards were full, and the apartment had been cleaned thoroughly enough almost to sparkle.

Then came the letdown.

Now what? she asked herself on the fifth morning as she sat sipping her coffee on the balcony. There were two and a half months to get through before she could start classes at the University of Hawaii, and though there were hundreds of places on Oahu to visit, she wasn't in the mood to go sightseeing. She wanted to do something constructive.

I suppose I could audit some classes at the university, she mused, and was aware of a certain excitement rising inside her that forced her to acknowledge why that particular idea had occurred to her. Asa was supposedly lecturing at the university, and the thought of slipping into one of those lectures to see him at work was almost irresistible.

He wouldn't have to know I was there if I decide it's wiser to avoid the risk of getting involved with him again, she thought reflectively. *I could slip in and out without drawing his attention.*

Carolyn was often amazed these days at how easy it was becoming to give in to her own desires. She decided with rueful amusement that she apparently had a talent for self-indulgence she'd never suspected existed. But now that she had the chance to please only herself for the first time in her adult life, she seemed to be getting rather good at it.

She also realized, however, that a strong dose of loneliness went along with her present freedom. She felt it most strongly at mealtimes and when she got into bed at night. For years, meals had been accompanied by Julie's chatter, and at bedtime, her routine had always included checking on Julie before retiring to her own bedroom. Now there was no one to talk to—no one to worry about—no one to care how her day had gone—and Carolyn knew there would come a time when the self-indulgence she was enjoying now wouldn't satisfy her.

Better get used to it, she thought realistically. *There may never be a man in your life, and your only opportunity to play mother again might rest with spoiling Julie's children.*

That sort of thinking made her restless, and Carolyn abruptly slid her chair back and headed for the kitchen. When she'd washed up the small pile of dishes in the sink, she went to her bedroom, dressed in jeans and a tailored blue shirt, slipped her feet into a pair of sandals, ran a comb through her hair, and put on a minimum of makeup.

When she was ready, she let herself out of the apartment and headed on foot for the university, hoping the walk would use up some of the excess energy that seemed to be surging through her veins.

At the administration office of the university, she inquired about auditing some classes and was granted permission.

Then, as casually as she could manage, she asked, "Are there any interesting lecture series going on I can attend?"

"Are you interested in China?" the polite young clerk responded.

Carolyn suddenly found an obstruction in her throat that prevented her from speaking, so she merely nodded.

"Well, Dr. Asa Bradley will be giving the last of a series of lectures on China this afternoon at three," the young woman said helpfully, and when Carolyn expressed interest, she was told where the lecture would be held.

Outside again, Carolyn walked without having any idea of where she was headed. All she knew was that she had five hours to get through before she could see Asa, and that when she did see him, she must decide whether she would permit him to see her, or whether it would be best to take one last look at the man she couldn't have and disappear without risking the sort of heartbreak he'd caused her before.

Asa was in an exceptionally good mood. Leilani and Jimmy were sitting quite close to the front of the auditorium and the lecture was going well.

He was talking about religion in China today, explaining how the restrictions had loosened in the last few years and how a great deal of the population, while educated to scorn the opium of the masses, still visited the shrines and temples and even went through the ancient rituals.

He was opening his mouth to explain the basic tenets of Taoism when he froze for an instant, unable to believe his eyes. At the back of the auditorium, just slipping into her seat, was a woman who was either Carrie Winters in the flesh or someone resembling her enough to be her double!

Asa fought to get his concentration back and somehow managed to continue his talk. But as he spoke, his mind was wrestling with the choice he knew he was going to have to make when the lecture was over. Was he going to concentrate on Jimmy Li and try to make the most of this last opportunity he would have to convince the young man to take him to his grandfather . . . or was he going to head for the rear of the auditorium as fast as his bad leg would take him to find out if Carrie was really back, and if so, why.

CHAPTER SEVENTEEN

At the end of Asa's lecture, Carolyn sat paralyzed in her seat, grateful for the cover the young men and women who were milling around her gave. She hadn't expected to remain unmoved at seeing Asa again, of course. But she hadn't expected to react quite as violently to the sight and sound of him as she had either.

She couldn't have repeated a word of what he'd told his audience. But she had the sound of his voice and what he was wearing and the look of his face and the grace of his body committed to memory, all of which were holding her where she was as she tried desperately to decide what to do. The crowd was thinning out, but there were a few young people clustered around Asa at the front of the auditorium, so she still had a few moments to make up her mind. It was courage she lacked—the courage either to stand up and walk toward the man she loved or slip away without speaking to him . . . without touching him, no matter how innocently . . . without gazing again into those dark eyes of his that seemed to see into her soul.

By the end of his lecture, Asa had hit upon a way to keep both Jimmy and Carrie around until the young people who wanted to speak to him were gone. Gesturing for the ones who were coming toward him to excuse him briefly, he made his way the short distance to where Leilani and Jimmy sat waiting until he was free. As they looked up at him with curiosity on their faces, he leaned down and spoke to them quietly.

"I'd like a favor," he said, and before they were through nodding their agreement, he added, "There's a woman in the back row, center section. No, don't turn around yet!" he said quickly as both Jimmy and Leilani started to crane their necks around. "She's tall and blond and has on jeans and a blue shirt. She's a friend of mine, but she may not intend to come up and speak to me. I'd like you two to go invite her to have coffee with us when I'm done here. All right?"

Jimmy shrugged his affirmation and Leilani nodded, her large dark eyes wide with curiosity.

Then Asa straightened and went back to the podium to answer more questions. As he did so, Asa unobtrusively kept an eye on Jimmy and Leilani's progress toward the back of the auditorium. He was relieved to see that Carolyn was still in her seat, but he could tell from the look on her face that she might not be much longer. And he didn't have time to deal with the question of why he was so afraid she would disappear without his having a chance to talk to her.

With her eyes fastened on Asa, Carolyn finally forced herself to stand up, but her legs felt unsteady and her mind even more so. She still didn't know what she was going to do as she stepped out into the aisle, and when a young man of Asian ancestry and a lovely young woman who was staring at her with overt curiosity stepped into her path, she stared at them blankly.

"Miss . . . ?" Jimmy started to give her his message, then paused as he realized Asa Bradley hadn't told him this woman's name.

"Yes?" Carolyn responded, her voice unsteady. She couldn't imagine what these two wanted with her, and she wanted to be left alone to wrestle with her decision, but she was too innately polite to be rude.

"Dr. Bradley sent us," Leilani spoke up. And when Carolyn reacted to Asa Bradley's name with a startled jerk, the young woman's beautiful eyes started to sparkle with understanding. As far as Leilani was concerned, her curiosity was satisfied. Asa Bradley and this beautiful haole woman had a romantic relationship. It was as simple as that.

"What . . . ah . . . ." Carolyn paused to swallow, her eyes darting from Asa at the front of the auditorium, who had his back to her now, to the young couple who were barring her way. "Why?" she finally got out.

"He wants to talk to you," Jimmy Li said politely. "He said we'd all go to coffee together when he's done here."

Carolyn closed her eyes briefly in relief at having the decision taken from her . . . and at knowing that Asa wanted to see her again.

When she opened her eyes, one look at Leilani's smiling, knowing expression told her the young woman had figured out the sort of relationship Carolyn and Asa had shared, and Carolyn flushed slightly and turned her gaze to the young man, who was merely looking at her with muted curiosity.

"Who—?" Carolyn started to ask who the couple was and why Asa had chosen them to convey his message, then she merely shrugged, smiled faintly, and held out her hand to Jimmy Li. "I'm Carrie Winters," she said simply.

Jimmy took her hand, shook it briefly, and gave a sort of half bow. "I am Jimmy Li." He introduced himself with a formality that seemed strange in one so young.

"And I'm Leilani Rodriguez," the young woman said smilingly, holding out her hand to be shaken.

Carolyn did so, feeling slightly embarrassed by the young woman's air of knowledgeable mischievousness. But Leilani's smile was irresistible, and after a moment Carolyn was smiling back.

"Rodriguez," she repeated, somewhat puzzled by the combination of Hawaiian and Spanish names.

"I'm Hawaiian and Filipino." Leilani grinned. "Jimmy's Chinese."

Carolyn nodded, relaxing. "Are you students here?" she asked.

Jimmy now had his hands clasped behind him like an elderly professor and as he nodded, Carolyn had to suppress a grin at his serious manner.

"We're sophomores," Leilani volunteered, and now she was unabashedly looking Carolyn over from head to foot, studying the way she did her hair, her makeup, even the way she stood.

"It's nice to meet you," Carolyn said politely. "I'll be starting as a freshman here at the spring semester."

That earned her a startled look from both young people, and Carolyn shrugged, her smile somewhat rueful.

"I wasn't able to go to college right out of high school," she explained. "Have you two known As . . . ah . . . Dr. Bradley long?" Carolyn at last gave in to her curiosity about why Asa had chosen these two to bring her his message.

"Not long," Jimmy responded, shaking his head. "We came to hear his lectures, and he invited us to have coffee with him. We talked."

Then Jimmy glanced behind him and nodded his head in that direction. "Dr. Bradley is coming now," he said simply, and Carolyn was immediately thrown into a state of confusion as she followed the direction of Jimmy's gaze and saw Asa limping toward them.

As always, his limp took her slightly by surprise and tore at her heart. When she looked at his rugged face and powerful body, she automatically expected to see him walk with a purposeful self-confident stride. She was positive that was how he must have walked before his injury, which made it all the more distressing to see him hampered now.

Leilani echoed her thought. "It's too bad about his accident," she said in a low murmur to Carolyn, and when Carolyn gave her a puzzled look, Leilani looked puzzled in her turn. "His automobile accident," she said, as though trying to prompt Carolyn's memory.

"Oh, yes, his accident," Carolyn said, turning away as she felt her cheeks beginning to heat up with resentful embarrassment. Why was it, she wondered grimly, that Asa had told this slip of a girl, who apparently barely knew him, how he'd gotten hurt, when he hadn't volunteered the information to her?

Maybe Leilani had the courage to ask him straight out, her mind proposed as an answer, making her feel even more resentful and uncomfortable as she remembered how many times she'd wanted to ask Asa, but had been discouraged by his hostile manner when she'd asked him any personal questions at all.

Carolyn was unaware that her thoughts had brought a cool, distancing look into her eyes or that she was unsmiling as Asa came to a stop a couple of feet away.

Asa's expression was hard for Carolyn to interpret. He was smiling faintly, but his gaze was almost blank when he nodded at her.

209

"Carrie," he said quietly, as though they'd parted only the day before instead of several weeks ago.

Carolyn hesitated, then nodded back. "Hello, Asa," she said just as quietly, forgetting Jimmy and Leilani entirely for the moment as she stared into the dark eyes that, despite their lack of expression, provoked a light and boneless feeling inside her, the way they always had.

"Shall we have something to drink?" Asa then proposed, smiling at each of them in turn in a way that made Carolyn feel as though she meant no more to him than these two students did. Suddenly, she wanted to run away home. The pain she had endured when parting from him the first time surged through her all over again.

But his fingers were circling her arm now, and though his expression was merely pleasantly neutral, Carolyn had the curious impression that he had known what she was thinking and had taken her arm to keep her with him.

"My lecture wasn't up to par, was it, Jimmy?" Asa said lightly as the four of them started walking toward the cafeteria.

Jimmy looked uncomfortable and Asa smiled at him with easy encouragement. "You don't have to worry that you'll hurt my ego," he shrugged. "I just had my mind on other things today." And as he said this, he glanced at Carolyn, whose eyes widened with understanding before she hastily looked away.

Jimmy caught the silent exchange between Asa and Carolyn, and then his expression lightened and he began smiling, too. "Well," he said almost apologetically, "your other ones were perhaps just a little better."

Asa grinned. "Only a little?" he said teasingly.

Jimmy didn't answer, but his smile broadened.

"I thought it was wonderful as always," Leilani put in loyally, her eyes solemnly supportive as she turned them on Asa.

"Thank you, Leilani," Asa responded in a gravely polite tone.

Carolyn noted the way Leilani was looking at Asa and felt a tingle of jealousy slide down her spine before she caught herself up. What was the point of being jealous of Asa Bradley? she wondered, her feelings turning toward a muted, simmering anger. After all, as he'd pointed out more than once, he wasn't the marrying kind.

By the time they were seated in the cafeteria, however, waiting for Jimmy to bring their drinks, Carolyn's mood had turned again. What was the point of being angry with Asa either? He had made things plain all along. And he hadn't asked her to come back to Hawaii. She had come on her own, with the clear knowledge that there was nothing to hope for where Asa was concerned. And yet immediately upon being close to him again, she'd begun to weave exactly the same fantasies about him that had trapped her before. It wouldn't do. It had to stop right now.

Gradually, as she forced herself to accept reality, Carolyn began to relax. Leilani was chattering away about one of her classes, which gave Carolyn the opportunity to study Asa in an unobtrusive way with a new objectivity. He was still clean-shaven, she noted. And his eyes looked tired, which touched the tender part of her heart as powerfully as his male sexuality could touch the rest of her.

But just as she was cautioning herself not to think such thoughts, he turned his head slightly and gave her a sweeping glance that contained such possessive sexual energy that it swept away any good intentions she'd been about to form.

Then Jimmy approached the table, bringing a tray of drinks with him, and Carolyn was able to recover a little of her equilibrium, though not all of it by any means.

"To the end of my lectures," Asa said, his smile rakish as he raised his cup of coffee as though in a toast.

"No, no," Jimmy protested. "I cannot toast that. I would attend more if you would give them."

Asa took a sip of coffee, then put his cup down and shrugged. "The university has something else scheduled, I think, Jimmy, but thanks for the compliment."

Jimmy looked unhappy, and Asa felt a surge of hope. Was Jimmy unhappy enough about the end of the lectures to want to continue the relationship?

"I hate saying good-bye to people, though," he said spontaneously, only afterward realizing how Carolyn might take his words, "so if you and Leilani aren't busy tomorrow night, how about coming to my place for dinner? I'm not much of a cook," he grinned, "but I know someone who'll cater it for me."

Leilani looked delighted. Jimmy looked at Carolyn in an embarrassed fashion, since Asa hadn't invited her as well.

But then Asa turned his head and smiled at Carolyn in a casual way. "You're invited, too, of course, Carrie," he said lightly.

Carolyn, however, suspected from the belatedness of the invitation that Asa was only being polite—that he didn't really give a damn whether she came or not—and she was suddenly angry, though she took care not to show her anger.

"I'll have to check my schedule," she replied vaguely, giving Asa an absent look as though she weren't all that interested in the invitation. "I think I already have another commitment."

She was momentarily stunned when something flashed briefly in Asa's eyes that resembled a rather fierce sort of possessiveness a man might display to a wife who had stepped out of line. It was gone so quickly, however, before Asa looked away, that Carolyn felt bewildered. Was she imagining things? she wondered. Surely, she must be!

Asa was a little stunned himself. When Carolyn had spoken of "another commitment," an image of her with another man had flashed through his mind, and the resulting jealousy he felt shook him far more than he would have cared to acknowledge if he could have helped it.

He had intended to talk to her alone after Jimmy and Leilani departed anyway and find out what she was doing here. Now, he knew he wasn't going to be able to resist trying to find out if she'd met someone else . . . someone who could offer her what he couldn't.

"I would be happy to come," Jimmy now said in a gravely formal tone.

"Me, too!" Leilani responded a lot more exuberantly, earning a glance of reproval from Jimmy in the process.

Asa saw a stubborn expression come into Leilani's eyes that strengthened his conviction that the two weren't going to be able to maintain a relationship. They were simply too different to be compatible.

For a few more moments, as they finished their drinks, Jimmy questioned Asa about some points in his lecture, but, as though sensing the atmosphere that was building between Asa and Carolyn, he didn't linger.

"Come, Leilani," he said as he got to his feet. "I'll help you study for your test in World History tomorrow."

Leilani looked somewhat reluctant to leave, as well as a little resentful about having to study, but she got to her feet and gathered her books up.

"Where is your apartment, Dr. Bradley?" she then asked. "If we are to come to dinner, we have to know where to come, right?"

Asa smiled and nodded, and reached in his pocket for a piece of paper on which to scribble his address.

Jimmy reached for it, beating Leilani to the punch.

"Come about seven," Asa said with easy graciousness. "I'll look forward to seeing you."

Leilani gave him a brilliant, somewhat flirtatious smile, Jimmy nodded politely, and then the two young people walked away, leaving Carolyn and Asa at the table alone together.

Asa didn't waste any time. Fastening his eyes, in which there was an intent expression, on Carolyn's face, he asked without preliminary, "What are you doing here?"

His abruptness aroused Carolyn's resentment, but she kept her tone calm. "I decided to live here for a while," she said simply. "I missed Hawaii when I got home, and since there was nothing to keep me in Kansas City and winter was coming on, I came back."

"For how long?" Asa asked.

To Carolyn's sensitive ears, he sounded almost grim, as though he didn't like the fact that she'd come back. She bristled slightly.

"Does it matter?" she said coldly. "Surely that's my business."

Realizing that he was creating the wrong impression, Asa grimaced, then took a deep breath and said in a softly intimate tone, "It may not be any of my business, Carrie, but it matters to me. I've missed you. I'm glad to see you again."

Carolyn stared at him, feeling uncertain about what he was really feeling, but unable to keep from softening toward him.

"I missed you, too," she said quietly, then quickly added, "But I didn't come back expecting—"

She flushed and stopped speaking, and Asa reached over and placed his fingers over her wrist, creating instant havoc inside her as he stroked her skin in an erotic manner.

"Maybe you didn't expect anything," he said softly, "but I do."

Carolyn inhaled a sharp breath, and her eyes were wide and questioning as she looked into Asa's.

"Where are you staying?" he asked, his voice deepening into a husky burr, his eyes a warm caress as he scanned her face.

Carolyn swallowed. "I . . . I have an apartment near here," she said shakily.

"Close enough to walk?"

Carolyn nodded, staring now at Asa's hand on hers, feeling her senses begin to wake up and stretch with expectation.

"Show me," Asa said, his voice as softly confident as any man's might have been who saw what he did in Carolyn's eyes.

Carolyn's nerves were stretched to the breaking point by the time Asa closed the door of her apartment behind him and set his briefcase down, so that she actually jumped when he came up behind her and turned her toward him.

He cupped her face in his hands as he stared into her eyes for a long moment in a way that made her pulse race, then his hands slipped into her hair and held her as his lips descended to capture hers, and Carolyn's body relaxed into a shuddering wave of relief that the preliminaries were over. She was back where she belonged, and Asa's hungrily demanding mouth was telling her he wanted her as much as she wanted him.

"How long have you been here?" he demanded between one devouring kiss and another. "Why didn't you call me when you arrived?" was the next question, delivered in that same deep, demanding rasp that thrilled her, but again his mouth was on hers before she could answer.

Then Asa seemed to lose interest in questions and answers, and his kisses became vivid demonstrations of the need that rode him until Carolyn took his hand to lead him to her bedroom, wrapped in the haze of her own desire. She stopped when she saw a tortured question in his eyes.

"It's all right," she reassured him quietly. "This time I'm coming to you protected."

Asa relaxed immediately, so caught up in his relief that there was nothing to interfere with his joy in making love to Carrie again, that he failed to notice a fleeting sadness in her eyes.

Carolyn wasn't saddened by the necessity to take precautions against pregnancy, though in her deepest heart she longed to have Asa's child. She was saddened because she knew she had no emotional protection against Asa. She was in love with him, and she didn't know how to stop herself from letting him break her heart again. She didn't even want to stop what was about to happen, though she knew the price she would have to pay. How could she help but know when she'd already paid it once.

There was no need for delicacy or subtle seduction in their reunion. Carolyn was locked too tightly in a desperate hunger to be one with Asa again to pretend to a shyness or reluctance she didn't feel, and Asa wouldn't have allowed such a pretense in any case.

His eyes devoured her as he removed her clothing without a wasted motion, and held her as he removed his own in the same way.

"Asa . . ." She said his name in a long, emotionally shaken tone of welcome as he bore her back onto the bed and then she was silent as he covered her mouth with his own as thoroughly as his body covered the rest of her.

She closed her eyes and her mind and clung to him, permitting her senses to rule her as she responded with everything in her to the familiar demands of his hands and lips. Some unconscious awareness deep inside her noted with joy that Asa's hunger for her was total—that his need for her held him in an unbreakable grip she didn't have to struggle to match.

"God, Carrie I've missed you." He murmured the words against her breast, his voice ragged and honest. "I've missed your love so much."

But before she could tell him the same, he moved his lips a fraction and the touch of his tongue on the tip of her breast drove the words from her mind and she could only gasp her response as her body shuddered with pleasure.

Her reaction seemed to drive him past caution and Carolyn could do no more than lie helplessly beneath him as he showed her with exquisite intensity how much he'd missed her, how glad he was to have her back.

Again, in the moment of completion, she heard him whisper his love for her and she believed him with all her heart. It was only much, much later, when they lay together in a state of temporarily satiated exhaustion that she wondered how Asa could love her so completely in the act of taking her body, and yet give no thought to sharing the rest of his life with her.

She turned such thoughts off quickly. That was old territory she had been over again and again in her mind when they'd been together before, and there was no solution. She was therefore left with the only resolution Asa would allow her. Live for the moment. Take what she could have of him for as long as it lasted. Then let him go when he required it of her.

Oh, Asa, she thought with the wistful sadness he so often inspired in her during the quiet moments before she dropped into sleep. *Why can't it be different? Why can't it last?*

She closed her eyes and went into the darkness without an answer, wrapped in the arms of a man who was unable to tell her why their love was doomed to end.

CHAPTER EIGHTEEN

They had a light supper of fruit and cheese on Carolyn's balcony, then sat with their coffee and enjoyed the caress of the evening breeze, the scent of tropical blossoms, and the beauty of the soft Hawaiian night descending around them.

In a way, Carolyn hated to disturb the companionable silence they'd been sharing by saying anything at all, especially when she was aware of how Asa would probably react to the questions she wanted to ask. But there was a limit to her ability to pretend they inhabited some sort of time warp when they were together, where the lives they lived when apart didn't matter.

It had worked before because there had been a definite time limit to their idyll. There was one now, of course, as well, but the difference was that Carolyn didn't know when the present idyll was going to end, and she could no longer tolerate being treated as though any knowledge of what Asa's life was like when he was apart from her was off limits.

"Leilani told me you injured your leg in an automobile accident," she said quietly. "Why did you never tell me about it?"

She was sensitized to Asa to a degree that she could tell he had stiffened with resistance at her question, though he hadn't shown his reaction in any visible way.

Asa had almost forgotten how Carolyn could catch him off guard with her directness. And Carolyn had guessed correctly that his first reaction to her question had been to stiffen with resistance. But as he thought about it, he realized his resistance lay as much in his reluctance to lie to her as to the necessity to maintain his cover.

"I'd rather forget about it," he finally answered with a part of the truth.

217

"I imagine you would," Carolyn agreed, still in that quiet, yet implacable tone. "But I was hurt to find out you'd shared something like that with Leilani when you wouldn't share it with me."

Asa closed his eyes and rubbed his forehead with his fingers, realizing anew the difficulties of a man in his position having anything other than a brief relationship with any woman, much less one like Carolyn whose basic character was innately opposed to having casual affairs in the first place.

"I didn't want your pity," he again told part of the truth. "It seemed easier not to talk about it at all than to have you start smothering me with sympathy."

Carolyn stiffened at the somewhat tactless way Asa chose to give his explanation, and had to bite back a tart rejoinder that would have precipitated an argument instead of a discussion.

"I'm sorry, Carrie," he immediately apologized in a gentle tone tinged with weariness. "It's just that I don't like talking about my leg and what it's cost me at all, and women—" He hesitated, sensing he was about to get himself in hot water again. "You have a soft heart, Carrie," he took another tack, "and it isn't pity that I want or need from you."

Reluctantly, for the time being, Carolyn ignored the part about what Asa wanted from her. She doubted that he actually needed anything from her or anybody else.

"What has it cost you, Asa," she asked instead, trying to keep her tone level and emotionless, "other than having to put up with the pain and a certain loss of mobility?"

"Isn't that enough?" he responded cynically. He was aware of the irony of sounding as though he were indulging in self-pity when he'd just told Carolyn he didn't want hers.

"I suppose," Carolyn agreed reluctantly, though she wasn't quite satisfied with Asa's answer. She could tell it was the only answer she was going to get, however, so she let it go.

There was a short silence between them while Carolyn gathered the courage to tackle Asa on another matter.

"Asa, what exactly do you want from me?" she then asked, though she feared the answer was all too obvious.

Asa remained silent. He knew she didn't really want to hear that he wanted the same thing from her he'd wanted when they

218

were together before: her company, in and out of bed, without questions and without a long-term commitment between them.

Now it was Carolyn's turn to sound wearily cynical. "I really didn't need to ask that, did I?"

Again Asa remained silent, and Carolyn's frustration brought her to her feet. She folded her arms and stepped to the balcony railing, looking out over the lights of Honolulu without seeing them.

Asa noted the way she was standing and identified the frustration, as well as the slight simmer of anger inside her. He got up and came to stand behind her, sliding his arms around her protectively as he rested his cheek against her sweet-smelling hair.

"Do you think I want to hurt you, Carrie?" he asked in a deep, soft voice that caught at her heart.

She shook her head, knowing with certainty that he didn't.

Asa was glad she understood that about him. But he also knew he was hurting her and though he selfishly wanted to have all of her he could have, he knew now was the time to spell things out for her again and leave the choice up to her.

"Carrie, I have a few things to do in Hawaii that will keep me here for a while . . . I don't know how long."

He felt her stiffen in his arms and he instinctively held her tighter as though to protect her against a blow.

"But eventually I'll be leaving," he forced himself to go on and tried to gentle the news by softening his voice. "If you want me to leave you alone the rest of the time I'm here, I will," he added, his own reluctance to stop seeing her evident in his voice. "But if you continue to see me, things haven't changed from the last time. I'm sorry, Carrie," he said with soft regret. "But I can't offer you anything more than whatever time we can have together before I have to go."

Carolyn closed her eyes and leaned back against the strength of Asa's body as she absorbed the pain his words brought her. She had expected to hear what she just had eventually, of course. But not so soon!

She felt bitter about her own foolishness in leaving herself open to this sort of heartache. But it was no good chastising herself for what she hadn't been able to help doing, and it was no good feeling bitter toward Asa for not offering her what she so desperately wanted. It wasn't his fault that she had again made the mistake of hoping the passionate love he displayed in bed was the sort that led to commitment, marriage, and babies.

"I'm sorry, Asa." She forced the words out by an act of sheer willpower. "I knew better than to do this to either of us. I just didn't seem able to help it."

Without replying, Asa tightened his arms around her for a moment, then turned her to face him. He studied her expression, hating himself a little for his part in putting that look of sad helplessness into her eyes.

"Would it be easier for you if we parted now?" he asked again, his voice gentle.

Without changing expression, Carolyn silently shook her head.

Asa understood that she was caught in the same trap he was. She wanted as much of him as she could have, just as he wanted all of her that time would allow him.

He started to kiss her, but Carolyn placed a soft hand on his cheek to stop him momentarily. When he looked at her inquiringly, she said, "Will you do something for me, Asa?"

He hesitated, fearing she might ask him to promise something it would be impossible for him to grant.

"If I can," he finally replied, wishing with a ferocity that startled him that he could give her anything she wanted.

"Don't worry." She gave him a faint smile. "I don't want much . . . merely that you tell me as much about yourself as you can. Things like where you grew up, what sort of little boy you were . . ."

Carolyn suddenly stopped speaking, and a line of puzzlement appeared between her eyes. Her own question made her aware consciously for the first time that there must be reasons for Asa's reluctance to talk about himself other than simple reticence. What was he hiding? she wondered anxiously. What could be so bad that he didn't want her to know about it?

Asa, however, was relieved by her request, and his assent interrupted Carolyn's thoughts.

"Sure," he said, smiling down at her. "I'll bore you to tears with tales of my childhood if you like . . . and you can tell me about yours."

Carolyn barely had time to note that it was only his childhood that Asa was willing to discuss with her before he pulled her closer and bent to cover her mouth with his.

For the first time since she'd met Asa, her response wasn't wholehearted, because her mind was filled with anxious questions.

Asa noted her unusual lack of enthusiasm, but he thought it was merely because he had forced her to face the unpleasant reality that they couldn't always be together. Instinctively, he redoubled his efforts to give her pleasure because something in him couldn't tolerate less than a total response from Carrie.

Carolyn's troubled mind was soon effectively subverted by Asa's kisses, and when he sensed he had succeeded in capturing her total cooperation, he led her to the bedroom.

As always, while making love, there was no room for anything extraneous to come between them. And since Asa's lovemaking that night was exceptionally intense and demanding, Carolyn was too exhausted to think by the time he let her sleep.

When she woke the next morning, he was gone and there was a note on her pillow.

"I'll see you tonight at my place," he'd written. "Come early and don't plan to leave. I won't be able to sleep without you."

But you'll have to one day, Asa, Carolyn thought as she brought her arm across her eyes, the note crumpled in her hand. *And so will I.*

"What's up?"

Asa and his contact, who had demanded a meeting at the Bishop Museum when Asa had called him early that morning, paused before a fierce-looking idol of carved ohia wood, one of three known to have been used at a *heiau* (an ancient Hawaiian temple) devoted to human sacrifice. There was no one around at the moment, but Asa had voiced his question in a barely audible tone.

"We think we've found him," the contact replied in a tone as quiet as Asa had used.

"Li Chang?" The news was so unexpected that Asa showed his surprise by speaking louder than he'd intended to.

His contact didn't comment verbally, but Asa grimaced as the other man hastily looked around them to make sure no one had heard Asa's exclamation.

"Sorry," he said with a shrug. "Where?"

"You won't believe this, but he was spotted in one of those hole-in-the-wall restaurants in Chinatown," the contact replied, shaking his head as though he couldn't believe it himself.

"Which one?" Asa quickly asked.

"It doesn't seem to have a name," the contact grunted, "but it's owned by an old fellow named Feng."

"I've been there," Asa nodded. "Was Li followed?"

"Our guy tried," the contact answered, sounding annoyed, "but despite Li's age, he managed to lose the tail. But at least we know for sure he's here and in what general area. And if he got careless enough to dine out once, maybe he'll do it again, and meanwhile we're keeping our eyes open around the rest of the area."

"He's not the type to get careless," Asa responded thoughtfully, then fell silent as a family group consisting of mom, dad, and two rowdy children walked toward them. Asa and his contact moved by silent agreement toward a display of brilliantly colored feathered cloaks worn by Hawaiian royalty in a bygone age.

"Who knows what someone will do at his age. Maybe he's gone senile," the contact ventured with a shrug.

Asa shook his head. "It's more likely he took a deliberate risk. Remember, as a high official in the Chinese Communist Party, he hasn't been used to having his activities circumscribed. He may be getting restless. Or," Asa added, his thoughtfulness growing more pronounced, "he may just be issuing his own version of a challenge to us."

The contact frowned. "That doesn't make any sense," he said skeptically.

Asa shrugged. "Li Chang's known to have a sense of humor," he said, "as well as a fairly substantial ego for a Chinese."

"What does that mean?" The contact, who had no special knowledge of China or its people, sounded disgruntled.

222

Asa glanced at him absently. "The Chinese are group oriented," he explained. "Any purely selfish desires are frowned upon. The family's needs always come first, followed by the needs of their immediate community, then the needs of China as a whole, though the Communist Party has been trying to change that order around. In their language, words that might connote something like 'I want' have a negative connotation."

"Okay, okay." The contact, looking bored, held up a hand. "So what does all that tell us about Li Chang?"

Asa smiled faintly. "I'm not saying that Li isn't family oriented or patriotic. He is. It's just that he has a more healthy regard for his own desires than is usual for his people. He was smart enough to keep on top for a lot of years, despite the fact that he allowed his family to emigrate to the United States, which normally would have had an adverse effect on his political ambitions. I have an idea he even enjoyed pitting his wits against his fellow Party members. It may well be that his present obscurity is proving boring for him, and he can't resist stirring things up a little. After all, what has he got to lose? My hunch is he came here to make peace with his son and die in the bosom of his family, anyway. Maybe it's just taking him longer to die than he counted on and he's passing the time by having a little fun with us."

The contact looked even more impatient. "So he's playing a cat and mouse game?" He snorted. "That still doesn't make any sense. He has to know his chances of winning the game are almost nil."

"Maybe he doesn't really care that much about winning anymore," Asa suggested. "Maybe he even wants to be caught. China and the United States aren't desperate enemies anymore, and anything Li Chang tells us now wouldn't necessarily make him feel like a traitor, the way it might have in the past. But he's not the type to give that kind of prize to someone he can't respect, and if we can't catch him, we won't have his respect."

The contact sighed and shook his head. "I'll let you try to get in his head," he said cynically. "All I care about is finding him. How are things going with the grandson, by the way?"

"He and his girlfriend are coming to dinner at my place tonight."

"Good." The contact nodded, then something about Asa's expression made him frown. "You got something in mind to crack that family loyalty thing you say those people live by?"

Asa's expression was now blank. As a matter of fact, an idea had just occurred to him, but he had no intention of sharing it. The risks were high, and he knew the contact wouldn't find them acceptable.

"Nothing special. I'm still trying to win young Li's trust," he answered. "You'll hear from me if I get anywhere tonight."

The contact nodded, then looked around to make sure they were still alone.

"And we'll keep looking for old Li around Chinatown," he said. "I guess that's it for now then."

Without another word, he walked rapidly away, leaving Asa to stand staring absently at a small sign near a red-and-yellow cape, which explained that the garment had been handmade from the feathers of birds that were now extinct and had taken years to create, since each bird furnished only one feather of sufficient brilliance to adorn a chief's cloak.

Shaking his head at mankind's vanity, Asa finally walked away, aware that he was committed to an act of vanity of his own, and that if his idea didn't work, he not only wouldn't get any feathers in his cap from his superiors in the Agency, he might just turn out to be a human sacrifice instead.

As Carolyn knocked on Asa's door that evening, she was joined by a young, white-jacketed Chinese man carrying two huge sacks in his arms.

"This Dr. Bradley's apartment?" the young man asked jauntily, his white smile slightly flirtatious.

"Yes, it is." Carolyn nodded, looking curiously at the sacks in his arms. "Is that our dinner?"

"Wonton soup, rice, sweet-and-sour pork, chicken almond, hot tea," the young man rattled off obligingly, his dark eyes inspecting her with cheerful admiration at the same time.

Carolyn smiled, but Asa opened the door before she had time to say anything else.

"Carrie! Come in!" he said, his eyes greeting her as warmly as his voice had sounded. "And Charlie," he added with a grin as he spotted the young man beside her. "Got everything, my friend?"

"Everything you ordered." Charlie nodded, following Carolyn inside as Asa stepped back to let them in.

In Asa's small kitchen, Charlie quickly emptied the sacks, talking all the while. "This stuff's hot now, but if you aren't gonna eat for a while, you better warm it in the microwave." He paused and looked around. "You got a microwave?" he asked.

"Nope, but I've got an oven." Asa grinned, amused by Charlie's astonishment that anyone in this day and age could operate in a kitchen without a microwave.

"Suit yourself." Charlie shrugged as he neatly folded up the now empty sacks. "That'll be thirty dollars, Dr. Bradley."

Asa fished some money out of his pocket and paid Charlie, adding a generous tip that made Charlie smile with satisfaction.

"Thanks, Charlie," Asa said as Charlie folded up the money, stuck it in his pocket, and headed for the front door.

"For you, anytime!" Charlie responded cheerfully, just before he shut the door behind him with a bang.

"He was Chinese, right?" Carolyn asked.

"Third-generation." Asa smiled, coming to put his arms around her. He began to kiss her forehead, her eyes, her cheeks with a petal-soft grazing of his lips that made Carolyn tingle.

"Do you know him personally?" she asked, though she was beginning not to care whether she received an answer or not.

"I sometimes eat at his family's restaurant," Asa murmured absently as he concentrated on nuzzling her ear. "They don't usually cater, but they made an exception for me."

Carolyn thought, *Doesn't everyone . . . especially me?* But Asa was kissing her mouth now and it ceased to rankle that Asa Bradley had the ability to make people—especially Carolyn—do things for him they wouldn't do for anyone else.

"I wish I had time to make love to you," Asa murmured huskily against her neck.

"I wish you did, too," Carolyn said, her voice languid and smiling.

"Later," Asa promised before taking her mouth in another kiss that left her weak at the knees. "Come on," he said when he'd let her go, his eyes teasing her over her aroused state. "Help me set the table."

Jimmy Li and Leilani arrived a few moments later. Jimmy seemed politely uneasy at first, while Leilani unabashedly examined Carolyn's silk print dress with envy before turning her curious eyes on the living room of Asa's apartment.

"You have a nice apartment," she commented when Asa handed her a glass of sangria.

"Thank you." Asa smiled at her, then moved back to the kitchen to finish reheating their dinner, leaving Carolyn to entertain the guests.

"Are you from the mainland, Ms. Winters?" Leilani asked, making Carolyn feel slightly ancient in the process.

"Call me Carrie . . . please," she said with a smile as she sat down on the sofa beside Leilani. "Yes, I'm from Kansas City," she said in answer to Leilani's question.

"Have you been here long, Carrie?" Leilani promptly accepted the invitation to use Carolyn's first name and continued to indulge her apparently inexhaustible curiosity.

"About a week this time," Carolyn said lightly. "I was here in August for a vacation and loved it so much, I decided to come back and stay for a while."

Leilani looked from Carolyn to Asa, whose back was visible in the kitchen, an expression on her face that told Carolyn the young woman had her own ideas about what had brought Carolyn back to Hawaii.

Carolyn decided to ignore Leilani's instincts. She turned to Jimmy.

"What are you studying at the university, Jimmy?" she asked, smiling in a way she hoped would put him at ease. He still seemed slightly uncomfortable.

"World History now; I will eventually study International Law," Jimmy answered politely.

"Well, the world seems to be getting smaller every day." Carolyn nodded. "That seems like a wise choice to me." She turned to Leilani. "And what about you, Leilani? What are you studying?"

Leilani grimaced slightly. "I haven't decided yet," she said, then flashed Jimmy a challenging look, as though daring him to comment on her indecisiveness.

Jimmy said nothing, however, though Carolyn thought she saw a flash of impatience in his eyes before he looked away from Leilani and toward Asa.

"May I help you, Dr. Bradley?" he called, getting to his feet to walk toward the kitchen.

"Sure, Jimmy," Asa responded.

Carolyn thought Jimmy's discomfort eased considerably when he had received permission to escape from the company of two women, and her guess was confirmed when Leilani leaned toward her and whispered, "He's no good at socializing. It makes him impatient and nervous."

"He seems to be a very serious young man," Carolyn whispered back.

Leilani nodded, a somewhat petulant expression in her eyes. "Too serious," she commented succinctly, then turned her attention to Carolyn's dress again. "Did you buy that here?" she asked.

"No, in Kansas City," Carolyn answered, resigned to satisfying Leilani's curiosity without losing her patience.

A couple of hours later, after dinner had been eaten and the dishes cleared away, Carolyn wasn't particularly pleased when Asa took Jimmy into his bedroom, explaining that he wanted to show him a new book on China he'd picked up at a bookstore that day, leaving her to the mercy of Leilani's curiosity again.

During dinner, Leilani had concentrated on a mild flirtation with Asa, which had annoyed Carolyn, amused Asa, and lit a flame of jealousy inside Jimmy. Carolyn wondered if Asa had taken Jimmy away to calm him down. She wasn't sure Leilani deserved any help in soothing her boyfriend's ruffled feelings, but at least when the two men were together, she didn't have to watch Leilani flirting with the man she loved.

In the bedroom, while Jimmy looked over the book Asa had handed him, Asa watched, getting his thoughts together for what he was about to do.

"May I borrow this when you've read it?" Jimmy asked, looking up from the book at last, only to go still at something he saw in Asa's face.

"You can keep it, Jimmy," Asa said calmly, holding the young man's eyes with a steady look. "I bought it for you anyway."

"You bought it for me?" Jimmy responded cautiously, his glance sliding away from Asa's for a moment before he faced him again.

"I thought you'd enjoy it," Asa nodded, "since it contains a whole chapter on your grandfather's role in the Chinese government after the Party took over."

Jimmy was silent for so long that Asa began to wonder if his gamble had failed. It didn't look as though Jimmy was going to respond at all. He merely stood staring at Asa, his face and eyes absolutely blank. But at least he hadn't denied that Li Chang was his grandfather, Asa noted.

"Did you make my acquaintance in order to get to my grandfather?" Jimmy at last broke the silence. His tone wasn't accusing, merely flatly emotionless.

Again, Asa nodded, his steady gaze never wavering from Jimmy's face.

"You work for the government?" Jimmy asked.

Asa didn't answer directly. "I have no wish to harm your grandfather, Jimmy," he said in a level tone. "I just want to talk to him."

Jimmy firmed his jaw. "I will not take you to him," he said in a flat, stubborn tone. "Not even if you threaten me with arrest."

"I'm not asking you to take me to him," Asa responded quietly, "and I have no intention of arresting you. I'm not with Immigration, and I'm not a policeman. I'm just a man who wants to talk to your grandfather. All I want you to do is ask him if he wants to talk to me."

Jimmy's head tilted slightly as he studied Asa's face, his eyes suspicious. "You are not having me followed?" he asked at last.

Asa shook his head. He didn't feel it necessary to explain that he had vetoed his contact's suggestion that they do just that. He had figured Jimmy would catch on quickly and lead them on a wild goose chase.

"It wouldn't do you any good anyway," Jimmy said with a hint of belligerence in his voice.

"But I'm not—"

"Now, Leilani!" Jimmy said sharply, and though Leilani whitened a little and looked as though she were about to argue again, in the end she didn't. She got up and accompanied Jimmy to the door instead, but not in a way that conveyed meekness. Just the opposite, in fact.

Carolyn was on her feet, looking from Jimmy to Leilani to Asa with confused surprise.

"Good night, Carrie," Leilani said stiffly. "Good night, Dr. Bradley," she added, turning to Asa and giving a little nod in his direction. "Thank you for dinner."

"You're welcome, Leilani," Asa said quietly.

Jimmy said nothing, and his expression was remote as he opened the door and ushered Leilani outside, closing it firmly behind them.

Carolyn turned to Asa, her eyes wide. "What was that all about?"

Asa shrugged, then leaned his shoulder against the doorjamb with his hands still in his pockets. His expression looked as remote as Jimmy's had, and Carolyn felt a sinking sensation, thinking Asa was in one of his moods where he was impossible to talk to.

To her surprise and relief, after a moment he came to her and put his arms around her, holding her as though to give her comfort. Her or himself, Carolyn wasn't sure which.

"I hurt his feelings," he said so quietly she could barely hear him. "I'm good at that, aren't I?"

Carolyn drew back to study his face, and saw something in his eyes that melted her heart. She put her arms around his neck, kissed his cheek, then looked into his eyes again, her own showing him how much she loved him.

"If you are," she whispered softly, "you also have some beautiful ways of apologizing."

Asa held her eyes, suddenly aware of how unbearable it was going to be when she wasn't there to soothe him the way she was now, or love him, despite the fact that he didn't really think he deserved her love, or send the passion surging through his loins the way she would in a few minutes when he took her to bed.

"I love you, Carrie," he said quietly, his voice steady and convincing, the expression in his eyes absolutely sincere.

"I know, Asa," Carolyn answered, meaning that she knew he loved her in his own way if not in the way that would allow them to spend the rest of their lives together. "And I love you."

"I'm glad," he said huskily, and kissed her with a wealth of tenderness.

The kiss then turned passionate and soon Asa was leading Carolyn to his bedroom, where he undressed her with slow deliberation and began to show his love in a way he considered was more convincing than words.

He took his time, exploring her with a thoroughness that left her no secrets while it lifted her to new levels of pleasure. And when she lay temporarily satiated in his arms, he began it all again . . . and again.

At last, needing to give as much as she was getting, Carolyn copied Asa's patient inventiveness and found a new sort of excitement in leading him to a convulsive explosion that left him shuddering in her arms.

And afterward, when his breathing had quieted and he could again tell her how much he loved her, there was more conviction in his voice than Carolyn had ever heard before. As a result, her belief in his love strengthened, but so also did her bewildered grief over his inability to make a permanent commitment to her.

How could anyone love so much, she wondered bleakly, and yet plan to walk away from that love? And how was she going to stand it when Asa was no longer here to tell her he loved her with his words and his body, because he had disappeared from her life and thereby demonstrated that there was something he must love more?

CHAPTER NINETEEN

It seemed to Asa as though he'd just gotten to sleep when the sound of the telephone ringing brought him abruptly awake again.

"Hello?" he answered groggily as he rubbed his free hand over his eyes to try to clear his vision enough to decipher the glowing hands of the clock on the bedside table. It was still dark in the bedroom.

"My grandfather has consented to talk to you," Jimmy Li responded in a stiff voice. "I will pick you up in thirty minutes." Then he broke the connection and all Asa heard was the sound of the dial tone buzzing in his ear.

"Asa?"

Carolyn's voice sounded muffled, and he could tell she was only half awake, which didn't surprise him considering his behavior for the last two nights. He'd been making love to her with all the enthusiasm of a child who had only a short time to eat all the candy in the candy store.

He hung up the phone, leaned over to kiss her cheek lightly, and whispered, "Go back to sleep."

His eyes were adjusting to the dim light in the bedroom and he smiled as he watched her snuggle further under the covers and return to sleep with a faint smile on her lips.

Turning, he glanced at the clock, discovered it was 5:30 A.M., and got out of bed as gently as his leg would let him. He grabbed the clothes he'd discarded on the floor the night before and quietly let himself out of the bedroom.

Because the last two nights had tired him as much as they had Carolyn and he wanted to be especially alert for the coming interview with Li Chang, he took the time to start a pot of coffee before he pulled on his clothes.

Then he wrote Carolyn a quick note, explaining that he had something to do and that he might be away all day. He knew she wouldn't be pleased by the message, and was surprised to find that he wasn't as pleased as he'd expected to be himself that his gamble with Jimmy had paid off. He couldn't remember ever preferring to be with a woman rather than carry out an assignment, and he frowned slightly at the implications of his feelings.

Of course, this wasn't quite the same as the fieldwork he'd been used to, Asa tried to tell himself. There was no real element of danger connected to it, and though he knew his superiors expected to learn a great deal from Li Chang, Asa wasn't as confident that what the old man might agree to tell them would be of any great significance. He could be wrong, however, and he knew it.

He shrugged and limped over to the balcony to keep an eye out for Jimmy as he drank his coffee. As he stared out at the early-morning light, he was surprised again to find himself remembering all the sheer drudgery that had gone along with the fieldwork he had loved so much in the past. There had been so many hours of boredom he'd had to endure, simply waiting for something to happen . . . someone to come back in and report to him. The times when he'd been in any real danger were actually few and far between.

What the hell are you doing? he asked himself with a puzzled frown as he wondered why his thoughts were taking the direction they were. *Are you trying to make yourself feel better about having to take a desk job that will make even this assignment look exciting?*

He didn't have a chance to finish sorting things out, however, because Jimmy Li, driving a battered-looking yellow Honda Civic, had just pulled up to the curb in front of his apartment.

Asa drained the last of his coffee, set the cup down on the coffee table as he headed toward the front door, grabbed his cane, and let himself out of his apartment.

A few minutes later, he sat in the passenger seat beside Jimmy, who headed the Honda in the direction of Chinatown.

"Good morning, Jimmy," Asa said in a quiet way, calling attention to the fact that the young man hadn't said a word to him since picking him up.

Jimmy was driving with an intense concentration that made Asa think he wasn't used to driving an automobile, and even when Asa spoke to him, he didn't look away from the street in front of the car.

"I tried to talk my grandfather out of seeing you," Jimmy responded, his tone grudging and disgruntled.

"Why?" Asa said in a mild tone of muted curiosity, though he thought he knew the answer. Jimmy might tell himself he wanted to protect his grandfather from any danger, which was probably perfectly true. But Asa thought it likely that Jimmy was also still suffering from a bruised ego at having been used.

Jimmy did glance at Asa then, a scowling look on his face.

"My grandfather is dying," he said tightly. "He only came here to make peace with my father. It's not right to subject him to a third degree."

"And have they made peace?" Asa asked quietly.

Jimmy nodded and then glanced at Asa again with a small light of triumph in his eyes. "And because he has, he isn't worried about any threats the government here might make to deport him. He's a brave man," he said proudly. But then he frowned, and his voice was anxious as he added, "But the government he used to be a part of will regard him as a traitor if he does go back—that is, if they'll even let him back into China."

Jimmy shook his head, still looking unhappy. "I just don't want him bothered by anybody," he said, a trace of grimness in his voice.

Asa's mouth tilted in a faint smile. "Obviously, your grandfather doesn't mind being . . . bothered," he suggested.

Jimmy scowled again, but he didn't answer, and for the rest of the drive he stayed silent while Asa mulled over what he wanted to say to Li Chang.

Jimmy parked the car in front of a rundown apartment building, jerked the keys out of the ignition, climbed out of the car in a stiffly angry manner, and stood waiting for Asa to join him on the sidewalk.

Asa didn't hurry. He knew better than to give Jimmy the

impression that he was a supplicant rather than the possessor of a certain amount of power. Jimmy's contempt was easily aroused, but so was his respect for anyone older who had authority.

The hallway of the apartment building was as shabby as the exterior and there was a heavy odor of cooking lingering in the air. Asa thought Jimmy looked embarrassed as he led the way up a rickety stairway to the second floor, but his face was blankly impassive by the time he knocked twice on one of the upstairs doors and opened it without waiting for an invitation.

With a thoroughness born of long practice, Asa quickly inspected the small living room of the apartment and found it sparsely furnished but clean, before his eyes settled on a tiny, wizened man with a small, pointed white beard who sat at a cheap wooden table just outside the small kitchen area. There was a pot of tea on the table and the old man had his hands wrapped around a chipped white cup filled with the aromatic brew. His eyes, as alert as those of a much younger man and containing a slight sparkle of amusement, inspected Asa as thoroughly as Asa was inspecting him, but he said nothing. Asa limped across the linoleum floor to stand across the table from Li Chang.

Asa gave a bow of respect and uttered a traditional Chinese greeting in flawless Mandarin. As he did so, he noted simultaneously that Jimmy Li seemed to be startled by his fluent use of the language, and that the sparkle in Li Chang's eyes fairly danced for a moment as he nodded his head in response to the greeting and gestured with one of his tiny hands for Asa to be seated at the table.

When Asa had sat down, Li Chang smiled affectionately at his grandson and said in heavily accented English that held a tremor of age, yet didn't conceal the natural authority of a man who was used to being obeyed, "Please to go into the bedroom and leave us alone to talk, my grandson. We will call you when we are done."

To spare Jimmy's feelings, Asa didn't look at him to see his reaction, but he could almost feel Jimmy's resentment as the young man muttered something inaudible and walked away toward a door on the other side of the room. When it had closed behind him, Li Chang returned his attention to Asa, staring at him in a keenly interested way that failed to ruffle Asa's composure or provoke him into speaking first. This seemed to please the old man.

"You are CIA," Li Chang finally stated, speaking in Mandarin.

Though the old man paused as though waiting for Asa to affirm or deny his assertion, Asa did neither. He merely sat, politely waiting for Li Chang to go on. This, too, seemed to please Li, judging by the relaxed smile he finally gave Asa.

"What does it matter?" Li waved one of his tiny hands in dismissal. "I agreed to see you in order to pass on a message to your superiors. Will you have some tea?" he asked politely, changing subjects with skillful smoothness.

"Thank you," Asa replied in Mandarin, nodding at the teapot. He was feeling strangely relaxed. Li's personality was almost exactly as Asa had pictured it from the reports he'd studied about him. He was an unusual man indeed, almost Western in his willingness to get straight to the point rather than indulge in a formal ritual of obscure fencing before angling toward what he wanted to say.

His hand trembling slightly with age, Li poured the tea and handed the cup to Asa, who gave the half-nod, half-bow customary in China as he accepted it and brought it to his lips for a sip. Despite the chipped cup, the tea was excellent, as Asa had somehow suspected it would be. Li Chang might be living in a state of genteel poverty in this rundown apartment, but his standards hadn't slipped in other ways.

"You may tell your superiors that I will talk to them," Li Chang now said with the dignified authority of a man used to power, "but I have one condition."

"And that is?" Asa asked politely, keeping his expression blank.

The old black eyes were shrewd. "I realize that the American government will not be willing to let me go back to China to die, nor will my government allow my reentrance into the country of my birth while I am alive," he said, seemingly unconcerned by either obstacle in his path. "I accepted that when I came here to make peace with my son and his family."

Asa nodded. He thought he knew what Li Chang wanted now, and his mind was already calculating how likely he was to get it.

"I have served China all of my life," Li Chang said now, his eyes looking into the distance for a moment as though he were reliving all those years of service. "And though I necessarily became a member of the Party, and behaved as though it meant as much to me as to the rest of the members, I never really cared about ideology. I saw in Mao and the movement a chance to change things for the better in my country, and that was what I cared about. And I believe I was right to support Mao, in spite of the mistake of the Cultural Revolution."

Li Chang's wrinkled face crinkled into a grimace, as though he were remembering those chaotic years with distaste.

"How did you manage to survive during the Cultural Revolution?" Asa asked. He couldn't help it. His curiosity was riding him hard.

Li Chang shook his head. "The same way I always did." He shrugged. "I became used to living two lives as a young man— the outward life and the inner one. And I have always kept in mind one basic truth."

"And that is?" Asa inquired.

"Everything revolves in a cycle, and everything passes," Li Chang responded with a smile.

Asa nodded.

"The Cultural Revolution was inevitable," Li explained. "When you make the sort of changes we did in a civilization as old as China's, upheavals are to be expected. I was glad when that particular one was over, however." He grimaced again. "So much of it was senseless. Things are better now."

Again Asa merely nodded, waiting for Li Chang to get back to his condition for talking to the American government.

"It was necessary that I make peace and explain some things to my son," Li Chang now said, his black eyes on Asa's again. "He did not understand what I did. His mother . . ." Li Chang's eyes again took on that remote expression as though he were gazing into the past. "His mother was educated at a mission school and she hated and feared Communism. She did not understand what I was doing either. How could she? Knowing her beliefs, I couldn't take the risk of telling her."

Li Chang issued a sigh that seemed to shake his entire body, and paused to sip his tea. Asa sat quietly sipping his own, making it easy for the old man to talk by remaining silent.

"Our marriage was arranged," he went on, "and I was not in a position at the time to object without revealing to our families my ultimate goals. Though she was an excellent wife, a comely woman who gave me much pleasure, I knew the marriage was a mistake, and when it came time to join Mao openly, I gave her the choice of staying with me or leaving for America. As I expected, she chose America, and though it lost me the confidence of my comrades for a while, I helped her and our son leave."

Li Chang told his tale with deceptive simplicity, but Asa thought he detected a certain wistful pain in the old man's aged voice. His conclusion was strengthened at Li Chang's next words.

"I chose not to marry again," he said simply. "I devoted my energies to the struggle of freeing China's people from as much of the poverty and injustice they had suffered as I could."

Li Chang paused again and his black eyes inspected Asa.

"You wonder why I tell you all this?" he asked when he'd lowered the cup. He didn't give Asa time to answer, however. "I lived most of my adult life without being able to be myself," he said simply. "It is a relief to be able to speak candidly at last."

Asa could understand that and his nod and look were sympathetic.

"Ah, perhaps that is the reason I have run on so much to you," Li Chang said with a twinkling look in his eyes. "You, too, I think, have lived a life where you were not what you seemed to be."

Asa smiled faintly, but again he didn't admit to Li Chang the nature of his profession, though he was aware that he didn't really need to.

"I will not speak like this to the men you will send to question me," Li Chang added. "I will stick to the facts they will want to know."

His glance and voice sharpened as he added, "You will understand, and you will make those who come after you to understand, that I am not a traitor to my country. I will tell them things that can do China no harm, and I will keep to myself what might. They will think they can learn more than I wish to tell. Let them. They will not, and I think you are a man who understands this."

Asa didn't answer directly, though Li Chang was right concerning Asa's opinion.

"And your condition for talking at all?" he inquired.

Li Chang's smile was slyly complacent. "I think you have guessed. You are a man worthy of respect, and I could wish you would handle my questioning. But governments seldom do the sensible thing, and they will no doubt send me someone who does not speak my language and knows nothing of value about my country. But that will only make it easier for me and will be their loss." He shrugged without concern.

"Is it that you wish to be buried in China," Asa said without a questioning inflection in his tone, and was rewarded by a pleased chuckle from Li Chang.

"Did I not say you had guessed?" he said. And then his mood sobered and he nodded. "If I have that promise, I will talk. If not, tell them to do what they wish with me. I have not long enough left to live to let it worry me."

"I'll do the best I can," Asa assured the old man, who nodded wearily and seemed suddenly to lose interest in the discussion, reminding Asa that Li was in his seventies, and that though he seemed to have aged gracefully, his vigor was somewhat deceptive.

There was just one more thing Asa wanted to know before he left Li in peace.

"Did you go out to a restaurant recently to put us on your scent?" he asked, giving Li an admiring smile.

The elderly man's smile was the only answer he gave, but Asa was satisfied that it was Li who had instigated this meeting rather than Asa's request to Jimmy that had brought it about. Li wanted something, and in his pragmatic, good-humored way, he had set about getting it. Asa didn't think Jimmy understood that, however, and he regretted that the young man he'd considered a good candidate for the Company's recruitment would probably be too angry to be amenable to an approach.

Li Chang now seemed suddenly to wilt, and his voice, when he called out to Jimmy to let his grandson know the talk with Asa was over, was weak.

Jimmy came quickly into the room and Asa got to his feet, wincing a little as the blood raced back to his injured knee, bringing pain with it.

Li Chang saw Asa's expression and stared at him curiously for just an instant before turning his attention to Jimmy.

"You did well to bring this man to me," he said, indicating Asa with a slight gesture of his hand. "He is a man to be respected. You must not blame him because he used you to find me. I would have done the same in his position."

Jimmy greeted this statement with a form of confused, reluctant belligerence that made Asa give a mental shrug.

"Please wait outside," Li Chang now said to Asa in a rather querulous manner that Asa thought was due more to the old man's fatigue than to any desire to assert his authority.

Asa bowed his head in a gesture of respect, limped to the front door, and let himself out into the hall.

He heard the murmur of voices through the thin door without being able to distinguish the words, and then Jimmy joined him, now looking more confused than belligerent.

"He says you're going to send other men here to talk to him," he said to Asa somewhat accusingly.

Asa nodded. "He wants me to, Jimmy," he replied, though he didn't expect Jimmy to believe him or, if he did believe, to let Asa off the hook for instigating all this.

"That's what he said," Jimmy nodded, his forehead furrowed. "I just don't understand why."

"Because he wants to be buried in China, Jimmy," Asa said gently. "Didn't he tell you that?"

Jimmy looked surprised, and Asa shrugged, wondering if Li Chang hadn't said anything about what he wanted to Jimmy because it might hurt his grandson's feelings.

"He came here to make his peace with your father and the rest of your family," Asa said quietly, "but he's Chinese, Jimmy. He's spent his entire life in China, working to make things better there. It's home to him, as much as Hawaii is home to you."

Jimmy thought about it a minute, then gave a reluctant nod. "I guess I can understand that," he admitted. "But there's so much I wanted to ask him about. I haven't been able to talk to him as much as I wanted to because we were afraid one of your people would follow someone here and find him."

Some of Jimmy's belligerence was back, but Asa merely shrugged. There was nothing he could do to change the fact that a man like Li Chang was too important to a lot of people to belong solely to the family he'd been apart from for the last forty years.

"Let's go," Jimmy now said, sounding despondent, and he remained silent as they got in the car.

When Jimmy started heading toward his apartment, Asa quietly asked to be let off near a pay phone.

Jimmy gave him a sharp look, but he shrugged and pulled into the curb when he saw a pay phone near the street.

Asa stooped and looked in the window at Jimmy before Jimmy could drive away.

"I'm sorry you had to be involved in this, son," he said quietly. "Your grandfather understands why this had to be done. I hope you'll understand too one day."

Jimmy merely stared at him thoughtfully, and Asa raised a hand in farewell, then straightened and headed for the pay phone as Jimmy drove away.

When his contact answered, Asa's message was brief.

"I've spoken to Li Chang," he said without inflection. "He'll talk but he has a condition to be met first."

"What condition?" the contact demanded, and Asa could tell he was angry because Asa hadn't contacted him first before meeting with Li Chang.

"He wants to be buried in China," Asa said simply. "See if you can fix it. I'll be at my apartment when you've found out something."

He hung up in the middle of a question from the contact, hailed a taxi, and was back at his apartment by nine o'clock.

Asa stood by the bed, a faint smile on his lips and a look of tender appreciation in his eyes as he stared at Carolyn sleeping peacefully.

He started unbuttoning his shirt, and when he was naked, he lifted the sheet and slid in beside her, then gathered her in his arms to hold her close.

He wasn't aroused yet. It just felt good—peaceful—to hold Carolyn like this and savor the soft warmth of her body against his. She stirred a little, shifted slightly to accommodate her position comfortably with his, and without waking, settled down again.

He looked at her slightly parted lips, soft with sleep, the delicate blue veins in her eyelids, the sweep of her dark lashes against the smooth skin of her cheek, and couldn't resist placing his mouth where his eyes had rested . . . softly, with only a breath of pressure.

Then he rested his head against the tousled cloud of her hair and closed his eyes, content for the moment to hold her while she slept. He was tired himself.

Carolyn began to wake, however, and his eyes came open as she stirred again, stretching a little in his arms. Her breasts brushed against his chest as she pushed one of her knees up between his thighs, and Asa's manhood was suddenly stirring as though it had a life of its own.

He watched, fascinated, as her lids blinked open sleepily, once, twice, before she was fully awake and staring into his eyes with a warm welcome in hers and a drowsy smile on her lips which widened as she felt Asa's hardness against her knee.

"How long have you been awake?" she murmured.

He gave a slight shrug with one shoulder, making a mental note to dispose of the note he'd written her that was still on the kitchen table.

"Long enough to get impatient?" she teased, her voice husky with sleepiness. Then a yawn caught her, and Asa laughed softly as he bent to kiss the corner of her mouth.

"Sorry," she mumbled when the yawn was over.

"Why?" Asa whispered, rising up on his elbow and turning her on her back. "You don't have a thing to be sorry about."

"Not even keeping you waiting?" Carolyn whispered back, her drowsy eyes laughing at him as she inspected his face with pleasure. She could feel his full arousal against her thigh and her blood was heating up in response to it.

"I think I stay this way even in my sleep," Asa teased, bending to kiss her forehead, her eyes, her cheeks.

Before he arrived at her mouth, Carolyn spoke again. "Sometimes you do, but not all the time," she said.

Asa raised his head and looked at her, one eyebrow arched in an expression of inquiry.

"Sometimes I wake up in the night and look at you," Carolyn confessed, her smile informing him that she wasn't making an apology for spying on him in his sleep.

"That's not fair." He grinned.

"Why not?" Carolyn's eyes roved his face, and her question was posed in an absent tone.

"Because you can tell what I'm dreaming about," Asa mocked teasingly, "but I can't do the same where you're concerned."

Carolyn's answering smile was sweetly feminine. "Then, you'll just have to take my word for it that I dream about you a lot," she teased back as she ran her hands over his shoulders and locked them behind his neck.

"Describe one of your dreams about me and then maybe I'll believe you," Asa responded, his voice deepening sexily.

"That would embarrass me." Carolyn shook her head.

"Then show me one of them," Asa persisted, shifting his body over hers and pressing himself between her thighs. His eyes darkened with satisfaction as his action brought a small gasp of pleasure from Carolyn.

"All of it?" she asked, sounding slightly breathless now.

"All of it," Asa responded in a deep soft command.

Carolyn studied the dark heat in his eyes and the growing sexual tension in his face, and as her response to Asa's masculinity sang through her veins, she nodded, her gaze taking on a drugged look of compliance.

"It will be my pleasure, Mr. Bradley," she whispered, and then her hands pulled his head down and her mouth slanted across his. Asa shuddered slightly as her tongue slipped wetly between his lips, but when he would have taken over the aggressive role as a matter of instinct, Carolyn resisted, pushing him off her and over onto his back.

"This is *my* dream, Asa," she reminded him quietly, and something in her voice and eyes made a shaft of pure animal sensuality stab through his loins.

He made himself relax and lie back as Carolyn came up on her knees and made a place for herself between his legs.

"So it is," he said, his voice roughening into a ragged demand. "But if you take too long to finish your demonstration, I may not last the course."

"Won't you?" she said on a soft laugh that bubbled up from her throat in a way that entranced him. "But maybe that is part of my dream, Asa, darling. Did you ever think of that?"

Asa swallowed and closed his eyes, hanging on to his control with everything he had.

"How do you expect me to think at all at a time like this, woman?" he said in a voice that had grown almost savage with the need that consumed him.

And with a smile of commiseration for his aroused state, Carolyn bent and kissed his arousal for the first time. He jerked in exquisite response to a touch that was soft as a breath but totally devastating.

Carolyn lost control of the waking dream then, as Asa's hands cupped her head and he guided her in an exploration that fascinated her as much as it drove him faster and faster toward a shattering climax.

By the time he lifted her in a mighty display of strength and drove himself into her as she settled onto his thighs, Carolyn was shaken by the power she had unleashed in Asa. But it wasn't long before her body had surrendered totally to the pleasure of his driving thrusts and she was going over the edge of the delicious precipice he'd made her scale and crashing to the other side on a wave of sensation so intense, she would later be incredulous that the experience had really happened.

A long time afterward, when she had her breath back and couldn't remain silent any longer about what she'd felt, she whispered her doubt that it could ever happen that way again against the warmth of Asa's neck.

She felt his chest move in a silent wave of laughter and without saying a word, he showed her, step by delicious step, not only that it could happen again, but that there were infinite variations to making it happen.

Had it not been for someone pounding on the door to Asa's apartment some time later, Carolyn would have been content to add unendingly to the wealth of experience she was gaining at Asa's instigation. Carolyn was not at all pleased by the interruption in her lessons, and she was aware on a deep level that something had happened between them she was certain Asa hadn't counted on. They were now entwined in a need for one another so strong, she doubted he could really leave her the way he'd planned to . . . or if he could, that anyone else would ever free him of the desire to have again what they'd shared together just now.

CHAPTER TWENTY

When Asa, wearing only a terry-cloth robe, opened the door to his apartment, he found his contact standing there, his cheeks flushed with anger, his flat gray eyes as cold as a dawn on the north Atlantic in winter.

Reading that expression correctly, Asa spoke before the other man could.

"I've got someone with me here. She's in the bedroom. Keep your voice down."

The contact clenched his jaw but said nothing until they were in the kitchen and Asa was pouring his uninvited guest a cup of coffee.

"What the hell's going on with you?" the contact demanded in a snarling rasp he kept barely audible. "You were supposed to let me know the minute anything broke on this case."

Asa handed him his cup of coffee and the contact took it, then stared at it as though wondering what to do with it.

As Asa poured himself a cup of the brew that was now an oily black after having been left to heat for several hours, he was asking himself the same question. Where was the professionalism he'd prided himself on for so many years? Didn't he give a damn whether Li Chang talked to his superiors or not? Maybe it was just that he was certain Li Chang wouldn't tell them much of significance, he thought. Or maybe he was more burned out than he'd even begun to suspect, he added wryly.

"The grandson called me at five thirty this morning," he said in a calm voice as he leaned back against the kitchen counter. He paused and sipped his coffee, aware that the contact was shifting on his feet in an impatient way but ignoring it as he grimaced at the taste of the coffee more out of habit than because he was really aware of how foul it was.

"He gave me thirty minutes to get ready." Asa shrugged. "I decided to wait and see what was up instead of calling you."

The contact puffed up angrily again. "Your orders were to . . ."

But Asa lifted a hand in an impatient gesture and interrupted, alerted as much by the sharp tone of his own voice as by his feelings that his nerves weren't under his usual control.

"Do you want to hear what happened, or do you want to stand there and tell me I screwed up the job!"

The contact subsided abruptly, but his fuming gaze told Asa he wouldn't waste any time reporting on Asa's conduct to their superiors.

"The old man wants to talk to us," Asa went on in a more level tone, "but only if we can fix it where he can be shipped back to China for burial when he's dead."

"Is that likely to be soon?" the contact responded sarcastically.

Asa shrugged and studied the oily brew in his coffee cup. "I don't know. I don't know what's wrong with him."

"Then do you mind telling me where we can pick him up so we can fill in the little details like that you neglected to find out?"

The sneering sarcasm in the other man's voice brought Asa's head up, and the look in his eyes brought a quick transformation in his contact's attitude.

"Okay, okay," the man said in a much more reasonable tone as he gazed with wary caution at Asa and tensed his body as though he were preparing to receive a blow. "I'm a little peeved, that's all."

Asa didn't move and said nothing, and after a moment, the other man relaxed somewhat.

"So where can we pick him up?" he asked.

"You don't until you can promise him what he wants," Asa responded in a tone that was much too quiet for the other man's peace of mind.

The contact opened his mouth as though to argue, then

closed it again, but the expression in his eyes told Asa his temper was fuming.

"Have you ever worked in the field before?" Asa asked, his voice hardening.

The other man shook his head, and it was obvious to Asa that like a lot of other desk men, this one considered field men a breed apart, not to be trusted entirely except when out in the savagery of the front line of intelligence gathering where they belonged because they were half savage themselves.

Asa's smile was humorless. "You keep your word out in the field," he said softly, "because if you don't, you don't keep your agents—or you get a knife in the back some day when you aren't paying attention."

Or a bullet in the knee, he added to himself with silent fury that he had let it happen to him.

"I told Li I'd do what I could to get him what he wants, and I plan to follow through," he went on, his voice harsh, his gaze implacable. "And I told you to see what you could do about it. But if you can't handle it, I'll do it myself."

The contact's face flushed, and for a moment the expression in his gray eyes looked murderous. But Asa had taken the mettle of the man, and he knew he had nothing to fear from him other than some inevitable political backstabbing, and Asa couldn't care less about that.

He straightened, indicating by the gesture that the interview was at an end.

"I'll be in touch," the contact said, making it obvious with his tone that he was looking forward to passing on to their superiors what he considered abnormal behavior, even for a field man.

"I'm sure you will," Asa said dryly, and watched as the man pivoted on his heel and stomped across the living room to the door, which he slammed behind him with relish.

Asa shook his head in a mild gesture of amusement. He knew what he'd done hadn't been necessary and that he would no doubt have to pay for it by enduring a lecture from one of his superiors, if he got off that cheaply. But somehow, he just couldn't care. There wasn't much he could think of that he did care about for the time being . . . except Carrie.

Stifling a tired sigh, he returned to the bedroom to find it empty. Carolyn was in the bathroom taking a shower.

Asa threw himself on the bed, intending to wait for Carrie and spend the rest of the day exactly as he'd spent the morning after returning home from his visit to Li Chang: numbing his mind by pleasing his body. But he was asleep long before Carolyn returned to the bedroom, and was unaware that she stared at him for a long time before she gently covered him with a sheet and kissed his forehead, then dressed and left for her own apartment, intending to be back before he woke again.

For the second time that morning, the ringing of the telephone brought Asa out of a deep sleep, but when he'd fumbled the receiver off its hook and growled a groggy hello, he found his old boss, Don Hubbard, on the other end of the line.

"You've got yourself in a peck of trouble," Hubbard said in a mild tone that told Asa Hubbard himself didn't hold what he'd done against him. But Hubbard was a former field man, which explained his tolerance.

"Yeah, that's what I figured," Asa said heavily as he rubbed at his eyes with the fingers of one hand. "What's the scoop?"

"They want you back here immediately to let the doctors give you a physical and psychological evaluation," Hubbard drawled. "Ain't that a bitch?"

"Hell," Asa sighed with resignation. It was no more than he'd expected, but he didn't like it. "What about Li?" he asked.

"It's been fixed," Hubbard informed him. "He'll rest in peace in China if we have to blow his ashes across the border with a wind machine, though we hope it won't come to that. So tell your friendly local representative where Li is, then catch the first plane you can get to D.C."

Asa gave a mirthless snort of amusement. "They aren't wasting any time, are they?" he drawled. "What are they afraid of, that I'm so messed up I'm about to defect?"

"Nah, they're talkin' burnout," Hubbard said. "Are they right?"

Asa hesitated, then shrugged, though he was aware Hubbard couldn't see him. "Hell, I don't know," he finally said. "Maybe

I am. I never wanted to get close enough to a desk to spit on it, much less sit at it."

"I know the feeling," Hubbard responded. "But you get used to it, Asa. You can get used to anything when you don't have a choice."

"And I don't?" Asa asked thoughtfully.

Hubbard was silent for a moment. "Well, you know what the doctors said," he then replied in a carefully casual tone, "but they can be wrong, I guess."

Asa heard the real answer in Hubbard's tone, however. Fieldwork was out for Asa Bradley as far as the Agency was concerned.

"I'll tell my friendly buddy here where he can find Li Chang." He changed the subject, speaking with dry sarcasm, "but not until I've assured Li Chang myself that he's getting what he wants. I don't think our local representative has the type of personality to inspire confidence in anyone as sharp as Li. Who's going to do the actual questioning anyway, do you know?"

"If I did, I couldn't tell you, Asa," Hubbard said quietly with a slight chiding note in his voice. "You know the rules."

"Yeah, I know the rules," Asa responded somewhat bitterly, "but you might pass it on that if they send some fool who can't speak Li's language and doesn't know a damned thing about China, they're going to get exactly what they deserve. He'll make mincemeat out of them."

"Probably," Hubbard agreed, "but that's not your concern, is it, Asa."

It wasn't a question and Asa closed his eyes and tried to overcome the frustration he felt.

"I'll see you tomorrow," Hubbard said quietly, but with a tone of authority Asa recognized as implacable. "Don't worry about the apartment. Just pack your bags and walk out. It'll be taken care of."

"Sure," Asa replied with no inflection at all in his voice.

When he'd hung up, Asa lay where he was for a moment getting control of his anger. When he thought he had, he sat up, reached for the telephone and dialed an airline. After making a reservation for five o'clock that afternoon, he got up and showered, planning how to break the news to Carolyn. He was almost grateful that there wouldn't be time to make a long job of it . . . not even time for second thoughts.

Carolyn returned to the apartment just as Asa had finished dressing, and she knew the moment she saw his face that something was very wrong.

She looked at him, her eyes huge and frightened and filled with questions, and Asa stared back at her without saying a word.

"Are you leaving me?" she got out, her voice sounding strangled to her own ears.

"This afternoon," Asa answered quietly, and took a deep breath when he saw Carolyn's face whiten while her body flinched against the news. He took her in his arms and she clung to him with a desperate strength that made him feel more wretched than he'd ever felt in his life before, even when they'd told him his leg wasn't going to heal.

"I'm sorry," he whispered against her hair, "but there's nothing I can do about it, Carrie—nothing at all."

But was that really true? Asa found himself wondering with bitter self-disgust. If he could give up his hopeless fantasy that he would one day be allowed to do fieldwork again, what was to stop him from marrying Carrie Winters other than his own stubborn belief that he wasn't supposed to have a wife and a family like normal people?

Carolyn was desperately trying to recover from the shock of learning that she was going to lose Asa so soon. She felt numb and panicked in turn, until she was afraid she was losing her mind.

"Asa . . . please . . ." She heard herself start to beg him to stay, and she quickly bit off the words rather than humiliate herself that way. "No—" She pulled back in his arms and shook her head, unaware that her eyes were wild with the emotion consuming her. "I'm sorry—don't listen to me—it's just such a shock."

She became aware she was beginning to babble, and she clenched her teeth together to keep from saying anything else.

Asa's dark gaze was soft with concern for her, and Carolyn

swallowed and avoided his eyes until she thought she could speak with a modicum of reasonableness.

"Shall I drive you to the airport?" she asked, her voice shaking with her effort to control herself, then she immediately shook her head again. "No . . . I can't do it." She took back the offer. "I can't stand there and watch you get on a plane . . ."

Then she was sobbing in Asa's arms, and he held her tightly, feeling helpless and angrily frustrated, and ripped to shreds inside with self-disgust over what he had done to Carolyn when she was the last person in the world he'd wanted to hurt.

When she'd cried herself into a state of numb exhaustion, Carolyn lay slackly against his body, gathering her strength to get through the good-byes that had to be said.

"I love you, Carrie," Asa whispered softly against her hair, and that brought her head up.

She stared at him with surprised indignation.

"How can you say that?" she demanded in a tone of incredulity. "How can you *possibly* say that?"

Asa looked at her, and recognizing that anger was perhaps the best emotion she could feel for the moment, didn't attempt to argue with her.

Carolyn's whole body was trembling with rage, and her eyes were wide and accusing. Then it was suddenly all draining away from her as she realized what she was doing.

She lowered her head and raised a hand to her forehead, rubbing her fingers hard against her skin as though to rub some sense into her brain. When she looked at Asa again, her eyes were empty.

"I'm sorry," she said tonelessly. "I'll go now, Asa, and leave you to pack."

"Carrie . . ." Asa lifted a hand, wanting to stop her, then he dropped it, but he continued to look into her eyes. Then, very deliberately, he said again, "I love you, Carrie. I always will."

Carolyn felt her mouth move into a faint smile, though the reaction was automatic more than anything else.

"I love you, too, Asa," she said in that quiet, toneless voice that cut through Asa like a knife. "Take care of yourself . . . please."

She turned around then, knowing she had to move fast if she was going to move at all, and forced her legs to take her to the door, her hand to open it. She hesitated, wanting to take one last look at the man she loved, then rejected the wish. If she looked at Asa again, she wouldn't be able to leave.

And as the door closed behind her, she realized she was grateful that Asa had made it easier for her by not saying good-bye. That was one word she couldn't have stood to hear right then . . . a word she hated with a passion she doubted would ever abate.

Asa stood for a long time staring at the closed door that had shut him away from Carrie before he began to grate a long string of self-condemnatory curses between his clenched teeth.

He was silent and grim, however, as he threw his clothes into a single suitcase and did what was necessary to get ready to leave the island of Oahu for the last time. When he was ready, he picked up the phone and called his contact.

Without speaking an unnecessary word, and without bothering to show the contempt he felt for the man, he gave Li Chang's address and asked to be met there.

"I'll need someone to drive to the airport with me and take the car I've been using," he said in a flat, level tone. "See to it."

When he'd hung up, he picked up his suitcase and reached for his cane, and he didn't look back as he headed for a future that couldn't be anything but cold and empty, unless by some miracle of medicine, his leg healed—or by some miracle of common sense he came back to find the woman who could make him stop caring that he was an ex–field man now, and as such, entitled to the sort of normal life the people he'd sworn to serve took as a matter of course.

CHAPTER TWENTY-ONE

Asa sat in a noisy Washington, D.C., bar across from Don Hubbard and lifted his glass of whiskey to his mouth, draining it as though it were water. When he set the empty glass down, he signaled the waiter for another, then sat staring with empty eyes through the window at the April thunderstorm pelting the sidewalk outside.

Watching him with a practiced eye, Hubbard shook his head. "You wantin' to get fired, Asa?" he drawled, and when Asa didn't so much as blink, he confirmed Hubbard's suspicion that Asa Bradley didn't give a damn anymore. But he was too good an agent to lose, so Hubbard set out to keep him.

"You're goin' about it in the right way, if that's what you got in mind," Hubbard said.

Asa glanced at him, his expression blank, but Hubbard knew he was listening, even if he didn't appear to care for the content of the conversation.

"You sweat about your old network too much—even though everybody and his brother has told you they haven't been blown and they're doin' just fine without you—" Hubbard was speaking with deliberate brutality. He wasn't here to soothe Asa Bradley's wounds, he was here to shock him into taking charge of his life again—"and you sure as hell ain't doin' a job worth the bucks the U.S. of A. is payin' you, are you, old buddy?"

Asa clenched his jaw, but Hubbard didn't flinch from his cold look.

"Well, hell, every man is entitled to wallow in a little self-pity at one time or another in his life," Hubbard went on, and now his expression was as cold as Asa's, "but I'm here to tell you it's gettin' old, buddy—mighty old."

The waiter appeared and set another whiskey down in front of Asa, who drained it and signaled for another before the waiter had had time to step away from the table.

Hubbard abruptly lost his patience, and his expression and voice were hard enough to convince any man as experienced as Asa that his career was on the line.

"You ain't gonna be a field man anymore, Asa," he bit out in a low, rasping voice. "It ain't gonna happen, so you can put away those fantasies you been havin' about your leg healing up and everything turning up roses. Put 'em away and do it quick, because you got one last chance to save yourself, boy, and I'm about to tell you what it is, so listen up!"

Asa took in a deep breath, intending to express the savage anger that rode him as a result of Don Hubbard's brutal declaration by telling his boss and old-time friend to take a flying leap straight into hell, but some last spark of common sense stopped him.

At last it got through to Asa that Hubbard had to be worried indeed if he was resorting to a style of manipulation that was foreign to his normal practice.

Slowly Asa relaxed, letting the denial and tension that had gripped him a moment earlier go.

"All right, Don," he said wearily. "I get the message."

"Do you?" Hubbard demanded. "You want me to believe you're gonna accept the truth at last and give up thinkin' you're ever goin' back to the field?"

Asa stared at nothing for a moment, letting the truth Don Hubbard wanted him to accept find a niche inside him he could live with. Then he turned to face Hubbard, his eyes steady and calm, and nodded.

Hubbard leaned back in his chair and gave a sigh of relief. "You had me worried there for a while, boy," he admitted.

Asa had to smile at the way Hubbard called him "boy" and "son" when he wasn't more than ten years older than him. But he understood. Hubbard had the old network runner's sense of responsibility toward anyone he supervised.

"You know that's the first time you've smiled since you got back from Hawaii?" Hubbard snorted.

Asa shrugged. "I guess it is," he agreed quietly. Then he

studied Don Hubbard's face with a faint gleam of interest in his eyes. "What's this job you're talking about?"

And Hubbard grinned with a relief that brought an answering glimmer of a smile from Asa.

"I thought you'd never ask!" Hubbard exclaimed with good-natured mockery, and he looked up and signaled to the waiter for another bourbon and soda before he got down to business. "You know that jerk in Hawaii who got your ass in a sling a while back?" he asked Asa, and at Asa's grim nod, Hubbard smiled a smile that was as amiable as a cobra's. "Well, he's done wore out his welcome in paradise, son, and we're gonna need a replacement for him right quick. You know anybody that hates desk work and winter and can stand another stint of duty in the tropics—and speaks good enough Chinese to take over questionin' an old man who's had it up to here with everybody else we've sent to talk to him?"

Asa stared at Hubbard sitting there with a smug expression on his homely, likable face and felt a surge of happiness. He cleared his throat. "It may be that I do know someone like that," he said in a voice he didn't recognize as his own.

"Well, glory be, ain't that just fine, now," Hubbard said, smiling a complacent smile that made Asa grin for the first time in months. "You just tell whoever it is that fits that description to start packing his suitcase and preparing to leave for paradise as quick as can be, you hear? Otherwise, some other lucky stiff—like me, for instance—might get in ahead of him and snatch this prize assignment right out from under his nose."

Asa tilted his head back and laughed, surprised to find that he still knew how.

Hubbard just sat there smiling, until suddenly an indignant look came over his face and he stretched his neck around looking for their waiter.

"How the hell does a man get a drink in here when he has something to celebrate?" he demanded testily.

Asa held up his hand, snapped his fingers and brought a waiter running toward their table. Don Hubbard glared at Asa's success, and it was Asa's turn to smile complacently.

"The secret is to bribe 'em, Ron," he said in an approximation of Hubbard's southern drawl. "Works every time, but a man as cheap as you wouldn't know that."

"You're darned tootin' I wouldn't!" Hubbard gave a curt nod of his head. "And if you had four kids to get through college on a civil servant's salary, you'd know it, too."

"Give me time, son, give me time," Asa said with a wink before the two of them roared with laughter and had everyone in the place staring at them like they'd gone completely out of their minds.

Carolyn let herself into her apartment and tossed her books down on the nearest chair before hurrying to her bathroom to turn on the shower while she hastily got out of her jeans and shirt.

It wasn't so much that she was looking forward to spending time with her American History professor, though he was a nice enough man, as the fact that she was too innately polite to keep him waiting. And she did expect to enjoy the Bishop Museum arts and crafts festival he was taking her to see.

She was working hard on her studies these days, and in her free time she was developing a talent for concentrating on the many distractions Hawaii had in abundance to take her mind off . . . other things. And she was actually beginning to think she was eventually going to become reconciled to a life without husband and children if no one ever came along who could compete with her memories of Asa Bradley.

Carolyn was putting the final touches to her makeup when her date knocked at the door and she gave herself one last quick inspection in the mirror before hurrying to let Bob Wilson in.

Her smile was in place as she swung the door open, and she was saying, "Hello, Bob," before she noticed it wasn't Bob Wilson standing on her doorstep looking at her with an intensity that made her breath catch in her throat and her face whiten with shock.

"Asa—" She said his name as though he'd been dead and had suddenly come back to life, which was what it felt like to her at seeing him again so unexpectedly.

"Who's Bob?" were his first words to her, spoken in a possessive tone that only increased her confusion.

"What?" She knew she sounded stupid, but she was so off base, she couldn't help it. Her mind kept telling her over and over again that what she was seeing couldn't be real.

"I said . . ." Asa started to repeat his question and then thought, To hell with it. "Never mind," he said as he caught Carolyn's arms in his hands and pulled her close to his body with a force that stunned her. "Whoever he is, he's going to be disappointed when he finds out you belong to me."

Then his mouth was on hers and Carolyn felt the familiar shock of contact that told her she wasn't mistaken after all. There was only one man whose kiss affected her like this, and if it wasn't Asa Bradley devouring her mouth as though he was starved for the taste of her, she wasn't Carolyn Winters.

There had never been a transformation to equal hers in the history of the world. She was certain of it. Every sense that Asa had drawn into sharp, vibrant life six months before and that had been steadily atrophying since he'd left her, suddenly blossomed with an incredible vigor.

"God, Carrie . . . hold me . . . yes . . . yes . . . yes . . ." Asa's deep, ragged voice echoed inside her, synchronized to the beat of her heart. And then he was kissing her again, his tongue an exquisite instrument eliciting complete response from her, his hands moving restlessly on her body owning her senses more surely than she did herself. There wasn't a thing in the world she wanted more than to take Asa inside of her so that she could feel him as he was meant to be felt.

"Let me love you," Asa whispered, his voice as potent an intoxicant for Carolyn as the rest of him. "Oh, Carrie, let me show you how much I've missed you . . . come on . . . come with me." And whatever else he might have said as he was drawing her toward the bedroom was lost to the sound of knocking on her front door.

Both of them went still, Asa with the tenseness of a predator, which startled Carolyn out of her state of bemused sensuality more than the knock on her door had.

"Is it the Bob you were expecting?" he said harshly. "Don't answer it—maybe he'll go away."

Carolyn blinked at him, then shook her head as though she were coming out of shock.

"I can't do that," she said in a hoarse whisper. And as she was clearing her throat, Asa answered impatiently.

"Of course, you can! Who the hell is he, anyway?"

Carolyn stared at him, trying to clear her head so that she could think. The knock came again, and she instinctively turned her head to look at the door.

Asa uttered a curse that made her jump!

"Asa!" she exclaimed, quickly turning back to him.

"Oh, hell!" he exclaimed, letting go of her arm at last. "Open the door and send him away. I've dreamed of making love to you every night for six months, and I'll be damned if I'll be put off by some—"

He couldn't seem to think of the word he wanted, but Carolyn didn't notice. Her mind had stuck on the irony of his statement that he'd been wanting to make love to her every night for six long months! While she had been lying in her bed crying her eyes out every night for three of them because he had walked away from her as easily as he might have any other woman!

A senseless, mindless fury suddenly filled her entire body and it was all she could do to keep from hitting him across the face with every bit of her strength.

Asa saw the look in her eyes and his pupils widened with a wary kind of shock.

"Carrie?"

Before she could open her mouth and scream her anger and her righteous indignation and her hurt at him, the knock on the front door came again, and she pivoted to stride toward the door, glaring at the rigid panels with a fury that matched what she was feeling toward Asa.

When she swung the door open, Bob Wilson took one look at her face, his smile died a sudden death, and he automatically stepped back a pace.

"I can't go to the festival with you, Bob!" Carolyn practically snarled at him, unable even to feel guilty about the fact that he hadn't done a thing to deserve such treatment from her. "Call me tomorrow. I'll be in a better mood by then . . . I hope!" And she stepped back and slammed the door in his face before pivoting to face Asa again.

Asa stood his ground, prepared to bear the brunt of the storm as patiently as possible. He'd used the few seconds Carolyn had been getting rid of Bob, whoever he was, to figure out what had happened to her. And when he had, he couldn't honestly blame her for being furious with him. She couldn't know that this time, he would neither be sending her away nor going himself.

"How dare you!" She spat the words at him as she paced menacingly toward him, her hands clenched into fists, her expression livid. "How *dare* you come waltzing back into my life expecting me to go through it all again!"

"I don't ex—"

"Don't speak to me!" she yelled. "Don't say one word to me!"

Asa took a breath, spread his hands, and began to step back a pace for every one Carolyn took forward, thinking life with Carrie was certainly going to be interesting. Funny, he'd never suspected she had a temper to match Attila the Hun's under all that cool blond beauty. Hadn't he thought at one time that she was too dignified to have any feelings as passionate as she had displayed in bed the last time they'd been together and such as she was showing now?

Asa couldn't help smiling as it dawned on him that Carolyn's love for him was in direct proportion to the fury raging through her, but he quickly erased the smile when he saw that it only enraged her further.

"That's right!" she snarled. "Smile, Asa! Why not? What does it matter that you've broken my heart twice and were intending to do it a third time? I'm just the sort of stupid female to put up with it, aren't I? I was falling right into your arms again, wasn't I? Oh, damn you, Asa, how can you smile like that when you've hurt me so much I wanted to die?"

It was the first time in her life Carolyn had ever lost control of herself so completely or used language that normally would have appalled her, and she abruptly covered her face with her hands and burst into tears of pain and humiliation and frustration, sobbing with an abandon that was as complete as her anger had been seconds earlier.

Asa couldn't stand it. He took three quick steps forward and wrapped her in his arms, ignoring her inadequate twistings and the pounding of her fists as she attempted to make him let her go.

She realized she was sobbing the words over and over again, "Let me go! Let me go! Let me go!" only when Asa turned her face into his shoulder and forced her to stop.

"Never!" he said with a fierceness that was quietly spoken, but no less forceful for the lack of volume. "Never again, Carrie. Believe me, I'm not going away from you again, and neither are you going to leave me!"

Carolyn heard the words, but she didn't really believe them, despite the fact that Asa sounded so sincere it was a temptation to. But he'd sounded sincere every time he'd told her he loved her, too, most especially so just before he'd walked out of her life each time.

She was crying so hard that Asa didn't attempt again to convince her that he was here to stay this time. He merely held her, and stroked her and murmured the sort of soothing sounds he hadn't even known he knew how to utter, until she was too exhausted to cry anymore and hung limply in his arms.

Then he wiped her closed eyes and damp face with his handkerchief and kissed her mouth with a tenderness that brought her eyes open in a wary stare.

"Don't look at me like that," he whispered with a smile that only increased her wariness, it was so temptingly honest. "I don't deserve it anymore."

Carolyn would have liked to move away from the warmth and temptation of Asa's body, but she had an idea he wouldn't allow it, so she settled for giving him a cold look as she asked, "What are you doing here, Asa, and how long do I get the pleasure of your company this time?" She pronounced "pleasure" as though it were a dirty word.

Her sarcasm failed to change the warm way he was looking at her, and she began to get very nervous about his intentions.

"I'm here to talk you into marrying me and having my children," Asa said simply, "and I expect to be around a long time if you accept."

Carolyn moved her head slightly to the side, eyeing him from the corner of her eye with all the trust she might have shown a convicted criminal.

"You don't believe me." Asa nodded, interpreting her look in the only way any sane man could. "Well, that's regrettable, but I imagine you'll change your mind when I take you to get the license."

"What license?" The question came grudgingly. Carolyn didn't trust the belief steadily growing in her heart and mind despite everything she could do to stifle it.

"The marriage license," Asa responded patiently, though his hands on Carolyn's waist displayed a restlessness that conflicted with the patience in his voice.

Carolyn thought about that for a moment, then said with a calmness she distinctly didn't feel, "I don't even know what you do for a living besides lecture on China when you feel like it."

Her distrust escalated when her statement caused Asa to look away momentarily. Then he shrugged and when his gaze returned to hers, it was steady and relaxed.

"I work for the CIA, Carrie," he said as offhandedly as he might have announced that he was a plumber.

Carolyn closed her eyes and shook her head with sad disbelief. "Sure you do," she said dryly, and when she opened her eyes again, they were beginning to blaze with renewed anger.

Asa looked at her thoughtfully. All the time he'd been trying to hide his occupation from her, it had never once occurred to him that she wouldn't believe him if he made an outright confession. It was amazing!

He raised one of his hands, slipped it into his inside coat pocket, and produced his wallet, which contained his identification. Flipping it open, he held it under her nose.

Carolyn gave him a suspicious look before glancing at the open wallet. Then she blinked. She blinked again. And her expression when she raised her eyes to his at last was absolutely stunned!

"I couldn't tell you before," he said apologetically. "But now that we're going to be married—"

"Is that why you sent me away . . . why you had to leave yourself?" Carolyn interrupted, her eyes as wide as a child's on Christmas morning.

Asa nodded. "I didn't think I could offer you anything as

long as there was a chance I could return to the field. But I've accepted now that the leg isn't going to heal enough to . . ."

Belatedly, Asa realized that his explanation wasn't the most flattering way to put things, and the look in his eyes became somewhat chagrined, though Carolyn didn't seem to be taking offense.

"Go on," she urged him. "I want to hear this."

"Oh, hell, Carrie, I couldn't have forgotten you even if I could have gone back to the field. It would never have been the same, though I tried to convince myself it would be." His expression turned rueful. "In fact, I never thought I'd be grateful for this damned leg wound, but I've got to admit—"

He stopped speaking as Carolyn's face whitened.

"How did you really hurt your leg?" she asked in a horrified whisper.

Asa sighed, wishing they could get past this discussion and just make love. "I was shot." He admitted the truth, however, figuring he might as well get it over with now.

"Asa—"

Strangely, Carolyn's long, drawn-out pronunciation of his name in a pained whisper that showed the depth of her empathy, comforted Asa rather than made him uncomfortable.

"Don't worry about it," he said, pulling her closer. "It may keep me out of the field, but I've showed you it doesn't hinder me in bed, haven't I?"

Carolyn slid her hands up his broad chest to cup his face, her eyes swimming with tears of love for him.

"Show me again," she whispered as she came up on tiptoe to press her mouth against his in a slow, exquisite demonstration of how much she wanted him.

Asa responded wholeheartedly for a moment, then drew back to search her eyes. "First tell me about Bob," he said quietly.

Carolyn smiled and shook her head. "He's my American History professor," she said soothingly.

"And he tutors you at home?" Asa's expression was doubtful.

"No. I've been out with him a couple of times," Carolyn admitted, her heart glowing with satisfaction when Asa greeted her statement with a stiff look of jealousy. "But only casually," she assured him. "I haven't made love with anyone since you left, Asa. I haven't wanted to make love with anyone else."

"Neither have I," Asa confessed softly as he began to relax. "And I'm very impatient to make up for lost time."

Before Carolyn could tell him how much his confession meant to her, Asa swept her tightly against him and slanted his mouth over hers, and she had to show him instead, which wasn't, by any means, a hardship for her, either during the kiss or during the almost frantic physical reunion that followed it. She was as starved for Asa's love as he was for hers, and neither of them was capable of wasting time with preliminaries.

Afterward, as they held one another tightly, Carolyn had a thought that brought her eyes open, and when Asa saw the serious expression in them, he asked, "What is it? What are you thinking about?"

"I need to know how you feel about starting a family right away, Asa," she answered, a hint of anxiety in her tone.

"Why?" he countered with a smile. "What's the hurry?"

"I'm not young enough to wait," Carolyn explained soberly. "So I'd like to have babies right away, if that's all right with you."

Asa made a show of inspecting her smooth, youthful face for age lines in order to give himself time to think. He wanted to please Carolyn—give her anything she wanted—but he also wanted her to himself for a while.

"Stop that!" Carolyn demanded. "I'm not old enough to have wrinkles."

"You seem to be betwixt and between," Asa suggested teasingly.

"No." Carolyn shook her head. "I'm bewitched and bothered again and wondering how soon you're going to do something about it. But first," she added with mock sternness as Asa, with a wicked smile on his lips, started to move his hands on her body in an intimate fashion, "I need to know how you feel about children so we can either get started or . . ."

"Carrie," Asa interrupted her, his eyes dancing with loving humor, "one thing at a time. Let's concentrate on us right now and talk about babies later."

"But—"

She got no further as Asa's mouth covered hers, and, predictably, it wasn't long before she forgot everything else but the sheer sensual joy Asa gave her.

A long time later, when she could talk again, Carolyn looked lovingly into Asa's eyes and stroked a gentle finger over his cheek.

"I'm glad you're back, Asa Bradley," she said with quiet sincerity. "But I'll kill you if you ever go off and get shot again or leave me for more than twenty-four hours straight."

Asa gathered her up in his arms and nuzzled her neck. "I can't promise either of those things, Carrie," he said seriously, "but I don't expect them to happen, if that makes you feel any better."

Carolyn sighed and accepted defeat as gracefully as though she had a choice in the matter, then reverted to the subject that had been on her mind earlier.

"Can you at least promise me that baby I want sometime in the very near future, so I'll have some company if you do have to leave me again?"

Asa's smile over her tenaciousness tickled her neck, and she began to giggle.

"I'll give the matter very serious consideration," he said smoothly, and moved his mouth lower to an area where it didn't tickle at all.

CHAPTER TWENTY-TWO

Asa winced as Carolyn's fingernails dug into his hand for the third time in five minutes as she nervously clenched and unclenched her fingers.

"Hey, take it easy," he said humorously, trying to lighten her mood. "This is your sister we're meeting, remember, and I thought you said she had a charming personality."

"She does when she isn't mad at me," Carolyn answered, her tone absently anxious.

Asa shrugged. "Well, I said you could blame it on me that I dragged you to the altar too fast for her to come to the wedding."

Carolyn shook her head. "It isn't just that, though that's enough to hurt her feelings and make her mad by itself. She hasn't said so, Asa, but I know she's worried that I'm not going to love her like I used to now that I'm married to you. I'm all she's got, remember, and she's been upset ever since I moved to Hawaii and left her without a home."

"Won't she be happy for you, though, Carrie, because *you're* happy and because you're going to have a baby?" Asa asked, frowning as he began to think this little sister of Carolyn's was going to turn out to be a spoiled, selfish brat.

"Eventually." Carolyn nodded, still with an anxious expression on her face, "but it will take a while for her to adjust."

Asa shrugged. Even after four months of marriage, he was still wrapped in the euphoric state of a man on his honeymoon, finding himself surprised over and over again at how satisfying marriage could be with a woman he grew to love more every day.

Because he wanted to please Carolyn, he hadn't told her he

hadn't been quite as thrilled at the news that she was pregnant as she was, simply because he didn't want to share her with anybody just yet, not even his own son or daughter. Then, when he'd learned her sister was coming for a month-and-a-half visit, he'd had to pretend to be enthusiastic about that as well. Now, he glumly suspected he was going to be locked in a secret battle for supremacy in Carolyn's affections with a young woman who might be as determined to make trouble as he was to keep the peace.

"There she is!" Carolyn cried and dropped his hand so quickly to dash forward and meet Julie that Asa felt astonishingly bereft.

He watched, keeping his expression carefully neutral as his wife headed for a young woman whose pretty face bore an expression as carefully neutral as his, and who was dressed in an offbeat style he didn't consider particularly attractive. The neutral expression disappeared when Carolyn caught Julie up in her arms and hugged her with an intensity Asa envied. Now the young woman's green eyes were filled with tears and she was hugging Carolyn back so hard, Asa feared for the baby his beloved was carrying.

He made himself stay where he was and let the two of them get their greetings over with in privacy, but he was relieved when Carolyn turned, gestured in his direction and started pulling Julie with her to meet him.

Calling on the charm that had come so easily to him before he sustained the wound to his leg, and which marriage to Carolyn had restored, Asa smiled warmly at Julie Winters and held out his hand, trying to ignore the fact that she was staring up at him with a reserved expression of caution. He noted that her resemblance to Carolyn was slight, and thought it might have been easier to feel the welcome he was about to express if she had looked more like his wife.

"Welcome, Julie," he said in his deep attractive voice. "It's good to meet you at last."

Julie smiled with her mouth only and nodded. "It's good to meet you at last, too," she replied, but Asa didn't think she meant it any more than he had, and he gave a mental sigh of resignation that the battle had begun.

267

Carolyn was looking from Julie to Asa and back again and wondering why, when they were being so polite to one another, she had the feeling there was something not quite right.

Puzzled, and more than a little annoyed that the two people she cared most about in the world weren't as thrilled with one another as she was about each of them, she smiled a bright smile, took Julie's hand in one of hers and Asa's in the other and said, "Let's get your luggage, Julie. I know you're going to love Hawaii. Did I ever tell you that Mom and Dad brought me here on vacation once before you were born?"

By the time the three of them reached the house Carolyn and Asa had bought at learning Carolyn was pregnant, she felt exhausted at having to chatter ceaselessly in an effort to keep a conversation going. Asa had been as silent as a sphinx all the way home, and though Julie had uttered a word of reply now and then, she had kept staring at her new brother-in-law out of her unblinking green eyes as though inspecting him for flaws.

As Asa carried Julie's bags to her room, Carolyn pretended she had to go to the bathroom and disappeared out of their sight in order to cry a few quiet tears of frustration before she had to recoup her diminished resources and provide referee services between her husband and her sister again.

In the spare bedroom Julie would use during her visit, Asa set the bags down and straightened to find Julie staring at him again.

"I hope you'll be comfortable here," he said politely. "Carrie worked hard to fix the room up for you."

At that, Julie looked away for a moment before she turned back to him, a slight glimmer of hostility in her green eyes.

"I always wanted to be the maid of honor at her wedding," she said with stiff resentment.

Asa thought his new sister-in-law was more like his wife than he'd thought. She had the same blunt way of getting to the point as Carolyn did.

"I'm sorry it wasn't possible," he said quietly. "Carrie would have liked it too."

Julie glared at him. "Then why couldn't you wait?" she demanded.

"Because I couldn't do without her that long," Asa responded with the simple truth. "I love her too much. And she was so anxious to have a baby we both thought it better not to wait."

Julie looked shocked. "You mean . . . ?" she started to ask, then gulped the question down though her eyes clearly showed that she found it almost impossible to believe that *Carrie*, the soul of propriety during the years when Julie had been growing up, could have behaved so indiscreetly with a man.

"That's exactly what I mean." Asa gave a faint smile and shrugged his broad shoulders, aware from the way Julie was studying him now that she was trying to discover what it was about him that could have derailed Carrie's principles so quickly and thoroughly.

Julie became aware from Asa's expression that she'd been staring at him a little too blatantly, and she looked away and cleared her throat.

"Well," she said faintly, "what do you know?"

Asa smiled more naturally at her then and said with quiet purposefulness, "I know we both love the same woman. I know neither of us wants to make her unhappy and that neither of us is going to give her up. So what do you say we make a pact to put her first while you're here and do the best we can to keep our mutual jealousy under control."

Julie looked at him in a startled fashion, an embarrassed flush stealing over her cheeks. "What makes you think I'm jealous of you," she said with muted belligerence.

"Because it's only natural that you would be . . . and because I recognize what I'm feeling myself in you." Asa sighed, raising a hand to rake it through his thick, dark hair in a gesture of frustration.

Julie remained stubborn for another moment, but when Asa dropped his hand, leaving his hair ruffled in an attractive way the female in her recognized as being almost irresistible to her own sex, she began to understand what it was about Asa Bradley that appealed to Carrie.

A faint smile began to tilt her lips, and Asa noted it with a sense of wary hope.

"Well," she said practically as she began to shrug off the light cotton jacket she wore that reached almost to her knees, "I

269

guess you're right. I've known for a long time that Carrie needed a baby to take care of to be really happy, and I even advised her to have one with or without marriage. I guess it's better with it, right?"

"In my completely biased opinion, yes," Asa responded humorously.

Julie paused, looking at him speculatively. "Are you a little jealous of the baby, too?" she asked bluntly.

Asa opened his mouth to deny it, then shrugged instead.

At last, Julie displayed the charm Carolyn had assured him she had in abundance. She grinned happily at him and nodded. "Me, too," she confessed.

Asa threw back his head and laughed, with Julie joining in, and that was how Carolyn found them when she reluctantly came out of the bathroom.

She stared at her two loved ones blankly for a moment, then her smile broke out like sunlight.

"Oh, thank goodness!" she exclaimed, gathering up both of them in her arms to give them a relieved hug. "I was afraid I was going to be trapped in the middle of a family fight for the rest of the summer."

Over her head, Asa winked at Julie, who grinned back at him before giving Carolyn an impudent look of mischief.

"If you think this was bad, wait till the baby comes," she said lightly. "It better be a charmer or Asa and I are going to throw it out the window."

Carolyn abruptly drew back, a look of shock on her face as she gazed at Asa and Julie in turn.

Asa shrugged. "You're a valuable commodity, sweetheart," he said unrepentantly. "We're afraid there's not enough of you to go around."

Carolyn glared at the both of them. "I never heard of anything so idiotic in my life!" she declared indignantly. "Haven't either of you learned that love stretches to fill the need?"

Solemnly, Asa and Julie shook their heads at her, and Carolyn rolled her eyes at the ceiling before fixing them with a look of disgust. "Well, take my word for it, it does!" she declared, and turned on her heel to go to the kitchen and fix lunch.

"You think she's right?" Asa asked Julie thoughtfully, his

mind casting back over the few months Carolyn had been in his life, forcing him to change his whole outlook on relationships.

"She'd better be," Julie sighed, "because I have the feeling one baby isn't going to satisfy her."

"I have the same feeling," Asa commented as he headed for the door, "and since that's the case, I'd better reassure her that it's all right with me if she wants a dozen kids."

"Is it all right with you?" Julie asked doubtfully.

"Hell, how do I know?" Asa paused at the door to grin back at her. "Until I met your sister, I didn't even believe in getting married. If she could change my mind about that, there's no telling what she'll have me thinking in a couple of years."

Julie chuckled and turned away to unpack her things as Asa went to the kitchen to find Carolyn.

She was at the sink slicing tomatoes, and Asa came up behind her to slip his arms around her waist. He kissed her temple and spread his hands on the new curve of her stomach with possessive indulgence.

Carolyn glanced up at him over her shoulder, and the warmth in Asa's eyes turned to concern as he saw that she'd been crying.

"Hey, babe," he said with soft tenderness, "don't take me and Julie seriously. I'm not saying I won't be a little jealous of your time when the baby comes, but I bet I end up loving it just as much as you do."

"I know." Carolyn nodded, looking away and sniffing back another tear.

"Then what's the matter?" Asa frowned, tilting her head with his hand on her cheek so he could look into her eyes.

"I don't know," she said simply. "I just felt like crying."

Asa's bewildered expression made her laugh through her tears.

"You're not unhappy?" he asked, a cold chill running through him as he thought about what it would be like if she were.

She shook her head, wiped her hands, and turned into his arms, draping her arms around his neck.

"Maybe I'm just happy because my husband, the former king of independence, loves me enough to resent the time I'm going

271

to be spending with his own son or daughter," she said sooth-ingly.

Asa relaxed a little. "You aren't angry with me for feeling that way? I don't expect it will last, you know."

"I don't expect it will either." Carolyn smiled complacently. "I think you're going to be a real pushover as a daddy."

Asa bristled slightly before he gave a smile that Carolyn couldn't resist coming up on tiptoe to kiss away.

"Well, all I know for the time being," he said huskily when she let him up for breath, "is that I've turned out to be a real pushover as a husband, and as much as I like making babies, you may be right about the sort of father I'll turn out to be, too."

"Of course I am." Carolyn nodded, planting another quick kiss on his lips before she turned back to her tomatoes.

Asa leaned back against the counter to watch her, loving the way she held her tongue between her teeth with each slice of the knife, amused at himself for turning into the sort of man who could be content just to watch his wife slice tomatoes.

Then the telephone rang and he straightened up to answer it, aware as he crossed the kitchen that, for some reason, his knee seemed to be getting better day by day.

He sobered immediately when he heard Jimmy Li's distressed voice on the other end of the line.

"What is it, Jimmy?" he asked quietly. "Is your grandfather worse?"

"He's dead," Jimmy responded, trying hard to keep the tears from coming.

"When?" Asa asked gently, feeling as saddened by Li Chang's death as he'd expected to feel. He and the old man had become good friends underneath the wily adversarial nature of their relationship wherein Li had enjoyed trying to keep as many secrets as possible from Asa, and Asa had enjoyed just as much trying to pry them out of him.

"This morning," Jimmy choked out. "I was with him. The last thing he said to me was to remind you of your promise. Was he talking about being buried in China?"

"Yes." Asa nodded sadly, though Jimmy couldn't see him. He glanced up as Carolyn, alerted by the tone of Asa's conversation

272

that something was wrong, came to put her arms around him. He pulled her close and rested his cheek against the top of her hair. "I'll see to making the arrangements, Jimmy," he said calmly, "and I'll be in touch when everything is set."

"Thank you," Jimmy responded with dignity.

When Asa hung up, Carolyn gazed up at him, questioning him with her eyes.

"I'm afraid I'm going to have to go to China, Carrie," he said gently. "Jimmy's grandfather died this morning, and I promised to have him buried in his homeland."

"You mean the *real* China?" Carolyn asked, worry tingeing her voice and dawning dismay in her eyes.

Asa cupped her face in his hand. "Don't worry," he said with firm assurance, his gaze steady and calm. "It isn't like the old days. We have the Chinese government's agreement to bring Li Chang back to be buried as long as we keep it quiet. They don't want it known he ever left."

Carolyn swallowed against the fear clogging her throat. "But do they know who you are . . . what you do?" she asked anxiously.

"No," Asa answered firmly, "and they're not going to. As far as they'll know, I'm just a government bureaucrat taking care of the mundane business any bureaucrat handles."

"How can you be sure of that?" Carolyn whispered, her hands tightening on his arms.

"Carrie, don't," Asa said with quiet authority. "I'll be back. I promise you that."

Carolyn shut her eyes and leaned weakly against his chest. "I'm going to hold you to that promise, Asa," she said shakily.

Asa smiled and held her close. "You do that, honey," he told her gently. "I want you to."

Julie came into the kitchen then and stopped short when she saw the way Asa was holding her sister and the look on Carrie's face.

"What's the matter?" she asked, alarmed by the atmosphere she could sense between them.

Asa straightened and gave Carolyn a warning squeeze on her arm. "Not a thing, Julie," he said with a calm smile as he watched Carolyn get herself together in response to his warning touch. "In fact, from your point of view, it couldn't be better. I've just learned I have to leave on a little business trip, so you'll have Carrie all to yourself for a while."

Julie wasn't necessarily convinced she was being told the truth, but she sensed it was important that she play her part convincingly.

"Now that's the kind of brother-in-law I've always wanted to have," she said with teasing smugness. "The kind who knows enough to make himself scarce when I want my sister to myself."

Asa and Julie laughed, and after a minute Carolyn managed to produce a quavering smile of her own. But she was under no illusions that she was going to enjoy Julie's visit as much as she'd intended to—not when her heart was going to China with Asa and wouldn't return to her until he brought it back along with the rest of him.

A few days later, Asa stood on the runway of an obscure Chinese airport and watched with respectful sobriety as the casket containing Li Chang's body was removed from the plane and carried to a nearby truck.

"We regret your visit must be so short," a stiff Chinese official said to him in English.

Asa knew better. The truth was that the Chinese government had never told their people that Li Chang had left the country, and the hero's burial they planned to give him would be complicated by the presence of an American who obviously mourned him as much as they did.

"I regret it as well," Asa said quietly, speaking in English. He didn't think it was a particularly good idea to let his reluctant hosts know how thoroughly he understood their language. "Li Chang was a man worthy of respect."

The official looked at him sharply, and Asa knew the man was wondering how close Li Chang and this American had been, particularly how much Li Chang had told the American government.

"When your plane has been refueled, you will be flown to the border," the man said, and giving Asa a curt bow, he walked away toward the truck which held Li's body.

Asa watched as the truck disappeared down the lonely road, then began to walk around in a casual fashion as his eyes inspected the countryside around him. There was nothing much to see, but Asa nevertheless felt the familiar tightening of his nerves that had always greeted his secret excursions into Chinese territory.

As he walked, he noted again that the ache in his leg had lessened, and he frowned as he wondered why. Had the doctors been wrong? And if they had been . . .

Asa stopped short at that thought, staring blankly at the empty Chinese countryside as he carefully began searching out how he felt about the possibility that he might someday be fit for fieldwork again. The issue wasn't simple anymore.

He had enjoyed his sessions with Li Chang, but they were over now and he wasn't even sure what his next assignment would be. But if it was as deadly boring as his time in Washington had been, the attraction of a field assignment would escalate sharply. Only there was Carolyn to consider now and soon there would be a child to consider as well: two people whose lives would be as affected by his decision as his own would be.

Asa absently walked back toward the plane, his hands in his pockets, his head down, his mind back in Hawaii with Carolyn. He was remembering the fear in her eyes when she'd learned he was coming to China. It was the first time they'd been separated since their marriage, of course, but that wasn't what had been bothering her, he knew. She had been facing the terror of losing him, and when he turned that around, and realized how he himself would feel in such a situation, he knew he couldn't put her through that sort of terror on a regular basis.

His decision made, Asa lifted his head and found himself staring directly into the eyes of one of the last Chinese agents he had recruited before getting shot—a man who hadn't really proven himself and who shouldn't be here on this remote Chinese airstrip if he was still working secretly for the American government.

Every instinct Asa had honed over years of maintaining just enough advantage over his adversaries to keep himself alive sprang into life. The visual duel couldn't have lasted over ten seconds, but it was the longest ten seconds Asa could ever remember experiencing, before the other man, who was manning the hose that was pumping fuel into the plane's tank, smiled a faint smile, then turned back to watch the hose that was his apparent responsibility.

Asa knew he was insane to press his luck, but he couldn't resist moving closer to the man. He ambled toward him in a fashion he took care to make seem casual, though every muscle in his body was tensed for action. When he was near enough to speak without being overheard by the pilot and copilot who, were relaxing over cigarettes a short distance away, he placed a hand casually over his lips so it couldn't be seen that he was speaking, and murmured a standard greeting he'd used with the man before, speaking in Mandarin.

Without raising his head, the man answered in the same language, in a voice almost too soft to be heard.

"All goes well, my friend . . . all goes well," a standard formula Asa had devised for agents in place to use to let him know that nothing was wrong.

Then he straightened with his back to Asa and began unclamping the hose from the opening on the plane. Asa moved away, relief surging through him that the chance he'd taken hadn't resulted in the man, who could have been turned, raising a hue and cry for his arrest.

He didn't look at the man as he wound the fuel hose around a carrier and drove it away, and a moment later the pilot and copilot had tossed their cigarettes aside and were coming toward the plane. Asa was the only passenger, and later, as he sat in lonely possession of the entire cabin of the plane as it carried him toward Hong Kong, he put his head back against the seat, closed his eyes, and accepted the fact that he didn't belong in the field anymore.

The chance he'd taken with the man at the airfield was a stupid mistake—one that could have resulted in his own arrest or in blowing the cover of a man who deserved better from him if he really was still on the CIA's payroll, which Asa intended to find out for sure when he got back to the States.

Asa knew he never would have made such a mistake in the past, and it was just such a lapse in judgment that could make Carolyn a widow and his child an orphan if he ever did return to the field. He was past it, he thought with sober acceptance, and whether he got the full use of his leg back or not, the Agency would be making a mistake to send him back where he didn't belong anymore, and he would be making a bigger one by accepting such an assignment.

A little over a day later, Asa walked into his own home feeling nothing but glad to be there. He felt even better when Carolyn came running from the kitchen at the sound of the door and threw herself into his arms.

"Oh, Asa!" she said, holding him with fierce possessiveness. "You're back! Thank God you're back!"

"Have you been praying for me to come back safe?" he asked with a smile as he held her tightly and savored the sweet softness of her in his arms, the clean smell of her hair, the total welcome he sensed from her that made him feel as though he didn't belong anywhere else but here.

She nodded, and her eyes were moist with tears of gratitude as she leaned back to study his face intently, assuring herself that nothing had happened to him she had to worry about.

He kissed her eyes, then found her mouth and his kiss expressed everything he was feeling. When he raised his head at last, the tears were gone and Carolyn was looking at him with exactly the expression he wanted to see. He smiled and turned her under his arm, intending to take her to bed for an even better reunion, but he'd forgotten about Julie, and before they'd taken a step, his sister-in-law came into the room and stopped short in surprise.

"Back already?" she said, giving him a mock scowl. "I thought you'd be gone a lot longer."

Asa sighed resignedly, then smiled with suspicious magnanimity as he took his revenge in the only way available to him for the moment.

"I came back early just so Carrie and I could take you out to dinner for a special treat tonight, Julie," he said lightly.

"Oh, yes?" she answered, sounding pleased by his thoughtfulness. "What's the special treat?"

"Sea slugs," Asa answered with a great deal of unworthy satisfaction and was rewarded by a look of complete repugnance on his sister-in-law's pretty face.

"You must be kidding!" she exclaimed in a sour tone that matched her look.

Asa squeezed Carolyn's arm to alert her that he wasn't serious, since she was looking at him with an expression that matched Julie's, but his voice when he replied to Julie was absolutely serious.

"Oh, no," he shook his head. "It's a delicacy the Chinese prize highly, I assure you."

Julie wrinkled her nose in disgust. "Are we talking about the same kind of slimy little creature that prowls people's gardens in the summer that you sprinkle salt on to make them shrivel up?" she asked incredulously.

"Not exactly," Asa said in a grave tone of authority. "This kind of slug prowls the bottom of the ocean, and the Chinese regard them on a level with shark's fin soup, birds' nests, silver tree fungus, and jellied moose nose. If you were served a menu like that in China, you would know you were a very honored guest indeed."

Julie shuddered and looked to Carolyn for help. "Has he lost his mind?" she asked her sister quite seriously.

Carolyn, though she knew Asa was putting Julie on, looked a little green at just listening to him describe the sort of food the Chinese considered gourmet fare.

"I don't think so," she answered Julie cautiously, then looked at Asa to see how long he was going to keep his joke going.

"I admit the slugs are something one has to develop a taste for," he said, still sounding perfectly serious. "They seem a little gooey and rubbery at first, and some of them look like shaggy loaves of brown bread. But the great thing about them is that they take on the flavor of whatever they're cooked with so . . ."

"Asa, stop!" Carolyn said faintly, and when Asa looked at her, he immediately regretted his unfortunate sense of humor. Carrie had a hand over her mouth and looked as though she were going to get sick at any minute, a state she had endured all too often during the early months of her pregnancy and just about gotten over.

"Hey, hey," Asa said in alarm. "I'm sorry, honey. I was only kidding, remember?"

Carolyn looked at him with mute reproach while Julie glared at him and came to take Carolyn's arm to lead her away from Asa and toward the living-room couch.

Under his breath, Asa said a word he knew Carolyn didn't approve of before he quickly paced to the couch where she was now reclining with her eyes closed. He knelt beside her, ignoring Julie, who continued to glare at him as though he were a beast who didn't deserve a decent woman for a wife.

"Forgive me, honey," Asa said, gently stroking her hair away from her temples. "I forgot about how easily you get nauseated."

"Obviously," Julie said just loud enough for him to hear.

Carolyn opened her eyes and smiled at him weakly. "It's all right; I'm feeling better now, Asa. I'll get up in a minute and cook us a decent supper."

"No, you won't," Julie said grimly, glaring at Asa again. "I'll cook the dinner tonight, and you can bet it won't be anything Asa likes to eat!"

When Julie had stomped away in the direction of the kitchen, Asa shook his head and tried to keep from laughing.

"Go ahead, laugh," Carolyn whispered, and when he looked up, he saw she was having a hard time keeping from laughing herself.

"If I do," he whispered back, "that impertinent little sister of yours will put poison in my food and get rid of me entirely."

"I know." Carolyn nodded, then had to cover her mouth with both hands to keep from laughing so loud Julie would hear her.

"You want her to poison me?" Asa demanded in a threatening whisper.

Carolyn shook her head, almost strangling on her laughter. "I just wanted to keep her busy in the kitchen for a while so we could sneak into the bedroom," she gasped out before she had to cover her mouth again with her hands.

"Ahhh." Asa nodded, his eyes beginning to gleam with appreciation of the idea. "No sooner said than done," he added as he got to his feet, leaned over Carolyn, and lifted her into his arms.

As he sneaked past the kitchen door, then carried her rapidly to their bedroom, Carolyn was trying so hard to keep from making any noise that she didn't even think about the fact that Asa's leg had made it impossible for him to carry her like this before.

It was only when he laid her down on the bed and stepped back to get out of his clothes that her eyes widened and her giggles died an abrupt death.

"Asa!" she exclaimed softly as she sat up and got to her feet, staring at his leg with incredulity. "Your leg! What's happened to it?"

"I don't know." He shrugged, grinning as he continued to take off his clothes. "Have you been praying about that, too? Maybe you've got a special talent for intercession on behalf of poor crippled-up husbands who need a helping hand."

"Oh, Asa, don't joke about it," Carolyn chastised him absently, still staring at his leg with wondering amazement.

"Yes, ma'am," he said meekly, but his expression wasn't meek at all as he began to undo the buttons of her blouse. "Anything you say, ma'am," he repeated huskily as he drew the blouse down her arms and stared at the burgeoning sweetness of her breasts. "Anything at all . . ." His voice died away as he unhooked her bra, then touched what he'd uncovered with reverently possessive hands.

Carolyn reached up to circle his neck with her arms, her gaze loving. "I'm so glad your leg's better, Asa," she said soberly. "I hurt for you every time I see you limp."

"You never said anything." He shook his head, staring at her wonderingly.

"You told me once you didn't want to be smothered with pity," she said simply.

"I said a lot of things before I accepted how much I loved you," he said softly, bending to wrap her closely in his arms. "But now that I know it hurts you to look at my limp, I'm sorry I'm not a hundred percent healed. The limp's still there, just not as bad."

"I'm glad for any improvement . . . for your sake," Carolyn whispered, then added, "And it wasn't really pity I felt for you,

Asa. I just was outraged that someone so perfect had to endure the injustice of an injury he didn't deserve."

Asa closed his eyes, holding her tightly without answering. Then he lifted her back on the bed, finished undressing her, and made love to her with a gentle strength that left her trembling in his arms and hoping Julie's cooking skills were as inadequate as she remembered them. If they were, there would be time to experience again the wonder of being loved by a man who managed to combine gentleness with strength so effectively, humor with intelligence so heartwarmingly—love with a passion that always left her wanting more . . . and more . . . and more.

A few days later, Asa learned from Don Hubbard that the agent he had seen at the airfield in China had been discovered by the Chinese government six months earlier, turned into a double agent the CIA was feeding disinformation on a regular basis, and had identified Asa Bradley to his Chinese superiors as the American who had recruited him for the Agency shortly before Asa had had to leave his post due to the gunshot wound which had ended his career in the field.

Asa never discovered why the Chinese hadn't arrested him and taken him prisoner when he'd made his trip to their country as a dead man's escort, since, with the right pressure applied —and Asa knew every man had his breaking point—he would have been a prize that would have enabled them to discover every agent the CIA had operating in China, past and present.

He presumed it was a matter of prudence, since he had been granted entrance to China as Li Chang's escort and it would have created a crisis of trust of major proportions between the two countries if he'd been taken prisoner under those conditions. Or maybe it was just a matter of luck. Or maybe it was Carolyn's prayers that had saved him from spending the rest of his life in a Chinese prison, had they let him live past the brutal questioning it would have taken to break him.

In any event, the question of Asa's returning to work as a field man in China was closed for good, and Asa had only one regret about it all that had nothing to do with his inability to return to the work he had once loved. For reasons of security, he couldn't tell his wife that he would have elected to stay with her had the door to China remained wide open to him for the rest of his career. The ties that bound him close to home had grown far too strong by now to have permitted him to break them for any reason short of death.

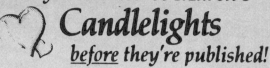